Other Works by David A. Wells

The Sovereign of the Seven Isles

- THINBLADE
- SOVEREIGN STONE
- MINDBENDER
- BLOOD OF THE EARTH
- CURSED BONES
- LINKERSHIM
- REISHI ADEPT

The Dragonfall Trilogy

- THE DRAGON'S EGG
- THE DRAGON'S CODEX
- THE DRAGON'S FANG

The Dragon's Fang

Dragonfall: Book Three

by

David A. Wells

THE DRAGON'S FANG

Edited by Carol L. Wells

www.DragonfallTrilogy.com

The Dragon's Fang

Chapter 1

"We're being watched," Derek said, pulling the curtain aside ever so slightly.

John extinguished the lamp and went to the next window over.

"Who's out there?" Imogen asked.

"Not sure," John said, peering out the window. "They don't look like Dragon Guard."

"I doubt it's Boggs either," Derek said. "He's not that subtle."

"So who then?" Imogen asked.

"And why are they just watching us?" Olivia added.

"Both good questions," Derek said, moving to a window on the side of the house. He peeked out and sighed, easing the curtain back into place. "More over here."

"Are we surrounded?" Imogen asked.

"Pretty sure," John said, going to the back door and checking the lock.

"That might explain why our friends haven't come back yet," Derek said.

"What do you mean?" Olivia asked.

"If they noticed that we're being watched, they probably wouldn't make contact," Derek said. "Odds are, whoever's out there wants the egg and they know it's not here so they're waiting for Ben to return."

"If Ben didn't notice them, Homer would've," Imogen said. "Sometimes I think those two can read each other's minds."

"Kayla would've seen them too, no question," Derek said.

"So what do we do?" Olivia asked.

"We wait," John said with a shrug. "It's all we *can* do."

Derek nodded reluctantly.

"Who else might know about the egg?" Olivia asked.

Imogen closed her eyes, shaking her head. "The Sage," she said. "He'd be able to feel its presence."

"Isn't he supposed to be on our side?"

"He's probably on his own side," John said.

"So, if we assume that the Sage's people are out there, then it's a good bet the meeting didn't go well," Imogen said.

"It also means they don't have our people," Derek said.

"Makes sense," John said.

"So again, what are we going to do?" Olivia asked.

"Nothing we can do."

"He's right," Derek said. "If we make a move, we'll probably end up in a fight and they outnumber us at least two to one. As long as they're watching us, all we can do is watch them right back."

"Is there another way out of here?" Imogen asked.

"Sure—a tunnel," Derek said.

"Really?" Olivia said. "Another tunnel?"

"This is Alturas, there's always a tunnel."

"Nice to know there's a way out," John said, "but we probably ought to sit tight."

Imogen nodded. "Just so long as they don't move against us."

"Agreed," Derek said. "We should post a watch."

Imogen woke, sitting up as she rubbed her eyes. "What time is it?"

"Just before dawn," John said quietly from his place beside the window.

"I didn't sleep worth a damn," Olivia said, lying on her back and looking at the ceiling.

"Me neither," Derek said, rolling to a sitting position and reaching for his boots. "We still have company?"

"Yeah, but just one guy," John said. "He showed up about an hour ago and the rest of them left."

"I wonder what changed," Imogen said.

John hesitated for a moment. "Could be they got our people."

"Yeah," Derek said. "I'll slip out and ask around. Maybe one of my contacts knows something."

Imogen jumped when Derek returned an hour later, appearing noiselessly from the back room where the tunnel entered the house.

"Sorry, didn't mean to startle you," he said.

"Any news?" John asked.

"Yeah, but I'm not sure what to make of it. According to one of my contacts, Boggs lost several men last night in a running fight. And another contact claims that a Dragon Guard Dominus was killed along with several of her men."

"Nash?" Imogen said.

"Sounds like it. Tall blond with a chip on her shoulder."

"That's good news," John said,

"Maybe," Imogen said. "Depends on what happened to Magoth."

"There is that," John muttered.

"That's where it gets a bit sketchy," Derek said. "Things went quiet, except for the higher-ups in the Dragon Guard—they got pretty worked up and went underground with almost a thousand men."

"Do you think Ben would've gone for the bunker without us?" Olivia asked.

"If he couldn't get to us, he might have," John said.

Imogen nodded. "I think we have to assume that he did."

"So where does that leave us?" Olivia asked.

"Waiting," John said.

"Agreed," Derek said. "When they return, it's a good bet we'll need to be ready to move fast."

"I feel so helpless," Imogen said quietly, pausing for a moment before looking up. "What if they're in trouble? What if they need our help?"

John sighed. "No way to know … and little chance of finding them."

Imogen went into one of the empty bedrooms and started drawing a circle on the floor. John followed, leaning against the doorframe.

"What do you have in mind?" he asked, after she'd finished and stood to inspect her work.

"I'm not exactly sure," she said as she sat down cross-legged in the center of the circle. "I guess I'm going to try to manifest more information, if that's even possible."

"Well, they say anything's possible," he said. "Never put much stock in that idea until recently. Let me know if I can help."

She smiled her thanks and closed her eyes. When she returned to the main room some time later, the tension was palpable. Olivia was pacing and Derek was watching out the front window. John was making a sandwich, seemingly less concerned than the rest.

"Hungry?" he asked.

"Actually, yeah. How long was I back there?"

"Couple hours," he said, pushing a plate across the table for her and going to work on another sandwich.

"Thanks," she said, taking a seat. "I'm not sure what good that did, but I feel better."

"That's enough," he said.

"For now," she said, taking a bite.

The day dragged on, tension and uncertainty hanging in the air like smoke.

"Where are they?" Olivia said as she looked out the front window. "They wouldn't just abandon us."

"Not without good reason," Derek said.

"Yeah, and most of those reasons are really, really bad."

"I know how you feel but there's nothing we can do," Imogen said.

Olivia huffed, turning back to the window. "It's almost dark. They should've been back by now."

Nobody answered.

Later that evening, when Imogen lay down to sleep, she sighed, shaking her head. "At what point do we go looking for them?"

"I'll see if my contacts know any more tomorrow," Derek said from his post at the window.

"That's not going to help me sleep tonight," Olivia muttered.

"Is our guest still watching?" John asked.

"Yep," Derek said.

Imogen felt like she was floating—drifting in the fugue state between waking and sleep. There was someone there, an indistinct form hovering over her, but she couldn't bring herself to wake up. She felt a tug at her neck. Then something crawled across her cheek. She woke with a spasm of revulsion, swatting at the bug she thought was crawling across her.

But it wasn't a bug. It was a man. He wore a bandana across his face that matched the color of his black hair, which only served to draw attention to the spark of intelligence in his dark eyes.

He put his finger over his lips as he backed away.

Imogen sat up, only then realizing that her amulet was missing. He slipped it into his pocket as he slowly, quietly retreated.

"Stop!" she shouted, surging to her feet.

He turned for the back door.

She fumbled for her sword, but he was too quick, reaching the exit before she could bare her blade.

An arrow zipped past her, followed by a yelp of pain as it sliced through the man's arm. Then he was gone—vanishing into the night.

John was up, another arrow nocked. He reached the back door and scanned the shadows, turning back to Imogen and shaking his head.

"Damn it!" she said. "He stole my amulet!"

"Derek is down," Olivia said, kneeling next to him. She plucked a dart out of his neck and held it up. Then she checked his pulse. "He's alive."

John closed and locked the door, then went to the front window.

"The watcher is gone."

Imogen looked at him sharply.

"That's too much coincidence for me," Olivia said.

"Me too, but why would the Sage steal my amulet?" Imogen asked.

"Power," John said, still looking out the window.

"This is a pretty advanced-looking dart," Olivia said, holding up the weapon for John and Imogen to inspect.

"Looks like a blow dart," John said.

"With a refillable poison reservoir," Imogen added.

"That guy was probably the best thief the Sage could afford," John said.

"Damn it," Imogen said, her hand going to her forehead. "What are we going to do now?"

"Derek's going to be out for a while," Olivia said, kneeling beside him again.

John sighed. "We wait."

Imogen went to her bed, lay down and quietly cried herself to sleep.

She woke feeling somehow numb, as if her senses were diminished in a way that she couldn't quite put into words. She sat up, her mind sluggishly focusing on Derek. He was awake and sitting up, sipping a steaming cup of tea.

"How're you feeling," she asked.

"Stupid," he said. "I have no idea how he got the drop on me. I know that door was locked, but he got it open without me even noticing."

"Don't beat yourself up," Imogen said without much energy. "He got the better of us all."

Derek nodded, clearly not persuaded.

Time passed slowly, the tension welling up periodically but always resulting in the same conclusion—*wait*.

"If they're not back by tomorrow morning, we should head for Shasta," Imogen said.

"I'm game," Olivia said, "if only to do … something."

"If that's what you want," John said, "but we should leave a message for Ben in case he returns."

Imogen closed her eyes and turned around, walking toward the back door … and then she froze.

"What the hell?" Olivia said.

"We've been made," John said.

Derek backed away from the door, a knife in his hand. "Head for the tunnel," he whispered.

Nobody moved, all eyes locked on the metallic man standing outside the back door, just his head and shoulders visible through the window. The shiny half bubble covering his face began to peel away, slivers of metal separating from his helmet and reattaching to his shoulders.

His eyes met Imogen's and he smiled.

"Hello, my name is Colonel Kaid," he said. "Director Boyce asked me to deliver a message."

"Director Boyce? You mean Ben?" Imogen asked.

"I do," Kaid said. "Perhaps it would be better if we spoke inside."

Imogen blinked, hesitating for a moment before heading toward the door.

"Are you sure about this?" Derek asked.

"I'll bet he could get through the door without an invitation," John said, moving to stand with Imogen.

Kaid entered, scanning the room in a glance, then turned to Imogen and nodded politely.

"Thank you for your hospitality, Imogen," he said. "Ben wants you to know that he's holed up in the bowels of Mt. Shasta. He's safe, but as of the last report, he was badly wounded and in need of healing. Fortunately, the facility he occupies is well equipped."

"Did they go for the door?" Derek asked.

"Yes," Kaid said, bowing formally with a smile. "They woke me … and pissed off a bunch of dragon minions in the process. From there, we went to Shasta. I dispersed the army, and Ben and the others fought their way through the base to the bunker and found the Codex."

"Why didn't you go in with them?" Olivia asked.

Kaid shrugged. "I'm all tech and there was a lot of magic flying around inside that mountain. Besides, I have a line on some weapons that just might fry the wyrm once and for all."

"What does Ben want us to do?" Imogen asked.

"For now, stay put and keep your heads down," Kaid said. "He'll find you as soon as he can." He produced a small leather pouch from his metal suit, splinters moving and shifting to bring it to the surface. "Ben said you could probably use this."

Imogen dumped the contents of the pouch onto the table, almost twenty gold coins, all exactly the same.

"It'll certainly help," she said. "How long do you think he'll be?"

"That's hard to say," Kaid said. "He'll need time to heal, and then he has to get out. That mule, Saint Thomas, is still inside with a bunch of stalkers. Also, some guy Ben called the Warlock went in too."

"None of that is reassuring," Imogen said.

"Apologies, I was shooting for honest."

"Fair enough, Colonel," she said. "Thank you for helping Ben."

"My pleasure," Kaid said. "Time I was on my way."

"Wait," Olivia said.

"Yeah, what about everyone else?" Derek asked.

"Ellie, Kayla, and Hound are alive and well, a bit banged up, but they'll be fine."

He turned without another word, walked out onto the porch and flew straight into the air and out of sight above the clouds.

"Quite a suit," John said, heading for the front window to see if anyone was watching the house.

"Can we trust that guy?" Derek asked after locking the door.

"I think so," Imogen said. "These coins are definitely from Ben."

Derek frowned and then shrugged. "If you say so."

Imogen sat down and sighed. "I feel better but I still want to do something."

Olivia nodded.

Imogen pursed her lips, her brow furrowing. "I feel different … like something's missing."

"Your magic?" John asked.

"I think so," she said after a moment of reflection. "I never noticed it before. It's so subtle, but now that it's gone I feel like something is off."

"Do you think you'd be able to tell if magic got close?" John asked.

She frowned, nodding slowly.

"Maybe that's a silver lining," he said.

"Maybe, but I'd rather have my amulet back."

"I'll go out after dark and see what I can find out," Derek said.

"So back to the waiting, then," Olivia said.

Derek returned late, smelling of alcohol. "A few of my contacts are reluctant to talk without some lubrication." He walked unsteadily to a chair and sat down.

"Learn anything?" Olivia asked.

"Big fight at Shasta. Bunch of dead Dragon Guard." He chuckled. "Lightning from the clear blue sky, they said. Didn't know what hit 'em."

"Anything about our people?" Imogen asked.

Derek shook his head slowly. "Saint Thomas isn't back yet, though. That has the Dragon Guard worried."

"Maybe they got him," Olivia said.

"We can hope," John said.

"Oh … the mountain caved in … a lot."

Imogen looked at John with sudden worry.

"Kaid said there was a fight and that Ben had reached the bunker," John said.

She nodded. "I just hope he can get out."

"Also …" Derek said, holding up one finger. Everyone waited. "Oh yeah, Lulu and Juju are in town … bad juju." His eyelids drooped.

"I think you need a nap," John said.

He nodded without opening his eyes.

Derek groaned as the light woke him.

"Morning, Sunshine," Olivia said.

He took several deep breaths and sat up, resting his face in his hands. "I feel awful," he moaned.

"Drink this," Imogen said, handing him a glass of water.

He nodded his thanks and downed the entire glass. "Thank you. I haven't been this hung over in a long time. My guy was scared. It normally takes a drink or two to get him talking, but last night he outdid himself. I just hope his head hurts as much as mine does."

"You mentioned something about juju," John said. "Got the impression it wasn't good."

"No … Lulu and Juju are Adara Coven assassins," he said, sighing as he shook his head. "Odds are, they're here for Kayla."

"Why Kayla?" Olivia asked. "Everyone else is after Ben."

"Her family derives its power from the wyrm. If it gets out that one of their own turned against him, they'll lose standing, or worse."

"Adara Coven?" John asked.

Derek nodded. "Magic is forbidden to all but the priesthood … but the dragon looks the other way when it comes to the coven. Though I suspect he might take more interest if he knew the extent of their activities."

"So we add another enemy to the list," John said. "What are the odds they'll find us here?"

"Can't imagine they're looking for us," Derek said.

"So back to the waiting, then," John said.

"For once, that sounds good to me," Derek said, easing himself back onto his bedroll and closing his eyes, one hand on his forehead.

Chapter 2

Two days later, a few hours after Derek had left on his daily information-gathering trip, Imogen stood up, quickly looking around with a hint of fear.

"What is it?" John asked.

"Magic," she whispered.

Derek entered the room slowly, a wary look on his face. Someone entered behind him, a hooded cloak obscuring his identity.

Everyone came to their feet, weapons at the ready.

Derek motioned for them to hold, though his face told a different story.

The man pulled his hood back and smiled his most charming smile.

"I'm so glad you're safe, Imogen," Frank said, going to her and hugging her as if nothing had changed between them.

She shoved him away and drew her knife. "Give me one reason I shouldn't gut you right now," she said, her eyes flashing.

His expression fell as he shook his head, sorrow and sadness replacing his smile as he held out open hands.

"I know what you must think," he said. "And I can't say I blame you. Just give me a chance to explain."

Imogen lowered her blade. "Start talking."

He nodded. "The Warlock spelled me." His eyes went distant for a moment. "I can remember everything I did, but I can't remember why I did any of it. It was so strange. He would suggest these horrible things, and at the time, it seemed like the most natural thing in the world." He looked at Olivia, his eyes welling up a bit. "I'm so sorry about Baxter. I would never have done that. You have to believe me."

Her face hardened. "Do I?"

He closed his eyes tightly, a tear slipping down his cheek.

"I understand if you don't trust me," he whispered. "How could you?"

Nobody answered.

"All I can say is, I'm sorry. I didn't have a choice. The Warlock's magic is so powerful. I just couldn't resist it. I'll leave if you want me to."

"No," John said. "We've got some questions."

Frank nodded, another tear sliding down his face, his composure breaking as he faced Imogen again. "Ben is dead." He started crying openly. "My brother is gone."

Eyes darted around the room but everyone remained silent.

"What do you mean?" Imogen asked.

He took a deep breath and motioned to the table. Everyone sat down, except John, who remained standing with an arrow nocked. Frank seemed to ignore him.

"The Warlock took me into the mountain. There was a big fight with one of the dragon's mules. And then Hoondragon arrived. Ben and Ellie fought him." Frank shook his head. "I was impressed—they were so good, I thought they might actually beat him. For some reason the Warlock sent me to help them. I got behind Hoondragon and managed to slip a knife through the cracks in his armor." He snorted bitterly. "That just made him mad. He swatted me away like a doll. Then Hound blasted the ceiling with a grenade and everything collapsed. All in an instant they were gone, crushed under a hundred tons of stone. All I could do was watch."

Olivia started to say something, but Imogen stopped her with a look.

"That's quite a story, Frank," she said. "How did you get away?"

"Hoondragon's sword," Frank said, pulling his cloak aside, revealing the black weapon.

Everyone shared furtive looks.

"Somehow, it wasn't buried when the ceiling collapsed. When I picked it up, the Warlock's hold on me broke ... I was free."

"What about Kayla?" Derek asked.

"And Hound?" Imogen added.

"They were on the other side of the cave-in ... with the Warlock. If they survived, they probably work for him now."

The room fell silent.

"I know this isn't what you wanted to hear," Frank said. "But there is good news. I can kill the dragon with this sword. It's that powerful. I'll help you get your baby back, Imogen." He reached across the table and squeezed her hand.

She flinched almost imperceptibly.

Olivia broke the tension with a chuckle, shaking her head. "You played me once, why should I believe you now?"

He sighed. "I guess that's fair, but honestly, you just got caught between two brothers having a squabble. It was really nothing more than that."

She snorted derisively.

"Suit yourself," he said, turning back to Imogen. "I have a plan, but you're not going to like it."

She pulled her hand back and crossed her arms. "Try me."

He sighed, nodding to himself. "We surrender to the Dragon Guard."

"Here we go," Olivia said, shaking her head.

"I know, I know," Frank said, holding up both hands to forestall further protest. "The thing is, they'll obey me. This sword gives me rank and standing—they have to do what I say. So we get a dozen of them to escort us to Denver. Believe me when I tell you that'll be a lot safer than trying to dodge them all the way there."

"How do you know they'll listen to you?" Imogen asked, leaning in with interest.

"Because they already have."

"Shit," John muttered, going quickly to the window.

Imogen stood. "What have you done?"

"Nothing," Frank said. "You're safe. They didn't follow me."

"Anything?" Derek asked, checking the side window.

"Not yet," John said.

"Why don't you tell us how you and the Dragon Guard wound up being fast friends," Olivia said.

He glared at her. "They're not my friends, but I did run into a squad of them on my way back here from Shasta. They had me surrounded. I thought they were going to kill me, but then they saw the sword and everything changed. The squad leader called me 'Lord Hoondragon' and offered to escort me to Legate Rath here in Alturas. When I refused, he bowed respectfully, gave me some food and water and sent me on my way. I'm telling you, this sword is the key."

"Magic sword or not, there's no way in hell I'm going to turn myself in to the Dragon Guard," Derek said.

"I don't know you," Frank said, an edge in his voice. "And I wasn't talking to you." He turned to his aunt. "Imogen, I can get your baby back. Ben's dead…" he stopped, his eyes focusing on her. "It's odd that you aren't more upset about my brother's passing." He looked over at Olivia. "And you don't seem to be too broken up about your sister."

Olivia snorted. "That's because I don't believe you."

He took a breath and sighed, shaking his head. He turned back to Imogen. "You too?" he asked.

She shook her head.

"We're family, Imogen. That has to count for something."

"You'd think," she said.

He nodded to himself, looking down at the table. "I guess all I can do is prove my loyalty. I'll leave if you want me to, but I'd rather stay and keep you safe."

She stared at him for several moments and then nodded slowly. "You can stay, for now."

"We really should be trying to get out of this town," he said. "The Dragon Guard will be looking for you."

"Why's that?" John asked.

"They lost Ben in the mountain but they know he had friends. Sooner or later, they'll come for you, all of you. It's not safe here."

"Lot of that going around," John said.

Imogen leaned back in her chair and looked up at the ceiling. After a few moments, she said, "Ben told us to wait here, so we wait."

Frank shook his head sadly. "I'll do whatever you want to do, but Ben's not coming back. We have a limited window of opportunity to run. If we miss it, I don't know if I can protect you."

"I thought you said that sword makes you important," Olivia said.

"It does, but not more important than the egg. They won't stop looking."

"We wait," Imogen said.

Frank nodded reluctantly.

Just after dawn the next morning, he pulled Imogen aside. "My plan is our only hope," he said quietly but intently.

"Bullshit," she said, walking away.

He kept his distance until noon. Then he said, "We can't stay here. Sooner or later, they'll come looking for me."

"What the hell, Frank?" Imogen demanded.

"The sword. The Dragon Guard know I have it. I have to report to Legate Rath, and *soon*, or they'll come looking."

"And there it is," Olivia said.

"I told you I ran into a patrol," Frank said.

"Did they follow you?" John asked.

Derek shared a look with Imogen—she nodded. He left through the escape tunnel.

"No," Frank said, shaking his head. "I was careful."

"We should get ready to leave," John said.

He and Imogen and Olivia went to work packing and gearing up. Frank sat down at the table and watched. Several hours later, Derek returned with two cloaked figures following him.

"Again?" Imogen asked, as everyone faced the new arrivals.

"They didn't give me much choice," Derek said.

Dom stepped into the light and pulled his hood back, staring intently at Olivia. Kat tossed her hood back and holstered her pistol.

"Where's your sister?" Dom demanded of his younger daughter.

Olivia went pale, glancing ever so slightly at Frank. Dom frowned, clearing his throat as he took in the room. Kat rested her hand on her weapon.

"You shouldn't have come here," Frank said, pulling his cloak aside and revealing Hoondragon at his waist, his left hand resting easily on the hilt.

"Shit!" Dom said, darts coming off his wrist and racing toward Frank. Before they could find their mark, Frank drew the sword and dodged to one side, deflecting one dart while avoiding the other two. He crashed through the back door and raced out into the street, calling out for help.

"Dragon Guard," John said, looking out the window.

Dom called his darts back as Frank took command of a platoon of advancing soldiers, waving them toward the house.

"Time to go," Dom said, taking Olivia by the arm and propelling her toward the back room and the escape tunnel. "Where's your sister?" he snapped.

"Mount Shasta," Olivia said over her shoulder. "She's alive and safe."

They filed down the narrow staircase and into the escape tunnel with Derek bringing up the rear. In the small room at the far end of the tunnel, he pulled up a rope concealed along the ground and heaved. A creak, then a groan, then a thunderous crashing reverberated into the room as the tunnel collapsed, drowning out the shouts of the first soldiers to find the entryway.

Dom started for the stairs.

"Wait!" Imogen said, grabbing his arm and turning him back toward her. "Why did you attack Frank?"

"That's not Frank anymore, that's Hoondragon. That damn sword is calling the shots now." He didn't elaborate, instead turning back to the stairs and motioning for Kat to take the lead.

Imogen looked back at the collapsed tunnel and shrugged to John as she followed Dom into the empty house above. It was cold and dark, the only sounds their footfalls and the distant shouts of soldiers searching for them.

Dom headed for the front door.

"Wait ... not that way," Derek said, motioning for the back door. "The alley is less exposed."

"Good," Dom said, after taking a look through the small broken window that occupied the top quarter of the door.

They slipped out of the house and into the night, moving quickly but as quietly as possible, Kat in the lead. She stopped just inside the shadows at the end of the alley, peering up and down the street.

"Stop!"

Everyone looked back. A lone soldier stood at the other end of the alley, pointing at them with one hand and waving for more Dragon Guard to join him with the other. A single dart separated from Dom's wristband and accelerated toward the man, hitting him in the face so hard it drove through his skull and knocked his helmet off as he fell backward.

"Let's go," Dom growled.

They weren't twenty feet from the concealment of the shadows when two dozen Dragon Guard rushed from behind the houses across the street, fanning out to surround them, bright blue tongues of flame igniting from the barrels of their rifles.

"Ambush!" Dom said, darts leaping from his wristband, killing two Dragon Guard in a matter of moments.

Kat shot another two.

Then Dom's darts fell to the ground.

Someone started clapping as the sounds of men running echoed up the alley from behind.

"Quite impressive," a priest said, stepping out into view. "Let us see how formidable you are without your tech."

Dom drew the Dragon's Fang, even though the situation looked nearly hopeless. Imogen drew her sword, searching for an escape and seeing none.

"You're beaten, Dragon Slayer," the priest said, smiling broadly, his eyes never leaving the sword. "Surrender or I'll burn you all."

It wasn't an idle threat. Dragon Guard surrounded them, rifles at the ready.

"I'd rather burn than be eaten by the wyrm," Dom said, the point of his blade never wavering.

"I'm sure my master would like to have a conversation with some of your companions, but I'm equally certain that he will forgive me for killing you when I bring him the sword that killed his brother."

The priest raised his hand and the Dragon Guard took aim.

"Last chance," he said.

Dom smiled and started to advance.

"Stop!" Frank shouted, breaking through the cordon, Hoondragon in hand.

The priest looked annoyed but he nodded respectfully. The Dragon Guard relaxed their aim.

"I need them alive," Frank said.

"All of them?" the priest asked.

"Well, no, just her," he said, pointing at Imogen.

She glared at him.

"Excellent," the priest said. "Perhaps a bargain is in order. If the woman and the Dragon Slayer surrender, I will release the rest of you. You have my word."

Dom snorted derisively.

"Very well," the priest said, muttering arcane words under his breath as he extended his hand toward them. Tendrils of dark magic curled around his hand and then shot toward Dom and Imogen. Dom raised the Dragon's Fang between himself and the magic, absorbing the spell with little effort, but Imogen was struck in the chest. She arched her back and began shaking violently, then crumpled to the ground.

A moment later a shot rang out and the priest's head exploded, spraying blood and brain onto the Dragon Guard standing next to him.

"Now!" Dom shouted, his darts coming back to life, targeting three of the enemy standing between them and a row of houses.

Dragon Guard all around raised their rifles.

"No fire," Frank shouted. They hesitated, several slinging their weapons and drawing swords as the cordon collapsed.

Dom met the first Dragon Guard, driving the Dragon's Fang through his breastplate with a single thrust, dropping the corpse in passing as he propelled Olivia toward the gap he'd just created in their line.

John shot Frank, the arrow piercing his left shoulder and sticking out his back. Frank screamed, rage flashing in his eyes as he closed with John, Hoondragon slashing through John's bow and taking his left hand off at the wrist. He grunted in pain as he went to his knees.

"Run!" Dom shouted, darting through the hole he'd made in the cordon, nearly everyone following as the cluster of Dragon Guard converged on them.

"What about Imogen?" Olivia asked, looking back in near panic.

"I didn't come here for her," Dom snapped, shoving her forward.

They raced between the houses and into another alley running the length of the block, turning toward the sound of a whistle.

Dom stopped for a moment as the first of the Dragon Guard reached the alley, a single dart felling the man with a thought. More came, too many more.

Halfway down the alley, someone in the shadows called to them.

"This way."

Kat turned into a yard without hesitation, following the voice. Olivia looked back at the platoon of enemy soldiers coming for them, the nearest falling from another of Dom's darts. Her father reached her, directing her toward the house. She fled between two dilapidated buildings, frowning in confusion at the man crouched in the middle of the gap between the two houses. He looked familiar.

It was Cleve, a brush rifle slung on his back.

"Olivia, this way," Zack said, adding to her confusion. He was crouched in the shadows in front of a house. "Good to see you," he said.

"Zack, is that you?" she said, smiling brightly.

"Hi, Olivia," he said, his blushing visible even in the dim light.

She kissed him on the cheek. "I didn't think I'd see you again," she said. "Tell me everything."

"Later," Dom growled as he crouched in the shadows next to them.

Cleve quickly joined them. "Claymore's set. Cover your ears."

"Wait, where's Imogen?" Zack asked.

"Lost," Dom said, nodding to Cleve and holding up a hand, watching for the first man to round the corner. When he made a fist, Cleve pushed the button on a small handheld device, and the world shook as the directional mine showered the cluster of Dragon Guard with steel pellets, tearing them apart in a blink.

Dom smiled his approval at Cleve.

"Time to go," he said.

"There's a tunnel entrance not far from here," Derek said. "It leads to the edge of town."

"We have to go back for Imogen and John," Olivia said.

"No, we don't," Dom growled. "I didn't come here for them, I came for you and your sister." He turned to Derek. "Lead the way."

Derek looked torn, but he nodded after only a moment's indecision, leading them into the night.

Frank stood over John and Imogen, shaking his head sadly.

"This could have been so much easier. All you had to do was listen to me." He bent down slowly and picked up John's left hand by a finger, wagging it in front of him for a moment before tossing it into the bushes. He motioned to a couple of nearby Dragon Guard.

"Hold his arm and burn his stump," he said, wincing from the pain of the arrow still sticking through his shoulder.

John screamed as the fire cauterized his wound. Imogen sat up, gasping for breath as if she'd just emerged from water, her eyes going wide in horror when she registered John's missing hand. She scrambled to her feet, sword in hand.

"What did you do?!" she shouted, lunging at Frank.

He parried her blade easily, dancing out of range, the sudden movement causing him to yelp in pain.

"Take her," he snapped.

Dragon Guard converged on her, their armor easily defending against the one attack she managed before they disarmed her and bound her hands behind her back.

"Behave or I'll take his head," Frank said, leveling his sword at John.

Imogen looked at Frank with murder in her eyes. "I'll kill you for this," she said coldly.

"I doubt it."

A sudden explosion drowned out everything else for a moment.

Frank sighed, shaking his head. He motioned to a couple of Dragon Guard. "Go see if there are any survivors. The rest of you, form up and escort us to Legate Rath."

They marched through the empty streets, every step taking them closer to their final defeat.

"I'm sorry, John," Imogen whispered.

"Me too," he said. "I was just a few inches off."

"Your hand," she said, a tear slipping down her cheek.

He smiled at her, genuine happiness in his eyes. "We'll get through this together," he said.

"How can you be so calm after what he did to you?"

He looked at his blackened stump and then at her. "I always wondered how it would happen."

She frowned, shaking her head in confusion.

"Quiet," one of the Dragon Guard said, hitting John in the back. He stumbled forward but kept his feet. He and Imogen shared a look and fell silent.

Frank led them to the Dragon Guard headquarters in Alturas. As they entered, Legate Rath stood waiting for them. He surveyed the prisoners briefly, then fixed his eyes on Frank.

"Report, Sword Bearer."

Frank bowed to him.

"I've captured the Wizard's daughter and one of her companions."

"I doubt very seriously that that's going to be enough for our master," Rath said. "Where's the egg?"

"Buried under Mt. Shasta."

"Along with Hoondragon, I presume."

"Yes," Frank said. "He was crushed when one of my brother's friends blew up the room they were standing in. I retrieved the sword and escaped."

"And Saint Thomas?"

"Unknown."

"Tell me about your traveling companion."

"The Warlock?" Frank said. "He comes from an alternate earth and is very adept at wielding magic. He offered to teach me in exchange for my help. I agreed and we pursued my brother into the mountain."

"What is his purpose here?"

"He wants to kill our master and take this world for his own," Frank said.

Rath nodded, smiling and then chuckling. "Ambitious."

"Yes, and dangerous, especially now that he has his staff back."

"He took it from Saint Thomas?"

"With my help, yes," Frank said, wincing in apparent distress from his honesty.

Rath smiled again. "You wanted to lie to me, didn't you?"

"Yes," Frank said, his eyes going a bit wild at the words coming out of his mouth.

"And you feel a strange compulsion to travel east to our master, do you not?"

"Yes," Frank said, frowning deeply.

"You are the bearer of the sword, but you are not yet Lord Hoondragon," Rath said. "Only our master can give you that high honor. But first, you must prove yourself to him."

"What do you mean?" Frank asked, a hint of alarm in his voice.

"The previous Lord Hoondragon fought in our master's arena for an entire year without a single defeat before he was given his title. You must prove your capability and your loyalty before you will be so named."

"How?"

"Through service," Rath said. "It's a shame you don't have the egg. I'm sure that would buy you favor."

"I have *her*," Frank said, pointing at Imogen.

"Yes, the Wizard's daughter is a prize, but she's little more than a means to an end. Tell me about your brother."

"He's still in the mountain," Frank said, glancing inadvertently at Imogen.

"So he was alive when last you saw him."

"You lying bastard," Imogen said, falling silent when Rath fixed her with his gaze.

"Yes, but he might be trapped," Frank continued.

"Might be?"

"It's a big place. There could be another way out."

"Indeed," Rath said, nodding thoughtfully. "Since the sword compels you to travel east, I will give you a gift. There is a rebellion in Battle Mountain. Crush it without mercy and perhaps our master will be merciful to you."

"By your command," Frank said, bowing respectfully.

"You will leave at dawn with a company of my finest men to escort you," Rath said. "Wouldn't want you to get lost along the way."

Chapter 3

"Tissue repair eighty-seven percent complete."

The impersonal voice sounded very far away.

"Temporary paralysis released."

Ben became aware of a dull ache in his side, then an awful taste in his mouth.

"Are you back?" Homer asked, worry and anxiety in his voice.

"I think so," Ben thought numbly.

He felt a cold nose on his cheek and then Homer licked him, whining softly.

"Easy," Ellie said. "Don't try to move."

Her voice was far away too, but thick with emotion. He felt her holding his hand.

"He's waking up," she said more loudly.

Ben struggled to open his eyes. It seemed to take a long time. The world was blurry and he couldn't quite understand what he was looking at. He blinked a few times and the picture became clearer. Ellie sat next to him, smiling with pure joy through the tears on her face.

"I was so scared," she whispered. "I thought you were going to die."

He tried to move but his body wouldn't obey. He tried to speak but his mouth was too dry.

"Easy, just lie still, you still have some healing to do," she said.

"I don't like it when you leave," Homer said.

"Me neither," Ben thought to his dog.

He focused on his breathing, taking a mental inventory of his body.

"Your internal injuries are healed, but there is still significant bruising," the augment said. "Move with caution."

He tried to speak again but only managed to cough, which all too suddenly transformed the dull ache in his side into stabbing pain.

"Here," Kayla said, handing Ellie a cup of water.

She gently wet his lips and then drizzled a few drops into his mouth. He struggled to swallow, working the moisture around and beseeching her for more with his eyes.

A few more drops and he was able to swallow.

"Help me sit up," he mumbled.

Hound gently lifted him into a sitting position while Ellie put a few pillows behind him. He winced again, but nodded his thanks.

"You gave us quite a scare," Hound said.

"How long?" he whispered.

"A week," Ellie said, offering more water.

He nodded, drinking slowly and carefully lest he start coughing again.

"You okay?" he asked Ellie.

She nodded, smiling sympathetically, wiping a fresh tear from her cheek.

"You saved me," she whispered.

"Good," he said, closing his eyes. "I'm going to rest some more."

He woke some time later, still groggy but feeling less pain.

Homer sat up and laid his chin on Ben's hand. "Feeling better?"

"Yeah, but still not great."

"You survived," Homer said. "That's all that matters."

Ben smiled at him, scratching his ear.

"Hungry?" Ellie asked, seeing that he was awake.

"Yes ... more now that you mentioned it."

"Be right back," she said, disappearing into the other room for a few moments before returning with some food.

He slept again after eating, waking in the evening, hungry again. After another meal, he tried to get up, grimacing at the ache in his side.

"Go easy," Ellie said, helping him to his feet and letting him lean on her. He made it to the table in the other room before sitting down again.

"Wow, lying on your back for a week takes a lot out of you," he said.

"I'm just glad to see you on your feet," Hound said.

"Me, too," Kayla added.

"Anything happen while I was out?"

"Not a damn thing," Hound said, coming to his feet and pacing.

"I tried to access base security," Kayla said. "Unfortunately, this section is the only area that still has power, so we can't see what's going on out there." She gestured vaguely upward.

"How soon will I be fit to travel?" Ben asked his augment.

"Another day of bed rest. Two would be better."

He turned to Kayla. "Any word from Kaid?"

"Not since he reported delivering your message to Imogen."

He closed his eyes, shaking his head. "I'll bet she's worried sick."

"Yeah, Olivia's probably not real happy with us either," Ellie said.

"As long as they're safe."

"I'm sure they are," Kayla said. "Derek knows Alturas as well as anyone. He'll keep them out of sight."

Ben started to catalogue all of the threats and obstacles they faced, feeling a wave of tiredness wash over him.

"We still have so much to do," he said.

"Right now, all you have to do is heal," Ellie said, laying her hand on his. He nodded.

"I can probably heal while I read," he said. "Could you bring me the Codex?"

He'd taken only a cursory look at the Dragon's Codex upon their arrival, his focus at the time entirely on Ellie and her wound. He spent the next several hours carefully examining every page, copying the contents into his augment's perfect memory and then translating every word and symbol for a more thorough study. His friends left him alone, though it was clear that they were as curious about its contents as he was. After a first read, he went to bed with his head swirling from all of the new information that he'd absorbed.

He woke the following morning with a much clearer picture of the Codex … and greatly improved mobility.

"You look like you're feeling better," Hound said, when he came to the table.

Kayla put a plate of food in front of Ben with a smile.

"Thank you," he said, then nodded to Hound as he took a bite of stale rations.

They all ate silently and quickly, all eyes turning to Ben after Hound cleared the table.

"So…" Ellie finally said.

Ben nodded, smiling. "There's a lot of it that I don't fully understand," he said. "Most is probably beyond me anyway, but there are a few things we might be able to use."

"I took a look through it after you went to bed last night," Ellie said. "Couldn't make sense of any of it, though. I thought it odd that there's only writing on one side of each page."

"I thought so too," Ben said. "Unfortunately, there's no explanation."

"One thing I did notice," she said, opening the book and sliding it in front of him, pointing to one of the symbols. "This keeps coming up and it's one of the symbols in the magic circle."

Ben nodded. "That rune represents the dragons as a race. The chapter on the magic circle says that there are seven magical races in the heavens and that they made a treaty eons ago that included the magic circle as a universally recognized protective spell. Each symbol within the circle represents one of those races."

"Does it say if any of those races are friendly?" Kayla asked.

Ben shook his head. "It doesn't say much more than that, except that all of those races are very old and very powerful."

"Maybe one of them would help us," Ellie said.

"Maybe, if we knew how to ask, but I doubt it," Ben said. "Of all the spells in the book, the circle is the easiest to use and the most necessary for everything else.

"The section on manifestation is interesting. Basically, the combination of will, a clearly pictured outcome, and a belief that your desired result will become reality is all that's necessary to change the world—provided you can access magic through a dragon artifact.

"It talks a lot about meditation as the most effective means of successful manifestation. I didn't really understand it all, but the basic idea is that meditation allows you to insert your desired vision into your subconscious mind, and that's where I get a bit lost. It says that the subconscious mind is a non-local energy field that exists everywhere in the universe at once and that it creates the illusion that our conscious mind experiences as reality."

"And you think *you're* lost," Hound muttered.

"I know, it's a bit out there, but then we're in a fight with a dragon … and a guy from another version of earth, so who am I to judge? Anyway, since consciousness creates the illusion that we experience as reality, we can cause it to create the reality we want by deliberately and persistently imagining the outcome we desire and then believing that it will become real.

"Apparently, people can do this without dragon magic, but to a far lesser degree, and only after a lot of practice."

"Can we manifest a dead wyrm?" Hound asked.

"Probably not," Ben said. "I suspect that the dragon knows more about this than we do, and he hasn't manifested our destruction."

"Not for lack of trying," Kayla said.

"No, but that brings me to the next part—manifestation usually occurs in the most ordinary way possible, through mechanisms that are already part of reality and that seem completely mundane."

"Like you finding all those gold coins," Hound said.

"Exactly. They don't just appear out of nowhere in my hand or my pocket, but they do appear."

"So how is manifestation going to help us kill the dragon?" Hound asked.

"I'm not sure it will," Ben said. "Although, I suspect it will help us get close enough to take a shot. My grandfather used it often to make seemingly small changes that added up to big differences. Hopefully, I'll be able to do the same thing, and I think I have an advantage that he didn't." He tapped the side of his head. "My augment allows me to visualize anything I want with perfect clarity. I need to play with it a bit, but I think that might help me manifest on a whole different level."

"I hope you're right," Hound said. "So what else you got?"

"Well, there's the section on healing, which is just a more specialized form of manifestation. I think we all know how that works," he said, gently probing his side. "Another section in the chapter on manifestation talked about creating an avatar."

"Like the Sage's winged woman?" Ellie asked.

"Yep," Ben said. "Apparently, the avatar spell is derived from an ancient meditation practice from Tibet. Tibetan monks would visualize a god in vivid detail, day in and day out for years, until it became real to them. So real that they could talk to it and even feel its touch. Some were even rumored to be visible to other masters. Once they had created their god, then they had to destroy it, willing it to vanish from their awareness entirely. Those who accomplished the entire exercise were said to realize the truth of reality—that what we perceive is truly an illusion produced by the mind and that the mind is capable of molding that illusion to suit our needs or desires.

"With the help of dragon magic, the process is apparently much easier and faster, as well as more substantive."

"You think you can make an avatar that can kill the wyrm?" Hound asked.

"I don't know about that, but I bet I can create one that will help us."

"The Sage's avatar made a pretty good spy," Kayla said.

"I'd rather have an assassin," Hound said.

"Yeah, I'm pretty sure that's where the next chapter comes in," Ben said. "Summoning. Really, most of the book is about summoning other-worldly beings to do the summoner's bidding. There's a whole list of named beings complete with methods for calling them, bargaining with them, and even compelling them to service.

"I understand more now about how my grandfather summoned Magoth. First, he called on his guardian angel, which the book says is a manifestation of the divine presence within each of us. Since demons are creatures of darkness, the light can compel them to serve one who is protected by their guardian angel. Unfortunately, that path takes time and a lot of prayer.

"The book is pretty clear about not summoning named demons without your angel's protection, but it does have a list of lesser beings that can be summoned and bargained with for services or information, which, of course, my grandfather warned me never to do."

"Probably good advice considering how Magoth turned out," Hound said.

"Yeah, I don't want to go down that road again," Ben said. "Unfortunately, most of the rest of the spells depend on summoning something or other to work. There's one for possession, both voluntary and forced."

"You mean you can put a demon into another person against their will?" Kayla asked.

"Yeah, the stalkers are one example, even though they kill the host during the process. Other, more powerful beings, can possess people while they live, imprisoning them in their own mind, helpless to do anything but watch the demon use their body for its own ends. Others can be invited in to coexist with the host, allowing them to retain their free will, or most of it anyway, and often lending them extraordinary powers, but at a price."

"That's terrifying," Ellie said.

Ben nodded. "I think we should consider possession magic off the table. I don't feel good about any of it."

"Agreed," Ellie said.

Hound and Kayla nodded.

"Summoning is also used to create prepared spells," Ben said. "Basically, a being is summoned and a bargain is struck for some service to be performed at a later time on command. When the spell is cast, the service is rendered. We've seen some of the priests use magic like this.

"It does mention that manifestation can be used in the same way, but only by very advanced and talented practitioners, and then usually with far less spectacular results.

"Summoned creatures are also instrumental in creating enchanted items, though the process is usually pretty involved. One section describes how the Dragon's Fang was enchanted by Sephiroth. It took days and several summonings."

"So the bottom line is, there isn't some magical formula in there for killing the wyrm," Hound said.

"I'm afraid not," Ben said, "but there are a number of things that we can make use of."

"I'm starting to understand why Cyril was so fond of tech," Hound said. "It works without a bunch of strings attached."

"Yeah, I was hoping for more too," Ben said.

"What about all the rest of the stuff in the vault?" Kayla asked. "I had a closer look while you were out. There's a big chunk of dragon bone, three scales, a vial of blood, and a box full of gold and gems."

"We'll take what we can," Ben said. "A few of the summoning spells call for dragon's blood, plus Sephiroth used a few drops of his own blood when he enchanted the Dragon's Fang, so that's probably important. The scales and the hunk of bone are probably too big to carry without drawing attention, but we might be able to break off a few smaller pieces of bone."

He got up, feeling much steadier on his feet, and went to the vault. The bone looked like a leg bone that had been shattered a few feet down from the ball joint. Ben inspected it, nodding to himself.

"Stand back," he said, lifting it over his head. He slammed it onto the floor and a few small shards broke off. He set the large bone back on the shelf and gathered the smaller pieces.

"These should do," he said. He handed the two largest pieces to Ellie and took the three smaller pieces for himself. He scanned the room, locating his jacket, then went to work cutting a seam in the cuff so he could insert one of the shards. After he'd sewn it shut, he inspected his work.

"It's not pretty, but it'll hold," he said.

"Good idea," Ellie said, picking up her weapons belt and going to work incorporating the smaller bone into it while Ben inserted a second bone shard into one of his boots.

After Ellie finished her task, she frowned at the larger fragment, then smiled, placing her sword and scabbard on the table. She attempted to unscrew the pommel, but it wouldn't budge. She frowned, handing it to Hound.

He shrugged and gave it a try, but still it remained in place.

Kayla handed him a wrench from a nearby cabinet. After a bit of effort, the pommel broke free, revealing a small hollow space in the hilt of the sword.

"My father said they made these swords like this so they could be turned into a spear if needed—just like the Fang." She wrapped the bone in a piece of cloth and worked it into the handle, replacing the pommel cap and tightening it with the wrench.

"Hey, what do you know? I have a magic sword."

Ben chuckled. "I'd forgotten all about that. When I was younger my grandfather insisted that I learn a spear form. He even showed me the screw-off pommel, but I never gave it much thought because I liked the sword forms so much better." He gestured for the wrench and went to work adding a bit of dragon magic to his blade as well.

"So, we have the book, and you two are all magicked up," Hound said. "What's the plan?"

"We head back to the surface first thing tomorrow morning. Then back to Alturas to get the egg and find our friends. After that, we go east."

"I can't help but wonder what happens once we get close to the wyrm. That book didn't really solve our problem."

"Honestly, I'm hoping our course of action will become clearer once we get to the Mountaintop."

"You know what they say, hope in one hand…"

"Maybe Kaid has made some progress," Kayla said.

"Maybe … computer, contact Colonel Kaid."

The computer went to work. After a few minutes, Kaid's disembodied voice crackled to life over the facility's speakers.

"Hey, Ben, how're you doing?"

"Much better. I was out for a while, but I'm back on my feet."

"Glad to hear it. What's your status?"

"We're still in Shasta but we'll be headed back to Alturas in the morning. Our plan is to head east from there."

"Did you find what you were looking for?"

"Sort of," Ben said. "We have the Codex, but there's nothing in it that will give us the kind of advantage I was hoping for."

"I might have the weapons we need," Kaid said. "I found the base I was looking for and a few of the weapons I was hoping to find. After a rather pointed conversation with the locals, they agreed to help me get them into orbit. The first is set to launch day after tomorrow."

"What kind of weapons are we talking about?" Hound asked.

"Kinetic orbital strike weapons," Kaid said. "Imagine a crowbar forty feet long and two feet thick with reentry shielding and a guidance system. Once we get them into orbit, we can call them down onto a target at will. Yield should be in the twenty-kiloton range."

Hound whistled. "Now there's a weapon. How many we got?"

"Three," Kaid said. "We'll have to make sure our shots are on target, but they should ring the wyrm's bell pretty good."

"Sound's like it," Ben said. "That's really good news. Now we just have to come up with a way to lure the dragon out."

"I'm sure that egg of yours would get his attention," Kaid said.

"True, but he would just send some of his minions. We'll have to stir up a bunch of trouble before he'll show up himself."

"Somehow I think you're the perfect man for the job," Kaid said.

"You're probably right about that. The wyrm seems to be fixated on me and my family. I'll figure something out."

"Good man, I'm sending the launch codes and the projected trajectories of the weapons. You're authorized to fire on the dragon, but only on him. We can't afford to waste these on anything else."

"Understood," Ben said, his augment receiving the codes and the intended orbital path of all three weapons.

"I also found a skiff," Kaid said. "It's got a few mechanical problems, but I'm pretty sure I can get it into fighting form."

The specifications of the skiff came up in Ben's mind's eye. It was an orbital vehicle capable of carrying eight people plus the pilot and copilot, powered by a vacuum energy drive and propelled by a gravity engine. Ben whistled, willing an image of the vehicle to be projected onto the facility's screen.

"Any chance you could give us a ride?" Ben asked.

"Not anytime soon," Kaid said. "The weapons are first priority. Afraid you're on foot for now."

"Fair enough."

"Hey, it looks like your fancy spaceship has some guns on it," Hound said, examining the image on the screen.

"Indeed it does," Kaid said. "A high-end laser and a missile rack. Unfortunately, I haven't found any missiles yet, but there are still a few areas of the base I haven't searched, so keep your fingers crossed."

"You had me at high-end laser," Hound said.

Kaid chuckled. "Past that, I've found an armory with some pretty good stuff, plasma rifles and a box of ex-plus."

Hound whistled. "I like the sound of all of that."

"Yeah, unfortunately, none of it will work against the dragon," Kaid said. "I reviewed the records of the group that was operating out of this base. They tried everything they had, except the orbital weapons, and nothing made a dent. They were on a mission to retrieve a few components they needed to launch when they were attacked by one of the dragons. Their skiff went down and they were all killed. The data stream cuts out when the dragon lit the crash debris on fire.

"At any rate, I'll be in touch once I'm overhead," Kaid said. "You stay alive in the meantime."

"We'll do our best," Ben said.

The line went dead.

"Sounds like he's had more luck than we did."

"Twenty kilotons on the wyrm's neck sounds pretty good to me," Kayla said.

"That has to kill him, right?" Ellie said.

"One would hope," Ben said. "And if the first one doesn't, maybe the second or third one will."

"Now we just have to figure out a way to lure him out into the open," Kayla said.

"We could kill one of his high priests," Hound said. "That worked for the Warlock in Rogue City."

Ben nodded. "I'd like to avoid destroying an entire city if we can help it though. Maybe we kill a priest and then use the egg for bait somewhere out in the desert."

"That sounds like a one-shot deal, with a pretty high price if we miss," Ellie said.

"There is that," Ben said. "We have some time to think about it and more than enough to do between now and then."

Chapter 4

Ben felt the tension in the pit of his belly rise with the elevator as it ascended. When it came to a stop he reasserted his magic circle and mentally checked his weapons. The Codex was wrapped in his blanket and stowed in his pack, the Oculus was in a leather pouch all its own inside the larger satchel at his waist lest he touch the gemlike artifact and inadvertently trigger another vision of the future.

He'd considered using it again, but his courage failed in light of the memory of Ellie tied to a post, at the wyrm's mercy. He felt a twinge of guilt that he hadn't told her about that, and a rush of terror at the possibility that his vision was a true and inescapable glimpse of things to come.

He looked to his friends, each nodding in turn.

"Open the door, already," Homer said. "I have to pee."

"You could have gone before we left."

"Are you kidding? They made me go in a box … like a cat."

Ben stifled a chuckle.

"It's not funny. Dignity matters."

Ben willed the door to open, immediately sending a drone out to survey the room. He nodded to his friends. Homer was the first out, finding a wall to lift his leg on right away. Ben sent his drone ahead, accessing his map of the base and plotting a route to the surface.

They had taken the vial of blood as well as the gold and gems but left the scales and the large fragment of bone, locking the vault before departing. Ben willed the elevator to descend back to the facility and then commanded the computer to secure and power down.

Before he set out, he reached out with his mind, feeling for magic. He found plenty, but all of it was theirs.

"Looks like we're clear," he whispered, turning on his flashlight and leading the way into the labyrinth that was Shasta Base. They reached the top of a set of stairs not ten minutes later to find a section of the corridor collapsed and impassable. Ben frowned, accessing his map.

"This wasn't caved in on our way down," he said.

"I don't think we came in that way, did we?" Hound asked.

"No, but it leads to a staircase…" His voice trailed off, the hair on his neck tingling. He spun, directing his light down the hall, catching the red eyes of the Warlock's shadow for just a moment before it disappeared into the black.

"Was that what I think it was?" Hound asked.

Ben nodded. "He's nothing if not persistent," he said, turning the other direction. "Looks like we're headed this way."

They ascended, working their way back to the room that Hound had partially collapsed, the room where Ellie had been shot. Ben covered his light as they approached the corner, stopping to send his drone around and up the corridor into the large room, searching for danger, movement, or light, and finding nothing but a mostly collapsed ceiling and mounds of dirt and rubble.

He did a more thorough search of the large chamber, finding only one exit that was still passable. He checked the map again, searching for a course that would take them out.

"It's clear," he said, moving again. They passed through the room quickly, eyes darting to the gaping blackness above them and the ceiling stones that had not yet fallen.

The exit took them into an unfamiliar section of the base, room after room, most of the doors still closed and locked. Ben passed them without stopping, relying on his drone and his magic to sense for danger. They reached a staircase and began to climb, ascending several levels before the stairs ended in a cave-in, forcing them into a corridor. Ben sent his drone ahead while he shined his light on the debris blocking the flight of stairs.

"That looks like scorching," Kayla said.

"Yeah, and that looks like the stone was melted," Ellie said, pointing at a portion of wall that was sagging like wax that had gotten slightly too warm to hold its shape.

Ben sent his drone to the end of the hallway, noting that it ended in a tee and that one of the paths was caved in as well.

"I think we're being herded," he said.

"Don't much like the sound of that," Hound said.

"Me neither," Ben said. "We're clear to the end of this hallway."

He kept his drone several hundred feet ahead of them, searching for any sign of a threat, but all he found was a series of collapsed passages, each bearing the telltale signs of extreme heat. As they traveled, he referred to his map frequently. With each forced turn they made, he became more certain of their destination, until they reached the top of a staircase and he stopped, sending his drone farther ahead, turning a few corners and finally arriving at the entrance of one of the base's enormous central-hub chambers.

"Shit," he muttered.

"What is it?" Ellie asked.

"Saint Thomas and a dozen stalkers."

"Long odds," Hound said.

"Yeah, but I'm pretty sure we have to go through that chamber to get out."

"Or we could double back and Bertha could blow a hole in a wall…"

Ben held his hand up urgently to silence Hound.

"Oh, God, your father is here, Ellie," he said, breaking into a dead run.

"What do you mean?" she said, rushing to catch up.

Ben didn't wait. He kept his eyes on the path before him, but his mind was focused on the drone feed. Dom, Kat, Cleve, Olivia, Zack, and Derek had just rounded the corner of a large vehicle passage on the opposite side of the chamber, drawing Saint Thomas's attention.

Somewhere in the distance Ben heard laughter, and then Thomas transformed into his true form, rising into the air on powerful batlike wings and bursting into fire. As one, the stalkers howled. Most were wolves, but there was at least one mountain lion in the bunch. The cat stayed close to Thomas while the wolves charged.

Ben rounded a corner, still another section of corridor to go before he reached the short hallway leading to the room. His legs burned. His lungs burned. His nearly healed injury pulsed with pain in time with his stride.

"Rufus, ex-plus," he shouted.

"Right," Hound said from somewhere behind him.

He could feel Ellie's fear, but it was easily overshadowed by her fierce need to protect her family.

Dom's darts came free, three slugs accelerating past the speed of sound into the nearest stalker wolf, peeling its head apart even as the impact flipped it over backward. The other stalkers ignored their fallen companion.

Cleve fired—loud, reverberating and powerful, the bullet tore into the chest of another wolf, nearly ripping its left foreleg off, leaving it useless and dangling as the stalker continued its frantic charge.

Ben drew his revolver, flipping the cylinder open as he ran and pulling a slug out, slowing momentarily as he pocketed the round and replaced it with a seeker. He reached the corner and slowed, deploying all of his splinters and forming them into a single dart, larger and far more powerful than any one on its own. His friends reached him moments later.

"Ten stalkers and Saint Thomas," he said, through his panting. "Dom is on the far side."

Another rifle fired several rounds in rapid succession. Another report from Cleve's heavy brush rifle, followed by two blasts from a shotgun.

"Hit Thomas hard," Ben said, rounding the corner and sprinting toward the room, sending the dart at the mule's back with all of his will. It streaked forward, moving with terrifying speed and force, hitting Saint Thomas directly in the spine, breaking apart inside his body and spraying out of his chest in four hundred metal splinters before falling to the ground in a bloody jumble.

Thomas fell forward, his fire extinguished as he landed on his face with a grunt. The stalkers turned, skittering to a stop and changing directions as their true purpose came into view.

Ben targeted the cougar and fired, guiding the seeker round into the beast's head and watching it explode in a spray of blood across Saint Thomas as he pushed himself up to his knees. The wounded mule tipped his head back and howled into the darkness.

His cry echoed into the corridors and passages of the base. Moments later it was answered by another howl, followed by another and then more still.

Shadow began to swirl around Saint Thomas. Hound raised Bertha and fired, launching an ex-plus charge into the center of the room. The explosion was deafening, sending a shockwave in all directions that caused a few of the ceiling stones to fall, stunning everyone in the room and even causing the charging pack of stalkers to flinch.

Thomas was blasted across the room, closer to the large passage that Dom and his companions were arrayed across. His broken body came to a stop, smoke mingling with swirling darkness. Ben could feel the magic, potent and terrible. He checked his circle, expanding it to a radius of thirty feet, flipping his revolver to his left hand and drawing his sword.

Ellie came up alongside him, giving him space to work. He could feel her mind within his, knew her intent even as she knew his.

The first three stalkers leapt at them and the battle was joined, both slipping to the left, avoiding the leaping attacks and the snapping snarling of each stalker as they closed, both striking cleanly, each taking a wolf in the back of the neck, killing them instantly, Ben nearly cleaving his target's head free from its body.

He tried to dodge as the third wolf hit him, knocking him off balance with the force of its lunge. He brought his blade up and across his face, blocking the snapping jaws as he went down. Digging the point of his sword into the ground for leverage, he wedged the blade into the beast's mouth and fired five slugs into its body, none fatal, but each forceful enough to shove the monster to the side. He slashed with his sword, slicing deeply into the muscles that held the lower jaw to the skull.

Hound fired at another advancing wolf, bowling it over backward. Ben rolled away and came to his feet, Ellie stepping in to finish the wounded wolf with a thrust into its eye.

Ben rushed forward to cover her side as the remaining three wolves closed the distance. He braced himself for the first, dancing to the side and hacking its head in half just behind the ears. Another crashed into him, knocking him to the ground again. Ellie kicked it in the side, leaping a moment later so Ben could roll under her, their minds flowing together in the heat of the battle. Hound fired again.

The last stalker leapt at Ellie. She thrust, catching it in the chest and turning it sideways as it fell, wrenching the sword from her hand and knocking her off balance. Ben regained his feet, dancing past Ellie and stabbing the creature. It backed off growling and snarling, Ellie's sword still jutting from its chest.

Hound stepped up and shot it from a range of ten feet, abruptly transforming its head into a stump of bone and blood. Ben scanned the room frantically for the next threat. His eyes fell on Saint Thomas, now back on his feet.

"How are you not dead?" Ben said, driving his sword into the stalker carcass so he could reload his pistol.

A bark drew his attention. Another stalker arrived, snarling as it approached from the far end of the room. A second was close on its heels.

Cleve shot Saint Thomas in the back of the head, the bullet passing cleanly through his skull and exiting his right eye socket, leaving a black, uneven hole in its place, and yet he still stood, black wisps swirling around him.

"What the hell?" Ellie said, incredulity and fear in her voice.

Another stalker arrived, the first two going to Saint Thomas.

"I must applaud you," he said. "You actually managed to kill me."

Ben and Ellie shared a look.

"You can't escape," Thomas said. "There are dozens of my pets coming. You can't withstand them all."

Ben flipped the cylinder of his pistol closed and retrieved his sword, wiping the black blood on the coat of the dead wolf.

A pack of six wolves arrived from another corridor some distance away from the passage where Dom stood.

Dom motioned frantically for Ben and his companions to circle Saint Thomas.

"I'm impressed," a voice said from the shadows on the other end of the enormous chamber, a patch of sunlight slowly growing over the form of the Warlock. "You actually managed to kill a mule. Not an easy feat."

"If he's dead, then why's he still talking to me?" Ben said, motioning for his friends to circle toward the Warlock and away from the other end of the enormous room where the stalkers seemed to be coming from.

"So much to learn," Thomas said. "And so little time. Tell me, where is the egg?"

Ben shot him in the chest with absolutely no effect.

"I'm starting to think he's not playing by the same rules that we are," Hound said.

"There is no way out," Thomas said. "Give me the egg and your companions can leave … you have my word."

Ben holstered his pistol and considered charging him. Were it not for the dozen or more newly arrived stalkers coming to Thomas's side, he probably would have. Dead or not, he'd be far less dangerous without arms or legs.

"The mule has a point, Benjamin," the Warlock said. "He'll be on his feet for another hour or so before death finally takes. And there are more stalkers on the way."

Ben glared at the Warlock.

"Of course, I could offer you salvation … for a price."

Saint Thomas turned to the Warlock, raising one hand to point at him. "Feed," he said. The stalkers leapt as one, charging toward the Warlock in a blood frenzy.

He stood calmly, laughing at them as they passed through the image of his form. He tapped his illusionary staff on the floor and black tendrils began to seep out of the light hovering over his head, each finding a stalker with unerring precision.

"Be calm," he said. Thirteen stalkers came to heel around him.

"Again, what the hell?" Ellie said.

"My people have a much older and more well-defined relationship with the beings that you call stalkers," the Warlock said with a smile. "Unfortunately, even my power is limited."

A mountain lion roared, entering the room with a coyote, both going to stand by Saint Thomas.

"Time is not on your side, Benjamin," the Warlock said. "I will transport you and all of your companions safely to the surface in exchange for the vial of dragon blood you carry … and a vial of your own blood."

"Don't do it, Ben," Dom shouted from across the room.

"You have little choice, Benjamin. And even less time."

Another pack of stalkers entered from the far side of the room, mostly wolves again, but a few bobcats as well.

"It's getting crowded in here," Hound said.

A crack echoed into the room, followed by a grinding noise, and then a section of the ceiling came free, crashing to the ground off in the darkness.

Ben looked at the Warlock. "How?" he asked.

"Smart boy," the Warlock said, his image wavering for a moment and then vanishing. The patch of bright light above his projection descended and expanded, revealing a doorway in the fabric of the world that looked like it opened into a grassy meadow bathed in sunlight. At the same time, the stalkers that the Warlock had mastered broke into a furious sprint toward Saint Thomas and his rapidly growing army of undead animals.

"Quickly, Benjamin," a voice said from far away.

"Damn it," Ben said. "Everybody through!" He raced for the doorway as the stalkers crashed into each other, spinning, whirling, snapping and clawing in a frantic battle. One of the big cats skirted the frenzy of claw and fang, bolting toward Ben. Hound fired, slowing it. Cleve fired, wounding it, but not fatally.

Ben reached out for his splinters and found them at his command once again. He formed two darts and attacked the cougar's hindquarters, tearing its right haunch from its body and leaving it limping into battle. Ben re-called the rest of his splinters with a thought.

"Hurry," he shouted to Dom and the others as he and Ellie faced the limping mountain lion, backing away as their friends raced past them to the portal. Dom stopped to stand with them.

"Go!" Ben shouted, his eyes never leaving the beast. It made a feeble attempt to lunge at them. Ben and Ellie moved in opposite directions and then attacked, each thrusting into the cat's neck, wrenching their blades up and out, severing its spine and dropping it dead.

Saint Thomas howled, black wisps of dark magic still swirling around him, and then he charged.

Ben and Ellie turned and ran for the portal. Everyone else was already through. Homer was waiting at the threshold, leaping through as they closed the gap, Thomas coming quickly behind them.

Ben was the last one to reach the doorway, falling forward as Thomas raked his back, tearing his coat and leaving bloody scratches in his flesh. The portal closed the moment he passed through. Everyone else stood around him, unmoving. He regained his feet and then realized that he was rooted to the ground. His feet were stuck, and he couldn't free them. He focused on his circle, but he still couldn't take a step.

One glance at his surroundings and he realized that he was standing in the middle of a magic circle drawn with blood. But this one was different. Within the circle there were a number of runes drawn on the ground, symbols that Ben had never seen before.

Off to the side, several hundred feet away, atop a small knoll, stood the Warlock, several corpses at his feet and two Dragon Guard standing nearby, both looking entirely possessed by magic. Another Dragon Guard stood just outside the circle.

That man approached Ben mindlessly, offering him a small glass vial. "Blood," he said, dully.

"And if I refuse?"

The runes began to glow, orange and hot.

"You will burn."

Ben clenched his teeth, then took the vial, sliced the edge of his hand and drizzled thick red blood into the small opening. He stuck his sword in the dirt and fished the vial of dragon blood out of his pouch.

"I figured this might come in handy ... but not like this," he said, handing both vials to the possessed Dragon Guard, who took them, turned and walked off toward his master.

The Warlock waited patiently for his servant, inspected both vials, bowed to Ben and then vanished over the knoll.

Chapter 5

"Now what?" Homer asked. "I'm still stuck."

"Me too," Ben said, directing a cluster of splinters at the edge of the circle and breaking the line of blood surrounding them. A moment later, his feet came free. He quickly stepped outside the circle, moving toward the knoll and sending a drone into the air to locate the Warlock, but found no trace of his other-worldly enemy.

He reached the knoll and noted the dead men, desiccated and drained of life, but saw no hint of where the Warlock had gone.

Hound arrived a moment later. "I'm really not sure what to make of that guy," he said.

"The only thing I know for certain is that we can't trust him," Ben said, sending his drone higher and surveying the surrounding area in an attempt to get his bearings. The glistening white peak of Mount Shasta told him that they were somewhere on the southeast slope.

Loud voices behind him drew his attention.

Dom was faced off with his daughters and all three were shouting.

"Maybe chasing after the Warlock would be safer," Hound said.

Ben nodded with a sidelong grin and headed back to the group.

"Both of you are coming home, right now!" Dom said.

"No, I'm not," Ellie said.

"Me neither," Olivia said.

"Like hell," Dom said. "You're coming with me if I have to knock you both out and carry you myself."

Ben stepped off to the side and waited.

"Good luck with that," Ellie said with a snort.

"You know you won't do that, Daddy," Olivia said.

"The Daddy's-little-girl routine isn't going to work this time," he snapped at Olivia. "Neither of you have any clue what you've gotten yourselves into. If you keep going the way you're going, you'll both end up dead."

"Maybe, maybe not," Ellie said. "At least we'll die for something worthwhile."

"Death isn't worthwhile, not for anything," Dom said, his voice dropping to a whisper thick with emotion. "I can't lose you too, I just can't."

"You won't," Ellie said.

"You don't know that. You're still young enough to think you're immortal, but you're not. This path you're on leads nowhere good. I know, I've walked it."

"Which is exactly why you of all people should understand how important this is," Olivia said.

"The wyrm has to go," Ellie said. "If we don't do it, then who will?"

"I don't care!" Dom said. "Let someone else fight the damn thing."

"Who?" Ellie asked.

"That's exactly my point," Dom said. "I don't see anyone else risking their lives to save the world. No ... most people just put their heads down and let the wyrm enslave them. The smart ones ran. Why should you risk everything for people who won't stand up for themselves?"

"Because somebody has to," Ellie said. "And we're not alone. All people need is the hope of success and they'll stand with us."

"Now you're just deluding yourself," Dom said. "People will take the easy way every time, even if it means accepting a collar."

"Not all of them," Olivia said.

"We certainly won't," Ellie said. "And why should we? After the way you raised us, how can you expect us to?"

Dom shook his head. "I don't expect you to submit, I expect you to come home. We'll leave the area, get as far from that damn wyrm as we can. You can live free. You can be safe and happy."

"And what about our children?" Olivia said.

"At least this way, you'll have a chance to have children."

Ben frowned as he scanned the group standing around watching Dom argue with his daughters.

"Where's Imogen?" he asked. Nobody answered. "Hey!" he said loudly enough to draw everyone's attention.

"Where's Imogen?"

Dom turned his glare on Ben, anger dancing in his eyes, but it was Zack who spoke.

"The Dragon Guard took her," he said. "John, too."

A thrill of fear raced up Ben's spine. He swallowed hard, taking a moment to absorb the implications.

"Frank helped them," Zack said, wincing a bit at his own words.

Ben's fear began to transform into anger.

"You made me a promise," Dom said, turning to face Ben.

"How was she taken?" Ben asked. "When and where?"

"You told me you wouldn't get my daughters involved in this fool's errand of yours."

"Yeah, and they listen to me about as well as they listen to you," Ben said. "I told them to go home, over and over, and yet here we are."

"You've put my family at risk," Dom said. "I have half a mind to put you down."

"Don't you dare!" Ellie said, moving to stand beside Ben.

"No, I haven't," Ben said, his own anger beginning to boil. "The dragon put your family at risk. And you put your family at risk when you raised your daughters with courage and morality. If you wanted them to slink away and hide, you should have taught them to be cowards."

"Watch your tongue, boy," Dom said. "My patience is wearing thin." His darts came free and began to orbit around his head.

"If you hurt him, I'll never speak to you again," Ellie said.

"And my patience is at an end," Ben said, accessing his augment. "Command override," he thought, taking control of Dom's darts, drawing them harmlessly into his hand and putting them in his pocket.

Dom's eyes went wide.

"First, don't ever threaten me again," Ben said. "Second, tell me what happened to Imogen."

Dom clenched his jaw, glancing to Kat.

"No, don't look at her," Ben snapped. "Look at me and answer my question."

Dom snorted, shaking his head. "Like Zack said, the Dragon Guard took her and John, right after your brother cut John's hand off."

Ben closed his eyes and put a hand to his forehead.

"Where did they take her?"

"How the hell should I know?" Dom said. "I didn't come here for her, I came here for my daughters. Maybe you should ask your brother."

"You can count on that," Ben said, handing Dom his darts and releasing control with a thought. "For what it's worth, I don't want to see harm come to your daughters any more than you do, but they deserve to make their own choices and I intend to respect that." He stopped, looking down for a moment before turning to Ellie.

"There's something you should know," he said. "I didn't tell you before because I was afraid that it might come true, that saying it aloud might make it real."

"What?" she asked.

"When I touched the Oculus, I had a vision of you tied to a stake in the dragon's lair."

She blinked. Olivia gasped. Dom closed his eyes and sighed, turning around and walking a few steps away before turning back with a look of resignation.

"The Oculus?" Dom said. "Where the hell did you get that damn thing?"

"I took it from the Sage after he stole the egg from me," Ben said.

Dom actually chuckled, albeit bitterly, shaking his head. "If this Sage is who I think it is, then good on you. As far as the vision goes…"

"Is it ever wrong?" Ellie asked.

"Not in my experience," Dom said, his eyes becoming glassy. "The thing is, the visions are rarely in context and always open to interpretation. Usually, the harder you fight to avoid a particular outcome, the more likely you are to make it happen. After the first few times we let it guide us, we decided it was more trouble than it was worth."

"So what does that mean?" Ellie asked, a tremble in her voice.

Dom sighed, shrugging helplessly. "It means the dragon is going to take you and tie you to a post. How or why or when, or what happens after that…" he shook his head, taking his daughter in his arms and holding her tightly.

"But I did change one of the visions," Ben said. "It showed us going back to the safe house. Ellie and Imogen burned in that vision."

Dom frowned, shaking his head.

"That's a new one," he said. "I don't pretend to understand how the Oculus works."

"I'm sorry, Ellie," Ben said. "Maybe your father's right. Maybe you should go home with him."

Dom let her go and turned to Ben, shaking his head. "You don't get it. That thing sees the most likely future, a terrifying prospect all on its own. Worse, it seems to zero in on stuff you don't want to happen. Trying to avoid it probably won't help. In fact, it might be the thing that causes the future you saw to happen."

Everyone fell silent.

"So we use it," Ellie said after a moment.

"What do you mean?" Olivia asked, coming to her side.

"If the wyrm is going to take me, then we use it against him," Ellie said.

"How?" Ben asked.

"I don't know yet," she said. "Maybe we can figure out where it is that you saw me so we can know where the wyrm will be and plan an attack."

"Bait? I won't use you like that."

"Doesn't sound like we have a choice," she said. "If the dragon is going to take me anyway, then don't let it be for nothing."

Ben shook his head.

"Maybe I *should* have raised you girls to be cowards," Dom said.

"No, you're wrong," Ellie said. "This is good. It means we'll get our shot."

"Uh ... you're forgetting just how big our bullets are," Hound said.

"He's right," Ben said. "There's no way in hell I'm calling down twenty kilotons anywhere near you."

"So we find another way," Ellie said, turning to her father. "You have the Dragon's Fang. Maybe that'll do it."

"If you try to stab the dragon with a sword, you'll get exactly one shot, and that's if you're lucky." Dom said. "Miss and everybody dies."

"So we won't miss," Ellie said.

"Easier said than done," Dom said. "You think that mule you killed downstairs is dangerous. He was child's play compared to the dragon." He sighed, shaking his head. "But then, I guess that doesn't matter anymore. The Oculus has set your course for you, like it or not." He turned to Ben. "So what's your plan, Wizard?"

Ben shrugged. "We're headed back to Alturas to retrieve the egg."

"You left the egg in a dragon city?"

"It's safe," Ben said. "After the Sage stole it from me, I was worried that bringing it here would be too risky."

"You've got a lot to learn about assessing risk," Dom said.

"Probably," Ben said.

Dom snorted, shaking his head again. "I don't like anything about this," he said. "Unfortunately, my headstrong daughters are right smack in the middle of it, so I guess I'm along for the ride."

"There's more," Derek said.

"Of course there is," Dom said.

"Lulu and Juju are in town looking for Kayla."

"Oh, shit," Kayla said. "That's not good."

"No," Derek said.

She started pacing, a deep frown creasing her brow.

"They work for the Adara Coven," she said, still pacing. "They want the wyrm dead just as much as we do, but they'll never admit it. And every time they have a chance to act, they back away in fear of reprisal. They'll hand me over to the family ... or just make me disappear, after they interrogate me, of course." She paced some more. "Mom will send someone, but she'll be angling to get me out of harm's way ... probably try and send me to another continent."

"Sounds like your mother is a wise woman," Dom said.

Kayla ignored him.

"Dad will send someone too," she continued. "He'll bargain for my life, sell out everyone he can to the dragon and I'll probably still wind up like my brother."

She stopped and faced Ben. "We can't stay in Alturas any longer than we have to, and I can't trust any of my contacts now. They'll all be terrified of the family."

"Any other enemies I should know about?" Dom asked.

"You met the Warlock," Hound said.

"Yeah, he's seems like he might be a useful enemy," Dom said. "Although you probably shouldn't have given him the blood you did. Now, all he needs is a good-sized piece of bone or a few scales and he'll be able to open a portal to his world. And that's liable to complicate things."

"I doubt any of us would be alive right now if he hadn't," Ellie said.

"Maybe so. But that dragon blood was important. Sarah, Imogen's mother, told me about a secret spell hidden in the Codex. She called it a failsafe. Said we should only use it if Sephiroth was killed—and that it can only be accessed with a few drops of dragon's blood applied to the back cover of the book."

"What the hell?" Den said. "Why didn't you tell me this before."

"And why didn't you use it before?" Olivia added.

"First, I never expected you to get this far. Second," Dom said, turning to Olivia, "Sephiroth wouldn't have allowed it, and after..." He shook his head sadly. "Well, I didn't have any intention of ever coming back here." He looked up at the mountain, his eyes haunted.

"What does the spell do?" Ellie asked.

Dom shook his head, his eyes still distant. "Don't know," he said, after a few moments. "But it wasn't good. I got the impression it was a trade-off between bad and less bad. Or maybe it was just Sephiroth's way of getting revenge from the grave."

"Either way, we need to see that spell," Ben said.

"Might be more trouble than it's worth. A lot of people think of Sephiroth as the good dragon, but he wasn't. He was just another wyrm, using us while we used him. Your grandfather and I always intended to kill him the second we took down the last of his siblings. I worried that he wouldn't have it in him to go against Sarah … but that's a story for another time."

Ben's augment drew his attention to the drone feed. A patrol was a mile out and headed in their direction.

"Time to go," Ben said. "Dragon Guard are headed this way. Anyone who's coming with me, we're leaving now." He turned and headed east, sending his drone to scout ahead.

Ellie gave her father a sympathetic look and then hurried to catch up with Ben.

"How's your back?" she asked, coming up alongside him.

"Hurts."

"Want me to take a look at it?"

"Yeah, but later," he said. "I want to get clear of the area before that patrol picks up our trail."

"We could set an ambush," Hound said.

Ben shook his head. "I'd rather they returned to their commander with nothing to report."

"Fair enough, but they'll probably find the Warlock's circle."

"I'll keep an eye on them. If they pose a threat, we'll deal with them."

"So, how about you tell me what's happened since you parted ways with Zack," Dom said. "He gave us a pretty thorough report of everything that happened up 'til then."

They talked as they walked, Ben letting Ellie and Olivia recount their journey while he focused on leading them through the wilderness toward his destination. After they completed their story, Dom began to question them, picking at every detail, searching for more information, focusing in on the Sage and Kaid in particular. After he finished his interrogation, he fell silent, seeming to brood over everything he'd learned.

Ben's drone gave him advanced warning of enemy patrols which led him to pick a somewhat meandering path, both to avoid contact and to obscure their trail. By midafternoon it became apparent that the Dragon Guard had deployed their forces to comb the woods surrounding Mount Shasta. The forest was thick with them. Fortunately, he didn't see any priests.

He stopped in a clearing and sat down. Nobody complained at the opportunity to rest. Ellie helped him take off his coat and shirt so she could clean and dress his wound. He inspected the three gashes in the back of his coat and frowned.

"I really liked this coat," he muttered.

"Any idea how that mule got back up after we killed it?" Hound asked.

"Magic," Dom said with a shrug. "Probably made a deal with some demon to possess and animate his corpse if he was killed." He chuckled humorlessly. "The upside is, he likely paid with his soul."

"Yeah, I'm not getting much upside out of that," Hound said.

"Me neither," Ben said. "I like the monsters I kill to stay dead."

Dom chuckled again, nodding. "What can I say, magic's a bitch. Just when you think you've got a handle on it, everything changes." He rubbed the stubble on his chin. "Of all the things you've told me, I'm most encouraged by this Colonel Kaid and his tech."

"Does that mean you'll help us?" Olivia asked.

He glared at her until she shrank a bit. "Yes and no. Ellie is caught up in this, like it or not. You aren't."

"But…"

"No," he said, silencing her with a raised hand. "I came here to protect you, both of you. That means you're going home, young lady."

Olivia frowned defiantly, shaking her head. "I'm a part of this."

"For now," he said, turning back to Ben. "As I was saying, Kaid's orbital weapons sound promising. Certainly better than trying to poke the wyrm with a sword."

"I think you're right, if we can lure him out into the open," Ben said.

"Or you could just blast his mountaintop into a crater," Dom said.

"It might come to that, but I hope not."

"This isn't the time for half measures," Dom said. "In a fight like this, you're either all in or you're all dead."

Ben nodded sadly, looking at the ground for a moment before replying. "I wouldn't be here if I wasn't ready to see this thing through, but I'd rather not kill a bunch of innocent people if I can help it."

"I get that," Dom said. "I even respect it. Just remember, you're the one who keeps talking about saving the future. And that's going to take some hard choices."

"I know," Ben whispered, shivering.

"All done," Ellie said, helping Ben put his shirt on. He winced a bit as he raised his arm.

"It looks a lot better than I would have expected," she said.

He nodded, tapping his head.

"We should get going."

The rest of the afternoon was spent walking quietly, avoiding still more patrols, once even hiding in a thicket while a Dragon Guard squad passed within fifty feet. By dark they'd traveled a dozen miles from the mountain, yet the patrols were still thick.

"These guys just don't give up," Hound said.

"I'll bet they'd rather wander around these woods for a year than report their failure," Dom said.

"You're right about that," Kayla said. "The wyrm has eaten people for less."

Ben accessed his drone and scouted the area, looking for enemy patrols and finding three camps within a few miles. "Let's keep the noise and the light to a minimum tonight," he said. "The Dragon Guard are too close to risk drawing attention."

They made a cold camp, ate stale rations and went to bed. Despite his fatigue, Ben found sleep elusive. He'd convinced himself that the Codex contained a magical solution for the wyrm. Now that he'd studied the secrets it contained, he felt let down. A part of him hoped that the blank pages, the secret spell, might be the answer he was looking for, but he didn't want to count too much on that possibility. Unfortunately, that left him with few options—Kaid's weapons or a swordfight with a dragon. Both options involved risks.

He found himself looking up at the stars and wondering where the dragons came from. They'd tried to conquer humanity before and failed. He intended to ensure that this attempt failed as well. But what of the next time? Was the world doomed to suffer their abuse forever?

"Really?" Homer said. "One dragon's not enough to worry about?"

"If they came before, they'll come again."

"Yeah, and you'll be long dead by then. Go to sleep."

"There has to be a way to stop them for good."

"No there doesn't."

Ben sighed, looking sidelong at his dog in the dark. As much as he hated to admit it, Homer was right.

He turned his mind to the one dragon that he might be able to kill and quickly found himself thinking in circles, revisiting all of his options again and again until he finally drifted off.

Chapter 6

Hound shook him awake just before dawn. Ben consulted his drone, still hovering several thousand feet overhead and found that the Dragon Guard were beginning to stir as well.

A distant howl shattered the morning calm. Ben knew in an instant that it wasn't a normal wolf. A big cat shrieked in answer.

"What was that?" Zack asked.

"Stalkers," Ben said, focusing his drone in the direction of the noise and zooming in, closer and closer, until he was looking at the entrance to Mount Shasta. Stalkers were emerging at an alarming rate, a cougar, then three coyotes, followed by two wolves. Fear fluttered in his stomach.

"They're emptying out of the mountain."

"All of them?" Ellie asked.

"Pretty sure," he said.

"That might be a problem," Dom said.

"Yeah," Ben said, sending another cluster of splinters into the air and assembling them into a second drone. "We should probably go."

They set out, moving more quickly and less quietly than the day before. Ben accessed his drones frequently, scanning the area ahead and then looking over his shoulder, as it were. The stalkers had vanished into the forest, but he knew it was only a matter of time before the creatures picked up the scent.

The Dragon Guard patrol directly in their path was another matter. He slowed and motioned for silence when it became apparent that evading them would take too long.

"Give me a minute," he whispered, sitting down and closing his eyes.

He sent his drones in closer, transforming one into a dart while using the other to see his targets. Both moved through the trees, the dart leading the drone by a hundred feet, closing with the enemy, quickly and silently. Eight men were having breakfast around a small campfire. Ben felt a brief twinge of guilt as he slowed his drone to a stop near their camp, sending his dart into the side of the first Dragon Guard's head with lethal speed. Blood sprayed across the man sitting nearby as the dart exited his companion's skull. He stood, crying out urgently. Ben redirected the dart at another, then another. Those still able rose in a panic, shouting, searching the forest for the enemy, taking up their rifles in vain as Ben killed them one by one.

The very one-sided battle lasted for less than a minute. All eight Dragon Guard lay dead, neat yet bloody puncture wounds through each man's head. Ben scanned the area and then sent his drone and dart higher into the sky, looking for other enemies close enough to represent an immediate threat. Finding none, he transformed the dart into a second drone and opened his eyes.

"Let's go," he said.

"What just happened?" Zack asked.

"I just killed eight people," Ben said sadly.

Dom looked at him appraisingly, nodding to himself before setting out.

Ben guided them around the camp, rationalizing that the route he'd picked was more direct, yet knowing in the back of his mind that he didn't want his friends to see the carnage he'd left scattered so casually across the forest floor.

It was one thing to kill in battle, up close and personal, but slaughter at a distance, so sterile and detached, seemed somehow to be a greater affront to his conscience. He found himself dwelling on it while they walked.

"Stop that," Homer said.

"What?"

"You know what. You chose to wage this war. And you did so for reasons that are just, though somewhat less than practical. There's no sense in beating yourself up over fallen enemies."

"It's just … it wasn't a fair fight."

"That's the best kind," Homer said. "You think the dragons agonized over the nine billion people they killed in one afternoon? I'll bet they didn't. They started this. If you're going to finish it, you'd better stop feeling sorry for them."

"I never wanted to kill people," he said after a time.

"You don't have to, you know," Homer said. "Hatch the dragon whelp and kill it, then run away and hide."

"You sound like Dom."

"Yeah, his priorities are more sensible than yours."

"What's that supposed to mean?"

"You're trying to save the world," Homer said. "He's trying to save his family."

Ben walked in silence for a while, mulling his dog's advice.

"I just can't let the wyrm get away with what he's done."

"Sure you can," Homer said.

"Where's this coming from?"

"Love," Homer said. "I don't want you to die. And you've made a good-faith effort at it twice this month."

"I'm not going to die," Ben said.

"And that's where you and Dom are different. He knows bad things can happen to him. You still think they only happen to other people, in spite of all the evidence to the contrary."

He fell silent, turning his options over in his mind yet again, and yet again coming to the same conclusions.

"I have to see this through."

"I know," Homer said.

Ben set a grueling pace, abandoning the quiet and hard-to-follow path he'd charted the day before in favor of covering ground as quickly as possible. A distant howl just after noon only served to reinforce his urgency.

"Do you think they found the circle?" Hound asked.

"And our trail," Ben said.

Another pack of wolves howled in answer. A cat screamed.

"Any chance we're getting close to that hole in the ground you're looking for?" Dom asked.

"Not even close."

"In that case, we're going to need a defensible position before nightfall."

"Or sooner," Hound said.

"If they come at us one at a time, I can probably defend without much risk," Ben said.

"Unless a priest shows up with them," Ellie said.

"There is that."

"We need to make better time," Dom said.

"On foot it'll take four or five days to reach Alturas, and that's if we push hard," Kayla said.

"We could turn south and head for the road," Derek said. "We might be able to find some horses."

"That road takes us pretty far out of our way."

"And we're bound to run into more Dragon Guard if we go that route," Dom said.

"Is there any way we could cover our tracks?" Olivia asked.

"I doubt it," Ben said. "Stalkers are hard to shake."

"What if we start a fire?" Zack asked.

"I'd hate to burn the forest down," Ben said.

"I'd hate to get eaten by a stalker," Hound said.

"It's dry enough," Dom said, scooping up a handful of needles from the forest floor.

Derek picked up some dried leaves, crunched them into pieces and let them fall. "The wind is at our backs," he said. "It'd push the fire right into us."

"For now, we keep moving," Ben said, setting out once again. He called one of his drones down to follow a dozen feet overhead while leaving the other at a thousand feet.

The gradual but steady slope of the mountain lent speed to their travels until they entered a field of fallen trees and had to slow to pick their way through the maze of haphazard debris. With the aid of his drones, Ben guided them through, but they lost time and nobody emerged without scratches to show for their efforts.

Almost as if on cue, a big cat screamed. Ben consulted his higher drone and picked out the stalker mountain lion as it leapt up into the remnants of a tree jutting from the far edge of the debris field.

He zoomed in with his higher drone as he sent his closer drone, transforming it into a dart, guiding it silently until he had a clear shot at the back of the possessed predator's head. With a thought, the dart accelerated past the speed of sound in a blink, striking the stalker just below the skull, severing its spinal cord and exiting through an eye socket.

The stalker flopped over, bounced once against the tree and then fell with a thud.

"One down," Ben said, re-calling his splinters and re-forming them into a drone.

"Good bet they've got a pin in us," Dom said.

"Yeah," Ben said, leading them back into the forest.

Twenty minutes later, Homer stopped, lifting his nose into the wind. "I smell wolves ... dead wolves."

Ben accessed his higher drone, picking out the pack of five loping toward them. He fixed that drone's sights on the enemy pack, then detached the two hundred splinters he had affixed to his boots, sending one up as a dart and attaching the second cluster to his left wrist.

"Five wolves about a minute out," he said, turning back and climbing up on a small boulder, waiting for his targets.

Dom spun up his darts, Cleve checked the chamber of his rifle. Everyone else spread out.

"Targets acquired," the augment flashed in his mind, marking all five as they burst into a frenzied sprint toward them, barking and snarling as they closed.

Ben sent his two darts, targeting the leading wolves, hitting the first in the mouth and killing it instantly. The second wolf flinched, causing the dart to hit him in the shoulder, ripping his foreleg free of his body and sending him flipping over backward in a spray of black blood.

Dom's darts came next, slamming into a single wolf in rapid succession, first wounding, then killing the beast.

Cleve fired, tearing into the chest of the fourth wolf, shattering its breastbone and then its spine, dropping the creature to the ground, alive but broken.

Silence fell onto the forest, the echo of Cleve's shot wavering in the distance. Hound fired next, bowling the last stalker over in a bloody mess. He advanced quickly, tomahawk in hand, hacking at its neck twice before giving his work a look and nodding approval.

"If that's the best they've got, I think we might be okay," he said.

"Until we have to sleep," Dom said, his darts coming to rest on his wristband.

"Or until they come at us en masse," Ben said.

"There's something wrong in the world when I'm the optimist," Hound said, wiping blood from his axe on the coat of the wolf.

"Well, shit!" Ellie said, pointing skyward.

A large bird circled overhead.

Ben smiled. "That's not nearly the problem it used to be."

"Might be an opportunity," Dom said. "Find a defensible position. Draw 'em in."

"We have to make a stand sooner or later," Ben said. "There's a knoll a couple of miles that way." He set out on his new course, checking on the bird with his drone to make sure it was following.

Sure enough, it maintained a tight orbit above them.

As the slope became steeper, the trees became sparser, revealing a glimpse of their destination ... a rock outcropping jutting from the base of the mountain, three sides sheer granite cliff faces falling a hundred feet into a steep scree field, the side in front of them a steep slope upward after descending into a saddle, culminating in a wide and level plateau with just a few trees leading up to it.

"I suppose this will have to do," Dom said.

The snap of a broken twig drew everyone's attention as a stalker coyote broke cover and charged.

It had gotten close.

Kat was its target. It lunged at her. She brought her rifle around to block, but Zack stepped up, aimed and fired his shotgun, blasting the coyote aside and stunning it. He took two steps closer, aimed and fired again, the blast slamming the beast's head to the ground.

"Thanks," Kat said, patting him on the back.

Ben chided himself as he accessed his high drone feed and scanned for other enemies, shifting into the thermal spectrum for a few moments before breathing a sigh of relief.

"We're clear."

They carefully moved down into the saddle as the slope increased, sliding from one tree to another to arrest their descent. The rocky ascent before them looked to Ben far more daunting than it had from a distance.

"You know I'm not a cat, right?" Homer said.

Ben ignored him, pointing at one of the fir trees near the base of the twenty-foot cliff looming ahead of them.

"Can we knock that tree down?"

"If we did it right, it would catch on that outcropping," Derek said.

"Make a nice ladder," Hound said.

Dom chuckled wryly, ambling over to the tree and drawing the Dragon's Fang. The blade was white, lustrous and nearly translucent, it tapered evenly from two inches in width at the hilt to a very sharp point.

He eyed the tree, chuckled again and nodded to himself, taking a broad stance, holding the fabled sword with both hands as he drew back smoothly and heaved himself into the stroke.

His body unwound like a spring, propelling the Fang toward its target. Driven by strength, fueled by will, and directed by intention, the pearl-white blade, glowing with reflected sunlight, slammed into the trunk, cutting through bark and wood, cleanly at first, but then with near explosive power.

Ben saw more. He watched Dom deliberately form a profoundly powerful intent, wind it up and unleash it into the tree by directing his entire will into the sword. He didn't account for failure. There was no thought or provision or consideration given to the possibility that he wouldn't succeed.

He swung the Dragon's Fang with everything he had.

The tree, sixty feet of needle and bough, jolted sideways as it came free of its root and stump, quivering in midair for a moment before gravity claimed it with a crash. It shook the ground, the violence of the impact reverberating up the tree in a wave before it slowly fell into the notch in the stone cliff face, lodging itself into place and providing them a way up.

Dom backed away, watching the felled tree warily, as if it might strike back.

"Looks good," Hound said, approaching from the side, testing the grounding and balance before climbing up the uneven ladder of limbs. He reached the top of the cliff and disappeared. Ben accessed his drone and watched him make a quick sweep of the plateau, returning a few moments later.

"We're good," he shouted down.

One by one they climbed the tree, Ben making a sling from his blanket to carry Homer. After taking a moment to survey their position, he found Dom standing at the top of the cliff looking at the tree.

"We probably ought to push that over," he said.

"Yeah, that bird's outlived its usefulness, too" Ben said, sending a detachment of splinters skyward. Less than a minute later, the aerial stalker was spiraling to the earth.

Ben found a limb to use as a lever while Hound started cutting several branches that were in the way. After a few minutes of work, the tree toppled over, flopping into the scree field and sliding down the mountain beside the knoll.

They spent the next hour clearing brush so they had firm ground to stand on, moving a couple of fallen trees to lay along the top of the cliff and stacking wood for a few bonfires. Ben checked his drone feed periodically, growing anxious that no more stalkers had arrived.

"I really thought we'd have seen another one by now," Kayla said, scanning the forest blanketing the slope of Mount Shasta.

"Yeah, I'm pretty sure that bird I shot down belonged to a priest," Ben said.

Dom nodded, frowning deeply. "We should post a watch and try to get some sleep," he said.

"It's not even dark yet," Olivia said.

"No, but we're probably not going to get much sleep tonight."

"You think they'll come at us in the dark?" Hound asked.

"Hard to say. Demons thrive in the night. If a priest has them on a leash, they'll probably wait until morning or even for some reinforcements. Those that are still stalking us on their own will come straight at us, day or night."

"You mean like that one," Hound said, pointing into the forest at another coyote peering through the brush.

Ben checked his drone feed. "Three more wolves are coming."

"Dogs I can handle," Hound said. "It's the cats that make me nervous."

"Me, too," Homer said.

Dom spun his darts up, whipping them around his head to build speed before unleashing them at the coyote, one after the other. Each hit hard enough to kill a normal animal, but it took all three to destroy the stalker.

Ben sent a dart to attack the approaching wolves, using his drone to guide the weapon. He caught them half a mile out and picked them apart, each wolf taking several strikes before going down, but all three succumbing in the end.

"I don't see any more coming," he said.

"That's some impressive tech," Dom said. "I can't help but wonder if things might have worked out differently if we'd had the balls or the desperation to use it back then."

"You ought to see what Kaid can do."

"I'm looking forward to it. For now, why don't you show me what you can do."

Ben shrugged. "You've seen the darts and the drones."

"Yeah, what else you got?"

"Kaid created a shield."

"And some pretty badass guns, too" Hound added.

"He said I don't have enough splinters to make a laser, never mind a plasma cannon."

"So show me the shield," Dom said.

Ben thought about it for a moment, chiding himself for not taking the time to explore his capabilities more thoroughly. Kaid had told him that creativity was the key to making his splinters more useful.

He accessed his augment and sent two hundred splinters to create a basic shield. They formed into a circular lattice about three feet in diameter and projected a slightly visible blue field between them. It hovered a few feet in front of Ben.

Dom nodded approvingly.

"Can you move it around?"

Ben thought about it and the shield moved according to his will. He sent it farther away, turned it so that the plane of the shield was level to the ground, brought it back to himself and touched it with his finger, feeling a slight tingle as he pressed against it.

"Not bad," Dom said. "Now let's see if it can take a punch."

Ben moved it away from him and angled it in front of Hound. Rufus smiled, drawing his axe and hitting the shield with the back hammer. It bounced off the blue tech barrier.

Dom spun his darts up and propelled them into the shield, nodding again when they bounced off, the blue field rippling as the lattice of splinters absorbed the impact.

"Nice," Ellie said.

Dom looked over at his daughter with a grin, drew the Dragon's Fang and stabbed at the shield. The blade penetrated the field, knocking several splinters out of position in the grid they formed and causing the entire shield to fail. A warning flashed in Ben's mind as his shield lost cohesion and became nothing but a small swarm of splinters floating before him.

"Can you bring it back?" Dom asked.

It took a moment but Ben was able to reconstitute his shield without difficulty.

"Good," Dom said. "It's important to know your limitations. See if you can push me away with it."

Ben frowned, chiding himself once again for failing to see the potential of his tech.

"Go on," Dom said.

Ben placed the shield between the two of them and gently moved it into Dom's chest. Dom turned his shoulder into it as Ben willed it forward. After a moment they came to an impasse, neither man nor tech gaining ground.

Ben let off.

"How fast can you move it?" Dom asked.

Ben turned it toward the edge of the knoll and propelled the shield forward very quickly, reaching combat speed in seconds, though not nearly the speed that his darts could achieve.

And so it went until the light began to fade, Dom offering suggestions for using the shield and Ben testing those suggestions. It wasn't long before he'd developed a whole new appreciation for the power of his splinters and for the depth and breadth of Dom's experience.

The darts and the drones were powerful, providing information and lethality, but the shield function was far more versatile. He could increase the size of the shield to five feet in diameter if he used all of his splinters. When turned level with the ground, the three-foot shield could carry just over forty pounds. He could spin it, creating a terrifyingly sharp saw-blade effect capable of slicing limbs from a tree with only a few seconds of effort. With a little practice, he discovered that he could launch two hundred splinters off his cuffs and form a shield very quickly, even propelling it with enough force to knock Hound off balance from a few feet away.

As darkness crept over the world, Ben began to wonder about the stalkers again. No more had arrived while he'd been training, and his high drone didn't show any more coming, and yet, he was certain that more had emerged from the mountain than they had killed … many more.

"How far can you see with that drone of yours?" Dom asked.

Ben shrugged. "Quite a ways. I haven't really tested its limits."

Dom fixed him with a hard look, then began shaking his head slowly. "Your grandfather would have just known what needed doing," he said. "But then, he had a few years on you. Send that thing up as high as you can and look as far as you can."

Ben felt a bit sheepish, accessing the drone feed as it rose into the air. He stopped at five thousand feet and began a slow sweep of the forest, switching to thermal imaging to penetrate the shadow of the mountain and the foliage blanketing the lower slope.

A cluster of men was camped about half a day away. As Ben zoomed in he began to make out the forms of animals, lots of them, except they didn't generate the same level of heat as living animals. Wolves and big cats mingled with a bear and dozens of coyotes.

"Looks like a priest has control of the stalkers, and he's accompanied by a squad of Dragon Guard."

He pulled out and scanned the terrain leading back toward the entrance to the base.

"And there are plenty more Dragon Guard farther out. Looks like they've all made camp for the night but I think they're moving to join with the priest."

Dom nodded, rubbing his chin. "Makes sense," he said. "The priest has to know we've made short work of the stalkers he's sent our way. Think your darts can get him from here?"

"I don't know. He's quite a ways out."

"Give it a try."

"All right," Ben said, taking a seat on a rock and closing his eyes. He sent another drone to join the first, transforming one into a dart as they covered the distance to the enemy camp, coming in several hundred feet overhead.

"I have a shot."

"Wait, won't that bring the stalkers right at us?" Zack asked.

"That's the hope," Dom said. "Take your shot."

Ben directed the dart down at the top of the priest's head, moving out of the night sky without a sound until it hit. The priest pitched forward into the fire. The Dragon Guard all came to their feet in surprise and alarm. Ben pulled his dart free and sent it back into the sky while he watched with the drone.

As one, the stalkers howled, screamed, and barked, all turning toward Ben and his friends and bounding into pursuit of their quarry.

He called his tech back. "Here they come."

"Light the fires and take positions," Dom said.

Hound began handing out several spears that he'd made, really nothing more than long pointy sticks … but enough to stop a charging stalker.

Ben brought one drone into orbit overhead while leaving the other a thousand feet up. It took several minutes before the onrushing horde of stalkers could be heard through the stillness of the night. Ben could feel the tension rising. He idly thought that he would rather have this fight during the day.

A pack of wolves came into view through his drone.

"Keep them off the plateau," Dom said. "Hold your fire unless you have a good shot, and watch each other's backs."

Ben looked over at Ellie. "Stay close."

"Always," she said.

Dom frowned.

The sound of a dozen wolves crashing through the forest reached them. Ben checked his drone feed. A memory of his first up-close and personal encounter with a stalker flashed through his mind, followed closely by memories of the haunting dreams that plagued him afterwards.

He set those thoughts, and the doubts that accompanied them, aside. He was far more capable now. He had the high ground and a defensible position. He looked over at Ellie again.

He also had more to lose.

The first wave of stalkers were all wolves. They came rushing down the slope toward the saddle and the rocky cliff that Ben and his friends stood atop. The first to break through the brush was hit by Dom's darts, all three in rapid succession tore into the beast, leaving it broken and bloody but still snarling and snapping.

Ben targeted the next with his dart, guiding the weapon more accurately and accelerating it more quickly than Dom's darts, hitting the wolf in the face and then exploding into splinters as it passed through the monster's head. The creature pitched forward and tumbled down the slope into the saddle.

Cleve fired, blasting another wolf sideways and wounding it severely. Ten more raced down the slope and leapt at the cliff face, momentum and dark magic carrying them higher up the cliff than Ben would have thought possible.

A few crashed into the rock, failed to gain any purchase and fell back to the saddle. A few more actually managed to find footing on the uneven face and propelled themselves toward the top. The first was knocked backward by Kayla and Derek, both stabbing down at it with their makeshift spears. It hit the ground and bounded to its feet, glaring up at them.

Hound blasted another in the face, toppling it backward.

One gained good footing and launched up at them. Ben sent the two clusters of splinters attached to the cuffs of his coat, transforming them into a shield and shoving the wolf backward. It wailed as it fell.

Another scrambled to the top of the cliff. Ellie reached over the log they were using for cover and stabbed it in the face. It fell backward.

More came, coyotes and a bobcat. The canines struggled to overcome the cliff, but the cat easily leapt across the saddle into one of the trees and then onto the plateau. Zack shot it in the side as it landed. It spun toward him. Olivia caught it with her spear before it could reach him, knocking the cat aside, the bloody tip of the spear sticking out of its back. Zack aimed and fired again, hitting it in the head and putting an end to its frantic thrashing. He reloaded.

Dom's darts returned to him, whirling around his head, whipping up speed before he launched them at another wolf that had managed to reach the plateau.

Ben kept his shield and drone in place while he targeted the enemy with a single dart, aiming carefully, targeting each in the head and usually hitting as he intended. Even when he missed a kill shot, the wound he left was debilitating.

If the wolves had a hard time scrambling and leaping to the top of the knoll, the coyotes were entirely helpless to climb the cliff, though not for lack of trying. Within a few minutes the first wave was defeated and Ben was directing his dart from one fallen stalker to another, ensuring that they would never rise again.

A cougar screamed, coming into view and leaping the saddle, clearing the low log wall they were using for cover and nearly landing on Hound. He spun, shooting the cat in the haunch before it could turn on him, firing again, then again, peppering the mountain lion with shot and doing damage but not enough.

It leapt at him. He rolled back and to the side, sacrificing balance and ground for range. Derek and Kayla both attacked the cat as one, stabbing it with their spears and pinning it to the log wall. Hound rushed forward, pressing Bertha's barrel into the neck of the cat. He fired. The beast's head came nearly free as it slumped to the ground.

While that battle raged behind Ben, another big cat landed right in front of him. He lashed out with his sword, catching the cat across the nose, causing it to flinch. Ellie stabbed over the log barrier and cut deeply into the side of its neck. It scrambled to the side, struggling to get its footing on the narrow strip of ground between the log barrier and the drop. Ben pulled his shield in quickly, angling it into the back of the beast, pinning its hind legs to the ground and preventing it from launching at him. Three darts whizzed past, hitting the cat in the face and knocking it backward off the edge.

A bear roared as it charged down into the saddle, crashing into the trunk of a young tree and toppling it into the side of the cliff, bringing it crashing down on Kayla and Derek. Both were knocked flat and pinned to the ground by the tree's branches. Cleve, Zack, and Olivia went to work trying to free them.

The bear started climbing. Ben hit it in the side of the neck with a dart, spraying splinters and black blood out the other side, but the bear kept coming. Hound leaned over the log barrier and shot it in the side of the head with buckshot, but the beast didn't fall. Another bobcat leapt the saddle, coming for Ben. His shield was out of position and his dart had yet to re-form. He danced to the side, slashing at the cat as it clawed at him, spinning and contorting in midair as it passed by.

Ben and Ellie moved as one, turning on the cat as it landed, Ben moving straight at it, leading with the point of his blade while Ellie circled, stabbing into its neck and driving it aside, drawing its attention as Ben brought the blade of his sword down onto the back of its head, killing it. They shared a brief glance of triumph before turning back to the fight.

The bear reached the top of the cliff a few moments after Derek and Kayla were pulled free of the fallen tree, both bruised and scraped. Hound loaded a round and took careful aim, but he was far too close. Before he touched off the round, the bear swatted the barrel away, causing the slug to hit the animal's shoulder instead of its head. It nearly fell, but managed to catch its balance and lunge into the log barrier, knocking the top log loose. Everyone backed away as their cover fell toward them.

Ben sent his dart at it again, willing his shield to begin spinning as the first dart hit it in the side of the head but not hard enough to penetrate the stalker's skull. He turned his shield sideways and directed it at the bear's neck, spraying black blood in a stream onto the ground as it sliced deeply into the beast.

It flailed, trying to get away, breaking free of the whirling blade, only to be met by Hound and another slug. This time the round hit the bear directly in the right eye and splattered the back of its head onto the low foliage, black blood glistening in the firelight.

Ben accessed his feed, taking in the battlefield with a glance. A coyote was awkwardly climbing the tree leaning against the cliff. Dozens more were coming.

"Hound, ex-plus," he shouted. "Other side of the saddle, on my mark."

Hound nodded, adjusting his rounds and moving for a clear shot. Ben directed his shield at the trunk of the tree about halfway down and began cutting. Cleve waited for the coyote to reach the top and then shot it in the face, killing it cleanly.

Ben focused on cutting the tree while also watching the onrushing pack of stalkers. They were moving in a cluster, all of them desperate to close the distance to their prey.

Ben looked to Hound. "Now!"

Bertha barked and then the world lit up. A bright flash followed by a shockwave knocked them all down, stunned and disoriented, blind in the dark. Ben clenched his eyes closed and accessed his drone feed. Broken and wounded stalkers were scattered all around but none were still coming for them. He scanned the darkness and sighed as he lay back, his eyes still closed.

As quickly as it had begun, the battle was over.

"Everybody okay?" he asked, without getting up or opening his still-blinded eyes.

"I think so," Ellie said.

"For the most part," Derek said.

As his eyesight came back, Ben regained his feet and surveyed the scene. The trees on the other side of the slope were blasted to ruin. Stalker bodies littered the landscape, their black blood staining the ground like splattered paint. He looked to his friends and nodded when he saw that all of them were alive.

The tree knocked over by the bear creaked and cracked, then broke and fell to the saddle. Ben called his splinters back.

"Anybody wounded?" Dom asked.

"Nothing too serious," Kayla said, prodding a gash on her arm.

"Let's get that taken care of," Kat said, retrieving her med kit and going to work patching up Kayla and Derek.

"Is that all of them?" Dom asked.

Ben consulted his drone, sending it higher, scanning for enemies in the dark.

"Looks like it," he said.

"Thank God for high ground," Hound said, reloading Bertha.

"And explosive shotgun rounds," Dom said. "That was quite a show."

"Yeah, Kaid gave Bertha a makeover. Prettied her up real good."

Ben turned his attention to the wounded stalkers and methodically put them down for good.

"Well, that went better than I thought it would," Dom said. "Without those stalkers on our heels, we should be able to stay ahead of the Dragon Guard without too much trouble."

Chapter 7

After the excitement of battle wore off, Ben felt a wave of exhaustion. He sat down next to the fire, resting his hand on Homer as he came to lie down next to him.

"I really don't like those stalker cats."

Ben scratched him behind the ear. "Me neither," he whispered.

"What was that?" Ellie asked, sitting next to him.

"Oh … just thinking out loud."

"You should get some rest," she said.

He nodded absently, staring into the fire. Not long ago, a small army of stalkers would have torn them apart, high ground or not. He'd acquired significant power over the past several weeks, but deep down, he knew that it wouldn't be enough. Possessed animals were one thing. As terrifying as they were, they didn't come close to the power of the dragon.

"Hey," Ellie said. "Where did you go? You looked really far away."

He nodded. "Thinking about the wyrm."

"Put that aside and get some sleep," she said. "We won today. That's enough for now."

He gave her hand a squeeze and went to lay out his bedroll.

Morning came all too quickly, Hound shaking him awake before the light of dawn had erased the stars.

"Already?" he muttered.

"Afraid so," Hound said.

Ben nodded and took a deep breath of the cool morning air, willing the fog to clear from his groggy mind. Within a few minutes they were all up and preparing to travel. Cleve looped a rope around a tree and they descended to the saddle.

Ben stopped for a moment to look at the carnage. Dead animals scattered the landscape, black blood splattered near each corpse.

Dom put his hand on Ben's shoulder. "It was them or us," he said.

"I know," Ben said. "Still sucks."

Dom chuckled, nodding. "That it does."

Ben pulled himself back to the present and sent his drone high overhead, scanning the distant forest for Dragon Guard. The nearest squad was already on the move, with many more coming behind them.

"Looks like we have a small army headed our way," he said.

"How far?" Dom asked.

"Probably five or six hours behind us."

"Good, we should be able to stay ahead of them."

"I'm half tempted to wait for them—pick them apart before they even see us."

Dom shook his head. "If a fight doesn't move you toward your strategic goals, then it's just a risk and a distraction."

Ben smiled sadly. "You sound like my grandfather."

"Who do you think taught me that particular lesson?"

Ben nodded. "I guess we'd better be on our way then."

The rest of the day was grueling and painful. They pressed forward, covering as much ground as possible without stopping to rest any more than was absolutely necessary. By dusk, everyone was exhausted to the point of stumbling. They made a cold camp, posted a guard rotation and went to sleep without much talk. Ben consoled himself with the knowledge that they had gained ground on their pursuers, partly from their dogged pace and partly because their enemy had stopped to search the battlefield.

He watched as the Dragon Guard came to the conclusion that their quarry had escaped the onslaught of stalkers without a single casualty. After that they seemed to move a bit more slowly.

The days that followed were more of the same, trudging through the forest, moving with all possible speed until it was too dark to continue and then collapsing from fatigue.

Ben felt a wave of relief wash over him when he found the entrance to the tunnel several days later. The Dragon Guard were still pursuing but they seemed to be more interested in making a show of their efforts than in actually catching their prey, which suited Ben just fine.

They stopped at the hole in the ground while Ben sent a drone in to investigate.

"All clear," he said, after a few minutes.

"I look forward to meeting this Kaid fellow," Dom said. "If he can do this, I can only imagine what other tricks he has up his sleeve."

"His tech is impressive," Ben said. "Unfortunately, it's completely vulnerable to magic."

"Maybe there's a way to fix that," Dom said. "You can keep your tech up and running within the confines of your circle. What if we could teach Kaid to do the same?"

Ben shook his head. "He doesn't have the gene."

Dom frowned, cocking his head questioningly.

"Magic can only be used by people with the right genetics," Ben said. "Kaid doesn't have it."

"Huh … that, I did not know," Dom said. He frowned for a few moments. "The Codex has an enchantment spell, doesn't it?"

"Yeah…"

"Maybe we can enchant something for Kaid to keep his tech working."

"Hadn't thought about that," Ben said. "I suppose it's possible, but I'm not sure how to do it."

"Why don't we both give it some thought. In the meantime, we'd better keep going."

They descended into the tunnel, taking care not to slip on the steep slope. It was quiet and dark, the air still and stale.

"Here we are again," Homer said.

"We're safer down here than we'd be on the surface."

"There are hundreds of feet of rock and dirt over our heads that could fall on us at any moment. How does that make us safer?"

"Okay, we're safer from the Dragon Guard down here."

"Whether we're crushed by rock or lit on fire, dead is dead."

"It'll be fine," Ben said, setting out by the glow of his splinter lanterns, silently crackling with electric blue light.

They walked in silence until they were once again exhausted and then made camp, going to their bedrolls without conversation and waking all too early the next day to continue their journey. By noon, they reached the elevator, still standing open just as they'd left it.

Once everyone had filed in, Ben accessed the base computer and commanded the enormous elevator to begin spiraling downward, paying close attention to their position relative to the room where they'd first entered the secret facility. As they neared, Ben slowed their descent until the floor of the elevator passed the ceiling of the room by a few inches, where he stopped their movement entirely so he could send in a drone.

At first he wasn't sure what he was seeing. The room was dark and the floor was uneven. He switched to thermal vision and frowned, still uncertain about what he was seeing. A tangle of plants had filled the room. Clusters were interspersed at irregular intervals, each sprouting a jumble of vines, some running along the ground and connecting with other clusters, others waving gently back and forth in the air, reaching a dozen feet in length or more in a few cases.

He moved his drone in closer to one of the clusters, stopping with a start when he realized that the vines were growing out of the chest of a dead man. He pulled back and scanned the entire room again, noting that the entrance had been completely walled up.

"Well, that's not good," he muttered, re-calling his drone.

"I smell death," Homer said.

"What is it?" Ellie asked.

"Some kind of vine has infested the whole room, and it looks like the Dragon Guard have built a wall across the doorway."

"We can't go back through the tunnel," Olivia said. "The Dragon Guard will be waiting for us."

"Let's worry about that later," Dom said.

"He's right," Ben said, activating the elevator again and refocusing on his circle.

As they began to descend, the room came into view. Hound swept the beam of his flashlight across the vines. They began to move, seemingly agitated by the light and noise. The long tendrils waving in the air began to sway back and forth while several along the ground started to slither like snakes toward them.

"I don't like the looks of that," Hound said.

"Me neither," Kat said.

One of the vines pulled back and then whipped toward them, snapping loudly. Something whizzed past Ben.

"What the hell?" Kayla said.

Another vine snapped.

"Ow … shit," Olivia said, pulling a thorn from her shoulder. "That thing bit me."

Several more snapped, vines whipping back and forth, sending inch-long spines like darts at them.

"Goddamn plant," Hound said, extracting a thorn from his thigh.

"I don't feel so good," Olivia said, staggering a little. Dom caught her as she slumped to the ground.

Ben sent all of his splinters forward, assembling them into a large shield.

"Everyone get behind me."

Hound wobbled and then fell over. Ben moved to cover him, his shield stopping several more thorns as the floor of the elevator passed the floor of the room. A vine slithered into the elevator, moving toward them with more assertiveness than a plant ought to have.

Thorns pelted the shield and the walls behind them as they descended, the elevator cutting several vines as its ceiling passed the room's floor. Ben pulled his shield back and went to Hound. He was out cold. He looked to Dom, still cradling his daughter in his lap.

"She's alive but unconscious," he said.

"What the hell was that?" Ellie asked.

"Whipvine," Dom said. "One of the wyrm's creations."

"Are they going to be okay?"

"Should be, if the stories are true, anyway."

"Anybody else get hit?" Ben asked, looking around the moving room. The others shook their heads. He turned back to Hound and inspected him thoroughly, searching for any more thorns, sitting back when he found none.

"I don't think I'll ever be able to pee on a bush again," Homer said, lying down next to him. Ben smiled at his dog.

The room came to a stop and the lights in the facility came to life.

"Let's get them into the infirmary," Ben said, motioning for Zack and Cleve to help him carry Hound. Dom picked up Olivia and followed behind them. Once the wounded were in cots and had been checked again for thorns, they left them to rest with Kat watching over them while Ben entered the restricted section and retrieved the egg. After a moment of indecision, he slipped it into his bag and returned to his companions.

"This is quite a place you've got here," Dom said, as Ben emerged through the force field protecting the inner sanctum where he'd found Kaid. "Any weapons?"

"Not anymore," Ben said. "Kaid was the real weapon. There's a fabrication machine in the other room that he used to make some grenades and ammunition for us, but he said it's all out of raw materials."

"Too bad," Dom said. "I was hoping for a flamethrower."

"How *are* we going to get out of here?" Zack asked.

"I have an idea about that," Ben said, heading for the elevator.

"Wait," Ellie said. "What are you going to do?"

"Kill the vines," he said.

"I'm coming with you."

"Stop! Both of you," Dom said. "What's your plan?"

Ben took a moment to explain. Dom nodded approvingly, frowning in thought for a moment before motioning for them to follow him. He led them into one of the rooms that had served as an office.

"This'll do," he said, laying a hand on a desk. "Help me get it into the elevator."

"Why?" Ellie asked.

He gave her a look.

She smiled. "The 'I said so' look doesn't work anymore, Dad."

He chuckled, shaking his head. "I don't recall giving you permission to grow up."

"Nope, but it happened anyway. So what's the desk for?"

"A shield. We tip it over and hide behind it while Ben does his thing."

"Huh, that's a pretty good idea," she said.

"I'm glad you approve. Now, let's get this thing moved in there."

Once the desk was in place, they sat down behind it and Ben started the elevator toward the entry room above, stopping once the elevator ceiling had passed the floor by a few inches. Three hundred splinters detached and floated into the room, forming a drone and a small shield. The vines began to become agitated again, but Ben ignored them, spinning his shield into a saw blade and going to work cutting each cluster free of the body it was growing from.

When he attacked the first plant, the rest began to flail, whipping this way and that, throwing thorns in every direction in a desperate bid to survive, but to no avail. The predatory and parasitic plant was defenseless against Ben's tech. He took his time, spending nearly half an hour cutting the vines down and then cutting them apart, leaving the room littered with black, thorny plant parts.

"That ought to do it," he said, bringing his splinters back and commanding the elevator to descend back into the facility. "Now we just have to get through the wall without bringing the ceiling down on us."

"I'm sure we can manage," Dom said.

Olivia and Hound woke an hour later, both still a bit unsteady.

"Never got my ass kicked by a plant before," Hound said, rubbing his face. "Not sure I'm going to add that one to my repertoire of stories."

"How're you feeling?" Ben asked.

"A bit foggy, but I'll be fine."

"Good, we should probably stay here for the night," Ben said. "I think we could all use the rest."

"Can't argue with that," Hound said, lying back down.

"Me neither," Olivia said, not bothering to sit up.

"Sure you're all right?" Dom asked, giving her hand a squeeze.

She nodded without opening her eyes. "Just sleepy."

He looked over at Kat. She nodded and settled into her chair. Dom looked to Ben and motioned for him to follow. He found a room out of earshot of the infirmary and sat down at the table, motioning for Ben to take a seat as well. Ellie joined them along with Kayla.

"Tell me everything you know about the Codex," Dom said.

Ben opened his mouth to speak and closed it again.

"I thought you knew more about it than I do," he said after a moment.

Dom shook his head. "I had a glance at it once, but I don't read dragon."

Ben frowned, accessing the facility computer and smiling after a moment of searching.

"I can do one better," he said. "How about I print you a copy in English."

"You can do that?"

"I just sent the file to the fabricator," Ben said. "The computer says it can make paper and ink." He got up and returned a minute later with a sheaf of papers.

"Here you go," he said. "I'd love to hear your thoughts about it."

Dom took the stack of paper and nodded approvingly.

"I'm going to find a quiet corner and meditate for a while," Ben said. Homer followed him. Ben switched the lights off in one of the laboratory rooms and sat down, crossing his legs. Homer curled up nearby.

Ben cleared his mind and listened to the silence for a few minutes, feeling the presence of the egg and the Oculus, noting the difference between them. Feeling the shards of bone that he'd incorporated into his clothing and sword took more focus and concentration. He found it difficult to pick them out through the magical noise of his more powerful artifacts, but after a while he was able to tune his mind into the different feel that each specific item evoked within him. The differences were subtle, almost imperceptible, but distinct when he applied his mind to the task.

He reached out, feeling in the distance for Ellie's magic. That took longer, and he was less certain if he was actually sensing the shards of bone she carried or if he was just imagining it. He made a mental note to pay closer attention to the way dragon artifacts made him feel, and also to take care to ensure that his circle was ever-present. If he could feel magic at a distance, so could his enemies.

He silenced his mind again, clearing away the clutter, dismissing memories that came to the surface, discarding his plans, hopes, and fears about the future, allowing himself to be completely present in the moment.

Once his mind was empty and quiet, he asked what his avatar should be and then listened, allowing the silence of his mind to swell and drown out everything else until he was no longer even aware of his body or his surroundings, only the silence.

An image came to him, suddenly fully formed in his mind, just a flash, but clear and distinct, bright and potent enough to etch the image into his memory. With a thought, he captured what he saw and transferred it into his augment, projecting a vision of the being in his mind's eye.

The image was of a man made of pure white stone, standing seven feet tall. He wore a white kilt and sandals, carried a large round shield and a broadsword. His powerfully muscled torso was bare. White feathered wings rose from his shoulders. His eyes glowed softly and his head was completely bald. He looked like Ben's idealized version of an angel of war.

"Augment, create a permanent projection of this avatar and allow it to learn and accumulate knowledge with experience. Begin with the qualities of honesty, loyalty, and reverence for life."

The computer in his brain went to work. He opened his eyes and was almost surprised when he could still see the projection standing before him.

"What should I call you?" he muttered out loud. "Maybe Gabriel?"

Homer grumbled.

"What?"

"That name's already taken."

"What do you mean by that?"

Homer rolled onto his back and started wiggling back and forth, scratching himself against the floor.

"You're a lot of help," Ben muttered.

Homer didn't respond except to roll over, curl up and close his eyes.

"I guess I'll have to think about your name," Ben said.

The projection stood stock-still, inanimate and oblivious.

"And I'll have to work on your personality too."

When he returned to his friends, he found Dom and Ellie engrossed in the Dragon's Codex while Kayla was sitting at one of the computer terminals studying a map of the Alturas Base.

He found Derek in the kitchen preparing dinner and went to work helping him, almost jumping with a start when he noticed his avatar following behind him. That was going to take some getting used to, he thought.

After he helped Derek serve the meal, he found a cot and went to sleep, waking the following morning feeling more rested than he had in days. They ate a hearty breakfast at a conference table, packed up and went to the elevator.

"I wonder if we can make use of these," Kayla said, squatting down to look at one of the Whipvine thorns on the elevator floor.

"If you're going to take one, make sure you put it in something sturdy so it doesn't accidentally poke you," Dom said.

She dropped her bag and fished out a small tin half full of sewing supplies, then went to work gathering up as many of the needlelike thorns as she could find.

"What did you have in mind?" Derek asked.

"I'm not sure, but these things are dangerous, and given our circumstances, maybe dangerous is a good thing."

Ben stopped the elevator with just enough space to send his drone into the room and found that the Whipvines were beginning to sprout anew from the dead bodies scattered about.

"Wow, those things *are* dangerous," he said, sending another two hundred splinters into the room and forming them into a shield so he could cut the vines down again. After he was satisfied that they posed no immediate threat, he raised the elevator to the level of the room.

"Be careful where you step," he said to Homer.

They followed the wall to avoid any of the thorns or remnants of the vines as they made their way to the far side where the entrance used to be. Ben sent the elevator down to the facility almost as an afterthought.

The wall across the entrance had been hastily built from brick and mortar. Hound wedged his knife between two of the bricks and pried out a small chunk.

"We ought to be able to make short work of this," he said.

Ben nodded, bringing his shield to the wall and carefully aligning it edge-on with a seam between two rows of bricks. Sparks flew as the spinning shield tore into the artificial stone. Once he was through he moved down one row. After a few moments he was able to knock a brick into the passage beyond.

A shout from the other side saved him. He jumped back a moment before orange fire washed through the small hole, splattering on the ground. Ben willed his shield to disassemble and sent the splinters through the hole, re-forming them into a drone and a dart on the other side.

There were a dozen Dragon Guard positioned behind sandbag barriers, all aiming their rifles at the wall, tongues of blue flame jetting from each barrel. One shouted a command to another. He picked up an ornate-looking glass bottle and smashed it into the ground. When it shattered, a shadowy form came free, rose into the air and howled as it fled down the tunnel.

Ben sighed. "I think they just sent a warning to Rath."

Another Dragon Guard fired at the brick-sized hole in the wall, but the fire that made it through fell harmlessly to the ground. Ben went to work methodically killing all twelve men, one by one, chasing the last three down the corridor as they ran for their lives.

"We're clear," he said, a note of sadness in his voice.

Hound went to work widening the hole, tearing out one brick at a time until the wall had weakened enough to push a large section over.

He stuck his head through and shined his flashlight this way and that. "Nice work," he said.

"That's not how it feels," Ben said. "Every time I kill a bunch of people, I feel like a little part of me dies too."

Dom took him by the shoulders and turned him to face him.

"Harden up," he said. "We're at war. Those people you just killed are the enemy. You're the one who wants to save the world, and that's going to take more killing. Worry about the dent you put in your conscience after the wyrm is dead. You hear me?"

Ben nodded, less than convincingly.

Dom didn't let up. "I'm not sure you do. You chose this, and now Ellie is caught up in your crusade, so you're going to wash your hands in blood until she's safe."

Ben felt a bit sick to his stomach but he nodded before turning away and stepping through into the corridor, waiting for Dom to follow.

"I just killed twelve people," Ben said, gesturing to the corpses scattered around them. "I don't ever want to get to a place where I like killing."

"First," Dom said, holding up one finger, "these aren't people, they're paper targets. Their purpose in life is to get knocked down." He took a breath and softened his tone. "Second, I don't think you have to worry about losing your conscience to this enemy. Just keep your goal firmly in mind. Don't look for people to kill, but don't be afraid to kill them if they're in your way."

A distant howl echoed out of the darkness.

"Sounds like we have some more trouble in our path," Hound said.

"Time to go," Dom said. "I hope you know your way around this place."

"I do," Ben said, tapping the side of his head and setting out, sending one drone ahead, another behind and deploying his remaining two hundred splinters as lanterns, illuminating the immediate area in electric blue light.

"The main tunnel heading east out of town is collapsed," Kayla said. "We can get to the surface on the east side through the basement of a tavern. The proprietor owes me a favor."

"You sure we can trust him?" Derek asked. "Lulu and Juju have probably paid him a visit."

"It's either that or we surface in the middle of town," she said.

"I vote for the edge of town," Hound said.

"Me too," Dom said.

Ben led the way, adjusting his course from time to time when Kayla warned him of collapsed tunnels or side tunnels that weren't on the map. They stuck to smaller passages in an effort to avoid the Dragon Guard patrols that seemed to be growing in number with every passing minute.

A few times they had to backtrack and take a less direct route to avoid soldiers that Ben saw coming through his drones. They kept their light dim and made an effort to move as silently as possible, but that did nothing to mask their scent from the pack of dragon dogs that were hunting them.

Ben knew that they could take them, but he also knew that it would be noisy. He consulted the map in his mind and found a nearby ladder.

"This way," he said, hurrying forward. The dogs were getting close, close enough that they could hear them barking and snarling as they raced through the dark, driven by the scent of their prey.

Ben rounded a corner and breathed a sigh of relief

"Hurry," he said, motioning for Hound to take the lead.

Hound didn't hesitate, climbing quickly, followed by each of Ben's companions in turn. The dragon dogs were close, their footsteps echoing up the passage. Ben watched them round the corner with his drone, glancing at Ellie as she began to climb. With Homer in a sling, Ben followed her closely. Howls of frustrated rage drowned out the pounding of his heartbeat as the dogs arrived, barking, snapping and snarling in fury that their quarry had escaped.

They climbed several levels, only setting foot on solid ground again when they reached the top of the ladder.

"We have to be careful," Kayla said. "There's a garrison on this level."

Ben nodded, keeping his splinter lanterns dim and heading out, picking his course carefully and moving with deliberate care to remain silent. After a few minutes of travel, he stopped, consulting his drones both in front and behind.

"We're boxed in," he whispered.

"I know where we are," Kayla said. "We can go for the surface, but we'll be exposed."

"If we fight, they'll get a bead on us," Dom said. "Better to take our chances above ground."

Ben motioned for Kayla to take the lead. She took them into a secondary tunnel that had been cut well after the construction of the base. It led to a dirt staircase that opened into a small basement.

"This house is abandoned," she whispered.

A muffled thump from upstairs caused everyone to freeze.

"Usually," Kayla said.

Dom motioned for Kat to take the lead, but Ben stopped her with a raised hand as he sent a drone upstairs.

"Looks like a couple of squatters," he said, looking to Kat again. She crept up the stairs quietly, slipped into the room and shot each of them with her dart pistol before they noticed her. Both men wobbled and then fell over, unconscious.

Derek went to the window and peeked out into the street. "Looks pretty quiet," he said.

"Rath probably has everybody in the tunnels," Ben said.

"We can hope," Ellie said.

"We need a plan," Kayla said. "If we go out on the street in daylight, we'll be spotted in a matter of minutes."

"Agreed," Dom said. "Is there a stable nearby?"

"Or a barracks?" Hound asked.

"Not close enough," Kayla said.

"These two will be out for about an hour," Kat said, gesturing to the squatters.

"The dragon dogs will probably pick up our trail and find this place before then," Ben said, going to the back of the house and peeking out the door, sending a drone out and up to have a look around.

"There's an alley back here," he said.

"Then what?" Dom said.

Ben consulted his drone feed. This section of town was mostly abandoned houses. He widened his search. "The neighborhood is mostly deserted. I think we're going to have to take our chances."

"If we get caught in the street, things are going to get bloody really quick," Dom said.

"If we stay here, we'll burn," Ellie said.

"Fair enough," Dom said. "Lead the way, Ben."

He consulted his drone, reaffirmed his circle, and stepped out into the backyard, moving quickly into the alley running between two rows of houses. A dog barked in the distance.

"He's just hungry," Homer said.

"Good to know," Ben said, moving quickly to the end of the alley, keeping his drone high and scanning the feed continuously. The street was empty. He rushed across into the alley on the other side, motioning for everyone else to follow, keeping his attention on his drone. A horse and cart was coming down the street parallel to the alley, but it was moving slowly enough to avoid.

He set out again without a word, weaving through the alleys and streets of Alturas, using his drone to avoid being spotted. Thankfully, this part of town was sparsely populated. After a few minutes he slowed, motioning for everyone to take refuge in the backyard of a small house with overgrown bushes.

"Patrol," he whispered.

"How many?" Dom asked.

"Six."

They kept quiet and still as the Dragon Guard worked their way down the street, going door to door. Ben breathed a sigh of relief when no one answered the door of the house they were hiding behind.

While he waited for the soldiers to pass, he considered his avatar. The white angelic-looking projection stood stock-still, almost like a statue, inanimate and empty. He made a mental note to work on that. While the tech in his head made it easy to visualize whatever he wanted, it would clearly take more focus and effort to transform the digital figment in his mind's eye into something more.

When the patrol had moved several houses down the road, he started to set out again.

Dom stopped him with a hand on his arm. "We're going to need a plan," he said.

Ben nodded. "There's a Dragon Guard warehouse and stables a few blocks from here. Looks like just a handful of soldiers and a few hands on duty at the moment. I thought we might borrow some uniforms, a few horses and a wagon."

"That's a good start," Dom said. "Then what?"

"We go north."

"Isn't there a big-ass army up north?" Hound asked.

"Yep," Ben said. "I figure another wagon headed that way won't get a second look. Once we're clear of town, we'll turn east."

"Well ... it's not a great plan, but it's better than anything I've got," Dom said. "Let's go."

Chapter 8

They continued toward their objective, drawing a few looks from people on the street as they moved into a more heavily trafficked part of town. Most people gave them a glance and then looked down, hurrying along their way. A few stared, until Hound stared back, and then they got really interested in their shoes.

Ben headed into an alley, stopping at the far end.

"Word will get back to the Dragon Guard soon," Kayla said. "Our heads are worth good money by now."

He nodded over his shoulder, consulting his drone feed again and holding up a fist as he crouched behind some bushes. He took a closer look at the warehouse and stables, marking the position of the guards—two at the main entrance, two at the stables' gate, two in the office and two on patrol. He could also see six workers, some loading supplies into a wagon, others harnessing four horses to it.

Ben took a moment to lay out his plan, then began moving toward a large house facing a side wall of the warehouse. He sent a dart through the window of the back door and then transformed it into a drone to search the house.

"What was that?" a female voice asked.

"Sounded like a window breaking," a male voice answered. "I'll go take a look."

Ben motioned to Kat, holding up two fingers. She nodded as the rest of them crouched along the back of the house under the windows. The door opened and Kat shot the man when he stuck his head out. Dom caught him as he fell, while Hound opened the door wide for Kat to enter. She moved like her name, gliding through the kitchen into the main room, firing her dart pistol again, rendering the woman sitting in an easy chair unconscious. Dom carried the man inside and laid him on the floor at the woman's feet.

Ben checked the couple to ensure they were unharmed and put a few silver drakes on the table next to the easy chair before going to the front window and scanning the street. Two Dragon Guard walked slowly along the length of the warehouse wall, stopping to inspect three empty wagons parked beside the building before continuing their patrol.

After they turned the corner and disappeared from sight, Ben opened the front door a crack and sent out two drones, parking one a thousand feet overhead and sending the other into the warehouse to scout ahead. Once he was satisfied, he sent his remaining two hundred splinters to a spot on the wall behind the wagons, formed them into a shield and spun it into a saw blade, cutting a hole into the wall just big enough for them to crawl through.

"We're good to go," he said, moving onto the front porch and scanning up and down the street, even though his high drone already showed him the road was clear. He darted across with Homer on his heels, skirted the wagons and pulled the three-by-three section of wall away, peeking through before crawling inside. His friends followed, Hound coming through last, propping the section of wall up to cover the hole.

Ben motioned for his companions to stay low behind the row of pallets lining the wall while he sent a drone and a dart to the office. Two Dragon Guard sat at their desks, both working on paperwork. Ben felt a twinge of guilt before he steeled himself and drove his dart through both their heads at almost the same instant. They fell forward with a simultaneous thud as their foreheads hit the desks.

"Two down," he said, motioning for Dom and Kat to move toward the stables while he, Ellie, and Hound moved toward the front entrance, leaving the rest to wait in hiding.

When he and his two companions reached the front door, Ben checked the position of the two door guards and the patrol with the drone still parked overhead, then pointed to Hound when he was satisfied.

Hound pushed a crate off a pallet. "Shit! Hey," he called through the door, "give me a hand in here!"

"What the hell did you break now?" a voice answered a moment before the latch lifted. A man stepped through.

"Where are you?" the guard asked.

"Over here," Hound said.

The second guard stepped into the warehouse following his companion. Ellie raced up and stabbed the second man in the back of the neck just under his helmet. He fell forward. His friend turned.

"What the…"

Ben's dart caught him in the left eye and knocked his helmet off onto the floor. He fell backward. Hound dragged one guard behind several pallets while Ben and Ellie carried the other.

Ben closed the door and they took their positions again. He cringed at a shout from the stables, holding his breath until things went quiet again, hoping that Dom and Kat had killed the guards quickly and subdued the workers.

A minute later a voice from outside carried through the door. "Hey, where did you two go?"

"They know better than this," another voice said.

The door opened and the two Dragon Guard on patrol entered, swords drawn, scanning the room. Ben took the first with a dart to the face. The second tried to cry out but Ellie silenced him with a blade across the throat.

Ben closed and locked the door while Hound and Ellie went to work stripping the men of their uniforms and dragging the bodies into a walkway between two rows of crates.

They rejoined their friends at the back of the warehouse. Kayla and Derek went to the office to strip the two guards there, while the rest went to work on the remaining two Dragon Guard. Then they carried all of the bodies into the warehouse and moved the six unconscious workers into the stables.

"Looks like they've got our wagon all hitched up and everything," Dom said.

Kat came out of the stables leading two horses while Cleve and Zack went in for the remaining four.

"That's all of them," Cleve said when they returned.

"Good," Dom said. "You two get them saddled while the rest of us unload some of the food from the wagon."

Within ten minutes, they had six saddled horses, four extra saddles, and a covered wagon half full of food and water.

Ben and Derek, Hound and Cleve donned the Dragon Guard uniforms while everyone else piled into the back of the wagon with Homer. Ben and Derek drove the wagon while Hound and Cleve each rode a horse. The remaining animals were tied in a string to the back of the wagon.

"Ready?" Ben asked, reaffirming his circle once again.

"We're good," Dom said from behind the canvas curtain.

Hound nodded, opening the gate. He closed it behind them and they set out, Ben keeping his drone five hundred feet overhead.

People hurried out of their way while Dragon Guard nodded respectfully or ignored them altogether. Ben felt almost invisible as he directed Derek through Alturas along a route designed to avoid larger patrols that were still clearly searching for them. They reached the edge of town quickly, coming to a checkpoint and a dozen soldiers inspecting a wagon on its way out of town.

Ben felt the tension rise as they approached the checkpoint, but the Dragon Guard commander gave them little more than a glance before waving them by the merchant's wagon. Ben nodded his thanks, but the soldiers had already lost interest. Derek drove past them without hesitation.

Once they were several hundred yards down the road, Ben started to feel the tension drain away. His plan had worked. Not two miles down the road, they came to another checkpoint, this one manned by six soldiers. The lead man held up a hand as they approached. Derek slowed the horses to a stop.

"You got paperwork?" the soldier asked, a hint of boredom in his voice.

Ben's mind raced.

"Sure thing," Derek said, pulling a leather pouch from under the seat and handing it to the guard.

The guard pulled out a sheaf of papers and flipped through them, nodding to himself before stuffing them inside the pouch and handing it back to Derek.

"Everything looks in order," he said, but then a questioning look overtook his face. "Where's your rune?" he asked, tapping the scar on his cheek.

"We're new recruits," Derek said. "They said we haven't earned the mark yet, and we won't unless we prove ourselves."

"That's not how it works," the commander said, his men becoming more alert by the second.

"Legate Rath said it was a new directive from the Mountaintop," Derek said with a hint of exasperation. "I'm just doing what I'm told, and one of the things they were pretty clear about is the importance of being on time. We're running behind as it is … can we speed this up?"

The commander looked uncertain for a moment but found his resolve, shaking his head.

"I'm going to have to inspect your cargo," he said.

Derek sighed. "At this rate, we'll never earn our mark."

"With that attitude, maybe you aren't ready for it yet," the commander said.

"Come on, man, just give us a break."

The commander ignored him, motioning for his men to take the reins of the horses and have a look in the wagon. Ben did a quick position check of the Dragon Guard, formulating a plan of attack.

Two soldiers went to the back of the wagon, one held the horses, one circled to stand, rifle at the ready, on Ben's side, while the commander and his remaining man stood glaring at Derek.

Ben felt for Ellie in his mind. Even in the calm before the storm, he could sense her intention. He watched through his drone as the two men at the rear of the wagon pulled the canvas aside and Dom and Ellie stabbed each in the face. The soldier beside Ben and the one standing with the commander raised their rifles, blue flame igniting in an instant. Ben deployed all of his remaining splinters, forming one hundred into a dart and killing the man beside the commander with a thought. The other two hundred he turned into a shield, forming just in front of the barrel of the dragon-fire rifle coming to bear on him. Orange flame erupted from the weapon, splashing into the shield, now not a foot in front of it, causing the fire to rebound and engulf the soldier in an instant.

Hound charged the commander as the man shouted a warning and tried to pull his rifle off his back. He wasn't quick enough. Hound hacked at the side of his neck in passing. The commander grunted as he was forced to his knees by the blow, still alive but bleeding profusely. He clamped a hand over the wound, but bright red blood flowed freely between his fingers.

Derek snapped the reins, causing the horses to lunge forward, nearly trampling the man holding their bridles. The guard only saved himself momentarily by leaping aside, putting himself in Hound's way. Rufus hacked at him, hitting his helmet hard enough to knock him over. Before Hound could turn for the killing blow, Ben brought his dart back and finished the man

Dom was out of the wagon, scanning for other enemy. Finding none, he came to Ben's side of the wagon.

"Any more coming?"

Ben sent his drone higher and scanned the area.

"Nothing."

"Good. Let's get these men and their gear off the road behind those rocks." He motioned to a boulder flanked by smaller rocks a hundred feet away.

Within ten minutes, the bloody scene was cleared and they were moving again. The tension was once again draining from Ben's body, this time leaving him feeling fatigued but more confident in his abilities and their chances of success.

"How did you have paperwork for this shipment?" Ben asked Derek.

"Kayla and I found it in the office. We've been smuggling for Adara Cartage for years. Paperwork is important."

Ben chuckled. "Good to know."

By midday, they came upon a broken-down and abandoned farmhouse well off the road. Derek guided the wagon toward the building and parked behind it, out of sight of the road. Then they loaded as much food and water onto the horses as they could and headed east toward a sparsely forested mountain range and the desert that awaited them beyond.

Ben breathed a sigh of relief when the first drops of rain began to fall.

"Speak for yourself," Homer said.

"It'll wash away our scent."

"I know, but I still hate getting wet."

They were traveling slowly along a narrow path that paralleled a small seasonal stream as they ascended toward a pass through the low range of mountains that stood between Alturas and the desert to the east. Ben kept his drone high overhead, periodically scanning for pursuers.

It felt a bit odd, not being chased. He started to wonder about the enemy behind him. Rath surely knew that they would head east. By now he also knew that they had stolen a wagon and gone north. Ben tried to get into the man's mind in an attempt to predict his next move.

If Rath had trackers or stalkers, they would be on their trail sooner or later. The rain would make their task more difficult, though not impossible. If Rath had a priest, and Ben had to assume that he did, it was likely that some form of magic would be employed to hunt them … what that might be, Ben could only guess.

Even with all that, Rath wouldn't leave their capture to chance. He knew Ben's ultimate destination, so he would send his soldiers in that direction, or at least enough of them to make things difficult. They would probably be waiting at Battle Mountain since that was the only real city between Alturas and Salt Lake.

For the moment, Ben knew that he could do little more than ride and watch for threats. He didn't have enough information to do much else. He consoled himself with the knowledge that things would become clearer in time.

At first he focused on his avatar, trying to imbue his imaginary friend with personality and purpose. While he could make the image in his mind do or say anything he wanted, it was still just a figment of his augmented imagination.

After a while, he turned his attention to manifestation, the one type of magic that he might be able to use to good effect. He'd been unwittingly using it all his life with his coin meditation, but that was too slow. He needed immediate results—something that he could use in a fight.

He saw a bird sitting in a tree, singing to the sky. He thought for a moment, using his augment to lend realism to his visualization, seeing the bird fly in his mind's eye.

Nothing happened. The bird sat singing as if mocking him.

He thought about his meditation, about the feeling of calm certainty he had when he sat still with his mind quiet. He relaxed as much as he dared while riding and picked out another bird, letting go of his anxiety and quieting his mind. He imagined the bird flying, feeling a conjured sense of joy at the sight in his mind's eye. A few moments later, the bird leapt into the sky.

He frowned, wondering to himself if he had succeeded or if the bird just wanted to fly. After a dozen more tries over the next several hours, he became convinced that he was getting better at the process. Much of it hinged on his state of mind. He had to be relaxed, focused, and clear-headed—his desired outcome vivid in his imagination, his emotional desire for that outcome strong, and his belief in it coming to pass unassailable. It was a bit of a mental juggling act that required a great deal of concentration. So much so, that he nearly fell out of his saddle more than once.

When they reached the top of the pass at dusk, they made a dark and cold camp. Ben did a patrol of the surrounding area with his drone but found nothing to be alarmed about except a young black bear foraging for food a few miles away.

"I don't like it," Hound said.

"What do you mean?" Zack asked.

"The Dragon Guard don't give up so easily."

"Unless they don't have any way of tracking us," Dom said.

"You really think we put that big a dent in them?" Hound asked.

"Hard to say. I figured they'd be on our tail, too."

"I'm worried about what we don't know," Ben said.

Dom chuckled softly with a note of sadness. "You sound like your grandfather."

"Yeah," Ben whispered. "I miss him."

"Me too, Kid. Me too," Dom said, patting him on the shoulder. "Get some sleep. We should move at the crack of dawn."

Ben nodded in the growing darkness. "I think I'm going to meditate for a bit first," he said.

He found a pine tree and cleared out a space inside its branches near the trunk, sat down and closed his eyes, smiling to himself as Homer curled up next to him.

After a few deep breaths he started quieting his mind and body, following a procedure he'd long ago memorized until he was aware of only his breath. Instead of focusing on his coin, he imagined his avatar without the help of his augment, seeing it in his mind in detail, holding the image as clearly as he could until his mind began to wander. When he caught himself thinking stray thoughts, he refocused on his avatar, seeing it vividly.

After an hour had passed, Homer nosed him on the cheek. "You need to sleep," he said.

Ben nodded, stroking his dog's head as he contemplated the spell he was attempting to cast, realizing that he had yet to add magic to the equation. He pondered his next step as he rolled out his blanket in the dark and lay down.

Drizzle began to fall, lightly but steadily soaking the forest. Ben listened to the water dripping from pine needles as he drifted off to sleep.

Chapter 9

Ben was running through the dark, his heart hammering in his chest, visceral fear driving him forward and yet he seemed stuck, as if he were running through mud. He didn't know where he was or how he'd gotten there. All he knew was that something was after him, something dark and powerful, hateful and ravenous.

He heard it coming … thudding, slimy footfalls—splat, splat, splat on the cold stone floor. He struggled to get away, to flee, terror overwhelming him, rendering his reason impotent and inaccessible. He searched frantically, looking for the thing stalking him in the black, but all he found was more darkness … and more fear. It was all around him, suffocating and surreal.

Somewhere in the back of his mind he knew he was dreaming, but the knowledge did him no good. He willed himself to wake up, tried to move, even searched for the moon, but there was no sky, no light, no sound save the footfalls of the beast in the dark.

It was close now, right behind him. He turned, reaching for his sword, but it wasn't there. He tried to access his splinters, but they were gone as well, along with the voice of the augment in his mind.

He saw a glimmer of light, green and sickly, as the thing came into view, the only illumination the glow coming from the multitude of eyes fixed on him, peering at him like a cat eyes a mouse.

He flailed frantically within the confines of his night terror, searching for anything that could help, any weapon, any source of salvation. The beast snarled, a hint of venom dripping from too many fangs, all sharp and long, as it crouched, preparing to spring.

Laughter in the distance echoed to his ears, human laughter, tinged with wickedness and gleeful malice.

Then a dog barked.

Homer was next to him, growling and barking at the beast. It hesitated, shrinking back as Homer lunged, snapping at the creature, growing in size in the space of a few steps until he was twice the size of the creature. He clamped down on the beast and it wailed, trying to retreat, but he held fast, growling and shaking.

Now the beast whimpered in fear, and the voice that had been laughing wailed with it.

Ben woke, catching a scream in his throat, Ellie kneeling over him and shaking him roughly.

"Wake up, Ben. Please wake up."

He reached for her, taking her in his arms and weeping on her shoulder.

"It was so real," he whispered.

"I felt it, too," she said, holding him, stroking his head as he cried. "You were so afraid."

Homer laid his chin on Ben's leg and whined. "That was close."

"What do you mean?" Ben asked his dog, still outwardly sobbing.

"It almost had you," Homer said. "But it's gone now."

"Everything all right in there?" Hound asked from outside the tree Ben had taken shelter under.

"Yeah," Ellie said. "Just a bad dream."

Ben thought about that for a moment and shook his head, still resting on her shoulder. He pulled back, just her outline visible in the dark.

"It was more than that," he said, reluctantly dredging the memory for more information, and his reason now intact, finding what he feared. "There was magic to it."

"What do you mean?"

"It wasn't an ordinary dream. Someone sent it."

"Damn," she whispered.

"Yeah," Ben said, wiping the tears from his face and taking a deep breath to steady himself. "I think I'm going to sit up for a bit and think this through."

"I'll sit with you," Ellie said.

Ben replayed the dream in his mind. With the fear now distant, he was able to pick out the feeling of magic that permeated the entire experience, the laughter … and Homer.

"Was that really you?" he asked his dog.

"Of course. That's what I'm here for," he said. "You should try to go back to sleep … it won't be back tonight."

"How do you know?"

Homer rolled over and licked his lips several times as he curled up and got comfortable.

Ben shook his head, wondering anew at his dog's origins.

"Would you stay with me?" he whispered to Ellie.

"Of course," she said.

They wrapped the blanket around themselves and closed their eyes. It took a while, but Ben finally slipped back into sleep.

Morning brought a cloudy sky and a sense of relief. The memory of the fear was enough to send a thrill of adrenaline into his stomach. It had been so real. Worse, he had absolutely no doubt that it would have killed him were it not for Homer's intervention.

"How're you feeling?" Ellie asked, making no move to extricate herself from his arms.

"I'm good," he said, more convincingly than he felt.

"What do you think it was?"

"I don't know, but it was powerful."

He searched his memory anew, consulting his augment and finding that there was no record of the event in its memory. "It didn't feel human," he added, after a moment.

She shifted so she could look him in the eye.

"Do you think it was the dragon?"

"No…" he said, frowning and shaking his head. "But it wasn't human. I'm sure of that."

"How do we fight a dream?"

"I don't know," he whispered.

People were stirring. The crackle of a fire and the promise of warmth lured them out.

Ben sat down on a rock and stared into the flames, replaying the dream again.

"How did you get into my dream?" he asked Homer.

"The same way I'm in your mind."

Ben eyed his dog and stroked his head, knowing from past experience that quizzing him would yield little or no information.

He turned his attention to his drone, doing a sweep of the surrounding area and finding it empty of potential threats.

"We clear?" Dom asked, after Ben refocused his gaze on the fire.

"Yeah, there's nothing out there," he said. "Seems strange."

"I'll take strange over surrounded any day," Hound said.

"Me, too," said Dom.

After a brief but blessedly hot breakfast, they loaded up their horses and set out. The ride down the other side of the mountain range took considerably less time than the ascent had taken, depositing them into a sage desert that stretched out to a large lake in the distance. With easier terrain, Ben let his mind wander to his avatar, dispelling the technologically generated image so he could attempt to conjure it in his mind with nothing but his imagination.

While he could visualize his coin very vividly in his mind's eye, his avatar was proving to be more difficult, but then he'd only been at it for a few days. His coin had been the focus of his meditation for years.

He began to alternate between his tech and his imagination, bringing his avatar into his field of vision and then trying to hold it in his mind after dispelling it with his augment.

That practice yielded better results, but not by much. He found that he was able to keep it in his imagination for a few moments, but it faded quickly. And then the sun was setting. He realized that they'd been traveling all day, and yet it felt like they'd only been on the road for a few hours.

"If we push, we can make the lakeshore by dark," Dom said.

They picked up the pace and arrived at the north end of an enormous lake just as the stars were beginning to sparkle.

A half moon rose while they made camp, brightly illuminating the night. Ben lay down, fretting over the threat of another night terror.

"Don't worry about that," Homer said. "I'll protect you."

"I don't doubt you, but it would be nice to know how."

Homer curled up next to him, ignoring the question.

"What the hell?" Kayla said from the edge of the lake where she was fetching water. "Ben!"

He was on his feet and moving in a blink.

Kayla and Derek stood tensely, facing an apparition of a young woman. She was floating a few inches off the ground and was translucent, like moonlight through smoke.

"Your family is worried about you, Kayla," the young woman said, her voice eerily haunting. "Come home. We'll protect you."

Ben approached cautiously, accessing his drone and scanning their surroundings. Ellie came up beside him, stopping short when she saw the apparition.

"What is that?"

"I don't know," Ben said, shaking his head.

"The family doesn't send you and your brother to protect people, Lulu," Kayla said.

"Not usually," the apparition said, "but these are unusual circumstances." She turned to face Ben. "There you are. We've been looking for you."

"Get in line," Ben said.

Lulu smiled, her silvery eyes seeming to pierce straight through him.

"You've done well so far," she said, "but your quest is a fool's errand. You can't hope to defeat the dragon alone. Perhaps, with our help, you might prove victorious."

"Don't believe her," Kayla said.

Lulu turned back to her, shaking her head sadly. "We're family, Kayla. Where's the loyalty?"

"Cut the crap, Lulu," Kayla said. "We both know that you're here to kill me."

"On the contrary, our mistress would very much like to have a conversation with you."

"I'll bet," Kayla said. "And after that, she'll kill me."

"Perhaps," Lulu said. "You had to know that this path you've chosen leads to death."

"Only if we lose," Kayla said.

"And you will. Even with the strength of the entire coven, we would not stand a chance against the dragon. How can you expect to fare better?"

"Because we actually want to win," Kayla said. "The coven and the family derive too much power from the wyrm. You don't really want anything to change."

"What I want is irrelevant," Lulu said. "I'm a loyal servant of the family, as you once were, and could be again. Deliver the egg to our care and all will be forgiven."

Kayla laughed, shaking her head. "What do you think, Ben. You want to give her the egg?"

"No … I think I'm going to hang on to it."

"There's your answer, Lulu," Kayla said.

The rest of Ben's companions had assembled behind him, watching the exchange in rapt silence.

"Is that a ghost?" Zack asked.

"No, Zack, I'm quite real," Lulu said.

"How do you know my name?" he asked.

She smiled, turning back to Kayla. "It's not too late. My offer stands … until it doesn't."

Kayla marched up to her and waved her hand through the apparition. "You're all talk," she said.

"Until I'm not," Lulu said. "See you soon." She faded out of sight, vanishing into the darkness.

"Don't much like the looks of that," Hound said.

"No," Dom said. "How close does she have to be to do that?"

Kayla shrugged. "I've heard stories about her and her brother, but the details are sketchy at best."

"What's her brother do?" Olivia asked.

"Juju's the scary one," Kayla said. "He can switch places with another person, take their body and use it for his purposes while they're trapped inside him."

"Possession magic," Dom said. "Not good."

"Why wouldn't the possessed person be able to use Juju's body?" Zack asked.

"Because Lulu has him tied down and doped up during the process," Kayla said. "They work as a team … a really deadly team. The coven only sends them when it's important."

"Can they mess with people's dreams?" Ben asked.

"Not that I know of," Kayla said.

"Will they give Rath our position?" Dom asked.

"No," Kayla said. "The coven wants the egg, if only to deliver it to the wyrm themselves."

"At least there's that," Dom said, heading back to camp.

Ben returned with him, lying down and worrying about the possibility of another dream. He was grateful to wake early the following morning without any trouble in the night.

The next several days flowed into one another, each a repeat of the previous. Long days traveling through desolate high desert. Ben focused on seeing his avatar, honing his concentration and imagination until the image began to take on an odd sense of realness. He knew it was just in his imagination, and yet the being was beginning to act seemingly of his own volition.

The desert was barren and unforgiving, but they had ample provisions and adequate water so the journey involved limited risk. Ben was vigilant nonetheless, keeping his drone deployed thousands of feet overhead, routinely scanning the wide open spaces for any sign of danger. Finding none, he started to wonder anew about his enemies' plans.

Whatever they had in store, Ben was certain of one thing—Rath wouldn't simply give up. Each day brought them closer to Battle Mountain. Ben became convinced that trouble was waiting for him there.

And he wasn't disappointed.

Half a day out, as they rode down a ravine, several dozen men seemed to appear out of the ground, coming up on both sides of them, brandishing a wide variety of weapons, ranging from rifles to bows to blades.

"If you go for your weapons, we'll cut you down," a man said, stepping out from behind a boulder.

Ben wondered how he could have missed such a large band of people. He had scanned the route with his drone and found nothing but dirt, rock, and sage.

He showed his empty hands, counting twenty-three men with his overhead drone, marking their positions, and realizing that he and his friends had walked into a well-designed ambush.

"We're just passing through," Ben said, noting that these people weren't Dragon Guard. In fact, they wore no uniforms at all, unless desert-colored clothing counted.

"Most people passing through are headed away from the Mountaintop," the man said. "Where're you headed?"

"Resupply in Battle Mountain and then on to Salt Lake," Ben said, calling his high drone down to about a hundred feet overhead.

"See, here's the problem," the man said, "there's a road a mile south that leads into Battle Mountain, and here you are, out in the middle of nowhere. Makes me wonder what you're really up to."

"Like I said, we're just passing through," Ben said.

Another of the men walked up to the first and whispered something to him.

"Looks like you have a few weapons," the first man said. "The kind of weapons the wyrm doesn't much like. People don't carry that kind of hardware without a reason."

"I can't help but notice that a few of your men are similarly armed," Ben said. "I suspect our reasons are much the same as yours."

"Cut the crap and tell me your business," the man said, raising a hand. His men took aim.

Ben looked over at Dom, who nodded slowly.

"We don't want any trouble," Ben said, looking around at the men positioned on the high ground above them. "You've got a pretty good advantage, with your position and all. Superior numbers too. The thing is, you don't understand what you're dealing with here. You might get a few of us, but if you attack, I guarantee you will die today."

Ben very deliberately pointed at the leader.

The man forced a smile. "Maybe, maybe not," he said, motioning for his men to lower their aim. He held Ben's gaze for a moment, scrutinizing him intently. "Did the wyrm send you?"

Ben started laughing.

The man and his companion shared a nervous look.

"No, the wyrm did not send us," Ben said. "In fact, that's the reason we took this route, to avoid his minions."

Another man came out from behind cover and hurried over to the first two. They conferred in hushed tones. Ben brought his drone down closer, listening to their conversation.

"We should take them."

"Why fight if we don't have to?"

"What if they tell the Dragon Guard where we are?"

"Maybe they could help us."

"How? There's only ten of them. We need an army."

"What does he mean, ten?" Homer asked.

Ben ignored him.

"Every man we can get is one more."

"We can't just let them go."

"No, but they don't seem to be afraid of us. Makes me nervous."

"Makes me wonder why not."

"Send a runner," the leader said. "Tell Varian what we've got."

The third man disappeared behind some rocks. The first two turned back to Ben and his companions.

"What do you need an army for?" Ben asked before they could speak.

"How…"

"Does it really matter?" Ben asked. "You need an army and you don't want the wyrm's minions to know where you are. Sounds like we might be on the same side."

The man and his companion shared another nervous look.

"What do you mean?" the leader asked.

"We're no friends of the dragon," Ben said.

"The dragon doesn't have friends, he has slaves," the man said. "Is he after you?"

"Something like that," Ben said. "That's why we aren't on the road."

"What did you do?" the leader asked.

"You first," Dom said, moving up alongside Ben.

The leader shook his head. "Tell you what, we're all going to wait right here."

Ben sent his drone higher, locating the runner and watching him disappear into the entrance of an old, seemingly abandoned mine not half a mile away.

"Fair enough," Ben said. "But if I see soldiers coming out of that mine you're holed up in, I'm going to start killing people."

The leader's eyes widened.

"You can't know that," he said.

"And yet, I do," Ben said.

"Who are you?" he asked.

Ben felt a surge of magic as a white, angelic-looking woman appeared beside the leader. The Sage's avatar.

"He's the Wizard," she said.

Dom growled under his breath.

"Hello," Ben said. "I'm glad to see that Magoth didn't dispel you permanently."

She shuddered. "That was unpleasant. Will you come with me? My master guarantees safe passage. There is much he wishes to discuss with you."

Ben looked over to Dom, who snorted derisively, then nodded, turning to the avatar.

"Tell your master," Dom said, leaning forward on his horse, "if he tries to pull any shit with me, I'm going to cut him in half."

"Master is aware of your presence and wishes to make amends."

Dom leaned in to whisper to Ben. "Be wary."

Ben nodded, then looked at the avatar and said, "Lead the way."

Chapter 10

They rode past the leader of the ambush without giving him a second look. The Sage's avatar led them to the mine entrance. A tunnel ran for a hundred feet into the mountain and then opened into a large room with a stable, three passages leading out and a shaft descending into the earth with makeshift stairs leading into the darkness. The Sage and the Thief were there to greet them, along with another man that Ben could only guess was Varian. He had the look of a man who'd lost too much. Half a dozen armed men stood behind them.

"I sense that you've done as I asked and found an artifact," Ben said, making no move to dismount.

"Indeed," the Sage said, nodding a bit too respectfully. "This is Varian, the leader of the Battle Mountain resistance. And I believe you've met my acquaintance, the Thief."

"What do you want?" Dom said, glaring at the Sage.

"Tactful as ever," the Sage said. "It's good to see you again, Dragon Slayer, even if you did abandon the fight so many years ago."

"Call me Dom," he growled. "I won't answer to that moniker anymore."

"As you wish. I would ask that you call me Sage for reasons you know all too well."

Dom grunted.

"I didn't expect to see you here," Ben said.

"Nor did I expect to be here," the Sage said. "But events have forced my hand."

"What's your business?" Varian asked, a hint of wariness in his voice.

"Like we told your men out there, we're just passing through," Ben said.

The Sage started to speak, but Varian silenced him with a stern look.

"I want to hear it from them," he said, his eyes never leaving Ben. "Tell me, why are you here?"

Ben looked over at Dom, and then at Ellie. Both nodded.

He took a deep breath and let it out slowly.

"I'm going to the Mountaintop to kill the wyrm."

Varian stared at him for a moment. A few of his men snickered under their breath.

"A bold claim," Varian said. "What makes you think you can do that?"

Ben shrugged, shaking his head. "Ultimately, I guess it comes down to will."

"Your will is no match for dragon fire," Varian said.

"Nevertheless, that's my intent," Ben said. "Why are you hiding in this mine?"

"Because the dragon and his priests are destroying our home and taking our families," Varian said, clenching his jaw. "They took my brother, his wife and children. Now … now, he's not the same. Something evil has taken hold of his soul, if there's anything left of it. And it's not just him. They've rounded up dozens of families and…" His voice trailed off. He shook his head, struggling to contain his rage and sorrow, motioning to the Sage.

"The dragon is building an army," the Sage said. "A priest came from Rogue City. Somehow, he's able to create human stalkers that are obedient."

Dread flooded into Ben's belly. He closed his eyes.

"Britney," he whispered.

"What do you know of this?" Varian asked.

Ben sighed, shaking his head.

"How about we see if we can't just pass right on through?" Dom said. "Like we planned."

"I want to know what you know about these soldiers," Varian said, ignoring Dom and looking pointedly at Ben.

"The first human stalker was a friend of mine," he said. "Her name was Britney. My brother betrayed her to the Dragon Guard and they turned her into something … inhuman."

"Do you know how they did it?" the Sage asked.

"No," Ben said. "She killed my grandfather and she tried to kill my brother, so I cut her head off."

"So they can be killed," a soldier behind Varian said.

Ben nodded numbly.

"How many do they have?" Dom asked.

"Several dozen," the Sage said. "Maybe up to a hundred."

A plan started to take form in Ben's mind. "How many people live in Battle Mountain?" he asked.

"A few thousand are all that's left," Varian said. "Not counting the Dragon Guard."

"What would it take to get them out?"

"What do you mean?" Varian asked.

"Could you evacuate the entire town? At night? All at once?"

"Why?" Varian asked.

"What are you thinking?" Ellie asked.

"We kill the priest, lure the dragon here and … boom."

"That would level the whole town," she said.

"What are you suggesting?" the Sage said.

Ben fixed Varian with an intent look, ignoring the Sage's question.

"Would you be willing to burn your whole town to the ground if it meant an end to the wyrm?"

"I'd burn the whole damn world to kill the wyrm."

"Good," Ben said, dismounting. "We have some planning to do."

"Can we talk about this?" Dom said, stopping Ben. "Up until now you've been running from the dragon's minions. This is an attack."

"Yeah, and it's about time," Ben said.

"I'm just saying, it better work."

"If you're willing to fight the dragon, then I'm willing to hear you out," Varian said. "Come with me. I'll show you what we're up against."

Ben followed him deeper into the mine, his friends, the Sage, and the Thief trailing behind. He stopped at the threshold of the large room, his breath catching in his chest.

"It's always a bit unsettling, isn't it?" the Sage said. "Now you see why I'm here."

It was the room that Ben had seen in his vision with the Oculus. This was where he would plan an attack against the dragon. One more proof that Ellie would be taken by the wyrm.

"Oh, shit," he whispered, closing his eyes.

"What?" Ellie asked.

"It's not going to work," he said.

"What do you mean?" Varian asked.

"My plan—it won't kill the dragon."

"You've had another vision," the Sage said.

Ben shook his head.

"I had several the first and only time I used the Oculus. One was of this room … of us planning an attack together. That was the last vision, the one I shared with you. But I also saw other things, a vision of an ambush that killed Ellie and Imogen at the safe house in Alturas. We avoided that one. The other was of Ellie chained to a post in a cinder cone—the wyrm was there. That one hasn't happened yet."

The Sage was staring at him with a mixture of alarm, jealousy, and wonder. "I've never had more than one vision at a time," he said. "Most often, I just see the last vision until it comes to pass."

"Well, maybe you were the problem all along, Sage," Dom said, clapping him on the shoulder in passing as he went to the table.

The Sage tried to hide his scowl. "Perhaps, if you had been more willing to include me in your plans, I would have been able to offer better advice."

Dom turned back to him, anger flashing in his eyes. "Your advice led us to the meeting that fell through," he said. "We were out on a wild-goose chase instead of in the bunker where we might have been able to save our families."

"Or die with them," the Sage said.

Dom's hand went to the hilt of his sword. "Tread carefully," he said.

The Sage held up his hands. "I don't mean to diminish your loss," he said, his tone supplicating. "That was a tragic and sad day for us all."

"Some more than others," Dom said.

"Clearly, you two have some history," Varian said. "And I don't give a damn about any of it. Either help us or get out."

Dom held the Sage with his eyes for a moment longer before nodding. "Fair enough," he said. "No sense opening old wounds."

Varian motioned to the large table in the middle of the room. A map of Battle Mountain and the surrounding area occupied the entire surface.

Ben took it in, accessing his augment for any more information about the town that it had to offer, which wasn't much. A single underground road passed beneath the town with only one access point. Most of the surface buildings in his augment's database weren't even represented on Varian's map. Only one stood out—it used to be a hospital. Now it served as the Dragon Guard headquarters. The building floor plan opened in his mind.

"The priest does his dark magic on the roof of the old medical center," Varian said. "The rumor is that his altar is a dragon's skull, but that's been hard to verify. He keeps his soldiers, and especially the human stalkers, inside the fortifications that the Dragon Guard have built up around the place."

"So they aren't using these new soldiers?" Ellie asked.

"No, and we don't know why," Varian said. "Dragon Guard from the town garrison run patrols … and abduct families to feed the priest's madness. His new soldiers just train in the courtyard, every day, all day."

"He's going to use them for something," Hound said.

"We assume that he's preparing to test them," the Sage said. "So far, we don't believe that they've faced combat."

"I guess it makes sense to use a methodical approach when building an army of super soldiers," Ben said.

"We don't really care," Varian said. "We just want them to stop taking our families."

"Why do they take whole families?" Olivia asked.

"We think they're sacrificed during the possession spell," the Sage said.

"Oh, God, that's horrible."

"Indeed," the Sage said. "Another atrocity as yet unaddressed."

"We have intel on a shipment of weapons and armor coming in tomorrow," Varian said. "Each time these shipments arrive, the Dragon Guard round up another twenty families. We're going to make sure this particular shipment doesn't reach its destination."

Ben nodded, looking at the map, his mind working on a more permanent solution.

"That might slow them down," Hound said. "But it won't stop them."

Varian shrugged, hands turned up helplessly. "We don't have the men to assault the compound, but we can't just hide. This, at least, is a target we can take. And it might slow them down enough to save a few more lives."

"Not saying it isn't a worthy objective, just saying it won't solve the problem," Hound said.

"If we could solve the problem we would have," Varian said.

"Can you get me closer to town without being seen?" Ben asked.

"Yeah," Varian said, "but I'm not sure what one man can do."

"For now, I need more information."

"Then what?"

"Then we make a plan to kill the priest."

Varian harrumphed, shaking his head. "What makes you think you can get close enough? And even if you could, then what? He's got magic."

"So do we," Ben said.

"So I've heard," Varian said. "I'm going to need more than that before I risk my men on hearsay."

Dom drew his sword and drove it through the table halfway to the hilt.

"Dramatic, as always," the Sage said.

Varian and his men stared at the mythical blade for a moment.

"So that's the Dragon's Fang, the only weapon to ever kill a wyrm," he said. "You have my attention."

"Like the man said, we need more information," Dom said. "Take us into town."

"Fair enough," Varian said. "We'll leave just before dusk. It's safer to approach at night. The Dragon Guard are hunting for us and there's word that Hoondragon arrived a few days ago to help them put us down."

Ben laughed bitterly, sharing a look with Hound. "Now why doesn't that surprise me?"

"Frank is getting to be a problem," Hound said. "Might be we have to put him out of our misery."

"Yeah," Ben said sadly.

"Wait, who's Frank?" Varian asked.

"My brother," Ben said. "Also known as Hoondragon."

"Your brother is the Dragon's hunter?" Varian said, his men becoming instantly more alert.

Ben shrugged helplessly. "We killed Hoondragon in Mount Shasta," he said. "My brother picked up his sword and now it owns him."

Varian regarded Ben intently for several moments. "I need you to be real clear about this," he said. "Your brother is our enemy. Where do your loyalties lie?"

"My brother betrayed me long before he picked up that sword," Ben said, somewhat deflated. "Before this is over, I suspect I'm going to have to kill him."

"It's a hard thing to kill your kin," Varian said. "You sure you have it in you?"

Ben shrugged again, shaking his head. "I really don't know," he whispered.

"At least you're honest," Varian said. "Know this, if we get a shot at him, we'll put him in the ground, no hesitation. You try and stop us, and there'll be trouble."

Ben nodded, another thought coming to the fore of his mind. "Was he transporting prisoners?"

"What do you mean?" Varian asked.

"Did he have a man and a woman with him?"

"Not sure, but I can find out," Varian said, motioning to one of his men, who left quickly.

"So, will you help us take down this shipment?" Varian asked.

"We'll help, but we're going to capture it and use it to get inside the fortress," Ben said. "The real target is the priest. What time is the shipment due to arrive?"

"Noon, tomorrow," Varian said.

Ben consulted his augment for telemetry on the orbital weapon, nodding to himself.

"That should work," he said. "Begin making preparations to evacuate the entire town tomorrow night."

"I'm still not sure about that," Varian said. "People are going to need a pretty good reason to abandon their homes."

"Once we kill the priest, the dragon will come and burn Battle Mountain to the ground," Ben said.

"That is a valid assumption," the Sage said. "I've seen it happen a number of times."

"Do we really want to lure the wyrm here?" one of Varian's men asked.

"Kill the priest and the dragon will probably come," Dom said. "Leave the priest and he'll keep taking your families."

"Where will we go?" another man asked.

"North," Dom said. "There are still some free territories up there."

Two men entered from a passage.

"Ah, you're the scout that saw Hoondragon arrive," Varian said.

The man nodded.

"Did he have prisoners? A man and a woman?"

"Yeah, a one-handed man and a really pissed-off woman," the scout said.

"Shit," Hound muttered.

Ben closed his eyes, bowing his head for a moment. "When can we leave for town?" he asked.

"A few hours," Varian said. "I'd offer you a meal but we don't have enough to go around."

"A place to rest is all we need."

Varian led them into a large cavern, propped up with stout timbers and dimly lit with a few lanterns. Dozens of people huddled in small groups. All were dirty and frightened. Children, women, and old men eyed them with suspicion and curiosity.

Ben's heart sank. More shattered lives left in the wake of the dragon's ambitions.

They sat down in a vacant corner.

"Tell me more about your visions," Dom said. "Sounded like the Sage was surprised at how much more information you got from that damn thing than he did."

Ben recounted everything he'd seen, leaving out no detail. The memory of the experience was surprisingly sharp even without consulting the augment.

"So you managed to avoid one of the visions," Dom said, after pondering what Ben had recalled. "But another, the room we were just in, that came true."

Ben nodded.

"And Ellie in the cinder cone, that hasn't happened yet," he said, frowning in thought. "I wonder if you get better information than the Sage does because you've got the egg."

"I don't know," Ben said. "I haven't wanted to use it again because I'm afraid of what I'll see."

Dom chuckled mirthlessly. "Don't often see such wisdom in one so young."

Ben snorted. "Not sure I'd call it wisdom," he said. "The Oculus might actually help."

"Or it might just show you something really shitty for you to worry about," Dom said.

"Begging your pardon, sir," a girl said from beside Ben. "Do you have anything to eat?"

She was dirty, her clothes were torn and ragged, and she didn't have shoes. Her big brown eyes were filled with a mixture of fear and hope.

Ben nodded dumbly, unable to move past the simple human need the poor girl was radiating like a plea for help. He handed her an apple from his bag.

Her eyes lit up as she took the piece of fruit.

"Thank you, sir," she said, before racing off.

Ben shook his head as he watched her go, returning to her mother with her treasure.

"One way or another, that priest is going to die," Ben whispered.

"Just remember, he's a means to an end," Dom said. "And who knows, maybe that crowbar you've got in orbit will put the wyrm down for good."

"Either way, his army of super soldiers isn't going to make it," Hound said. "At bare minimum, you get to piss him off."

"Doesn't take much to rile a dragon," Dom said.

Ben propped his pack against a wall and lay back against it, closing his eyes and trying not to think about all of the fear and suffering happening around him.

He felt himself drifting off to sleep and then he was in a dark forest. He knew immediately that he was dreaming, but there was a different quality to it— magic was near.

A rustling in the dark drew his attention. A pair of yellow eyes watched him intently. When he locked eyes with it, whatever it was, it charged.

He came awake with a start, sitting bolt upright and taking a deep breath.

Ellie stirred, looking over at him from where she had propped herself up beside him.

"You all right?"

"Another dream," he muttered. "This time, I knew it was happening right away and I was able to wake myself."

"What do you think it is?"

"Probably another minion," he said, easing himself against his pack and closing his eyes. Rather than try to sleep he turned his attention to his avatar once again, beginning with his augment's projection but then shifting to his imagination only.

He was making progress. While the white angelic being was visible to him even without technological assistance, it was still entirely dependent on his direction for action. Without him willing it, his seven-foot-tall imaginary friend would simply stand stock-still.

The Codex was clear that the casting of this particular spell was a process that often took a long time and required continuous effort. Ben started to wonder if it was worth it, chiding himself after a brief moment of doubt. If his avatar could provide him an advantage, even a small one, it was entirely worth whatever effort it cost.

He felt magic coming before he saw the Sage emerge from the passage. He stopped dead in his tracks, staring at Ben's avatar with a mixture of wonder and envy.

"Quite impressive," he said, his eyes never leaving the figure. "It took me many months to create my avatar, and I spent most of that time in deep meditation."

"Wait, you can see it?" Ben said, coming to his feet, a thrill of excitement lending him a burst of energy.

"Yes, I can indeed," the Sage said. "You've made remarkable progress in a very short period of time, especially considering all that you've had to contend with."

"I can see him, but he's just an extension of my imagination," Ben said. "How do I make him take on a life of his own? Like your avatar."

The Sage smiled, shrugging helplessly. "Time and effort. You must continue your visualization exercises until you come to believe that he has volition and personality. Only then will he truly manifest."

Ben nodded thoughtfully, hoping that his augment could help speed the process along.

"Varian is ready," the Sage said. "My associate will be joining you."

"The Thief?"

"Yes."

"That's quite the moniker," Ben said. "You understand that if he tries to steal from me, it won't end well."

"I assure you, we're working for the same ends."

"Uh-huh," Ben said, collecting what gear he would need.

"Reassuring, isn't he?" Dom said.

The Sage gave him a reproving look. "I know we've had our differences, but we face the same enemy. Surely, we can find a way to work together."

"That remains to be seen," Dom said, leaning back and closing his eyes "I'll be here. Try to stay out of trouble."

"Just a recon," Ben said, helping Ellie to her feet. "We'll be back before you know it."

They followed the Sage into the map room. Varian and the Thief were geared up and waiting.

"Is the dog really necessary?" Varian asked.

"He goes where I go," Ben said.

"If he barks at the wrong time, we're burned."

"He won't."

They left on foot, Varian leading the way. He took them north of town and circled to the east so that they could approach through the low range of hills that bordered the north side of town. As they approached a rise, Varian motioned for them to stay low. Ben had a single drone up several thousand feet, so he knew that they were in no danger, but he crawled to the vantage point just the same.

"There it is," Varian said, pointing to the five-story building surrounded by a high log wall and patrolled by several squads of Dragon Guard.

Ben kept his drone where it was and zoomed in on the roof. Sure enough, there was a magic circle etched into the floor and stained with blood. In the center was a dragon's skull, nearly intact. From this distance he could feel its magic if he concentrated.

Dragon Guard stood sentry at all four corners, but otherwise the roof was empty. Ben began a sweep of the perimeter, focusing on the seven guard towers interspersed at irregular intervals along the wall. Each tower was manned by two Dragon Guard, while the catwalk atop the wall was patrolled by a pair of enemy soldiers pacing between the towers. Oil lamps hung from posts on the walls and the towers, providing dim illumination.

Within the courtyard there were seventy-two men, each wearing identical black armor. They were training with swords, all in perfect formation, all obeying the commands of the Legate giving instruction. The men in the training field had the look of dark magic about them. Even through the drone, Ben could almost see the shadow on each man's soul.

He switched to thermals and his drone slowly descended, scanning the building for heat. The top floor was nearly empty save for a few sentries. He approached carefully, seeking out the priest, switching back to normal vision once he located two people in a large room on one corner of the building. He kept his drone at a distance but focused in on the room, angling for a view through one of the large floor-to-ceiling windows.

Frank lounged in an oversized chair next to another man wearing the robes of a priest. Each held a goblet and they were talking as if they were old friends, or at least Frank was.

"So what now?" Varian asked. "We don't dare get any closer."

"We don't have to," Ben said, switching back to thermal and inspecting the fourth floor. It held a number of rooms, some containing families. Only one contained just two people. He switched back to normal vision, but it was too dark to see through the barred windows. As much as he wanted to get closer, he didn't dare.

The third floor held only a few roving sentries. The second floor and the ground level were crawling with Dragon Guard, over a hundred by the looks of their heat signatures.

"One hundred and seven," his augment offered.

"Right," Ben thought, reminding himself to use his tech to its fullest potential.

He circled the facility with his drone, noting the stout walls and the ample guard. It was a fortress. There were two large gates and three man-sized doors, all of which were guarded by two men each and well lit with oil lamps, not to mention clearly visible from the nearby guard towers.

He did a full sweep of the entire facility, recording everything for later analysis, covering every foot of the wall and the surrounding terrain. Once he'd collected the information, he inched backward from the ridge and rolled over, looking up at the stars.

"What do you think?" Ellie asked.

"Won't be easy," he said.

"Looks like suicide to me," Varian said.

"One or two good men could get in quietly," the Thief said. "Getting out…"

"Yeah … I need to think," Ben said. "Let's head back."

They returned to the mine in silence. Ben made a list of objectives, trying to rank each in order of importance. Rescue Imogen and John. Rescue the families being held and awaiting a fate worse than death. Kill the priest. Capture the dragon's skull. Deal with Frank, maybe permanently.

That last one made him a bit queasy. He tried to put himself in his grandfather's shoes and found only a dual answer. As a grandfather, Ben knew that Cyril would have done everything in his power to save Frank, even from himself. As the Wizard, Ben wasn't so sure how his grandfather might have handled the threat that was his brother.

Hoondragon was master now. Ben didn't even know if that particular spell could be broken, but he decided that he had to try—he had to give his brother one more chance. Reason told him otherwise. Common sense told him to put him down. But…

Frank was his brother.

That had to mean something, even if only to prove to himself that he hadn't already washed away his humanity in a torrent of blood. He'd killed so many people. Somehow it seemed different when it was his own family. He wondered what that said about his slowly twisting sense of morality. The enemy soldiers that he'd struck down had families too.

"Stop that," Homer said.

"What?"

"Mentally flogging yourself over Frank. He's his own man with his own free will and he's chosen his own course. Let him bear the consequences for that. His burden isn't yours to carry."

"It's just … I'm not sure I can kill him."

"Then don't," Homer said.

"What if I have to?"

"Then you will."

"You make it sound so simple," Ben said.

"That's because it is. If you have to kill him, you will. If you don't, you won't."

Ben pondered his dog's advice while they walked in the moonlight.

"I guess you're right," he finally said. "Ultimately, it's up to Frank."

"Of course I'm right," Homer said.

Ben looked over at his dog and shook his head.

Dom was with the Sage and a number of other men in the map room when they returned. Hound sat beside the entrance with a jug in his lap.

"I need to know," the Sage said.

"You need to know what the Wizard decides you need to know," Dom said.

Neither had noticed them enter.

Ben looked at Hound quizzically.

"The Sage wants to know what your plan is. Dom won't tell him. They've been going round and round for half an hour now. Pretty good show."

He offered his jug.

"No thanks," Ben said.

Dom and the Sage noticed them.

"About time," Dom said, turning toward the exit. "Go harass him for a while."

"Ah, did you learn anything?" the Sage asked.

"I think so, but I'm tired and I need to think," Ben said. "We'll make a plan tomorrow."

"Please, allow me to be of assistance," the Sage said.

"I will … tomorrow," Ben said.

"Not much to tell," the Thief offered. "We didn't get close enough to learn a lot."

Ben left through the passage Dom had taken. He found him in the large room with the refugee families.

"Get what you needed?" Dom asked.

"I got what I could," Ben said. "Not sure if it's what we need."

Dom chuckled, lying back on his bedroll and closing his eyes. "If I didn't know better, I'd say we're at war."

Ben rolled out his blanket, lying down and looking at the cave ceiling.

"It looked pretty well fortified," Ellie said.

He nodded.

"Maybe you could kill the priest with one of your seeker rounds," she offered. "That way we don't have to go inside."

He shook his head.

"Frank was there," he said. "If he's there, then so are Imogen and John. Also, there's a half dozen families being held on the fourth floor."

"Shit," she said. "That complicates things."

"Yeah, we need to get inside, and I'm pretty sure we can manage that. Getting out…"

"We'll figure it out," she said.

He offered her his shoulder for a pillow, drifting off to sleep a few minutes after she curled up next to him.

Chapter 11

Ben was dreaming again, but this time there was more magic, more than he'd ever felt before, buffeting against his mind and washing over his will.

He was in a cavern. Water dripped in the distance. Green algae clung to stalagmites and stalactites, glowing with an eerie hue, casting dim light across the underworld expanse. His eyes stopped scanning when he saw the wyrm, black scales glistening like those of a serpent, piercing yellow eyes like those of a cat. The beast watched him, crouched as if prepared to spring, all too close.

Sudden fear gripped him. Laughter brought him back to his senses. A man stood next to the dragon, eyeing Ben like a spider eyes a fly caught in its web.

He felt the words in his mind rather than heard them.

"You have proven to be a worthy adversary," the dragon said. "I find that I have come to respect you … as much as I respect any human."

Ben looked around, searching for an exit or for other threats, as if the dragon wasn't enough. Looking down, he found that his weapons were gone. His fear began to grow.

"You can't defeat me," the wyrm said. "Surrender and submit to my will and I will make you more powerful than you can imagine. It is the only way."

A cascade of memories flashed through his mind—his grandfather, Britney, Imogen's baby … so much death and suffering. Anger supplanted his fear.

"Like hell. I can think of at least one other way."

The dragon started purring, an altogether unsettling sound.

"Defiant, yet still sensible enough to be afraid. Oh yes, I can smell your fear, even in this dreamscape. You reek of it. Deep down in your monkey brain, you understand that you are prey. Nothing more than a light snack, at that.

"Even still, you've bested many of my most potent servants. The blood of my ancestors must run strong within your veins. Serve me. There's nothing that I can't give you."

"How about my world back? All of it."

"This was never your world," the dragon said. "Your feeble and ephemeral species is nothing but an accidental caretaker, and then for only a blink in time. Your reason for existence was always to serve … most of you even embrace your enslavement."

"Bullshit!" Ben snapped. "Maybe some people accept servitude because the alternative is death, but nobody wants to be a slave."

"You were made to be slaves," the wyrm said.

"Made … by who?"

The dragon flicked his tongue at Ben, turning to the man beside him.

The man looked up at the wyrm, fear and confusion on his face.

"No, Master," he said. "I don't understand why, but I can't locate him."

Ben became more wary as the dragon tensed, cat eyes fixed and unblinking.

"Shame," the dragon said. "I would have treated you like a favored pet."

Ben's fear started to spike. He tried to wake up but couldn't. The wyrm's tongue flicked at him again.

"Death will come more quickly than you deserve."

Homer trotted up beside Ben out of the darkness, barking once.

The dragon recoiled slightly, snarling.

"How?" the man beside him said.

"You hold precious little sway here, serpent," Homer said.

The dragon roared in fury, sending a spike of terror coursing through Ben. He woke with a start, Ellie waking with him.

"What is it?" she asked, her hand finding the hilt of her sword.

He took a deep breath and let it out slowly. "Another dream," he whispered, struggling to regain his composure.

"A normal dream?"

"No ... very much not normal," he said. "I'll tell you about it in the daylight."

She nodded, easing back into his embrace.

"What just happened?" Ben asked Homer.

"I saved you from the dragon."

"But how?"

Homer rolled onto his back and started wiggling back and forth, snorting with no sense of self-consciousness whatsoever.

"What's gotten into him?" Ellie asked.

"I have no idea," Ben said, closing his eyes and trying to quiet his mind. Peace didn't come.

The more he tried to force his most recent nightmare from his mind, the more it consumed his thoughts. It raised so many questions. First and foremost: How was the dragon reaching into his dreams?

Ben suspected the answer to that question had something to do with the man who'd been standing next to the wyrm. His identity was another question.

He reviewed the dream in his mind, stopping at the brief exchange between the wyrm and his servant. The man had said that he couldn't locate Ben—small favors, he thought. But why? Another question.

The one point he was sure of was his vulnerability within the dream realm. That brought him back to his dog—again. Homer had always been a mystery. Sometimes he was forthcoming and helpful, but often, particularly in regard to his origin and purpose, he was frustratingly enigmatic. Regardless, Ben was sure that Homer had saved him again.

Perhaps, whatever magic Homer brought to the table was the reason the wyrm couldn't find him through his dreams. But then, it could also be his now-constant magic circle. Either way, it was a relief to know that his location was still unknown to his adversary.

For the moment, anyway.

Ben had every intention of changing that soon enough.

His mind turned back to the immediate task at hand. Lying in the dark, he called his recordings of the Rogue Priest's fortress into his mind and reviewed them in detail, looking for any weakness he might exploit to gain entry.

After several passes at the data he'd collected, he found himself wishing that he could fly. The bulk of the enemy was stationed on the lowest two floors, while his targets were on the top floors. He needed a way past all of the Dragon Guard and the possessed soldiers that wouldn't raise the alarm. And then he needed a way out.

"Perhaps a simulation would help," the augment said.

Ben blinked in the darkness. He'd used the battle simulator for training purposes several times in the past, but never with a situation as complex as this one.

"Can you do that?"

"I have enough data to compile a simulation with eighty-six percent accuracy," the augment said.

"Do it," Ben said. Several moments later he found himself standing in the map room outlining his plan to a simulation of his friends.

When his first attempt raised the alarm and led to his death, he twitched violently enough to wake Ellie again.

"What's happening?" she mumbled.

"Nothing," he said, the residual pain from his simulated death fading quickly. He wondered idly what time it was.

"An hour and a half before dawn," the augment offered.

With full command of the computer inside his mind, Ben had relegated it to the background. He began to wonder if that had been a mistake. It could offer so many capabilities, but it wasn't very good at offering suggestions, probably because it was designed to be used by someone who had been trained in its capabilities. Ben decided to make a better effort at engaging the augment in the future.

"Another dream?" Ellie asked, her voice thick with sleep.

"Sort of," Ben said, extricating himself from her embrace and sitting up so he could return to his simulation without disturbing her again.

Several attempts later, complete with simulated deaths, Ben concluded that a frontal assault was out. He managed to infiltrate the facility quietly, only to raise the alarm once inside. On a few of those attempts he reached the priest, but that was where the simulation broke down. The augment didn't have enough information or understanding of magic to accurately depict how the priest might fight, never mind the true strength and capabilities of the soldiers that he'd created.

One thing he did learn for certain, he would need to use his last ex-plus charge if he was to have any chance against the garrison of Dragon Guard.

After gaining as much insight as he thought possible through the simulation, he opened his eyes. Ellie sat nearby, watching him. She smiled gently.

"Hungry?"

He nodded. She handed him a bowl of porridge with some nuts and fruit. He smiled his thanks.

After he'd finished eating, Ellie said, "The others are waiting for you. I thought I might have to knock the Sage on his ass to keep him from disturbing your meditation."

He chuckled. "I was using the augment's simulator to run through plans of attack."

"Huh … any luck?"

"I'm not sure I'd go that far," he said, getting to his feet. "This won't be easy."

"Never thought it would be," she said, taking his hand as they headed for the map room.

"Ah, there you are," the Sage said, with a hint of annoyance. "I trust you slept well."

Ben snorted, shaking his head as he came to the table.

"Do you have something to write with?" he asked Varian.

Without a word, Ben drew a map of the compound, indicating the locations of the sentries, the priest, the families being held, the doors through the surrounding walls, the staircases within the building, and the number of soldiers.

"You managed to get a lot more information than I did yesterday," Varian said.

Ben nodded. "We have our work cut out for us. I see three primary objectives. First, we need to rescue the prisoners on the fourth floor. Second, we need to kill the priest. And finally, I want to capture that dragon skull."

"Oh, is that all?" Varian asked.

"Not entirely," Ben said. "I believe that my Aunt Imogen and a friend named John Durt are being held with the families on the fourth floor. Also, my brother is staying with the priest on the fifth floor. He wields the sword called Hoondragon."

Murmuring broke out among some of Varian's men. Ben let it run its course.

"I hear doubt, and I don't blame you," he said. "Truth is, we face a formidable enemy. And you don't know me any more than I know you, but I do know that our goals are the same. We all want to live in a world without fear, without persecution, and without enslavement.

"That world can't exist as long as the wyrm does. So that is my purpose. I intend to kill the dragon. Since he's not here right now, I'll settle for killing his minions."

Varian held up his hands to forestall his men's objections. They quieted after a few moments of protest.

"Bold words," he said. "And I think we can all agree about the sentiment—it's the *how* we have a few questions about."

"That's why we're here," Ben said. "My plan is complicated. It'll require a number of teams to accomplish very specific tasks, in just the right order, at exactly the right time. Will you hear me out?"

After a few more moments of discussion, Varian silenced his men again.

"We'll hear what you have to say, but we aren't making any promises."

"I wouldn't have it any other way," Ben said. He proceeded to outline his plan, step by step, assigning tasks to each small group of people, stopping objections and questions until he had nearly completed his entire presentation.

Suddenly, a man rushed in, drawing everyone's attention.

"Rath is coming!" he shouted.

"Report," Varian snapped.

"We made contact with a Dragon Guard scout team in the valley," he said. "Killed one, captured one. One got away."

"Damn it!" Varian said. "Are we pursuing?"

"Two men. He had a pretty good lead."

Ben sent two hundred splinters, forming two drones and navigating them along the ceiling of the mine.

"What the hell was that?" Varian asked.

"A weapon," Ben said, focusing on getting his drones clear of the mine. He sent them straight up once he was out, gaining elevation rapidly as he turned his focus on the valley where they'd first met the resistance. From there he zoomed in, searching for the horse's tracks, isolating them and following them back into the desert.

The rider was fleeing with all the speed his sturdy little horse could muster. Ben transformed one of his drones into a dart and lined them up, dart before drone, guiding the dart into the back of the fleeing scout's head in a gentle slope, killing him instantly, without warning.

He toppled off his horse.

"You'll find your scout by a cluster of rocks marking a bend in the road," Ben said, bringing his drones back into orbit overhead.

"I'm going to need you to explain just exactly how you know that," Varian said.

Ben nodded, detaching his remaining two hundred splinters and forming them into a shield. A moment of silence was followed by hushed muttering among the men in the room.

"This is technology from before Dragonfall. I can do quite a lot with it, actually."

He spun the shield into a blade and sliced a few inches off the corner of the table.

"I used this tech to kill the escaping scout."

The Sage shook his head, looking down at his feet for a moment. "I owe you an apology," he said. "Had I known what I know now, I would have behaved much differently. I hope you can forgive me."

"Forgive, yes," Ben said. "Trust, maybe. It all depends on your actions."

"I assure you, I stand ready to assist the Wizard in whatever way I can," the Sage said with a respectful bow.

Dom snorted under his breath. The Sage ignored him.

"I'm going to hold you to that," Ben said.

"As well you should," the Sage said.

Ben nodded, turning back to the table and scanning the faces watching him—their expressions were a mixture of respect and fear. His shield disassembled and the splinters attached themselves to his belt.

"Now, my plan begins by capturing the shipment … the very same shipment that you want to hit," Ben said.

"But then you want to assault the compound," one of Varian's men said.

"Yeah, that is a bit crazy," another offered.

"Yes, but we'll do that part," Ben said. "You don't even have to attack until after we're inside."

"Let's just start off with the highway robbery," Varian said. "See how things go from there."

Ben felt a chill, then a hint of unfamiliar magic. The Sage looked over at him sharply, then scanned the room. Ben saw his avatar flare into temporary view as she went to investigate.

"Agreed," Ben said, trying to identify the feeling he'd just had.

Three men entered, leading a Dragon Guard prisoner.

"The last man was found dead on the road, hole through his head," the lead man said.

Varian looked over at Ben.

"How many of his men is your Legate bringing?" Ben asked the Dragon Guard.

"All of them," he said, with a shrug.

"Rath is coming, indeed," Ben muttered, turning to Varian.

"One more reason to flee. You don't want to be here when that army arrives."

It was the Warlock's shadow. That's what Ben had felt.

"Can't argue with that," Varian said. "Get the word out about Rath's army."

Half a dozen men left in a hurry.

The Warlock was lurking in the shadows. Again.

Ben checked his drones, holding one at two thousand feet and sending the other straight up to ten thousand feet, before zooming in to the west and searching for the army. Sure enough, two dust plumes, one for the cavalry, a thousand strong and a day and a half out, the other marking five thousand infantry several days behind, but coming nonetheless.

"So, tell me about this shipment," Ben said.

Chapter 12

Ben saw the heavily armored wagon coming well before the scout signaled. It was alone, just like it was supposed to be, traveling on a small country road, just where they thought it would be.

They waited, allowing the wagon to get into the kill zone before toppling a rockslide down across its path, stopping it cold. The two drivers nearly went over the front, they reined their horses in so quickly. Ben killed them both simultaneously with two darts. There was a muffled commotion and then the side of the wagon came unhinged at the top and flopped over, slamming to the ground with a reverberating whack.

Two dozen stalker soldiers stood at the ready inside the wagon. They started to swarm out toward Ben.

"Ambush! Ex-plus! Now!" he snapped at Hound.

Rufus didn't miss a beat, ejecting the round in Bertha's chamber and loading an ex-plus charge, aiming into the rapidly emptying wagon and firing. The explosion was deafening, spraying broken stalker soldiers in every direction.

Ben grabbed Hound and motioned for him to follow, doing the same with Ellie, leading them away from the carnage. Varian and his men were on the other side of the ravine. Ben set a course for the rally point, working his jaw to pop his ears.

He didn't stop until he reached the first of two locations where they had agreed to meet after the mission. Ben scanned his drone feed, finding three men coming quickly.

Varian's men entered the small clearing without Varian.

Ben started scanning the surrounding area.

"He's coming," Ben said, picking him up as he left a house several blocks away. Varian arrived a few minutes later.

"Let's get back to base," he said. "Looks like your mission was a bust."

"What it was, was an ambush," Ben said. "Makes me wonder if the Rogue Priest knows what we're planning for tonight."

"Does it really matter right now?" Varian asked. "Let's get under cover and continue this conversation there."

"Fair enough," Ben said, sharing a look with Ellie. He could feel her senses heighten in response. Varian's men led the way back to the mine.

Fortunately, the ex-plus had been very thorough. The stalker soldiers had been utterly destroyed, leaving a bloody crater strewn with splintered wagon parts and little else.

Ben still felt a sense of unease. He tried to identify the source, but it was elusive.

"You all right?" Ellie whispered, pulling him aside.

"Something's wrong," he said. "I'm just not sure what."

"You mean besides the fact that there's a mole back at the mine, and we might already be burned?"

"Yeah, besides that," he said, gesturing to Varian with his head.

She frowned, taking a look around with fresh eyes, nodding her unspoken agreement to remain alert. They hurried to catch up.

Safely underground, Ben started to feel an even greater sense of unease. Magic and malice was close, but he couldn't quite put his finger on it until he looked directly at Varian. It was subtle, almost imperceptible, but undeniable once he focused his attention.

Varian was possessed.

Juju had taken hold of him.

Ben looked away, scanning for Kayla. She was across the room. He didn't let his eyes linger on her, moving on to Dom and offering him a cautionary look.

"So what now?" Varian asked.

"I'm not sure," Ben said. "I wasn't expecting your shipment to be an ambush."

"Me, neither," Varian said. "Let's take an hour and see what we can come up with."

Ben nodded, his skin crawling when he looked at the man. He began recording from the drone he'd parked a thousand feet overhead, looking straight down over the mine entrance, while he made his way to the cave where they'd slept.

"Be ready to move," he told his friends before sitting down and closing his eyes, focusing on his drone feed.

It didn't take long. Varian and Kayla left in a hurry, with Varian pointing a gun at her back.

Ben tapped Ellie and Hound and the three of them raced out of the mine. He tracked Varian and Kayla with his drone, staying far enough back to be undetectable. Varian took her to a house in town. Ben closed with a drone to get a better look, slipping inside the room without notice. Lulu was there, along with her brother, currently unconscious and in possession of Varian.

"Hello, Kayla," Lulu said. "I told you it would be less than pleasant if we had to come and get you."

"Let Varian go," Kayla said.

"That's up to you," Lulu said.

Ben hurried his pace, trailing Ellie and Hound behind him. Homer kept up easily. They slowed as they neared the house, approaching quietly. Ben motioned to the door and deployed two hundred splinters, waiting a moment for Hound to kick the door open before sending them into the room.

He followed his swarm into the house, directing it at the unconscious man on the bed, Juju in the flesh, transforming his splinters into a shield rotating like a saw blade, poised over his head.

"Let go of Varian and maybe we can come to an understanding."

Varian looked over at Juju's body, a frantic twitch of panic contorting his face.

Hound entered on Ben's heels, pointing his shotgun at Lulu. She held her hands up, palms out.

"Wait!" she shouted. "Just wait."

"Let go," Ben said, pointing at Varian.

He let go of Kayla.

"Nice try," Ben said, motioning for Kayla to get behind him. "Now let go of Varian."

Varian slumped to the floor.

"All right, all right, you win," Juju said. "Just don't kill me."

Ben withdrew the blade, disassembling it and re-calling the splinters.

"Here's what we're going to do," he said.

Ben looked at the battlefield again. He'd spent the afternoon preparing. Atop three nearby hills, he'd carved circles into the stone and then blessed them. On the nearest, he'd cut three circles, one inside the next, all three blessed with the intention to protect and conceal.

He had his teams in place. The town had been thoroughly warned to evacuate, though Ben suspected the people wouldn't begin to flee until he blew the barracks.

They watched the shadows grow longer, waiting for sunset.

As the last of the direct light vanished, they moved, using the cover of rock and trees to approach the fortress unseen. Ben stopped them behind a large bush, waiting for a pair of roving sentries to turn, then led them across a patch of moonlight and into shadow again.

He took his time, picking where they would stop and where they would run with the guidance of a single drone held close inside his circle. He brought them to the wall directly below one of the towers, not too far from a man-sized door in the back wall of the fortress.

Ben picked out his targets. Two in the tower. Two on the wall above the door. Two inside the door. Two in the next tower over.

He didn't have to worry about the two at the door. That left six.

He watched through the wall with his thermal vision. A man approached the sentries, timing his arrival to avoid the notice of the guards in the towers and on the catwalk. The man walked up without a word and stabbed the two door guards in the throat, one after the other, setting them up inside the enclosure, out of sight, before quickly unlocking door.

Ben led the way inside.

The Dragon Guard soldier handed Ben a ring of keys. "Everything is in place," he said.

"Good, wait here."

"Right," Juju said.

Ben and his team raced across to the corner of the building and the back staircase leading to the upper floors. They slipped inside and closed the door before the roving guard on the catwalk noticed. Even still, Ben waited for a moment just to be sure before he started heading up, one drone right over his head, the rest of his splinters attached and powered down.

He watched the second team stick to the shadows along the wall as they infiltrated the compound.

Homer, Ellie, Cleve, Zack, Dom, and Kat followed him as he ascended quietly but steadily. At each floor he slid a doorstop under the door and pressed it into place—not enough to hold for long, but enough to buy time if a guard heard anything and tried to investigate. He reached the fourth floor without raising the alarm and stopped, kneeling at the stairwell door, maneuvering his drone under the door into the hallway beyond.

"Two men," he whispered, "walking back and forth, up and down the hallway."

"Just tell me when they're about to pass each other," Kat said.

Ben nodded, taking hold of the doorknob, pulling the door open when the two sentries came shoulder to shoulder. Kat raced in and shot them twice each. Both tried to call out, slurring their words before they could finish them as they slumped to the floor.

Ben moved in quickly, racing past Kat to the far end of the hall, searching for other sentries. When he found none, he opened the nearest door. The small, dingy room was occupied by a man, a woman, and a young boy. All three eyed him with fear.

Ben put a finger over his lips. "We're here to get you out," he whispered, motioning for them to come to him.

They didn't move, still looking at him with fear in their eyes.

"Who are you?" the boy asked.

"My name is Ben," he said, squatting down so he could look the child in the eye. "I've come to help you and your family, but I need you to do something for me. Will you help me?"

"Hush," the father said to his son.

The boy remained silent but he nodded solemnly, innocence and hope in his young eyes.

"I need you to come with me, and be really quiet."

The boy nodded again, taking a step forward before his father stopped him, stepping between his family and Ben.

"Why should we trust you?"

Ben shrugged helplessly. "I have nothing to offer you except an open door," he said. "I can't make you walk through it, or at least I won't. What I can tell you is that this place is going to become a battlefield in a few minutes. You're not going to want to be here when that happens."

He stepped back into the hallway and went to the next room, opening the door.

A man stood ready to attack him, holding his blow when he saw Ben, a look of confusion washing over his face.

"Who are you?"

"I'm with the resistance."

Ellie came up beside Ben.

"We're here to get you out," she said. "Move quickly and stay quiet."

This family didn't need any more than that. They followed instructions without hesitation, moving to the end of the hallway and waiting with Cleve and Zack for the rest of the prisoners to be released.

Ben started to feel a sense of urgency building in his gut. He started down the corridor, unlocking and opening doors without stopping to talk to anyone, instead letting Ellie and Dom coax the prisoners out of their cells with the promise of escape.

Only when he opened a door and saw Imogen and John did he stop, smiling at his aunt. He went to her without a word, taking her in his arms and hugging her tightly.

"Ben?" she said. "Is that really you?"

"Yep, you ready to go?" he asked.

"Past ready," John said.

Ben turned to his friend and winced at the sight of his stump. "I'm so sorry about your hand," he said.

John shrugged, smiling with a measure of happiness that Ben had rarely seen in the Highwayman.

"One of these days I'll tell you about the fortune-teller and the vision of my future she showed me," he said. "But that's probably a conversation better had over a bottle … or two."

"I look forward to it," Ben said. "Cleve and Zack are at the end of the hall. We're going to move everyone out all at once."

"Frank is here," Imogen said. "He's with the wyrm now."

"I know," Ben said sadly.

"Listen to me," Imogen said, a hard edge in her voice. "He's my family too, and I'm telling you to kill him."

"I will if I have to," Ben whispered. "For now, let's just get these people out of here."

She nodded, putting a hand on his cheek before filing out and down the hallway.

Within a few minutes, the entire prison was emptied out, more than twenty people, afraid and anxious, were crowded at the end of the hallway. Ben hurried to the far end of the building, checking each room to ensure that they had everyone. Even the first family that he'd met was out in the hallway, waiting for a chance to escape.

As he turned back toward the group, the door behind him opened. He spun to face two Dragon Guard, both looked as surprised as he was.

"Intruder!" one shouted.

The other reached for his rifle, pulling it off his back as Ben sent two darts with all possible speed, accelerating them past the sound barrier in the space of a few feet, a loud crack reverberating down the hall an instant before both of their heads exploded.

The one with the rifle pulled the trigger as he fell backward, spraying fire at the ceiling. Ben scrambled backward to avoid the droplets of magical flame, narrowly escaping the splatter. The staircase ignited with a whoosh.

A bell rang somewhere in the distance.

"Go!" he shouted down the hallway, racing toward his companions as fast as he could run.

Cleve and Zack led the way through the door and down the staircase, followed by twenty-some panicked people.

When Ben reached the staircase, he smashed the window with his sword and sent two darts and a drone, moving them quickly toward the two men in the nearest tower, taking the tops of their heads off. He turned the darts sharply, using the drone behind them to target the two men on the catwalk, killing both with nothing more than a quiet thud. He pulled up and targeted the final two soldiers on the next tower over, killing them a moment later before calling his splinters back. The escape route was clear.

A shotgun blast reverberated up the staircase from below. Ben leaned out of the broken window, waiting and watching, holding his breath.

Several moments later, the door burst open and a steady stream of people raced toward the open door in the wall, where Juju, wearing the body of a Dragon Guard, waited, motioning for them to pass through quickly.

Another shot rang out from below and then Cleve and Zack were on the move as well. All of the prisoners were out and running for the wall ahead of them.

A terror-inducing roar shattered the night, stilling everything within earshot for a moment before creatures large and small made for cover. Ben felt the magic in the howl—it was a spell, and it had placed the entire compound on alert.

He looked down at the remaining people racing away from the building and through the gate. A single Dragon Guard emerged from the staircase and fired, a wave of orange death washing toward the door. Cleve and Juju were the last ones at the door. The fire struck them both.

Ben watched as the Dragon Guard's eyes went wide, Juju withdrawing from his body a moment before the fire reached him, hitting him full in the face and engulfing him in an instant. Fire splattered over Cleve's back, igniting his cloak and sending him tumbling through the door in a blaze. Ben couldn't tell if he was alive or dead.

He closed his eyes and made contact with the ex-plus charge, verifying its location and recalculating the structural damage that it would cause to the building—enough, but not too much.

The fortress was beginning to come to life, people shouting and alarm bells ringing.

"Hang on," Ben said, activating the weapon.

A moment passed. He could feel the process taking place.

The world shook.

First, a single sharp jolt. Then, a slow swaying accompanied by crumbling and crashing, falling and wailing.

The staircase was still intact.

His ex-plus charge, placed by Juju in a footlocker in the first-floor barracks, had hollowed out the first few floors of the building and slaughtered most of the garrison in a blink. In the distance, wagons raced out from behind cover at the signal, headed for the fleeing families as Varian's men moved to rescue their neighbors.

Aside from Cleve, the first phase of the plan had gone like clockwork.

The Dragon Guard that had fired the shot raced toward the door, raising his rifle again, but he was blasted backward by a shotgun.

"Young Zack is coming along nicely," Kat said.

"That he is," said Dom. Then he sighed and said, "I hope Cleve is all right."

"Me too," Ellie said.

"Yeah ..." Ben said, turning away from the window. "We ready?"

Everyone nodded.

Chapter 13

Ben set the carnage he'd caused aside and led the way up toward the roof. He had his circle firmly in place and his splinters all attached to his belt, save for a drone floating right over his head.

He burst through the door and came face to face with a stalker soldier. They both stopped for just a fraction of a second, both sharing a brief moment, eye to eye. Ben felt a sensation of being prey. As much as he didn't want to feel that way, the look in the eyes of the possessed man he faced said otherwise.

He transformed the drone overhead into a dart and propelled it into the forehead of the stalker soldier, spraying his brains across the roof, then drew his sword and took in the scene.

The Rogue Priest stood inside his circle, behind his dragon-skull altar, a glimmering field of magic surrounding him. He was enthralled, head tipped back as he barked a guttural chant into the night sky.

Frank stood off to the side, leaning casually against Hoondragon, magic surrounding him as well. Three more stalker soldiers were converging on Ben and his companions and several more were emerging from the staircase on the far side of the roof. Fortunately, they were armed with swords, no fire.

Ellie stood beside Ben to his left. Dom and Kat took the other side, darts orbiting over Dom's head and a light-but-fast rifle in Kat's hands.

Magic buffeted against Ben's circle. He could feel the priest's will tearing at his protections, searching for a way in.

Ben refocused on his circle, keeping his tech inside its confines.

"You're trapped, Ben," Frank said. "That's what this is … it's a trap. Why do you think you managed to get the prisoners out?"

"Superior tactics and a good plan," Ben said.

The three stalker soldiers fanned out behind Frank, each carrying a broadsword.

"Put that sword down and come with us. You're not yourself."

"You're wrong, Brother. I've never been more me than I am right now." He pointed Hoondragon at Ben. "Surrender or I'll put you down."

Ben reached out with his mind and found Ellie ready and alert. He looked over to Dom. He was dour and yet serene, the Dragon's Fang in his hand. Ben extended his magic circle out to a radius of twenty feet, pressing back against the magic buffeting against him.

"Attack!" Frank commanded.

The three stalker soldiers leapt forward, charging into battle.

Ben sent a dart into the first's head, tipping him over backwards, dead and still. Dom directed all three of his darts at the next, hitting him three times in the upper chest, standing him up straight. The soldier smiled. Dom moved in quickly, stabbing him in the face. The man was still smiling as he slumped to the floor.

Ben drew, spun and struck, killing the last of the three advancing soldiers with a lashing strike to the side of the head. He rebounded from that attack and lunged at Frank, with Ellie rounding on the dying stalker soldier at an angle to attack or pressure as Ben needed, their minds in sync, their swords working in unison.

Frank parried Ellie wildly, dancing in a contortion away from Ben's blade as they came to face him together, driving forward into his retreating action. Ben sent a dart at his brother, but it hit a surface not three feet from Frank and shattered into splinters, raining to the ground. A warning flashed in his mind as the augment went to work reinitiating the splinters. It would take several seconds before they were available again.

The battle would be decided with a blade—Hoondragon's domain.

Ben and Ellie engaged—attacking, feinting, parrying and positioning for each other to gain an advantage. They moved in unison, flowing together, body and mind, magic bridging the gap.

Their enemy was singular and masterful, avoiding and blocking, presenting weakness just enough to draw them in and blunt their attacks and then countering with ferocity the likes of which Ben had never seen in his brother before.

Frank was bound in a spell. It didn't take a Wizard to see it. The sword was the puppet master and Frank danced with devotion. He wore an expression of gleeful bloodlust as he pressed the attack.

His magical mastery of the blade easily held Ben and Ellie in check. Even together, they were no match for the skill that Hoondragon gave Frank.

He alternated, back and forth, attacking Ben, then shifting to Ellie. He seemed happy regardless the outcome, his blade moving easily and with certainty. Ben and Ellie fought together and yet all they could manage was a stalemate, both nearly taking wounds on multiple occasions while Frank remained unscathed and unthreatened.

Worse, his shield remained intact even within the confines of Ben's magic circle, a fact that he would have spent some time pondering were he not in a fight for his life. Fortunately, the magical barrier only seemed to defend against projectiles rather than blades.

Even with his attention firmly fixed on his brother, Ben couldn't help but notice the fight taking place all around him. The Rogue Priest continued to chant his spell, all the while protected by his magical shield. Out of the corner of his eye, Ben could almost see a thread of power extending from the priest to Frank, no doubt the source of his shield as well.

Dom sent his darts at the advancing cluster of stalker soldiers, this time taking care to aim for the face, felling three in rapid succession, while Kat fired her rifle, also aiming for headshots. In the first moments of the fight, they managed to kill several of the already dead soldiers, yet more came from the far staircase.

An explosion shook the night, Hound joining the battle, hitting the front gate of the compound with an ex-plus shotgun round, just as they'd planned, drawing what remained of the Dragon Guard garrison into a distraction while the real fight raged on the rooftop.

A moment later the priest shouted the final word of his spell. Ben felt the magic before he saw its effect, grabbing Ellie and leaping backward as a rift opened on the floor, beginning just outside of the priest's circle and running quickly toward Ben. He and Ellie fell backward, scrambling just out of range of the tear in the world, edges red and hot, the rift itself black as night, yet rippling as if it were filled with oily liquid. It ran for several dozen feet, ten feet wide at the midpoint.

He stared in wonder and horror, giving thanks in the back of his mind that Frank was on the other side of the rift. He and Ellie regained their feet, backing away. Frank looked this way and that, searching for a route to rejoin the fight and seeing quickly that he would have to circle the priest. He started moving.

The Rogue Priest seemed to come back to reality, no longer caught up in the spell he'd been casting. He turned to the edge of the roof and saw the resistance attacking his gates.

"Destroy Battle Mountain!" he shouted to the stalker soldiers in the courtyard. "Kill everyone!"

Dom had re-called his darts and was spinning them up around his head for another attack when they went dead, scattering across the rooftop in three different directions, leaving him to face an advancing group of stalker soldiers with only his sword.

The first reached him, attacking rather clumsily. Dom parried and then cut off the possessed man's arm, black blood splattering to the ground along with his sword. The stalker soldier didn't even seem to notice, hitting Dom across the face with his other fist, knocking him off balance while several more converged on him.

Kat shot the nearest in the face, attempting to shoot the next with only a click for her efforts.

"Shit," she said, moving to reload her rifle.

A sword thrust caught Dom across the outside of his shoulder as he struggled to regain his balance and footing, blood running freely down his arm.

Ben and Ellie rushed to his aid as another stalker soldier closed with him, hacking at him with single-minded determination. Dom retreated, blocking frantically. Ben extended his circle to surround them as he approached and sent two hundred splinters, forming them into a shield and spinning them into a blade, propelling it at the head of the stalker soldier as he raised his sword for a lethal strike.

The soldier's head came free and he slumped to the ground. Several more joined the fight, advancing quickly, bloodlust all but shining from their dark eyes.

The priest cursed, a wave of magic hitting Ben's circle and nearly overwhelming it. He had to pause his advance to direct his full attention to maintaining his magical protections.

Dom retreated as Kat raised her rifle again, firing several shots in rapid succession, felling the nearest two soldiers before they could close the distance to Dom.

Then she screamed.

Pain and fear echoing into the night. All eyes turned to see her on the ground, a black, slimy tentacle reaching out of the rift and wrapping around her leg, hot steam coming off the burning wound it had inflicted.

She struggled as it dragged her toward the rift's edge.

"Kat!" Dom shouted.

Ben redirected his shield toward the tentacle but his splinters lost cohesion as they passed out of his circle and scattered to the ground.

Kat turned her rifle on the attacking appendage but it did nothing except leave dark stains on the floor.

They all watched helplessly as she was dragged into the rift, disappearing beneath the darkness and vanishing entirely. The blackness closed over her a moment later.

Laughter interrupted the moment of stunned silence. The priest began clapping. All eyes turned to him as the remaining stalker soldiers advanced on them.

Then Frank rounded the magic circle to rejoin the fight.

Ben set the loss aside in his mind and turned his attention to the battle, calmness and grim purpose settling onto him.

He meant to kill his brother. Nothing less would do.

He lunged into the advancing stalker soldiers, deploying his remaining two hundred splinters into another saw blade but taking care to keep it within the protection of his circle.

While the stalker soldiers were nearly immune to wounds except to the head, they were not particularly bright, and they didn't have the benefit of fear or good sense. As they charged into the fray, Ben sliced them into pieces before they could get close enough to land a blow.

Engrossed in the battle before him, he failed to see Frank slip by and engage Dom and Ellie. Only when he felt Ellie's mind go silent did he realize his error. He spun, frantic and full of fear. His heart stopped when he saw her lying still.

"Ellie!" Dom shouted.

Everything seemed to slow. Ellie was down, her mind silent. Terror and rage welled up from the pit of Ben's stomach, but he was too far away to intervene. In that moment of distraction, Frank drove his blade through Dom's belly.

Ben heard the Dragon Slayer grunt, his mythical blade clattering to the ground, a look of triumphant glee on Frank's face as he held Dom up with his blade for a moment before withdrawing it quickly, allowing him to slump to his knees.

Frank raised Hoondragon overhead, magic radiating from the demonic weapon in anticipation of a kill stroke, but Homer darted in from the shadows and bit Frank on the back of the leg. He yelped, swiping at Ben's dog but missing narrowly as Homer scurried out of the way, tail tucked as he fled back into the shadows.

"Stupid dog!" Frank shouted, turning to search the darkness. "I'm going to kill you once and for all."

Ben charged, lunging at his brother with fear and rage, his unbidden battle cry was all that saved Frank from a stab in the back. He turned, blocking Ben's strike with a wild swipe, stumbling backward a few steps, turning his attention on Ben, backing away, Hoondragon held between them.

"Just you and me now, Brother," he said. "Bet you never thought I would beat you in a sword fight."

Ben stilled his emotion, calmed his mind and focused on the moment. There was no past, no future, only now.

"Ben," Dom said weakly, still on his knees, one hand holding his belly. Ben glanced to the side. Dom tossed him the Dragon's Fang.

It floated through the air, spinning tightly along its long axis. Time seemed to slow again as Ben flipped his own sword to his off hand and caught the only weapon to ever slay a dragon.

It felt good in his hand, like an extension of his body and mind. Magic, fierce and sharp flowed into him. It wasn't like the egg, or the Oculus. Each of those artifacts had its own distinct personality, the egg alive and potent, the Oculus tearing at the veil between seen and unseen. The Fang was different.

It was made to kill and it felt like it knew it, reveled in it even.

The Dragon's Fang was a weapon, singular in purpose and well-suited to its reason for existence. It was light and fast, moving almost as if driven by thought as much as by Ben's hand.

Frank's confidence faltered as Ben turned on him.

Ben knew his brother well enough to see the doubt in his eyes. "What's the matter, Frank? Afraid you've chosen the wrong side?"

Frank snorted derisively, shaking his head. "Not possible, the only side I've ever been on is my own."

He lunged.

Ben parried with his off-hand sword and counterattacked. They fought, a dance with death, one wrong step all that stood between victory and ruin. Ben threw himself into the fight—body, mind and soul, the Fang eager to be used, to strike and to kill. When it hit Hoondragon, Ben could almost see the darkness within the demonically possessed blade squirming, perhaps even writhing in pain, and yet the steel held.

They fought to a stalemate, each a match for the other. Ben realized quickly that he couldn't beat Hoondragon, so he opted for a different tactic. As he neared the priest's magic circle, he directed his attention to his avatar, projecting his angelic servant with all of his will and imagination, all of his need and intention.

The priest's eyes went wide, the distraction interrupting his spell and causing him to flinch with fear. Ben feinted, leading Frank to move in the wrong direction as he drove Dragon's Fang into the shield that protected the priest with all of his strength, using the blade to channel his will and determination to break the magical barrier.

It hit the shield and penetrated with a loud crack, the shimmering field shining brightly at the point of Ben's strike and then receding from that breach, evaporating quickly.

The priest shrieked as Ben leaped up onto the altar and stabbed him in the chest with the Dragon's Fang.

"Look out!" Homer shouted into his mind.

Ben fell forward off the altar and onto the dead priest, rolling to his feet as Frank brought Hoondragon down onto the dragon skull, leaving a deep scar across the top.

A loud crack, followed by a rumbling was all the warning they got before a section of the roof on the far end of the building collapsed. Fire rose in a whoosh from the gaping hole, casting an orange glow into the night. Both Ben and Frank struggled to keep their footing, the building shaking again a moment later and knocking Ben to his knees.

He scrambled to his feet just in time the see Frank reach the door to the staircase.

"You're such an asshole!" Frank said. "You couldn't just let me have this. It always has to be all about you."

Ben sent his shield, spinning like a saw blade at his brother, but Frank disappeared into the stairwell before the weapon could reach him.

And then Ellie groaned.

All thoughts of pursuing Frank vanished in the face of her need. Relief washed over him like a cool breeze.

She was alive.

He raced to her side, cradling her head in his lap, stroking her hair. Fire leapt out of the hole in the roof. He could feel warmth from the floor beneath him, fire raging within the hollowed-out building.

"We need to get out of here," Homer said.

The building shook again.

"Can you move?" he asked Ellie.

She was still a bit stunned, but the fog cleared quickly when she saw her father lying in a puddle of his own blood.

"No!" she cried, scrambling to his side. "Oh God, Daddy, I'm so sorry." Tears streamed down her face as she cradled her father's head in her lap.

"I'm not dead yet," he said, blood sputtering from his mouth.

She choked back a sob.

"What have I done?" she said.

"No matter what happens, I love you and I'm proud of you," he said, closing his eyes.

The building shook again, another section of the roof caving in as the fire began to consume it.

Ben called back his splinters, overriding Dom's darts and calling them to him as well. Then his eyes fell on the dragon skull. He raced to the altar and shoved the skull toward the edge of the roof, toppling it off of the wooden cradle that held it and sliding it with great effort toward the low wall. Once he was close, he went to the edge, peering over and breathing a sigh of relief when he saw the wagon, waiting and ready, the Sage and the Thief looking up at him expectantly.

He raised the Dragon's Fang and brought it down on the crumbling cement wall with all his strength. The blade hit with such force that it shattered a section a foot wide all the way to the floor. He moved a few yards to the side and hit it again, then pushed the section of wall over, letting it topple into the night.

Moments later he shoved the massive dragon bone over the edge, watching it tumble through the air as it fell, hitting the ground with a crash, the lower jaw coming free and clattering away from the rest of the skull.

The Sage waved up to him, then turned his attention to the magical artifact. As he and the Thief moved toward it, a rift opened in the fabric of space-time not ten feet from the larger part of the dragon skull … four men rushed out, taking hold of it and hurrying back into the rift.

The Warlock. Again.

Ben sent a drone and a dart, but he wasn't quick enough. The four men disappeared through the magical portal. A moment later a small leather bag was tossed through and then the rift closed.

"Damn it!" Ben shouted.

A Dragon Guard came around the corner of the building, seeing the Sage and the Thief before they saw him, raising his rifle. Ben redirected his dart and drone, re-forming them into a shield and angling it to deflect the gout that erupted from the dragon-fire rifle. Orange death splashed against the blue surface of the shield and sprayed against the wall surrounding the building.

Ben brought his shield up, spinning it into a weapon and then brought it down, slicing the Dragon Guard's hands off at the wrists, cutting his weapon in half and eliciting a scream of pain and terror.

"Get the jawbone into the wagon and take that man as well," Ben shouted. "We have wounded. Meet us at the staircase."

The Sage waved up to him as the Thief pocketed the small bag that had been tossed through the rift. Ben left them to it and raced back to Dom and Ellie.

"Time to go," he said, taking Dom by the arm and lifting him to his feet, wrapping an arm around his shoulder. He grunted in pain, his head lolled forward and his legs were limp.

"Help me," Ben said to Ellie, still on her knees, blood pooling around her and soaking her pants.

She looked up with anguish, the horror of her father's wound so sharp in her mind that Ben could feel it through their magical link.

"We can save him if we hurry," he said.

She blinked, her eyes shifting from despair to hope when she saw the fierce determination on Ben's face. She picked up her sword and regained her feet, taking Dom's other arm around her shoulders. They carried him to the stairs, recoiling from the smoke and heat that washed over them when they opened the door.

Ben sent a drone to scout the way, finding that the stairs were still intact.

"It's the only way," he said, plunging into the smoke.

His lungs burned, heat threatened to overwhelm him, flame seeped into the stairwell from under the doors at each floor, but they pressed on, choking and coughing with each step until they reached the ground, bursting into the night air with a gasp, stumbling and falling, dropping Dom hard. He fell with a thud.

The Sage and the Thief were there, both moving to help Dom into the back of the open wagon with the jawbone and the handless Dragon Guard, who was wailing in pain. They lifted the Dragon Slayer and nearly tossed him into the wagon bed. The Thief jumped onto the driver's seat and took the reins, while the Sage climbed into the back and began bandaging Dom's wound.

"Go!" Ben croaked, helping Ellie to her feet and moving toward the back gate of the compound, sending his shield at the bar still holding it fast and slicing through it quickly before using the shield to shove it open.

Hound and Olivia were waiting on the other side with a string of horses.

"What happened?" Olivia said, fear rising in her voice at the sight of her father bleeding and unconscious in the back of the wagon.

Ben and Ellie were still coughing from the smoke as they reached their horses and mounted.

"Is he dead?" Olivia asked, panic in her eyes.

All Ben could do was shake his head and motion for them to flee. He held on to his horse as they fled, focusing on staying in the saddle and taking in the fresh night air, each breath burning in his lungs but each less than the last. Hound led the way, guiding them to the rally point in the hills north of town.

Battle Mountain was burning. Shrieks of fear and wails of despair echoed into the night as the inhabitants fled the small army of stalker soldiers carrying out the last command that the Rogue Priest would ever give—Kill everyone.

Ben's plan had succeeded so far, but at a great cost, and there would be more carnage to come. He shoved the guilt and horror of such death and destruction aside and focused on breathing and riding.

"We have to stop," the Sage said.

The Thief reined in the horses, pulling the wagon to a halt. Everyone else slowed and circled on horseback, coming closer.

"I can't heal him on the move," the Sage said, laying one hand on Dom's wound and the other on the belly of the terrified and helpless Dragon Guard.

"Please don't," the soldier said.

The Sage ignored him, focusing on his spell, willing the wound that Dom had sustained to heal and offering the Dragon Guard up to bear that deadly burden. The man shrieked in agony as his belly opened, and then his eyes went wide and he slumped back into the wagon, dead.

Dom was still injured, though less than fatally. The Sage lifted the dead man over the wagon railing and let him fall to the ground.

"I've done all I can for now," he said.

"Will he live?" Ellie asked, emotion thick in her voice.

"Please say yes," Olivia said, streaks of dusty tears on her face.

"I believe he will, but he still needs more healing," the Sage said.

They set out again, heading for the set of magic circles that Ben had etched into the stone on one of the hilltops to the north of town. They reached the valley beside the hilltop in less than an hour, finding Varian and what remained of his resistance helping a large group of refugees, scared and confused people who had fled town before the stalker soldiers could finish them.

"Ben!" Imogen shouted from across the crowd. She came running.

"Are you all right?" she asked, taking him into her embrace. "I was so worried when I heard what you were trying to do."

He nodded, his throat still raw from the smoke.

"I'm helping with some wounded on the other side of the camp," she said. "I'll find you once they're taken care of."

He offered her a smile as she returned to her work.

Varian came up next.

"Is he dead? Did you kill the priest?"

Ben nodded again, trying to speak but failing in a fit of coughing. Varian handed him some water. He drank carefully, clearing his throat several times before he felt capable of speech.

"The Rogue Priest is dead," he said. "But Frank got away, and the Warlock took a large piece of the dragon skull."

"The priest is dead," Varian said. "That's what matters most."

"You and your people need to flee," Ben said. "The dragon is coming."

"I doubted you," Varian said, laying a hand on Ben's shoulder. "I don't anymore. I'll have these people on the move within the hour."

Ben nodded, going to Dom and his daughters. Both of them were sitting in the back of the wagon with their father, watching him while he slept, worry and fear etched into their faces.

"How is he?" Ben asked.

"The Sage says he'll survive," Olivia said.

Ellie looked at Ben, grime and soot on her face, but not enough to mask the anguish. She went to him and wept into his chest while he held her.

He said nothing, letting her cry until her sorrow was spent. She looked up, the tears washing away streaks of grime.

"I almost got my father killed," she said, her eyes welling up anew.

"No, you didn't," Ben said. "None of this is your fault."

"It feels like it is," she said, laying her face onto his chest again. "He wouldn't be here if it weren't for me."

The Sage came bustling up to them.

"The transport is prepared," he said, oblivious to Ellie's tears. "I've cut a magic circle into the back of a covered wagon to hide the jawbone. We'll take Dom and the artifact north, then head west as you've instructed."

Zack appeared out of the darkness, rushing up to Ben. "There you are," he said. "I heard you were back, but I had to see for myself."

Ben smiled at his friend. "It's good to see you, Zack. How's Cleve?"

"He's burned pretty badly. One of Varian's men is tending to him, but it'll be a while before he can ride."

Zack looked around, frowning. "Where's Kat?"

Ben closed his eyes and shook his head.

"Oh, no," Zack said. "She was nice to me."

"Me, too," Ben whispered.

"Ben," Dom said weakly from the back of the wagon.

He climbed up beside the Dragon Slayer. "I'm here," he said, "and I have your sword." He laid the Dragon's Fang next to him.

Dom shook his head. "Keep it. Use it to keep my daughters safe."

"It's your sword," Ben said.

"Not anymore," Dom said. "My days of fighting are over."

Ben nodded solemnly, taking up the magical blade once again. He looked up at Olivia and then over at Zack.

"I need you two to do something for me. I need you to go with the Sage and the Thief. Take Dom and Cleve home. Keep them safe."

Both shook their heads.

"I want to go with you," Zack said.

"Me, too," Olivia said.

"No, not this time," Ben said, raising a hand to forestall any debate. "If you want to help me, then this is what I need you to do. Dom and Cleve both need time to heal. Also, this jawbone needs to be taken someplace safe." He turned to the Sage.

"We'll see it done," he said. "Once we've located a suitable location, we'll begin quietly recruiting. This artifact will provide the basis for an entire guild of wizards."

"Thank you," Ben said, then turned back to Zack and Olivia. "If I fail, humanity will need a way to fight back. I need the two of you to help make that happen."

Zack started to object, but stopped when he saw the resolve in Ben's eyes. He smiled. "Who am I to argue with the Wizard?"

Olivia looked torn.

"Please, Liv," Ellie said. "I need to know that he's being taken care of and I trust you more than anyone."

She sighed, nodding. "I'm going to miss you," she said, hugging her sister. "You better come back."

"I will," Ellie said, sniffing back new tears.

"I think this is for you," the Thief said, handing Ben the small bag that had been tossed through the Warlock's rift.

Ben opened it and dumped the contents onto the tailgate of the wagon. There was a rolled piece of paper, sealed with wax, and a small glass bead. Ben broke the seal and unrolled the letter.

Dear Benjamin,

Once again I am in your debt. You are proving to be my greatest ally in this strange and wonderful world of yours. I can only imagine what we could accomplish if we worked together toward our common goal. I urge you to consider an alliance.

I know you don't trust me, and perhaps with good reason, but I want you to know that I no longer bear you any ill will. You have acted in the best interests of your people and your world. I understand and respect that.

If at any time you would like my assistance, simply crush the glass bead and I will endeavor to contact you.

Respectfully,
The Warlock

Ben laughed bitterly, handing the letter to Ellie.

She read it, her brow furrowing as she began to shake her head. "You've got to be kidding me."

"I wonder why he's reaching out now. He has everything he needs to open a passage to his world."

"Regardless, we're going to have to deal with him sooner or later," Hound said.

"Can't argue with that," Ben said, holding the glass bead up to the light of a nearby lantern. "But I have to wonder if we can make use of him somehow."

"Sounds a little bit like playing with fire."

"Yeah," Ben said, pocketing the bead. "Sometimes fire makes a pretty good weapon."

"Don't get me wrong," Hound said. "I like fire, but it's always wise to have a bucket of water handy if you're going to mess around with it."

Chapter 14

Kayla and Derek arrived on horseback, riding hard.

"Looks like your plan worked," she said, smiling broadly until she saw Dom in the back of the wagon. She dismounted, looking a bit sheepish. "Is he going to be all right?"

"He'll live, but it'll be a while before he's on his feet," Ben said, drawing her aside. "How did things go on your end?"

"I let Lulu and Juju go, with a warning," she said. "And I told them to deliver a message to the coven—the wyrm is going to die, with or without their help. It probably won't do any good, but I had to try."

"I thought you'd kill them both," Hound said.

"I considered it, but that's the kind of thing the family and the coven would take pretty personally. If and when we kill the dragon, I'd like to be able to live my life without constantly looking over my shoulder. Besides, I want them to tell the coven about what we did here. It might persuade a few of them to help us down the line."

"We can certainly use all the help we can get," Ben said.

A distant roar echoed through the fading darkness, the dragon arriving with the dawn. Everyone froze in place, fear evident on every face. The sensation of being prey settled onto Ben once again—a feeling he didn't like one bit.

He fought through the fear and reclaimed his senses as the remaining people taking refuge in the valley began to react, some with panic.

Ben climbed up onto the wagon and sent all four hundred of his splinters to float around his head as electric blue lanterns, drawing everyone's attention.

"Listen to me," he shouted, stilling the murmurs of fear in the crowd. "I need you all to stay here and remain out of sight." He didn't wait for the crowd to obey, instead jumping off the wagon and racing up the hillside toward his magical circles, reinforcing his circle of light as he ran, re-calling his splinters to his belt and the soles of his boots.

Another roar only spurred him to run faster. He reached his circles as the sun began to break over the horizon, casting long shadows from the pillars of smoke rising out of the remains of Battle Mountain.

He sat down. Homer sat on the ground next to him, whining once softly. Ben closed his eyes and projected three concentric circles of light atop the three circles he'd already carved into the stone. He took several moments to focus on his protections, ensuring that they were as firmly in place as he could make them.

And not a moment too soon.

A wave of magic hit his protections, collapsing the outer circle and causing the etching in the stone to melt, deforming the symbols and rendering the circle useless. New fear flooded into his stomach. With an act of will, reason struggling with animal instinct, he accessed his augment and checked the trajectory of the weapon.

"Three minutes until the launch window opens," the augment reported.

Ben deployed a single drone ten feet overhead and used it to zoom in, searching for the wyrm. The beast landed atop the now mostly burned-out hospital and tipped his head back, roaring in fury. Ben watched him leap back into the air and breathe fire across a swath of town, igniting those buildings and homes that had not been set alight during the battle.

The dragon flew gracefully, wheeling gradually to make another pass, deadly flame erupting from his mouth again, and then again, more of the town becoming fully engulfed.

"Launch window is now open."

Ben hesitated, wondering how many people had failed to escape. The dragon turned as if something had caught his attention. Ben refocused his drone and saw a thousand cavalry, led by Legate Rath, coming into view as they rounded a hill to the west of town and then began to assemble, watching their master lay waste to what remained of Battle Mountain.

Ben smiled to himself.

The dragon flew to his soldiers, landing easily before them, the Dragon Guard struggling to maintain control of their horses in the presence of the wyrm's menacing presence.

Rath approached on foot, alone, going to his knees when he reached his master.

"Activate firing sequence," Ben commanded.

"Weapon active," the augment said.

The dragon twitched, his head snapping back and forth, his gaze coming to rest on Ben. Fear flooded his belly. He held his breath. The dragon seemed to stare straight at him.

The wyrm roared, ignoring Rath as he took to wing, each stroke carrying him higher into the sky, his catlike eyes never leaving Ben.

"This had better work," Homer said.

"I know," Ben said.

A streak of fiery orange in the sky caught his attention.

"Close your eyes," he said to Homer. "This is going to be really loud and really bright."

Ben wrapped one arm over his head to cover his ears, a shoulder over one, a hand over the other, pulling Homer's head to his thigh with his free hand. He clenched his eyes shut and watched through the drone.

The dragon noticed the weapon, falling like a meteor, but he was far too late. It streaked through the morning sky, trailing fire behind it as the reentry shielding burned away. The wyrm roared with fury. Magic again washed over Ben's circles but they held.

Then it hit.

The sky lit up with a flash, argent light outshining the sun for a brief moment. A crack like thunder shook the world, primal and entirely beyond the scope of any normal experience. Ben felt a twinge of doubt, the deepest recesses of his mind and soul questioning whether anyone had the right to unleash such forces upon the world.

Fire and violence radiated away from the point of impact, igniting and shattering every building that remained standing, reducing them to smoldering kindling scattered like a handful of toothpicks tossed into the wind.

The shockwave hit next, a thump in his chest, felt more than heard. Ben focused on his drone feed, searching for the wyrm. His augment picked him out, drawing attention to the tumbling form of the dragon, flopping through the air, end over end, his wings rent and charred, his body limp and at the mercy of forces even greater than he. The beast hit hard, spraying dirt and rock, leaving a scar in the desert before bouncing and tumbling through the air for several hundred feet more before hitting again and skidding to a stop.

The dragon lay still, smoke rising from his scales.

A thrill of victory rose up from Ben's belly. He watched with rapt attention, his focus entirely on the wyrm, the backdrop a conflagration of smoke and flame rising in a column into the sky.

He had to remind himself to breathe. Seconds passed, then a minute.

The dragon moved.

Ben's heart sank, dread and hopelessness driving the triumph from his mind. How could any living thing survive such violence? His will threatened to abandon him. He'd done his worst and the enemy was still alive.

The wyrm flopped over, one wing, broken and tattered, rising into the air. The other wing rising a moment later, but it too was torn and useless.

Hound came rushing up, trailing several more people, then a crowd, all eyes on the destruction and then the dragon in the distance.

"Is he dead?" Ellie asked.

Ben stood, shaking his head. "No, but he's hurt. We need horses."

"You're not going down there, are you?" Varian said.

The dragon tried to roar, but it came out more like a wail. He tried to regain his feet, but one leg failed him, turning at an unnatural angle.

"He's wounded," Ben said. "We'll never get a better chance to finish this than right now."

"Damn shame we don't have another one of those things," Hound said.

"Yeah … I won't make that mistake again," Ben said.

"Looks like he's trying to get up," John said, shielding his eyes from the sun.

Ben watched the dragon struggle to regain his feet again, and fail once again. He flopped to the ground, falling still.

Maybe, Ben thought.

Magic flared around the dragon and a circle lit up, fiery red, burning into the desert floor surrounding his broken body.

"He's casting a spell," Ben said, his slowly building hope receding once again.

He frowned to himself, searching his arsenal for a weapon.

"Range check," he said to the augment, thinking of his seeker rounds.

"Within range," the augment said.

He drew his revolver and flipped the cylinder open, dumping the slugs into his hand and quickly replacing them with six seeker rounds, taking aim at about a forty-five degree angle into the sky and firing all six rounds in rapid succession, aiming for the dragon's left eye with every shot.

Moments passed. Ben found himself holding his breath again. The first hit, exploding on impact. The wyrm flinched. The second hit. He roared, this time with more fury than pain. A shockwave seemed to burst forth from him, the remaining four rounds exploding in midair as it washed through them.

The dragon slumped to the ground again.

Ben zoomed in closer, smiling to himself when he saw the bloody socket where his eye had once been.

"Made you bleed," he said.

The dragon reached into his mouth and snapped off a tooth, pressing it into the ground within his circle and then began making a kind of noise that Ben had never heard before. It was so far away that he couldn't make out the details, but it sounded like a language that was more complex than anything a human could ever manage to utter.

Arcane and alien words tumbled from the wyrm's mouth. Power emanated from his body with such intensity that Ben could nearly see it undulating through the air around him. Swirls of darkness began to form, growing into a cloud surrounding him, reaching up into the sky several hundred feet, spinning faster and more violently, taking up dirt and rock like a tornado.

When it seemed that it couldn't possibly spin any faster, a loud clap of thunder echoed through the morning and the spinning vortex of darkness burst away from the spot in all directions, dissipating in a matter of moments.

The dragon was gone.

"What the hell?" Ellie said.

"Yeah," Hound said. "I'm getting the impression that this isn't a fair fight."

Ben snorted to himself, shaking his head. "No, but we made him bleed," he said, smiling humorlessly.

"Oh shit, you're right," Ellie said. "We've got to get down there."

A crowd had gathered on top of the hill, all eyes on the spot where the dragon had fallen.

"Wait, I recognize you," Imogen said, pointing at the Thief. "You stole my amulet."

All eyes turned to her, facing the Thief with fury in her eyes.

Ben looked over at Hound and sighed.

"It's always something," Hound said.

"Is this true?" Ben asked, stepping up to the confrontation.

The Thief looked over at the Sage. He nodded.

"He was acting on my instruction," the Sage said, turning to Ben. "And I was acting on yours. You commanded me to obtain a dragon artifact. I did as you instructed."

"You son of a bitch," Imogen said.

"That's not quite what I had in mind," Ben said. "Give it back."

"Of course," he said, removing the amulet from around his neck and handing it to Imogen.

She frowned. "Just like that? You go to all the trouble of stealing it from me and then you give it back without even blinking."

"Yes," the Sage said. "The jawbone that Benjamin recovered more than makes up for it. And, after the display of raw power that I've just witnessed, my loyalty will forever rest with the Wizard. He is clearly humanity's best champion in this fight." He looked over at the rising mushroom cloud marking the spot where Battle Mountain had once stood.

Imogen glared at him but held her tongue.

"You're not going to like this," Ben said to his aunt, "but I need you and John to go with them."

"What?" Imogen said. "I'm going with you. My baby is still out there." Her voice broke. She swallowed hard and took a deep breath.

"I know, and I'm going to bring him home to you," Ben said. "But you have your father's blood. That makes you potentially very powerful. I need you to learn how to use magic." He turned to the Sage. "And I need you to teach her."

"By your command," the Sage said, bowing slightly but with genuine respect.

Imogen harrumphed, frowning deeply, but nodding agreement after a few moments.

Ben sent his drone higher, scanning the entire remains of Battle Mountain and finding Rath and his cavalry scattered across the desert, broken and charred. Nothing had survived the impact save the wyrm. All that remained was a crater and a column of smoke and ash. He sent the drone higher still, directing his gaze west and finding the infantry, still a day out.

"Varian, gather your people and flee north," he said. "Rath's infantry are still coming. The rest of you, wait here, we might find a scale or two to add to the pile."

"We'll make ready to move upon your return," the Sage said.

Ben headed for the few horses that had been tied off well enough that they hadn't been able to escape in panic. He tried to soothe the first animal that he came to, but she was still pretty frightened. It took a few minutes to get them calm. Then he and Ellie and Hound mounted up and rode toward town.

They reached the spot within twenty minutes. The circle was still intact in spite of the fact that a small crater of dirt and rock had been sucked up by the whirlwind of dark magic. Ben's heart sank when he realized that everything of the wyrm had been taken with the magic. He scanned the area and his sight came to rest on the spot nearly a thousand feet away where the dragon had first hit.

He mounted up again and rode to that spot, smiling broadly. A splotch of ground was stained with blood and there were several scales scattered nearby.

"Looks like we're in luck," he said, dismounting and handing his reins to Hound. He went to the blood stain and sank to his knees, retrieving the Dragon's Codex from his pack and laying it before him with the back cover facing up. A thrill of possibility raced up his spine as he took a small handful of blood-soaked dirt and pressed it into the middle of the cover, holding his breath expectantly.

Nothing happened.

He frowned, waiting, hoping, and praying.

After a moment, lines of red began to seep away from the center recess in the cover and magic pulsed from the Codex, the lines of red seeming to flow into the interior of the book.

Ben waited until the sense of magic faded and then opened the cover. There was writing on the page, red as blood, scrawled into the parchment as if the author had been in a hurry.

He recorded the page with his augment and then began turning page after page, capturing the contents of each in his mind's eye, preserving the knowledge within his augment for later translation and study. At first glance it was a summoning spell. He focused on getting the entire text into his augment's memory banks. For now, that was enough.

"Found a scale," Ellie said, holding up a blackened piece of the wyrm.

"Looks like another one over here," Hound said.

Ben brought his drone to a few hundred feet overhead and scanned the area, finding three more scales for his effort. He directed Hound and Ellie to where they had fallen while he scooped up the blood-soaked dirt and loaded it into his blanket. When he was satisfied that he'd gotten it all, he tied the corners, packed the Codex away and mounted his horse, cradling the priceless soil in his lap.

They returned to find Varian and his people gone and Ben's companions cooking breakfast over an open fire.

"Might as well have a hot meal while we have the chance," John said.

Ben laid the blanket full of bloody soil into the wagon with the jawbone and Dom. Ellie and Hound added five scales to the treasure trove.

"How're you doing, Dad?" Ellie asked.

He tried to smile, but it looked more like a grimace. "I think I'm going to make it," he said, taking her hand and giving it a squeeze. He looked over at Ben. "That was quite a show."

"Honestly, it was a bit more than I expected," Ben said. "I think if I'd had another shot like that, the wyrm would be dead."

"Probably," Dom said. "Next time."

"Yeah, next time I'll have two shots," Ben said, setting his pack on the back of the wagon and fishing out the Codex.

"Keep this safe," he said, handing it to Dom.

He nodded, taking the book. "You keep her safe," he said, looking over to Ellie.

"I will, with all my life, I will."

They shared breakfast, and then made ready to go their separate ways.

"There's a piece of dragon bone in the hilt," Ben said, handing his sword to Imogen, scabbard and all.

"Are you sure?" she asked.

"I only need one sword," he said, resting his hand on the hilt of the Dragon's Fang.

He turned to the Highwayman. "You won't be able to remotely target the seeker rounds," he said, handing John his pistol and holster with all of the bullets he had left. "But they'll still explode on impact."

"Thank you, Ben," John said.

"Keep her safe," Ben said.

John nodded solemnly.

Ben dug the Oculus out of his pouch, still stored within its own leather bag to prevent accidental contact, and handed it to the Sage.

"Use it wisely," he said.

"You are a man of your word," the Sage said. "Thank you."

They said their goodbyes and then set out in different directions. The Sage, the Thief, Dom, Cleve, Zack, Imogen, John, and Olivia went north in two wagons with the dragon artifacts. Ben, Homer, Ellie, Hound, Kayla, and Derek headed east on horseback.

Chapter 15

Ben kept his drone high while they rode, both to scout for threats and to survey the damage he'd caused to Battle Mountain. The destruction was truly awe-inspiring and terrifying at the same time. In all his life he'd never witnessed anything so destructively powerful—he wasn't sure he wanted to see such a thing ever again, never mind cause it.

His thoughts turned to the wyrm. The primal forces that had been unleashed against him had wounded him, yet the fact that he had survived was a testament to his power and resilience. The fact that he had simply disappeared from the battlefield was one more piece of evidence that Ben was in way over his head.

But then he'd known that from the start. And he found, upon reflection, that he was okay with that. His thoughts turned to the refugees from Battle Mountain. They had been through hell, even before he'd utterly destroyed their home. The suffering and fear that had been inflicted on them was simply unacceptable. People should never have to endure such abuse so that a few could have power.

As he turned it over and over in his mind, he found a deep sense of calm settle on him. He was riding toward a fight that could very easily end his life. He faced an adversary so formidable that the only sane course of action was to run away and hide. He was a terribly fragile, ephemeral being on a collision course with a creature of such power and ferocity that a mere glimpse was enough to paralyze with fear.

And none of that mattered.

He would be true to his conscience, come what may.

That left the how, which was far more problematic. He thought of the Codex.

"Translation complete," his augment said.

As much as he wanted to review the hidden spell, he knew better than to try to read in his mind's eye while riding a horse. It wouldn't do to fall off and break his neck. The thought made him smile wryly—fragile indeed.

"You know," Hound said, "the wyrm is probably going to send everything he has at us now."

Ben nodded, smiling more broadly. "Yeah, I think we probably pissed him off pretty good."

"My point is, we should think through how we approach Salt Lake."

"I figure that'll be dictated by whatever the dragon throws at us next," Ben said.

"Back to reacting," Hound said.

"Until we have another shot, yeah," Ben said. "It's all we can do."

They rode east until the only evidence of Battle Mountain's destruction was the dissipating mushroom cloud on the western horizon. Ben figured that the army behind them would be delayed by the sudden absence of leadership and by the crater in their path. He also assumed that they would send an advance party to hunt them—probably composed of the most powerful and dangerous men and creatures at their disposal.

Still, he felt he had some breathing room. As the sun set, orange and angry through the vanishing cloud of dust to the west, they made camp on the bank of a small, winding river that had cut a muddy path through the desert.

"What can we expect in Salt Lake?" Ben asked around a mouthful of his dinner.

Kayla shrugged, shaking her head, her face illuminated by the low but crackling cookfire.

"It'll probably be stirred up like a hornet's nest," she said. "I haven't been there in a few years, but the place is always swarming with Dragon Guard, never mind the constant machinations of the various factions of my family to curry favor with the dragon."

"Is there anyone who will help us?" Ellie asked.

"My mother," Kayla said. "She's hated the wyrm ever since he ate my brother. And she's got some pull, though not nearly enough to keep the rest of the family from handing us over if they catch us."

"I'm sure there are a few others in the smuggling community that will be sympathetic to our cause," Derek said.

"If they aren't paralyzed with fear."

"There is that," he said. "Hopefully, people will see what happened at Battle Mountain as a sign of the dragon's weakness."

"If they even know about it," Ben said. "I suspect the dragon isn't telling."

"Probably not," Kayla said. "But you'd be surprised how quickly information like that can spread, especially if Adara Cartage wants it to—and in Salt Lake my mother runs the whole intelligence operation."

"So how do we make contact with her?" Ellie asked.

Kayla winced. "I'm not sure we should. She's probably being watched, if not by the dragon then by my father's people."

"And you don't trust your father," Hound said.

"Sort of," Kayla said. "It's complicated. If he could protect me without anyone finding out about it I'm sure he would, but he won't risk the rest of the family for me. Mom, on the other hand, has always put her children first, even when it meant going against our father."

"Is there anywhere in town that might contain tech?" Ben asked.

Kayla frowned, falling silent for a few moments. "Hard to say. There are some underground facilities, but they're pretty tightly controlled by the family and the Dragon Guard. If there is any tech, it's either been destroyed or it hasn't been found yet."

"Maybe we just avoid the place altogether," Hound said.

"I'm not sure about that, either," Kayla said. "We need a way into Denver, and it's pretty heavily guarded. I was hoping to make contact with a few of the smugglers I know in Salt Lake and get them to help us."

"She's right," Derek said. "Last time I went to the Mountaintop, it was a fortress. I can only imagine how much worse it'll be now that you rang the wyrm's bell."

"Yeah, now that I think about it, the dragon will probably be dug in under Cheyenne Mountain. It used to be one of the control centers for the NACC military."

"You really think the dragon would hide in a hole?" Hound said.

"I do," Kayla said. "At heart, he's a coward. Plus, he's got time. If he really wanted to, he could just go to sleep for a hundred years and wait us out."

"I don't get the impression that he has the patience for that," Ben said.

"Probably not," Kayla said. "Still, you hit him pretty hard. I doubt he'll be willing to risk taking another shot like that."

"That just leaves his minions," Ellie said. "I like our odds against them better than I do against the wyrm."

Ben nodded. "I think I'm going to read the hidden spell and see what it can do for us. The rest of you should get some rest. We'll be on the move at first light."

He sat cross-legged and closed his eyes as he accessed his augment's translation of the spell. It was a summoning, and a powerful one. The first step was to call on your guardian angel, a profoundly powerful, involved and difficult spell in its own right.

Ben felt a bit deflated when he realized that the process was probably beyond him. Once again, his hope for an easy solution was dashed by reality.

As he read further, he came to understand exactly why Sephiroth considered this to be a last resort.

The spell called forth a being described as a storm god—a creature of lightning and wind with enormous power to shift the weather of the entire planet, causing storms of such magnitude that the world would be ravaged by wind and water for months on end, leaving nothing but a landscape scoured by floods and hurricanes in its aftermath.

These beings originated in an alternate but parallel plane of existence, one that the dragons could naturally see into and even meddle with. Such meddling was the source of enmity between both races, each hating the other with abiding intensity—the storm gods for the dragons' attempts to bind them into servitude, and the dragons because of the fear they had for their would-be slaves.

Then he reached the section describing why the dragons were afraid and a piece of the puzzle snapped into place.

Dragons were vulnerable to lightning.

Electricity was their weakness.

He'd always wondered why they hated tech so much. For the most part, they weren't threatened by it. The NACC had tried plasma cannons, lasers, and a wide variety of explosives against them, with precious little effect.

122   DAVID A. WELLS

Most of their advanced tech was powered with electricity, but Ben wasn't aware of any that used electricity as a weapon in itself. He queried his augment.

"Several experiments have been done in an effort to weaponize electricity, but all found it to be too costly in terms of energy consumption when compared to other weapon systems, and the effects were less predictable, difficult to target and lacked the range of plasma and laser weapons."

"So, no lightning gun, then?"

"No."

"Show me a map of NACC facilities in the Salt Lake area."

An image sprang into his mind's eye. There were a number of buildings that had once housed advanced technology, but were most likely gutted and useless. A few underground bases were connected to the one underground road that ran deep enough beneath the city to pass under the lake itself, but the number of surface access points was limited, and most of those looked like they would be in heavily controlled areas.

"Do any of these facilities have a quantum-communications link?"

"One."

A small area deep under the city lit up on his map.

"Do you know if it's still operational?"

"Unknown."

"Figures," Ben muttered under his breath.

"Hmm?" Ellie said, her voice sleepy.

He opened his eyes and lay down next to her.

"I'll tell you in the morning," he whispered, checking his drone feed before closing his eyes. They were in the middle of nowhere, with nothing anywhere nearby, and Homer would provide ample warning if anyone approached.

And he did.

Ben woke with Homer licking his face.

"There's someone out there."

Ben accessed his feed, scanning the night for a threat. It took a few moments to locate the squad of Dragon Guard marching by moonlight along the road to the south of them. Ben counted five men. He zoomed in and noticed that they looked a bit bedraggled. Their uniforms were dirty and smudged with soot. Only two had rifles. They were headed toward Salt Lake, probably refugees from the destruction that Ben had left in his wake.

Serves them right, he thought, as he soothed Homer and curled back up in his blanket. Dawn came all too quickly and then they were on the move again. While they rode, Ben detailed the contents of the hidden spell to his friends and explained why he suspected that electricity was the dragon's weakness.

As the morning passed into afternoon, they fell silent and focused on covering the distance while remaining out of sight as much as possible in such a barren landscape. Ben's attention turned back to his avatar. The angelic-looking warrior had become vivid in his mind's eye even without the help of the augment, but it had yet to take on a sense of realness. Always in the back of his mind, Ben knew that it was just a figment of his imagination. He suspected that he would have to overcome that belief before his spell would take on a life of its own.

Several days passed, one much the same as the next. They traveled across the sage desert, keeping to low places to avoid contact or detection, cooking over a small fire shielded from view, if they lit a fire at all.

They were camped in a dry riverbed, just finishing their meal, when Lulu appeared just outside camp, her form silvery and translucent. Ben felt her presence before he saw her, coming to his feet and scanning their surroundings, then relaxing somewhat when he saw who it was.

Kayla marched up to her.

"The Matriarch has sent me to find you," Lulu said. "Much has happened since last we spoke."

Kayla snorted. "I'll bet."

"Our family is in grave jeopardy because of you."

"Nonsense!" Kayla snapped. "If anyone is in jeopardy, it's because of the wyrm and you know it."

"Be that as it may, our family is being held responsible for your actions," Lulu said. "The dragon has decreed that we must offer up nine young children for sacrifice unless we can deliver you in their stead."

Kayla went slightly pale. Derek put a hand on her shoulder to steady her.

"The dragon claimed a thousand slaves in sacrifice to heal himself from the wounds that you inflicted at Battle Mountain," Lulu said. "He has since taken refuge in his lair south of the Mountaintop.

"A legion of Dragon Guard have been dispatched to Salt Lake to oversee the family's operations. There is great fear, and even greater anger that you have been so rash and reckless."

"Let me get this straight," Ben said. "You're mad at Kayla because the dragon is acting like a tyrant."

"We must live in the world as it is," Lulu said. "The dragon is the dominant power, and he is quite intolerant of disobedience or disloyalty. Kayla has demonstrated both—our family will be held to account for her transgressions."

"So fight," Ben said.

"To what purpose? The wyrm is too powerful."

"He is if you sit on your ass," Ben said. "There's only a handful of us and we made him bleed. What if there were more? What if the Dragon Guard couldn't go to sleep at night without fear of waking up with their throats cut? What if his priests couldn't step out into the street without someone stabbing them in the back? What if we all fought back?"

"Many more would die," Lulu said.

Ben shook his head sadly. "You and your brother are powerful. You could help us. Your whole coven could help us. And you might as well, because I'm not going to stop."

"None of us are," Ellie said.

Kayla swallowed hard and found her voice. "She's right. We're all going to see this through to the end, one way or another."

"How much damage will you see done to your family? Is your friend worth more to you than your kin?"

"You've got it all wrong," Kayla said. "My conscience is worth more to me than anything, and I can't sit by and watch the dragon enslave the whole world when there's even the slightest chance that I can do something to stop him."

Lulu smiled sadly. "I told the Matriarch that you would respond as you have, but she sent me to make you an offer, and a generous one. Come in and the coven will protect you and all of your friends. We will transport you to a distant continent where you can make a life for yourselves."

"Let me guess, all it will cost is the egg," Ben said.

"That is all the dragon wants," Lulu said. "Give him his prize and he will lose interest in you. Allow our family to deliver his prize and you will redeem our name."

Ben chuckled bitterly. "First off, I doubt the wyrm is going to forget the beating we gave him a few days ago. He can't let that go unanswered and you know it. Second, if I was going to sell the world for a comfortable life, I'd have done it already.

"Your precious master killed my grandfather, kidnapped my nephew, and turned my brother against me—this will only end after I've mounted his head on the wall.

"So you've delivered your message. Now I have a message for your Matriarch—pick a side. Either stand with us and defend humanity or get down on your knees and grovel to your master, knowing that every generation of human beings born from this day forward will suffer for your cowardice and inaction."

"And, Lulu," Kayla added, "remember what I told you when I let you and your brother go."

Lulu smiled with genuine affection. "It's a shame that we never got to know each other better. I suspect we might have been friends."

"Maybe … if, you know, you weren't a psychopathic killer," Kayla said.

"We are what we have been made to be," Lulu said, fading from sight. "You have a high price on your head," her disembodied voice said just before her presence vanished from Ben's senses.

"You all right?" Derek asked Kayla.

She nodded tightly. "In the back of my mind, I knew this was going to happen," she said. "The wyrm is nothing if not vindictive. The truth is, most of my family deserves their fate … but not the children."

"I'm sorry, Kayla," Ben said. "Do you think your mother will be all right? We could help her if she needs it."

"If I know her, she's already out of sight. Living in the shadows is practically a way of life for her."

"She probably has people looking for you," Derek said.

"I have no doubt of that. I'm just not sure if letting her find us will help us or not."

Ben hesitated for a moment.

"There's a facility under Salt Lake that might have a quantum-communications link. Could your mother help us get there?"

She nodded after a few moments of consideration. "It won't be easy, and that's if she decides to help us. After talking to Lulu, I was starting to think about finding a way into Denver without help. Salt Lake is about to become very hostile territory."

"I need to talk to Kaid," Ben said. "He might be able to get us a weapon that can kill the dragon."

Kayla nodded. "I know, I'm just saying, dealing with my mother is tricky, in a number of ways."

"She could probably arrange for passage to Denver as well as anyone," Derek said. "Also, she's got to be worried sick about you."

"I know," Kayla said again, quietly. "I didn't want to get her involved."

Derek faced Kayla squarely, taking her gently by the shoulders. "I know you vowed to never ask for your family's help again, but this is bigger than that."

She nodded, taking a deep breath and letting it out quickly. "First we'll need to make contact, which actually means getting word to her to make contact with us."

"And how do we do that?" Ben asked.

Kayla shrugged. "I know a guy."

"Almost sounds like we have a plan," Hound said.

"I think it still needs some work, but yeah," Ben said.

"We might have another opportunity," Ellie said. "With the Dragon Guard crackdown, there's bound to be some hard feelings. Maybe we could stir up some resistance."

"That would certainly keep them busy," Hound said.

"If the mood on the streets is right, my mother could help with that too, again, if she's willing."

"You don't think she'll help us?" Hound asked.

"She always has an agenda or two, and I'm pretty sure that the outcome she's looking for in this particular situation is my safety, whether I like it or not."

"Well, I would hope so," Ben said. "We should get some rest."

"Maybe post a guard, given our recent guest," Hound said. "And by that I mean I'm volunteering for first watch."

Chapter 16

The night passed without incident and the day that followed was another in a long string of similar days. Hound woke Ben for guard the following night. He sat up, nodding groggily that he was awake. The sky was clear and the air was crisp. In the desert the stars were particularly brilliant.

He heard a buzzing, dismissing it as the wind. But it persisted, growing louder by the moment.

And then it was overhead.

"Run," Ben said to Homer, as he bolted to his feet.

"Wake up!" he shouted, "We're under attack!"

His warning was too late.

A swarm of black, dragonfly-like insects descended out of the night sky onto the camp, their tails containing inch-long retractable stingers. The attack was as swift as it was vicious. Ben tried to fight back, deploying his shield, but without any effect. The swarm spiraled down in a vortex surrounding the camp and then collapsed in on them all at once. Only Homer managed to escape.

The insects attacked as one, stinging everyone with terrifying frequency, dozens of stings landing within the space of seconds—numbing, paralyzing venom spreading from each angry red welt.

As quickly as the swarm had arrived, it ascended into the darkness and vanished, buzzing and all.

Ben lay in an awkward position, one leg folded back underneath him, his arms outstretched, his face to the sky. He couldn't move. Pain radiated throughout his body, only the numbness of the venom masked the agony he knew he should be feeling.

Homer licked his face. "You look terrible," he said.

"I feel worse," Ben said, refocusing his mind on regaining control over his stubbornly unresponsive limbs.

"The venom has paralyzed you," the augment said. "I am metabolizing it as quickly as possible, but it will still be several minutes before you regain control."

Ben resigned himself to waiting, all the while wondering about his attacker.

He tried to access his drone, but found that his tech was unavailable—it had gone offline when he was stung.

"How's everyone else?"

"They're all breathing, but I don't think they're conscious," Homer said.

"At least there's that."

"Someone's coming," Homer said.

Helplessness washed over Ben. He was paralyzed, lying flat on his back out in the open … and whoever had just attacked their camp was coming.

He focused on moving his arms, then his legs, then on activating his tech. Nothing worked.

"Take the egg and run," Ben said to Homer.

"Are you sure?"

The clop, clop of an approaching horse floated out of the night.

"Yeah, hurry."

Homer took hold of the bag strap and pulled it up over Ben's head, then worked it off his body, got a better grip on it and ran off into the night, leaving Ben lying helpless, listening with rapt focus to each footfall.

It was one horse approaching slowly.

Ben felt a twitch in his hand, followed by a burning twinge of pain that radiated up his arm.

The man stopped at the edge of camp and opened the shutter on his lantern, shining its light slowly across each of Ben's friends. Then the light lingered on him.

"It's your lucky day, young wizard," the man said. "She told me not to kill you."

Ben thought there was something familiar about the voice.

The light moved on, finally landing on Kayla.

"There you are, my dear cousin."

Juju.

He dismounted. It sounded like he might have tied off his horse. Ben started to regain command over his eyes, stabbing pain accompanying the return of his control. He looked to the side, his head still frozen, facing straight up.

A Dragon Guard, possessed by Juju, was carefully maneuvering Kayla onto the back of his horse, tying her onto the saddle, belly down.

Ben twitched again, his arm coming back to life, one painful spasm at a time.

He tried to access his tech, but it still didn't respond.

Juju finished tying Kayla down, checked his work and nodded to himself. "I hope you know that this isn't personal."

He turned away after waiting a moment, and his gaze landed on Ben.

"Such a troublemaker," Juju said, coming to a stop at Ben's feet, looking down at him and shaking his head. "Someone thinks highly of you. I've been ordered not to kill you. Dumbest thing I ever heard." He stopped and looked Ben over again. "I am supposed to get the egg though."

He took Ben by one arm and rolled him over so he could pull his pack free.

Ben spasmed, his whole body jolting with pain. He focused on his coin, seeing it in his mind's eye, trying to distract himself from the intensity of the venom's enervation. Slowly, he regained his senses.

"Where is it?" Juju said, throwing Ben's empty pack to the ground.

Ben's hand found the hilt of his sword, some control over his arms was returning.

Juju grabbed him roughly and rolled him over onto his back again. Ben drew, turned the blade and stabbed Juju through the belly, gasping in pain from the sudden movement, his gasp drowned out by Juju's shriek.

He flopped backward, holding his belly as he scrambled to his feet and stumbled to his horse, nearly collapsing when he reached it, leaning heavily on his saddle while he took a few deep breaths.

He mounted up, grunting and then whimpering as he leaned over Kayla's body and coaxed his horse into a walk out of camp. Ben tried to get to his feet, but the rest of his body still wasn't working. Every attempt at movement brought a stab of pain, and when he could make his arms or legs move, they often didn't do what he wanted them to.

Minutes wore on, burning agony seeming to be the only path through the venom's paralysis. Five minutes stretched into ten before Ben was able to sit up, and even then it took another two minutes for him to get to his feet.

The rest of his friends were in far worse shape, angry red welts dotting their unconscious bodies.

Ben tried his tech again.

Nothing. His augment worked just fine, but he couldn't access his splinters.

Homer appeared out of the night, dropping the bag with the egg in it at Ben's feet.

"Nice," Ben thought to his dog.

It was well over an hour before they were in any shape to travel, and almost as long before Ben's splinters came back online. He wasn't sure, but it seemed like the venom had been disrupting his link. He didn't like the implications.

He sent up a pair of drones as soon as they came back online, searching for Kayla, scouring first the immediate area for a trail, then following the horse tracks and the occasional drop of blood as he retraced Juju's escape from camp.

He'd traveled for an hour, coming to a knoll along a deliberate path. Atop the rocky prominence, Ben found the Dragon Guard, dead from the wound that he'd inflicted. His horse had run off and there was no sign of Kayla. No tracks. No marks. Nothing, save a few large overturned rocks in the immediate area.

"Looks like we have another reason to contact Kayla's mother," Ben said.

"What did you see?" Derek asked.

"She was taken—like, poof, someone disappeared her. We'll follow her trail to where it ends, but there's not much to go on."

"Lulu mentioned the Matriarch," Derek said. "This is her, I'm sure of it."

"What will they do to Kayla?" Hound asked.

"Since they didn't get the egg," Derek said, "they'll try to leverage her against you. So ... they'll try to turn her, then they'll interrogate her, then they'll offer her in trade for the egg, which they won't make good on, by the way, and then they'll probably reach out to Penelope and try to enlist her against you in exchange for her daughter's safe return. This is bad."

"Then we should try to get to her first," Ben said.

"That'll never happen," Derek said. "The coven will already have a back channel established with her."

"Regardless, we have to reach out to her," Ben said. "Now more than ever."

"All right," Derek said after a long silence. "It would be better if we had something to show her."

"Let's go see if my drone missed anything."

They gathered up camp and made for the knoll. Ben used his splinter lanterns to gently light the way, keeping the illumination low to the ground. They found exactly what he expected—nothing. He located the horse Juju had ridden and they spent a few minutes rounding it up and calming it down before inspecting the saddle.

Ben found part of a strap that had been recently cut and untied it for closer inspection.

"So," Hound said, "Juju takes Kayla up to this rock, cuts her loose and she disappears, then he dies and his horse runs away. Do I have that right?"

"Pretty much," Ben said, pocketing the piece of strap. "We still have a few hours before dawn. We should probably try to get some rest."

They crested a gentle rise several days later and got their first look at the salt flats, gleaming white in the late morning sun. They had been traveling relentlessly, only slowing to ensure that they weren't spotted.

After going over his objectives, Ben had shifted his attention to his avatar, working doggedly to convince himself that the being was real. He felt that he'd made some modest gains. While his creation would act according to Ben's will, even continuing to perform assigned tasks without much direction, he was still an automaton without personality, self-awareness, or volition.

Some vital part of the spell had eluded him.

Concerns about Kayla intruded on his work with maddening regularity, drawing his attention into a pointless loop of *what ifs* and *could haves*. He pulled himself away from such thoughts when he noticed them, refocusing on the task at hand—manifesting an avatar.

The uniform vastness of the salt flats was enough to focus his complete attention back to the present moment. It was a force of nature stretching out before him, impassable and deadly. He had intended to cross in the night, but just seeing it changed his mind.

That moment of complete presence produced an unforeseen result. The avatar became more real. The effect was momentary, but it was powerful.

"So, north or south?" Hound asked.

"I like south," Derek said.

"Works for me," Ben said, his mind still mulling over what had just happened with his avatar.

South brought them to the road that ran through the salt flats and into the city. Ben scouted ahead and found a checkpoint along the road with half a dozen Dragon Guard lazing around under a canopy. The road was otherwise empty.

"They keep a checkpoint at the edge of the salt flats with a cistern full of water for travelers," Derek said.

"How thoughtful," Hound muttered.

"We could borrow their uniforms," Ellie said.

"That's risky," Derek said. "It doesn't look like it right now, but this road is actually pretty well traveled."

"Going around without being spotted will take half a day as flat as this place is," Hound said.

"Yeah, but going through lets them know we're here," Ben said. "I'd like to avoid that for as long as possible."

"Fair enough," Hound said.

They turned west, traveling parallel to the road for several hours before turning south again. At one point they had to stop and take cover while a caravan passed. Ben watched it go by with his drone—a dozen wagons, thirty-five Dragon Guard … and Frank.

Ben considered killing his brother right there and then. Had it not been for the Dragon Guard he might have, but given their other, more pressing concerns, he simply watched them go by.

"Looks like Frank made it out of Battle Mountain," he said.

"Now why doesn't that surprise me?" Hound said.

"What are we going to do about him?" Ellie asked.

"Avoid him for now," Ben said. "We have two objectives here: Get Kayla and get a message to Kaid with as little conflict as we can manage."

"Sooner or later…" Hound said.

"I know," Ben said.

"You don't have to do it," Hound said. "I'll pull the trigger if you want me to."

"No," Ben said, shaking his head sadly, "he's my brother. If it has to be done, I'll do it."

Hound shrugged. "Offer stands."

"Thank you," Ben said. "Hopefully, once the dragon is dead, Frank will become less of a problem."

"Wishful thinking isn't like you," Homer said.

Ben gave his dog a sidelong look.

"I think they've passed," Derek said.

They waited a few more minutes and then resumed their journey. Camp that night was cold and dark. Ben didn't want to risk any chance of being spotted. Morning came, bright and clear. He was starting to become anxious. The dragon wouldn't let Battle Mountain go without some type of retaliation. As yet, the wyrm had done nothing, or at least, nothing that Ben was aware of, and that's what made him nervous.

The dragon could wield magic with greater power than any human could match, and he understood what magic could do better, too. Ben couldn't help but wonder what was coming.

He looked down, a glint of light catching his eye as the sun broke over the horizon. He chuckled to himself when he picked a gold coin out of the dirt.

"You know, there are kings who would kill for that kind of power," Derek said.

"Yeah, if only I could figure out how to use it more directly," Ben said.

"Hold on to that thought," Derek said. "We're liable to need a fair amount of money to bribe our way through town, and a coin like that goes a long way."

They set out, heading south and east until they reached the edge of the salt flats.

"NACC technology detected," the augment said. "Orbital weapon command codes downloaded." An image of the globe and the weapon's orbit flashed into Ben's mind's eye.

"Looks like Kaid's been busy," he said. "He just put another weapon up."

"Good," Hound said. "Bigger guns are better."

They skirted the south end of the salt flats, heading north and east until they reached a small range of hills, rugged and sparsely forested.

"We'll be able to get a pretty good view of town from atop these hills," Derek said.

"I see trees," Hound said.

"Yeah, some green is nice for a change," Ellie said.

"Let's find a place to make camp in that grove," Ben said, pointing to a particularly dense cluster of trees clinging to the side of one of the more gentle slopes.

As they made their way through the forest and up into the mountains, the horses began to become skittish.

"I smell a cat," Homer said.

Ben consulted his drone. He had to switch to thermals before he could pick out the bobcat that was hunting them. It was circling to approach from downwind. Ben deployed a dart, guiding it into its target with relative ease and killing the stalker cat with a single well-placed strike.

A roar shattered the evening calm. Ben just got a glimpse of a mule launching into the air, its powerful batlike wings carrying it above the treetops with a few strokes.

Then the two hundred splinters outside of his circle went dead.

"Mule," he said, dismounting from his increasingly anxious horse and dropping his pack. His friends followed suit, letting their horses flee into the wild.

The mule rose into the sky, its black wings soaking in the last of the evening sun as it wheeled and dove toward them.

Hound fired. A sabot round tore through the mule's wing. It roared again and burst into flames.

Ben momentarily regretted his decision to give John his revolver as he drew the Dragon's Fang and readied for the attack.

The mule seemed to ignore him, focusing instead on Hound who was only too happy to engage, loading another sabot and taking aim, waiting patiently until the flaming dragon-man was twenty feet away before firing.

This round hit flesh, tearing a hole through the shoulder of the mule and disrupting its attack enough for Hound to roll out of the way.

The mule hit hard, one wing giving out from the injury and causing it to land awkwardly and tumble into the dry underbrush, igniting the hillside with a whoosh.

Ben extended his circle to twenty feet and deployed his remaining two hundred splinters as a shield, his mind and Ellie's flowing together effortlessly as they advanced on the flaming priest.

The mule roared, leaping into the air with a single thrust of its wings and coming down on Ben.

Ben waited, holding position until the last possible moment, slashing at the mule's ankle before diving to avoid the flaming monster as it landed hard, stumbling and falling forward, howling in rage and pain, its severed foot hitting the ground nearby.

Ellie darted in and slashed a gaping tear into the mule's one good wing. It spun on her, projecting a jet of fire, hitting her in the chest hard enough to blast her off her feet.

Panic flooded into the back of Ben's mind. He could still sense her, still feel her, but she was down. The fire still coming off the mule was hot enough to make breathing difficult. Ben ignored it, coming to his feet quickly, calculating the range to his target relative to the dimensions of his circle and then directing his shield like a blade at the back of the mule's neck. It hit hard, spinning and cutting through the tough scaled skin, but not deeply enough.

The mule pitched forward, yelping in pain, its escape from Ben's shield-blade only serving to bring it closer to Ellie, igniting her tunic. She rolled away from the beast to gain distance and to put out the fire.

Hound fired again, shot spraying across the mule's flank, drawing its ire and attention, but slowing its advance toward Ellie for the moment that Ben needed. He raced toward the back of the beast, leaping in the air and thrusting with all his strength, stabbing the mule in the spine and burying the Dragon's Fang nearly to the hilt as he followed the beast down and rolled to the side to avoid landing on its burning carcass.

The magical fire subsided quickly, but the dry brush that had been ignited was burning freely, flames spreading in all directions. Derek reached Ellie first, helping her to her feet and peeling off her still smoldering tunic in one motion. She looked down and breathed a sigh of relief at the unscathed ballistic shirt she wore underneath.

Ben retrieved his sword from the dead mule and re-called his splinters, save the one drone that he used to quickly locate their horses, re-calling it and deactivating it as well the moment he had their direction.

"You all right?" he asked, going to Ellie.

She nodded. "That was close. I'm glad the mule didn't aim for my face."

He gently touched her singed eyebrows before taking her in his arms.

"Hate to break up a tender moment, but the fire is growing," Hound said.

Ben nodded, locating his pack and retrieving it before the fire reached it. They moved away from the rising plume of smoke, searching for their skittish horses and finding them several hundred yards away, grazing on green shoots near a tiny seasonal stream.

"So much for camping in the forest tonight," Hound said, looking back at the growing blaze.

"All things considered, I'm glad we ran into that mule head-on rather that at night while most of us were asleep," Ben said.

"There is that," Hound said.

"There are a few burned-out towns south of Salt Lake," Derek said. "If we push we might find cover there by midnight."

"Not sure we have a choice," Ben said. "This fire is bound to draw some attention, and I can't help wondering if that mule was out here waiting for us."

"If it was, there are probably more where it came from," Ellie said.

"My thoughts exactly. Unfortunately, that means I can't risk using my tech to scout ahead."

"So, we're traveling blind," Hound said. "Better stay on our toes."

Chapter 17

They went south, heading away from the fire, looking for a way around the range of hills that they had initially intended to use for cover. Night fell, the ground dimly lit by the moon, so they slowed, finally dismounting and walking their horses to safeguard against a fall. Everyone was tired, their weariness growing into exhaustion as the night wore on.

"There," Derek said, pointing into the darkness. "We're close."

"Good thing, too," Hound said.

A few more minutes brought them to the edge of what had once been a small town, probably no more than a thousand people at its height. Now it was a field of broken and burned-out homes and buildings, only a few still intact enough to provide cover.

"That one looks promising," Hound said.

"Agreed," Ben said, looking at the remnants of what had once been a two-story brick building. When they got closer they had to adjust course to skirt a section of fence still standing guard against a child's ball rolling into the street. Ben nearly tripped over the remains of a rusted-out swing set, stumbling but catching himself before falling.

They led their horses to the building and then along one wall until they came to a double door that had long ago been torn open, one door lying in the weeds, the other hanging by one hinge at an awkward angle.

"Hear anything?" Ben asked Homer.

"Just the crickets."

Ben handed Derek the reins of his horse and approached carefully, looking into the large open room for several seconds before stepping inside. The roof was mostly intact, but there was enough damage to let the rain in—the result being a small forest of trees growing up through a gymnasium floor.

"Looks clear," Ben whispered.

They led their horses inside and tied them off to the trees before finding a dry corner to lay out their bedrolls. Ben was asleep within minutes, waking with a start when Hound shook his shoulder some time later.

Ben blinked several times, the confusion of sleep still clouding his mind, the light of dawn quickly burning away the haze in his mind.

A voice in the distance brought him to full alertness.

"Sweep the whole place."

"Dragon Guard," Hound whispered. "Looks like a platoon."

Ben nodded, setting aside his desire to go back to sleep and waking Ellie before sitting up to pull on his boots.

Derek hurried up from the door. "Three men are headed this way," he said. "How do you want to play this?"

"Quietly," Ben said, knowing even as he said the word that they would probably be discovered. "Looks like that corridor is intact." He pointed to one of the hallways leading deeper into the building.

"What about the horses?" Ellie asked.

"No choice," Ben said. "Get what you can and leave them."

They packed hastily, grabbing their saddlebags along with their packs before hurrying into the passage.

As they made their way down the dark and decaying hallway, once bustling with schoolchildren, they heard the Dragon Guard call out.

"We found horses."

They quickened their pace, muffled shouts urging them on. The corridor teed, the left passage leading to a broken set of glass doors opening to the school grounds, the right leading deeper inside the building. They turned right. Ben glanced behind him, wincing at the footprints they had left in the thick dust. Even without a stalker, the Dragon Guard would find their trail easy to follow.

The hall led past numerous classrooms, all dilapidated with disuse, before it turned. Ben approached the corner cautiously, peeking around and seeing another set of broken-out glass doors at the end of the hallway. He pulled his head back quickly when two Dragon Guard stepped inside.

There was a brief commotion, the sound of feet running, and other feet chasing, then a crashing noise.

"Let me go," a young voice said.

"Well, well, what do we have here?"

"Looks like a scavenger," another voice said.

Ben reinforced his circle and deployed a drone, taking care to keep it close, moving it just around the corner to see what was happening.

The Dragon Guard had a boy by the arm. He was dingy, his clothes were torn and unkempt, but he was feisty, struggling to free himself from the grip of the man holding him.

"A scavenger in no-man's-land, huh?" one of the Dragon Guard said. "I guess the stalkers haven't gotten the job done out here."

The boy kicked the man in the knee. He yelped and then hit the child across the face, knocking him to the ground. Ben clenched his teeth.

"Who else is here?" the Dragon Guard asked, putting his boot on the boy's chest.

"Go to hell," the boy said.

"Maybe we cut off your hand," the other one said. "I bet you'll talk then." He drew his sword.

"I'm not telling you shit," the boy said, still struggling against the man with the boot on his chest.

Both Dragon Guard laughed.

"Kid's got spirit, I'll give him that."

"Yeah, I think maybe it's time we stomped that out of him," the other said.

"I need you to bark once," Ben said to Homer.

His dog dutifully barked. Both Dragon Guard looked down the hall.

"Is that your dog, kid?"

"I bet he'll talk if we put a sword to his dog," the other said.

"Get up," the first one said, dragging him roughly to his feet.

"Let go of me!"

They all came toward Ben.

He turned and looked back at his friends, holding up two fingers.

Hound and Ellie nodded, drawing weapons. Ben stepped back and drew the Dragon's Fang.

"Where did the dog go?"

"I can't see him."

"Let me go!"

"Stop struggling or I'll take your hand, kid."

"Go to hell."

Homer barked again, standing well out of the way behind them all.

The men approached the corner, Ben monitoring their position with the drone that he had pressed up against the ceiling. He looked back. Ellie was right behind him, her sword out and ready, her mind melding with his as the moment of battle approached.

They came into range and Ben moved, Ellie coming around beside him a moment later.

Ben thrust through the first man's breastplate, stabbing him straight through the chest. Ellie stabbed the second man in the throat, her blade only penetrating an inch before he flinched backward, but that was enough. He fell to his knees, blood soaking the front of his armor, a look of panic and surprise on his face.

"You gonna cut my hand off now, asshole?" the boy said, kicking him in the chest.

The Dragon Guard toppled over backward, gurgling and sputtering.

"There're more coming," Homer said. "I think they found our trail."

"Time to go," Ben said.

The boy looked at Ben and his friends, scrutinizing them for a moment before nodding to himself. "Follow me," he said, turning and racing down the hallway without waiting for an answer.

Ben and Ellie shared a look, both shrugging, before they chased after the boy. He led them into a classroom with a mostly caved-in ceiling and crawled under some debris along a path that looked well worn.

They followed, somewhat more slowly for their size, Hound having the most difficulty squeezing through the rubble. The boy was waiting in what looked like a coat closet.

"Come on," he said, sitting on the edge of a hole in the floor before dropping through.

"Might as well," Hound said, following the boy into the floor below.

Ben lowered Homer down to Hound and then he and Ellie followed. They were in the school's basement.

"This way," the boy said, racing off.

He led them through a number of dark corridors, the only light coming from a few places where the foundation above had cracked, allowing in a sliver of sunlight here and there. They reached a room filled with old equipment. The boy led them behind one of the large boilers to a hole broken in the wall and crawled into a tunnel no more than three feet high.

Ben and his companions followed, struggling to keep up. They emerged fifty feet later in another basement. The boy was waiting impatiently.

"Keep up or I'll leave you behind," he said, racing up the stairs as soon as Ben emerged from the hole.

"Wait," Ben said. "Slow down."

The boy ignored him. Ben went to the top of the stairs, holding position until his friends had emerged from the tunnel.

In spite of his warning, the boy was waiting for them at the only exit from the pile of rubble that was all that remained of the building.

"Stay low and quiet," he said, once everyone had caught up.

Ben followed closely, obeying the instructions. The boy led them into the remnants of a narrow alley running between a block of two-story buildings that had once been a row of businesses. At the end of the block, he crawled through a cut section of chain-link fence and darted across the street, stopping to wait on the other side.

Ben peeked out, looking both ways before following. He could hear soldiers searching for them a block over. The boy led them to a ladder, up to the second floor of a mostly intact building, then down another ladder and into a small room with another hole in the floor. This one had a ladder leaning up against its edge.

Ben carried Homer down into the darkness. He turned to see two men pointing weapons at him, one a bow, fully drawn, the other a long spear.

"Who are you? And why are you here?" the first man said.

"Bradley, we told you not to show anyone where we are," said the other.

"They saved me," the boy said with a shrug.

Ben showed them his open hands. "We don't want any trouble," he said, "just trying to avoid the Dragon Guard."

"Isn't everybody?" the man with the spear said.

"If they're smart," Ben said.

"We're going to need that sword," the man with the bow said. "Can't have armed strangers in our home."

Hound landed next to Ben, leveling Bertha at the man with the bow.

"I'm afraid I can't give you my sword," Ben said, raising a hand to Rufus. "Like I said, we're not looking for trouble, just a place to hide until the soldiers move on."

The two men looked a bit worried, staring down the barrel of Hound's shotgun.

"More refugees?" a voice from the shadows asked.

"They're too well armed to be refugees," the man with the spear said.

"And they saved me from the Dragon Guard," the boy said, again.

"Lower your weapons," the man in the shadows said, stepping into the dim light.

The two men obeyed, reluctantly.

"They killed two of the wyrm's men," Bradley said.

"Is that so?" the leader said. "I suppose that makes us allies … or at the least it means we have the same enemy. I'm James."

"My name's Ben."

"You fleeing the crackdown in Salt Lake like everyone else?"

"Crackdown?"

"I guess not," James said. "In that case, what brings you through here?"

"We're on our way into the city," Ben said.

"That's a new one, at least lately," James said.

Ellie slid down the ladder behind Ben, coming up alongside him.

Then Derek dropped into the room as well.

"Tell you what," James said. "Why don't you and your friends come inside? We can share stories while you wait out the patrol. Just know, these people look to me for protection, so weapons or not, you won't survive if you attack us."

"Fair enough," Ben said.

"Right back at ya," Hound said, slinging Bertha.

James eyed Hound up and down and then nodded. "Follow me."

He led them to another recently dug tunnel that ended in a corrugated steel wall. He knocked three times and the wall moved aside, revealing what had once been an underground train station. Thirty-some people occupied the space, many of them families. Once inside, Ben saw that the corrugated wall was a section of an old shipping container bolted to the side of a sturdy wagon filled with rocks. Three men pushed the wagon back into place, sealing the passage once again.

James motioned for them to follow. All eyes were on them. Ben noted the desperation and fear. Most of these people had seen tragedy, and all too recently.

James led them into a smaller room with a long table and motioned for them to sit.

"I'd offer you food if we had enough to go around," he said. "But we don't, so I'm afraid water is all the hospitality I can spare at the moment."

"A place to hide is all we need," Ben said.

"So, Bradley, who wasn't supposed to be out on his own, by the way," James said, giving the boy a reproving look, "says you killed two Dragon Guard. Not an easy thing to do and live to tell about it."

"We caught them by surprise," Ben said.

"Doesn't hurt that you're well armed," James said, glancing over at Hound. "So, I guess I'll go first. A week ago, there were a dozen of us living here, just trying to stay out from under the dragon's thumb, so to speak. Then something happened and the wyrm's men started to go full jackboot on the people up in Salt Lake. Since then, there's been a steady stream of people coming through town. We've taken in a few here and there. Mostly, we let them pass by.

"You, on the other hand, come into town, kill two of the wyrm's men, and you say you're headed *into* Salt Lake. That makes you different, maybe dangerous."

"We're looking for a friend," Ben said. "She's been taken by the Adara Coven and we think she's being held in Salt Lake."

James whistled, shaking his head.

"She must be a real good friend," he said. "I don't know many who would willingly risk drawing the attention of the coven, let alone go up against them."

"Loyalty matters," Ben said, shrugging.

"Definitely different," James said. "Maybe a bit crazy. From what I hear the city is swarming with Dragon Guard, checkpoints everywhere, random searches ... even summary executions. Something's really got the dragon pissed off. Rumor has it, a battle out west didn't go his way. Not sure how that works. It's been years since anyone even tried to stand up to the wyrm."

"It's about time someone did," Bradley said, standing near the door.

"Child, go find your mother—tell her what you've been up to before I do," James said.

The boy frowned at James like he was trying to will bad things to happen to him, then turned and stomped off.

"That kid's going to get himself killed one of these days," James said. "He is right though. If someone did kick the wyrm in the teeth, then good on them."

"I can't argue with that," Ben said. "Any advice about getting into town?"

James cocked his head for a moment, then nodded. "Yeah, don't. The roads are crawling with patrols and there are more stalkers roaming around than ever. We can hardly go out anymore. Makes gathering food that much more difficult."

"Does this tunnel go through?" Derek asked.

"I don't know for sure," James said. "We have it pretty well barricaded up, and nobody I know is fool enough to go exploring."

Ben consulted his augment, searching for a map of Salt Lake and its transportation system. Sure enough, they were on a main underground train line that ran all the way into and through town, provided the tunnel was still intact.

"Can you get us through your barricade?" Ben asked.

"Yeah, it'll take some work, but it can be done," James said. "Fair warning, once you're through, we won't be opening back up for you."

"Wouldn't expect you to," Ben said. "You give us passage into that tunnel and we'll be on our way right now."

"You know there are things in the dark—unnatural things."

"We know."

"All right, don't say I didn't warn you. Come on. The barricade is this way."

He led them to an old train car that had been rolled on its side and wedged into the passage. The space between the top of the car and the ceiling was piled full of chunks of cement and rocks.

James called for a few men to help him and they went to work clearing a section of the tightly stacked debris from atop a section of the car. The last piece was another section of corrugated steel that had been laid over a number of broken out windows.

"Up the ladder, into the car, down to the far end and out the front window," James said. "Or, you could just wait until the soldiers leave and go back to the surface. I know that would be my choice." He leaned in and whispered, "We hear things on the other side of this car sometimes. I wouldn't want to meet those things in a dark, tight place."

"We're probably safer underground," Ben said, extending his hand in thanks.

"If you say so," James said, shaking Ben's hand.

Once he and all of his companions were in the tunnel, Ben led the way, lighting the far side with his splinter lanterns, but taking care to ensure that they remained within the confines of his circle.

The tunnel was dark and still with only minimal debris littering the ground. Ben listened for a moment—silence. He smiled to himself.

"Underground ... again," Homer said.

"It's safer, for now anyway," Ben said.

They set out. The tunnel ran straight and level, the only noise the sound of their boots and the occasional drip of water seeping through the cement ceiling. They walked until Ben's augment told him it was dark outside and then made camp.

"I really thought we'd have met something unpleasant by now," Hound said.

"Me, too," Derek said. "Not that I'm disappointed."

"Still, we should be on our guard tonight," Ben said.

After a cold meal, he sat down to meditate. Instead of his coin, he returned to visualizing his avatar. The image had become second nature to him, bright and vivid in his mind, yet still not real. After half an hour, he turned his attention to the Codex, rereading the spell in question, looking for clues to help him succeed but finding nothing that he didn't already know.

He went to bed wondering if he was wasting his time. His guard shift was still and silent, so he passed the time using his augment to see his avatar, willing the angelic figure to practice fighting and flying—and then something odd happened.

He was quite suddenly the one doing the fighting and the flying—his point of view had shifted into that of the avatar. His eyes snapped open, dispelling the effect. He sat very still, turning the experience over in his mind. It was as if he had become the imaginary being that he was attempting to create, but that wasn't how the spell was supposed to work. He went back and read it again, just to be sure.

"Be careful with that," Homer said. "Leaving your body can be dangerous."

"Wait ... what do you know about this?"

"I just told you, leaving your body can be dangerous."

"How do you know that?"

Homer rolled onto his side and licked his lips several times before going back to sleep.

"One of these days you're going to have to explain how you know these things."

Homer started to snore.

Chapter 18

The following morning they continued on, Ben consulting his augment to see if the tunnel they were traveling through connected with the military system underneath Salt Lake. It didn't. The public transportation system and the NACC underground were entirely separate. They would have to surface to find an entrance into the facility he wanted to investigate.

They came to another station, but the surface access passage had collapsed, leaving them no choice but to continue through the blackness. Ben consulted his map. They still had at least another day of travel before they would be under the city.

"I'm worried about Kayla," Derek said.

"Me, too," Ellie said.

Ben felt a surge of guilt. She had saved him before she even knew who he was, and now she was paying a high price for helping him. He couldn't help but feel responsible for her plight. He tried to let the feeling go, turning his mind to those things he could control, which were precious few at the moment.

"Do you think her mother will hear us out?" he asked Derek.

"She'll listen, but only once she has us where she wants us."

"I don't much like the sound of that," Hound said.

"No," Derek said, "and you shouldn't. Penelope is dangerous, especially where her children are concerned."

"Dangerousness requires capability and intent," Ben said, remembering the words his grandfather had spoken to him during his many lessons. "We just need her to see things our way."

"You don't get to be the head of Adara Intelligence by letting other people tell you what to think," Derek said. "All we can do is give her the truth and hope."

"Any chance we could find out where they're holding Kayla?" Ellie asked.

"Slim to none," Derek said. "The coven is easily as slippery as Adara Intel. They have facilities and safe houses all over town. Kayla could be anywhere, if they even brought her here."

"Hadn't considered that," Ben said. "Who might know where she is?"

"Hard to say," Derek said. "Once we get into town, I'll see what I can find out. Until then we're in the dark … literally."

The day passed slowly, the still, silent blackness all-encompassing. They passed another station, this one intact. Ben started to wonder if the things that James warned about were just stalkers that had found their way into the tunnels. By the time they stopped for the night, he had convinced himself that that was the case.

He sat down to meditate, taking a moment to scratch a circle around himself on the floor and will it to protect him, overlaying the circle of light within his mind atop it before he closed his eyes and started descending into deeper states of consciousness. He imagined his avatar, focusing on the present moment, using his augment to conjure the being as clearly as if it were standing before him.

Once he had it firmly in mind, he tried to transfer his consciousness into his creation. Nothing happened. After several more failed attempts he thought back to the moment that he'd felt at one with his avatar. It had happened while he was practicing with his sword.

He went to work recreating the sequence, seeing his avatar making every move. And then he was there, working through the steps of his sword form, except he wasn't himself, he was a figment of his imagination made manifest by his will. He stopped, turning to look at his friends. They were oblivious to him, but Homer was looking straight at him.

"Can you see me?"

"Of course," Homer said. "If you're going to start doing this, you should have someone watch over your body while you're out."

"Won't the circle protect me?"

"Yeah, unless someone comes up and clubs you in the head."

Just then a silvery, translucent figure appeared, looked right at Ben's avatar and then screamed and floated straight through the wall.

"What the hell was that?" Ben said.

"A ghost," Homer said. "There are a lot of them down here."

"You can see ghosts?"

"Sure, I'm a dog."

Confusion and a moment of disbelief overtook Ben and he slammed back into his body, coming out of his trance with a jolt.

"Have you always been able to see ghosts?"

"Yeah."

"Why could I see it?"

"You were out of your body," Homer said. "You were where they live."

Ben's mind raced. Homer was rarely this forthcoming about such matters. He wanted to ask him a hundred questions, but the one that bubbled to the surface was the most important.

"Is my grandfather a ghost? Could I talk to him?"

"No, Ben. I'm sorry, he's moved on."

Ben felt sudden hope crash into disappointment. He nodded sadly. He would have given a lot to see his grandfather just one more time.

"You okay?" Ellie asked, when he lay down next to her.

"Yeah," he said, nodding in the darkness. He didn't bother to explain, instead taking her in his arms and closing his eyes.

The following day brought them to the edge of town, or at least that's what his augment's map told him. Stations started to become more frequent, though most were caved in or otherwise impassible. When they reached one with an intact set of stairs leading up to the street, they stopped to consider their options.

"We're under the south side of town," Ben said. "How close are your contacts?"

"I know a guy pretty close to here," Derek said. "Provided he hasn't closed up shop."

"Can we trust him?" Hound asked.

"No, definitely not," Derek said. "But he'll be able to get word to Penelope."

"What's he do?" Ellie asked.

"He runs a blacksmith shop, but he's really a fence and a smuggler."

"So he's a criminal," Hound said.

"Yeah, but then, so are we," Derek said.

"I guess that's a matter of perspective," Ben said. "Once we get to the surface, keep your heads down and your weapons hidden."

Ben led the way up the stairs, stopping in his tracks when he turned the corner at the landing and saw that the stairwell had been covered over. He slowed, approaching more cautiously. A low cement wall surrounded three sides of the staircase with the side where people would access the stairs walled up with brick and mortar. Heavy steel plates covered the top, sealing the entire passage off from the surface.

"What do you think is on the other side of this?" Ben asked.

"Hard to say," Derek said. "Could be the street or it could open inside a building. The wyrm's people made a push to cover over all of the access points to the underground a few years ago."

"So this is as good a place as any," Hound said.

"Yeah, at least this one isn't caved in," Ellie said.

Ben brought his light closer to examine the brick wall directly before him, nodding to himself after a moment's inspection.

He backed off a few feet, reasserting his circle before deploying his splinters into a shield and spinning it into a blade. A few minutes of work had stripped away the mortar between several rows of bricks, allowing him to easily pry the wall apart and create an opening large enough for them to crawl through.

He peered into a room, dark and musty, before wriggling his way inside and standing up. It appeared to be a storage room of some sort. Crates and boxes lined the walls and shelves. His friends followed him in as he went to the only door and listened.

A pair of footfalls approached, getting louder with each step, then passed and receded, leaving them in silence again.

"This complicates things," Ben whispered. "Let's see if we can get out of here without drawing too much attention."

He opened the door just a crack, peeking out into a hallway constructed from salvaged building materials. He considered scouting ahead with a drone, but decided against it. There were too many priests in town.

He stuck his head out and looked both ways, neither offering him an exit. He decided to go right, following the two people who had just passed by. The corridor teed at the end. Again, neither passage offered any hint of a way out of the building. The right passage ended in a doorway, while the left ended in another tee and included several closed doors on either side of the hall.

While he vacillated between left and right, the sound of footsteps prevented him from moving. He ducked back around the corner and deployed a drone, taking care to ensure that it remained within the confines of his circle while sending it to rest against the ceiling, offering him a clear view of the hallway.

Two men came from around the tee at the end of the left passage—one a Dragon Guard dominus, the other a Legate.

Ben looked back to his friends, motioning for silence and weapons at the same time. He pressed his back up against the wall and waited, hand on his sword. The two men went to one of the doors and entered. Ben breathed a sigh of relief.

"I think we're inside a Dragon Guard barracks," he whispered.

"Shit," Ellie said.

"Now I know exactly where we are," Derek said. "There are probably a hundred men in this facility, and that was before the Mountaintop sent reinforcements."

"All the more reason to find a quiet way out," Ben said. "Stay close."

He slipped around the corner, keeping his drone deployed directly above his head, as he crept down the hall and stopped next to the door that the two men had entered, pausing to listen.

"Terrorists have hit two more checkpoints, here and here."

"Any survivors?"

"Two from the first, none from the second."

"Did we get any of the terrorists?"

"No, the two men that survived said that fire bombs came from the rooftops, but they didn't see who threw them."

"Double the checkpoint guards, but spread them out on either side of the street. Also, send a request to the priests for more stalkers. I want one at each checkpoint to hunt anyone who attacks us."

"Understood, Legate. Our sweep of the abandoned neighborhoods to the south turned up a few resistance cells, but there was no sign of the Wizard."

"So we found his horses, but he vanished without a trace. Lord Ick is not going to be happy with that answer."

"Regrettably, I don't have better news. I've sent people to lean on our informants all around town. If he shows up, we'll hear of it."

"If he's smart, this is the last place he'll be."

There was a pause.

"Do you think it's true?" the dominus asked, lowering his voice.

"What?"

"Do you think the Wizard made the dragon bleed?"

"No!" the Legate said. "And you would be wise to keep such questions to yourself."

"Understood," the dominus said. "I have reports from patrols outside the markers."

"And?"

"Refugees are fleeing town and a few small groups have been found living beyond our protection."

"I trust they've been dealt with."

"All dead, as ordered."

Ben closed his eyes, hoping that James and his people weren't among them.

"Good, let's go over troop deployments for the coming week. I have word from the Mountaintop that we can expect another company in a few days."

"That should help us maintain order in this quarter."

Ben looked over to his friends and motioned with his head, slipping past the door with as much stealth as he could muster. He reached the end of the hall and sent his drone to look in both directions. Both passages ended in closed wooden doors.

He went right, coming to the door and listening quietly for a moment before slipping his drone just underneath it. On the other side was a barracks lined with bunks, all empty at the moment. One wall was lined with windows. A door in the center of the wall opened into a courtyard. Ben brought his drone up to eye level on the far side of the door. The courtyard was bustling with activity—Dragon Guard coming and going, saddling horses, assembling for patrol or guard duty. Dozens of soldiers. Ben thought it odd that none of the men were armed with dragon-fire rifles. Instead, they all carried crossbows and swords.

"Hey! Who are you?" a voice demanded from behind them.

They all turned as one to see a single Dragon Guard looking at them from the other end of the hall.

"Guards!" he shouted, raising his crossbow and firing. The bolt hit Rufus squarely in the chest, shattering against his breastplate. The Dragon Guard dropped his crossbow and drew his sword but made no move to advance.

Ben opened the door, hurrying into the barracks and scanning for an exit other than the door to the courtyard. He found none.

"So much for quiet," he said, drawing the Dragon's Fang and deploying all of his remaining splinters as two darts and a shield.

His friends followed him into the room, Hound slamming the door behind them and tipping a bunk against it before unslinging Bertha.

"Hit them hard and fast, stay together and head for the gate," Ben said, kicking the double door open and emerging into the courtyard filled with soldiers. For a moment time seemed to stop. All eyes turned to them, disbelief and surprise registering on the rune-scarred faces of the soldiers all going about their business.

The next moment, shouts of alarm rose up all around them. Ben ran for the gate, snapping the point of his blade into the face of the first man to challenge him. The soldier fell back screaming, blood leaking out through his fingers as he tried to staunch the bleeding.

Bertha blasted another charging soldier onto his back where he fell still, crimson pooling around his head and shoulders.

A squad that was formed up near the gate raced into the fray, swords drawn. Ben and Ellie met them head-on, minds syncing, swords moving in effortless cooperation, each fighting to complement the other.

Ben shoved one man aside with his shield as he parried the attack of another, turning his attention to yet a third when he felt Ellie strike at the man he'd just defended against, stabbing him in the side of the neck before moving to defend against another attacker. Hound fired again. Derek circled behind a soldier, quickly slicing his throat as he moved to stay close to Ben.

Ben killed a charging man with a dart while simultaneously engaging another in a brief bout of swordplay that culminated with the man losing his head.

He felt the bloodlust contained within the Fang coursing through him. The blade was made for the fight, reveled in the kill. He'd fought with the sword before, but never like this. The fury and rage and glory was intoxicating. He felt powerful in a way he'd never felt before. He wanted to kill. He wanted to strike his enemies down.

And it was so easy.

The blade moved with fluid grace, dancing and darting, cutting and piercing with ease. The Dragon Guard armor, usually so formidable, was no defense against the Fang. It cut cleanly with each thrust and strike. And with each, a man fell, his life draining from him into the dirt.

The bone-white blade turned red, leaving a trail of death in its wake. They neared the gate and Ben turned back to face the soldiers, a crossbow bolt glancing off his shield, another striking him in the stomach, but without penetrating his ballistic shirt. He staggered back from the force of the blow, much like getting punched in the stomach.

The lust was almost overpowering. He started to advance back into the compound even as more soldiers poured out of the barracks and into the courtyard.

"Come on!" Hound shouted, grabbing him by the shoulder and turning him toward the open gate. "Time to go."

Ben knew in his mind that he needed to flee, but in the depths of his being he wanted to fight, he wanted to kill. The power of it was nearly all-consuming. The righteous fury flooding into him from the Fang wanted more.

Ellie stepped in front of him, grabbing him by the shirt and looking him in the eye.

"We have to run!"

The spell broke. Good sense overcame his desire for carnage. He nodded, fleeing through the gate into the streets of Salt Lake City.

Another crossbow bolt hit him in the back, causing him to stumble forward. He redeployed all of his splinters into a large shield, placing it behind his team to protect against the bolts now coming at them.

"Ex-plus!" he shouted, pointing toward an alley leading between two buildings and off the main street.

"Right," Hound said, adjusting the rounds in his shotgun. After the others had all entered the alley, he fired, ducking into the narrow passage as soon as the round was away. The explosion was deafening—a crack that sounded like the world was breaking, followed by crumbling and wailing.

Ben struggled to keep the power of the sword under his control. He found himself hoping that more soldiers were waiting for them wherever the alley spit them out. His conscience chided him when he felt a pang of disappointment at the empty loading area behind a set of businesses.

He glanced back into the alley and let out a deep breath, cleaning his blade and sheathing it before calling his splinters back to his boots and belt.

"This way," Derek said.

A plume of smoke and ash rose up behind them as the barracks began to burn. They ran through several more alleys until they came to a main road, everyone stowing their weapons before they emerged onto the street, walking briskly.

There were a number of people about, mostly just citizens, all watching the cloud of smoke rising into the evening sky. Ben ignored them, instead remaining hypervigilant, expecting an attack from every direction—part of him hoping for another chance to lose himself in the fight, the better part of him feeling a sense of relief that it never came.

Derek led them down the street, keeping his head down and eyes averted when a patrol of Dragon Guard rode past without giving them a second look.

After a few minutes, they came to a corner and saw a checkpoint. Derek backed away and turned around, leading them into another alley running between two rows of businesses.

A mule roared from the sky. They all pressed up against the wall, hoping that they hadn't been spotted. A shadow passed overhead, followed by another roar receding into the distance.

"We need to get off the street," Hound said.

"Agreed," Ben said, just as an elderly man poked his head out of the backdoor of one of the businesses. Ben hesitated for a moment, until the sound of another mule overhead made his mind up for him. He pulled the door open and grabbed the man by the arm, guiding him into the back room of the small building.

"Stay quiet," he said.

The frightened man nodded tightly while Ben's friends filed in behind him and closed the door, Hound taking a moment to drop the bar into place and check the bolt.

"We aren't going to hurt you," Ben said. "Is your shop open?"

"Yes," the man stammered.

Ben looked to Derek. He nodded, going into the storefront, pulling the shades and locking the door.

"What's happening?" the man asked.

"Are you alone here?" Ben asked, ignoring the man's question.

"Yes, my wife usually helps out, but she had to run some errands."

"Good, we're going to stay here until dark," Ben said. "Where does that door lead?"

"To the cellar."

"Perfect, let's go."

They went downstairs, finding a low ceiling and musty air, but it was still and silent.

"Have a seat," Ben said, motioning to a nearby crate.

"Please, take anything you want, just don't hurt me. I don't know how my wife will get along without me."

"We aren't going to hurt you," Ben said. "We just need a place to hide for a while."

"So that's what all the commotion is out there," the shopkeeper said. "Are you with the resistance?"

"Something like that," Hound said.

"They'll be putting stalkers out just as soon as they get the streets cleared."

Muffled shouting from somewhere outside reached them. Everyone froze, waiting and listening. The noise subsided.

Ben fished out two gold coins from his pocket and put them on the crate next to the shopkeeper.

"Payment for the trouble we've caused."

The man looked at the coins, then at Ben.

"That's a small fortune," the man said, pocketing the coins quickly. "I don't know what you're up to, and I don't want to know, but I believe in value for value. You're welcome to stay until dark."

"And after we leave?" Hound asked.

"I never saw you. Hell, if I did report you, they'd just take these coins and probably beat me up for my trouble, or worse."

"Will your wife be coming back?" Ellie asked.

"No, she's headed home after she finishes her errands."

"Good. Will the Dragon Guard want to search your place?" she asked.

"They might bang on the door, but they usually move along if you don't answer."

"Usually?" Hound asked.

"Lately, in the past week, they've gotten particularly heavy-handed. Rumors are flying around town about the return of the Wizard and a battle out west. Whatever happened, it stirred the wyrm's men up like angry hornets. There's no telling what they might do now."

Ben felt the weight of his burden. The consequences of his actions were being borne by others. He sat down. "Tell me about the resistance."

"Not much to tell," the old man said. "Before, it was mostly just youngsters with too much time on their hands. Now, they've gotten more serious—fire bombings, ambushes, and a few outright assassinations. Needless to say, the Dragon Guard have overreacted with public executions, house-to-house searches, and curfews. They mostly leave me alone, but more than two young men walking down the street together is an invitation to be harassed."

"What's the mood of the people?" Ben asked.

"Bad. Nobody likes the wyrm or his thugs, but we've learned to live with their abuses. Now, it feels like the whole town is headed for a blow-up. Lots of people have left. The wife and I talked about it, but we wouldn't know where to go."

"Are any of these resistance groups well organized? Any more effective than the others?"

"Sure, the street gangs that used to deal in black-market goods. They've always been organized and disciplined enough to keep from getting caught. I suspect they're unhappy because the crackdown has put a dent in their business. Shame too, some of us depend on them to get stuff you can't find in the shops."

"What about Adara Cartage?" Derek asked.

"They're the only ones bending over backwards to behave. Since the legion arrived from the Mountaintop, Adara has been quiet as a mouse. Come to think of it, that might be why the black-market guys don't have much to sell."

"Probably," Derek said.

Muffled pounding silenced everyone.

"Open up!" a voice shouted. "Inspection."

Ben held a finger over his lips. The room fell deathly silent.

More pounding.

"Open up, or we'll break the door down."

"What do we do?" Ellie asked.

"We go out the back and let him answer the door," Ben said, turning to the shopkeeper. "Value for value."

He patted the pocket where he'd put the coins. "Never saw you, just closed up shop when I heard the commotion."

"Good man," Ben said, heading up the stairs.

He checked his circle, opened the door a crack and sent a drone through, breathing a sigh of relief when he saw that the alley was empty. They slipped out into the growing shadow of evening and headed away from the shop with haste, stopping only when they came to the road at the end of the block.

"How far to your friend's place?" Ben asked.

"Half a mile," Derek said.

The sound of horses silenced them, everyone pressing up against the wall, staying in the shadows. A patrol rode by. They waited for several moments before daring to breathe again.

"We aren't going to last long out in the open," Hound said.

"No, we're not," Ben said, eyeing the row of houses across the street. All of them looked lived in.

"There they are!" a voice shouted from the opposite end of the alley.

"So much for quiet," Hound said.

"Run," Ben said, racing across the street at an angle to obscure the soldiers' view. He went between two houses and smashed through a wooden gate into a backyard, heading for the low fence separating one yard from the other, scooping Homer up and dropping him on the far side before vaulting over himself, his friends all scrambling to keep up. They raced across the yard, out onto the far street and into the yard of another house across the way.

Shouting behind them spurred them to run faster, through one yard and into the next. Once they'd cut through three blocks of houses, Ben turned along the street, slowing to a trot to catch his breath. As they approached the corner, they saw a checkpoint at the intersection a block over. Six soldiers were roughing up four men, accusing them of being on the street when they shouldn't have been.

Just as Ben slowed and ducked behind a hedge, a group of a dozen men, all wearing makeshift masks, came out of a nearby yard and rushed the Dragon Guard, taking them by surprise and attacking them with clubs. The scene descended into a melee.

Ben considered avoiding the fight, but the Dragon Guard had killed three of the men quickly and were forming up to fight the remaining rebels, sword and armor against stick and mask. Before he could make up his mind, the rebels broke and ran, scattering in every direction. One man came in their direction, pursued closely by two Dragon Guard.

Ben looked over at Ellie, then Hound. Both nodded, following Ben to the end of the hedge, but staying low. A moment after the rebel ran past, Ben stepped out, sword in hand, catching the lead soldier by surprise and stabbing him through the heart. Ellie was right behind him, hacking at the second man's knee and sending him sprawling where Hound finished him with a stroke of his axe.

The rebel stopped and turned around.

"Who are you?" he said, surprise and relief in his voice. "Never mind, come on."

He didn't wait for them, instead racing off into the growing darkness. Ben and his companions followed. The man led them to the cellar door of a nearby house and down into the basement. Once inside, he pushed a large crate aside, revealing a recently dug tunnel.

They followed him into the tunnel, noting the slight downward slope of the passage. It opened into another basement. The man led them up the stairs, out into an alley and into what had once been an apartment building, but now had long been the home of squatters.

The rebel knocked on a door, waited, then knocked again. A few moments later the door opened and a young woman ushered them inside.

"Jacob, you know better than this," she said, closing the door and locking it with several bolts before pushing a blanket up against the crack beneath it to block the light from a single oil lamp.

"They saved my life," he said. "I couldn't just leave them out on the street. Besides, they can handle themselves. Vincent will want to meet them."

"Are you crazy?" she said. "He's made it abundantly clear that he doesn't want any outsiders anywhere near his business. I swear, Jacob, if the Dragon Guard don't kill you, Vincent will."

"Relax, Renee, we're safe. Nobody followed us."

She sighed, shaking her head at the young man before turning her attention to Ben and his friends, sizing them up quickly.

"You're definitely not the usual," she said. "Might as well make yourselves comfortable. The streets won't be safe until dawn—maybe not even then."

Jacob motioned to a worn sofa and a few old chairs.

"Thanks for your help," he said. "I'm not sure if I would have gotten away on my own."

"Why did you attack that checkpoint?" Ellie asked.

"They caught some of our friends," Jacob said. "We were just trying to distract the Dragon Guard long enough for everyone to escape."

"Looks like three of your people fell," Hound said.

Jacob looked down, nodding.

"Yeah, Vincent won't be happy about that, but we couldn't let the wyrm's men interrogate our people. Our whole network of safe houses and tunnels might be compromised."

"You'd think my brother was some kind of cartage spy or something," Renee said, pulling up a wooden chair. "I'd offer you something to drink, if we had anything to offer."

"Thank you," Ben said. "A safe place to wait out the Dragon Guard is all we need."

"So what do they want with you?" she asked.

"We just killed two of them," Ben said.

"So Jacob got you into this, too," she said, giving her brother a reproving look.

"No, I think it's fair to say that the dragon got us all into this."

"See, he understands," Jacob said. "Somebody's got to stand up to them. Might as well be me."

Ben shared a glance with Ellie. Her eyes mirrored his thoughts. This young man was going to get himself killed, and yet, Ben had to admire the courage, or foolishness, required to actually do something. Dom had asked where the people who wanted freedom were. Why nobody had risen up against the wyrm.

Maybe the time had come.

"You mentioned someone named Vincent," Ben said.

"Yeah, he's the boss," Jacob said.

Renee gave her brother a stern look. "You talk too much," she said.

"What? Maybe they'll help us." He turned to Ben again. "Vincent runs things in this part of town."

"What sort of things?" Hound asked.

"Used to be just contraband—tech and other old-world stuff they don't make anymore. Now, mostly he's running weapons and coordinating raids on the jackboots. That's what he calls 'em, anyway. Not sure why, but it sounds good."

Ben smiled to himself at the memories of lessons his grandfather had taught him about the history of governments before Dragonfall. Dragon or not, government and tyranny seemed to go hand in hand.

"How much of the population is with you?" Ben asked.

"Not enough," Jacob said. "Don't get me wrong, people hate the dragon, but they're afraid of him too."

"With good reason," Hound said.

"Somebody's got to do something."

"I'm not arguing," Hound said. "But it pays to be smart about it. You and your friends rushed a checkpoint with nothing but sticks, and it cost you."

"Yeah, that really wasn't the plan."

"Maybe we should let our guests rest before you say too much," Renee said.

Jacob frowned, but nodded nonetheless.

"Thank you again for taking us in," Ben said.

Renee nodded, motioning for her brother to follow her into the next room.

"Do you know Vincent?" Ben asked Derek.

"Yeah, we've done business a few times. He used to be a low-level black-market guy. When I knew him, he was all about the coin."

"Sounds like his priorities have shifted," Hound said.

"A lot's changed since the last time I was here," Derek said.

Ben nodded. "We stick to the plan and reach out to your contact as soon as possible. No sense getting entangled with the local uprising unless we can use it to further our objectives."

"You sound like my father," Ellie said.

Ben sighed. "I guess I'm learning a thing or two about being at war."

Chapter 19

Ben briefly considered meditating, but decided he needed the rest more so he settled down into the corner of the couch and closed his eyes. It felt like only a few moments passed before voices woke him.

"Something's happening out on the street," Renee said, peeking through a gap in the boards covering the window.

"I smell smoke," Homer said.

Ben came fully awake, going to the window and looking for himself. A squad of Dragon Guard on horseback were milling about on the nearest corner. He moved to another window and saw another squad a block down.

"They know we're here," he said.

A mule came into view, wings out and sword in hand.

"Yeah, they definitely know we're here."

"What the hell is that?" Renee asked.

Ben took another look, a thrill of fear flooding into his belly when he saw it. A creature of pure black, standing on four powerful legs, came to heel next to the mule. The beast had an oversized head with a dozen red eyes and a long snout lined with needle-sharp fangs. A row of spines ran down its back. A pair of tentacles sprouted from its shoulders, each ending in an odd-looking appendage.

"Trouble," Ben said. "Time to go. Do you two have a back way out of here?"

"Yeah, if they haven't found it yet," Jacob said.

"Grab anything you can't afford to leave behind and any weapons you have," Ben said.

He looked back out the window and the beast locked eyes with him, tipped its head back and unleashed a cackling howl that made his skin crawl.

And then it was coming—running straight for the wall that Ben was standing behind. He backed off, checking his circle and deploying a small shield as he drew the Dragon's Fang.

"Go!" he shouted.

The beast closed the distance all too quickly, slapping its tentacles against the outer wall. A section of wall turned bright red and then vanished, leaving a rough, charred edge around the opening.

The beast barked, drowning out the cacophony of footfalls coming their direction.

Ben backed away, deflecting one tentacle with his shield as it snapped out at him, narrowly dodging the other and lashing out at it with his sword. The blade cut it cleanly, the appendage flopping to the floor. The beast barked again, fury and pain, then the floor turned red and vanished beneath Ben's feet. He fell into the basement, landing on his feet but stumbling and falling a moment later.

"Ben!" Ellie shouted.

"Run!" he called back, scrambling to regain his feet while deflecting the tentacle as the beast flailed about blindly. Abruptly, the creature backed away, responding to a command from the mule. A moment later, orange fire washed into the room above. Ben leapt backward, protecting himself with his shield as he searched for a way out.

He heard Bertha and followed the sound.

"Run north," Homer said in his mind.

Ben obeyed, racing through the darkness, stumbling over debris but managing to remain on his feet. He glanced over his shoulder and saw the mule emerging from the small basement room he'd fallen into.

"You will not escape, Wizard!"

Ben kept running, coming to the end of the hall and scrambling up the staircase, crashing into the wall at the landing and turning to see Ellie at the top of the stairs, engaged with a Dragon Guard. They fought toe to toe, Ellie's blade deflected by the soldier's breastplate, his blade missing as she ducked.

Their minds synced the moment he saw her, she rolled away at his unspoken command. He sent a cluster of two hundred splinters at the man, peeling his face off in a violent attack. The Dragon Guard fell back screaming.

Ben reached the top of the stairs, calling his splinters back to him, taking care to keep them within the confines of his circle and forming them into a pair of darts.

"The mule's right behind me."

"This way!" Derek shouted.

Bertha erupted again from just outside the door.

They emerged onto the street, drawing the attention of two squads of Dragon Guard, each on opposite ends of the block.

Ben didn't wait, following Derek across the street. Derek leapt onto the porch of a house and crashed into the front door with his shoulder, smashing it open as he fell. Ben hoisted him to his feet on his way past.

They raced through the house, ignoring the voices from upstairs on their way to the back door. Orange light flared behind them. Ben kept going, heading for the broken gate in the back fence.

"Look out!" Derek shouted, pointing to the sky.

All eyes turned to the mule, descending toward Ben.

"I got your number, bitch," Hound said, firing a sabot round and hitting the mule squarely in the chest. The dragon's minion looked surprised, black blood flowing freely and splattering to the ground as it fell hard, going to its knees, one hand trying to keep its blood from oozing into the dirt.

The creature looked up at Ben, hatred and vengeance in its eyes as it raised its other hand and both wings. Ben brought his shield around just as a jet of fire burst forth, gushing into the flickering blue disc for several seconds before fading out. Ben swept in, taking the mule's hand with one stroke and then its head with another.

Dragon Guard and the beast stopped short, all eyes on Ben and the fallen mule. The beast shivered, its black flesh undulating for a moment before it slapped its remaining appendage against the back of the nearest Dragon Guard. The man flared red, a silent scream frozen on his face for a moment before he vanished. The beast turned and snapped its jaws on the thigh of the next man, taking his leg off with a single bite, swallowing the chunk of flesh whole while slapping another man with its tentacle.

The Dragon Guard all turned to defend against the sudden threat in their midst.

"Come on!" Derek shouted.

Ben turned and bolted into the alley, racing through the night, following where Derek led him, looking back over his shoulder frequently, always expecting to see some new horror, but only seeing the rising fire as it consumed the neighborhood.

Derek kept them off the main streets, sticking to the alleys and side streets, always favoring the shadows. The chaos that had only moments before surrounded them receded into the distance. The night was cool and the air refreshing.

"No, this way," Jacob said, motioning for Derek to follow. "There's a guard station that way."

Derek let Jacob take the lead.

Ben kept his splinters close, transforming one into a drone just overhead so he could keep an eye behind them while they ran. They threaded their way into an abandoned industrial park, dilapidated buildings and broken warehouses lined up in neat rows along wide streets overgrown with grass and weeds.

Jacob led them past a marker, pointing to it as they moved through the night.

"Keep an eye out for stalkers," he said, leading them into a partially intact building. They were only a few steps inside when lights hit them from several directions.

"Identify yourselves," a voice in the darkness said.

"I'm Jacob, one of Vincent's lookouts," he said nervously.

"Damn it, Jacob, what have I told you about strangers?" another voice said, as a man stepped out into the light, revolver in hand.

"Hello, Vincent," Derek said, a beam of light falling on him as he spoke.

"Derek, is that really you?"

"Yep, any chance we can take this conversation somewhere more secure? We need to talk."

"All right, but I'm going to need your friends' weapons."

"Not going to happen," Hound said, raising Bertha slightly.

"You don't have anything to fear from them—unless you try to take their weapons," Derek said.

"You vouch for them?"

"I do."

"All right, but you know what that means if they turn on us."

"I know. They won't."

Vincent scrutinized them for several moments before nodding slowly.

"Follow me," he said, leading them to a staircase hidden by rubble into the basement and then into a tunnel. After twenty minutes of walking through old service tunnels and a few newly dug passages, they passed another marker.

"We took that from outside of town," Vincent said. "Keeps the stalkers out."

Ben and Ellie shared an approving look. After another ten minutes, they reached an area with several rooms that looked like they had once been offices for a subway switching station.

"This place makes a good operating base," Vincent said, motioning to the tunnels going off in various directions. Several of his men moved to secure the area, while the four with the best weapons followed him into a large room and took positions at each corner. Vincent motioned toward a number of old plastic chairs surrounding a table with a badly scratched veneer surface. He took a seat at the head of the table and fixed Derek with his dark brown eyes.

"So, last I heard, you were running with that Adara girl in Alturas."

"Yep, things changed," Derek said.

"You should have seen them," Jacob said. "They killed one of those dragon men."

"Hush, Jacob," Renee said.

Vincent looked over at the two siblings and smiled wryly.

"That's why you two make such a good team—one's all enthusiasm, and one's all common sense." He turned back to Derek. "You really take down a mule?"

"Not me, them," Derek said, motioning toward Ben and Hound.

Vincent whistled.

"I could use people like you," he said. "Looking for a job?"

"I'm afraid we already have one," Ben said, giving Derek a questioning look.

He nodded.

Ben took the Dragon's Fang out of its scabbard and laid it on the table.

"I intend to kill the dragon," he said. "We took a shot at him in Battle Mountain, and damn near got him—made him bleed, at any rate. Unfortunately, that just pissed him off."

"Well, I'll be damned," Vincent said, "I always thought that sword was a myth. How'd you happen to come by it."

"Let's just say the Dragon Slayer is a family friend."

"Fair enough," Vincent said. "So what's your plan? You going to knock on the dragon's front door—ask him to come out and play?"

"Haven't gotten that far yet," Ben said. "At the moment, we're trying to figure out where that Adara girl you mentioned is. The coven took her."

Vincent's eyes widened and he shook his head slowly. "I try and steer clear of the coven. Those people don't get along well with others."

"Maybe you could put us in touch with Penelope Adara," Derek said.

Vincent harrumphed, then turned and spit on the floor. "Ever since the garrison arrived from the Mountaintop, cartage has rolled over and peed straight up in the air. Used to be we could do business with them, but not anymore. The wyrm's got them so terrified, they just sent nine of their own kids off to be dragon snacks. I mean seriously, what the hell is that? How does a person even do that?"

"Shit," Derek whispered, looking down at the table. "If you can't put us in touch with Penelope, then I need to go see a friend of mine."

"Whoa, slow down," Vincent said. "The streets aren't safe. It's like you hit a beehive with an axe handle out there. Stay here for the night, get some rest, make a plan."

"He's right," Ben said. "We can't be out on the street right now. That reminds me…" He turned to Vincent. "Do you have a map of this tunnel system?"

"There's one on the wall in the other room," Vincent said. "Cave-ins are marked."

Ben found the wall map of the old subway system and recorded it into his augment, overlaying the cave-ins onto the transportation-system maps he already had for Salt Lake.

Vincent came up alongside him while he examined the map.

"We have people being held here," he said, pointing to a spot on the map, "and the wyrm's men have a weapons store here." He pointed to another location. "We haven't had the firepower to take either of them, but with your help, I know we could capture the weapons."

"I admire your persistence," Ben said, "but I really do have people counting on me."

"Fair enough," Vincent said. "If you change your mind, the offer stands."

"Thank you, but I'm pretty sure I won't," Ben said before wandering off to find Ellie.

He lay down next to her and tried to sleep, her rhythmic breathing only serving to remind him of his inability to drift off. After pretending for a while, he sat up and began to meditate. Once he'd quieted his mind, he projected his avatar and then he became his avatar, his consciousness and awareness transferring into his manifestation.

He floated up through the ceiling and into the night sky, taking in the city from a much broader perspective. There were checkpoints everywhere. Patrols roamed the streets, particularly in the area of the destroyed barracks where they had first emerged. The fire was out, but smoke still rose from the charred remains of the building.

He thought about the map of town and the location of the underground facility that he wanted to find. Seemingly unbidden, the entire world rushed by and he found himself floating over that part of town. It was a disconcerting feeling to move so quickly, so unexpectedly. He lost focus and almost returned to his body.

Then he realized where he was and decided to do some reconnaissance, descending into the earth, floating through utter blackness, allowing his intuition to guide him until he emerged into a space that was no less black, but seemed to be intact. As he lamented the lack of light, he began to be able to see, a soft luminous glow radiating from everything in the room.

He was in an NACC facility. He scanned the room, which was lined with computer terminals along all four walls. A circular command center stood in the center of the area. All of the terminals were dark, and the room looked like it had been undisturbed for decades.

He located the door and floated through it, emerging into a hallway that only went for a few dozen feet before it ended in a cave-in. He floated through the rock and dirt, estimating that the obstruction spanned only ten feet or so before the corridor resumed. It led into a larger underground facility with multiple rooms and corridors leading off in all directions. This section looked like it had been stripped clean at some point. Everything of a technological nature was gone, and the tech that was built into the facility had been smashed or burned or both.

He looked for an exit and found a staircase leading up. At the top was a heavy steel door, locked and sealed. He drifted through it and found himself in another section of the facility, this one stripped of all tech as well, but currently being used as a laboratory of the most unspeakable kind.

People were being held in cages along the wall, mostly adults, but a few of them children. His anger began to rise.

There were a number of people in the room who were wearing white lab coats, most likely remnants from the old world. They were gathered around a table with a man strapped to it. He was clearly terrified.

Ben moved closer. One of the men in white extracted something from a jar with a pair of metal tongs.

It looked almost like a squid, only there was a darkness to it that Ben knew in a glance was unnatural. Two other men used metal hooks to force the terrified man's mouth open while the man with the squid carefully dropped the dark creature into the man's throat.

The man struggled against his restraints as the thing disappeared inside him. His eyes went wide in sheer terror, then his body began to convulse violently. Ben was fascinated and revolted at the same time.

The convulsions stopped and the man fell limp.

"Damn it," the man with the tongs said, shaking his head and turning to a colleague. "Serum number seventeen failed to keep the host alive during initial implantation."

The other man made a note on his clipboard before sighing to himself. "Do you really think this will work?"

"What I think doesn't matter," the first man said. "Lord Ick has assured me that it will work, and I have no intention of questioning him."

A door opened and a mule in human form walked in. "Progress report," he said.

All the men in white coats became a bit anxious. The man with the tongs set them down and bowed his head to the mule.

"Seventeen of twenty-five have failed," he said without meeting the mule's eyes.

The mule started to say something, but then stopped abruptly, looking straight at Ben and transforming into his true form as he did.

Ben was so startled that he snapped back into his body and opened his eyes with a gasp, his mind reeling. He lay down and closed his eyes again, accessing his augment's maps of the facility he'd just visited and tracing a route to the surface.

"Damn," he whispered to himself.

The entrance was within the prison where the Dragon Guard were keeping those accused of resistance—the same detention center that Vincent wanted to raid. Ben started to reconsider, drifting off to sleep as he evaluated his options.

He woke some time later with Homer licking him on the face. "People are coming," he said.

Ben rolled to a sitting position, nudging Ellie as he pulled on his boots.

"Hmm," she mumbled.

"Company's coming," he whispered.

He quietly moved to Hound and Derek, waking each with a gentle shake. "People," he whispered.

They all took positions around the room, covering both doors while they waited for those approaching to arrive. Not a minute later, a woman stopped at the doorway, looking into the blackness of the room, her frame illuminated faintly from behind.

She gave a hand signal, and the sound of approaching footsteps increased. Hound chambered a round, the distinctive sound of Bertha's action drawing everyone's attention.

The woman made another gesture and the approaching footsteps stopped.

"Make a move and I'll spray you all over that wall behind you," Hound said.

She tensed but didn't move.

Ben deployed a hundred splinters as lanterns and another hundred as a dart overhead.

"Penelope?" Derek said.

"Is that you, Derek?" she snapped. "I've been looking for you."

"I'll bet," he said. "We were trying to get to Rollo to send you a message."

She hesitated.

Ellie caught Ben's attention and motioned toward the other door. Faint shadows of men poised just outside fell across the floor.

"Seems like you brought a lot of friends," Ben said. "Why don't you step into the room, nice and easy."

She didn't move.

Hound smiled at her. "You heard the man," he said, his aim never wavering.

She gestured for the men in the hallway to hold and took a single tentative step into the room, scanning everyone in a glance. Physically, she didn't look like much, but her grey eyes conveyed a keen intelligence.

"You look a lot like Kayla," Ben said. "She's in trouble and I need you to help me find her."

"What?" she said, a flicker of confusion dancing across her face. She mastered it quickly.

"Kayla has been taken by the coven," Ben said. "I need to know where they took her."

She looked at Ben more closely, a deep frown creasing her brow. "Why?"

"She's my friend and she's in trouble," Ben said, as if the statement was self-evident. "I need you to tell me where she is so we can go get her."

Kayla's mother blinked several times, seeming to come to a decision. "Stand down, boys," she said, gesturing to a chair at the table.

The men outside the room acknowledged the order and backed off. Ben took a seat at the table with Penelope, while Ellie lit a lantern and Hound checked the doors. Derek pulled up a chair as well.

"So tell me, Derek, how did you let my daughter get caught up in this shit?"

He shrugged helplessly. "Kayla's going to do what she's going to do," he said.

Penelope snorted softly, shaking her head, a flicker of emotion on her face before she regained control. She turned to Ben.

"So, you're the Wizard. You look like you're about twelve. I mean seriously, what the hell are you even doing here?" she said, looking up with some exasperation. "And what are those things?"

Ben re-called the lanterns floating overhead to his belt, but left the dart.

"They're called splinters," he said. "Advanced tech. So far they've been pretty useful. As for why we're here—we were hoping to get transportation into the Mountaintop, but the coven waylaid us and took Kayla, so now we're here to rescue her."

Penelope laughed bitterly. "Of course you are," she said. "What I mean is, why are you doing any of this?"

"The dragon stole my Aunt Imogen's baby, so I'm going to rescue the child and kill the wyrm."

She looked at him like an arm had just grown out of his forehead, then sat back and laughed out loud. Ben waited while she struggled to control her mirth.

"I hate to break it to you," she said, "but the baby is probably already dead or worse. As for killing the dragon…" She started laughing again, but with a hint of bitterness.

"We almost got him in Battle Mountain," Ben said. "Made him bleed."

She threw her hands up and shook her head in dismay. "Of course! That was you!" she said. "Only a twelve-year-old with powerful toys would be so reckless. You know he killed over a thousand people to heal himself, right?"

Ben nodded, looking down at the table.

"That's the problem with young people," she said, "you can't see more than a step and a half ahead—no consideration for the unintended consequences of your actions."

"And the problem with old people is you want to sit on your ass and think the situation to death without ever taking action. Somebody has to do something. Might as well be me."

She smiled at him with just a hint of warmth. "I can see why Kayla likes you," she said. "And I know why she hates the dragon. The problem is, your idealistic nonsense has put my daughter in a really bad spot."

"They offered you a bargain, didn't they?" Derek said.

"Of course they did. Young Benjamin here, for her, hence the men in the hallway."

"So Vincent sold us out," Derek said.

"The moment you arrived."

"I guess that's what I get for trusting a criminal," Ben said. "Not that I had much choice."

"So what now?" Penelope said.

"That's up to you. Please know that I don't want to hurt you, but I will if I have to. And those men outside aren't enough to take me."

"Youthful confidence," she said. "Attractive, but foolhardy. You're going to get yourself and all of your friends killed."

"Maybe, but we'll die trying to do something worthwhile."

She chuckled again. "Oh, to be young and idealistic again. I remember the simplicity of it all. Unfortunately, the whips and scorns of time have a way of beating the idealism out of a person."

"Kayla told me about your son," Ben said. "You have to hate the dragon at least as much as we do, so why don't you help us?"

A flicker of rage in her eyes told Ben that he'd hit a nerve.

"You're right. I do hate the wyrm. But I have to consider the larger picture. Because of you and Kayla, nine of my family's children will be sacrificed. If it was discovered that I was helping you, the dragon would burn Salt Lake to the ground and hunt my entire family to extinction. I love my daughter with all my heart, but I can't trade my whole family for her."

"So tell us where they're holding Kayla and get out of our way," Ben said.

She frowned, looking down at the table for a moment, her eyes going distant.

"Can he really rescue her?" she asked Derek.

"If anybody can, it's him," Derek said. "He has powerful magic, and even more powerful tech."

She seemed to consider the situation for several moments, glancing over at Hound, who was still holding Bertha and watching the door.

"Doesn't look like I have much choice in the matter," she said. "She's being held in the basement of an old warehouse not too far from here, but she's heavily guarded, and there's always a member of the coven present."

"Draw me a map," Ben said.

Chapter 20

Ben zoomed in, scanning the front of the warehouse with his drone, held close to avoid detection. Penelope had provided him with all the information he needed to find Kayla, as well as transportation through a number of checkpoints in a supply wagon. He listened to each conversation as the driver addressed the Dragon Guard by name, chatting with him like an old friend, always ending the friendly encounter with a small bag of coins.

Clearly, security wasn't the only reason the Dragon Guard were interfering with the people of Salt Lake. The driver dropped them at the edge of the warehouse district, pointing them in the right direction and then rolling off without a second look.

They had made their way into a warehouse across the street from their target. The district was just beginning to come to life as people went to work. The two mercenaries standing at the door across the way looked alert—wary even, as if they expected an attack.

Ben switched to thermals. He counted fifteen heat signatures inside the building.

"I count seventeen," he said, "fifteen inside plus the two guards at the door. And there's no telling how many are in the basement."

"That seems like a lot," Ellie said. "Wouldn't so many armed men draw more attention than they want?"

"You'd think," Hound said. "The woman did say the place was heavily guarded."

"We should consider the possibility that we're being played," Derek said.

Ben looked over at him questioningly.

"Penelope is nothing if not devious. This might be a trap."

"Maybe, but what if it's not?" Ben asked.

"We need more information," Ellie said.

"I can't risk my drones, but maybe I can scout the place with magic."

A noise caught their attention. Someone was approaching the main door.

"Well, that complicates things," Ben said.

"I'll take care of it," Hound said.

"Gently."

"Now, how else would I handle a situation?" Hound said with a wry smile before trotting off to stand beside the door while the rest of them hid behind a number of crates.

The door opened and a single man entered. He was carrying a sheaf of papers and looked to be an ordinary businessman. Ben grimaced when Hound stepped up behind the man and took him in a choke hold. The man struggled for a moment before falling unconscious and going limp. Hound eased him to the floor, then tied his hands and feet before returning to the group.

"See, gentle," he said.

"I'm sure he agrees," Ellie said.

"Either that, or I introduce him to Bertha. Didn't think he needed a lump on the head."

"Fair enough," Ben said. "Keep an eye out while I meditate."

He sat, closing his eyes. It took some time to quiet his nerves and calm his mind, but eventually he was successful. His avatar came into his mind's eye without difficulty and he was able to transfer his consciousness into it with little effort. For all of his past struggle with this ability, it had now become relatively easy to accomplish.

His angelic-looking form floated out of the warehouse, across the street and past the two men standing guard at the door. The men inside were all armed with crossbows and looked as if they were waiting for a fight.

Ben started to think Derek was right. He began to search the large open space, looking for a way into the basement. Finding none, it occurred to Ben that he didn't need a staircase, so he willed himself to descend into the floor, searching the space beneath the warehouse for Kayla, but finding only blackness.

After he was certain that the building had no lower level, he returned to the floor above and saw Lulu in her silvery form talking to the men in the room.

"Your target is in the warehouse across the street," she said. "Send one squad…" Her voice trailed off when she saw Ben appear out of the floor.

"Go now!" she commanded.

Ben snapped back to his body, his eyes coming open as he came to his feet.

"Trap," he said. "They're coming."

"This way," Derek said.

They followed, running across the warehouse to a side door, emerging onto a street with a few people coming and going. They raced across and into the next building over. Ben scarcely noticed the type of business they ran through.

They raced through the building and out the far door onto the next street over. Ben kept his drone directly overhead, watching behind them for their pursuers, but so far, it looked like they hadn't picked up the trail. Derek led them down the street, turning at the first corner and then stopping to get his bearings.

They crossed and cut through another warehouse, a few of the men moving pallets shouting for them to get out. They passed through and kept going. After a few more minutes of following Derek, they came to a loading dock at the back of a smaller building that shared a block with another warehouse.

"This is Rollo's place," Derek said, going to work picking the lock. It took longer than Ben would have liked, but soon enough there was a click and the door opened. Derek slipped inside and held the door for the rest of them.

Ben was three steps into the back room of the business when Rollo, a big man with long scraggly hair and an oversized belly, came around the corner and aimed a double-barrel shotgun at his face. Ben froze, his hands up.

"Whoa!" Derek said. "It's me, Rollo. We just need a place to lay low for a while."

"Damn it, Derek," Rollo said, lowering the shotgun halfway. "You know better than that. I could have killed you. What the hell are you doing here, anyway? Last I heard you were out west."

"It's a long story. Are you alone?"

"I am for now, but a few of my men will be in shortly."

"Can you hide us?"

Rollo looked skeptical, rubbing the stubble on his chin.

Ben held up a gold coin. "I'll make it worth your while," he said.

Rollo smiled like the sunrise. "Now we're talking," he said. "Come with me."

They followed him into another room and down a staircase into a basement used for storage.

"Penelope know you're here?" Rollo asked.

"Yep," Derek said. "You still running for her?"

"Off and on," he said. "She pays better than most, but her business isn't enough to cover the bills, so I've been doing some other work on the side."

"Always looking for an angle," Derek said. "Glad to see you haven't changed."

Rollo shoved a large crate aside and motioned to the tunnel cut into the wall.

"Goes to an old utility-access tunnel," he said. "There's a small storage room you can hole up in, but don't wander into the tunnels. If you get lost, the rats are the only ones that will find you."

Ellie shivered. "I hate rats," she muttered.

"Thanks, Rollo," Derek said. "Do me a favor and take your time letting Penelope know we're here."

"I got some orders to put together before I send my delivery man out," he said. "Should take a couple hours, but you know as well as I do, she has a way of knowing things she shouldn't be able to know."

Derek shrugged. "All we can do is all we can do."

"Ain't that the truth," Rollo said. "Remember about the tunnels. Without a map that place is a maze."

Ben went first, ducking to pass through the twenty feet of tunnel before he stepped into a stone corridor. He accessed his augment and pulled up a map of the service tunnels beneath Salt Lake. This set of tunnels was separate from both the transit system and the NACC military complex much lower.

The room at the end of the hall was empty, but it looked like it was used frequently. The floor was clear of dust save in the corners, and the lantern sitting on the one small table in the corner still had oil in the reservoir.

"Well, that sucked," Ben said, dropping his pack and sitting down.

"Could have been worse," Hound said.

Ben nodded grudgingly.

"Doesn't get us any closer to Kayla, either," Derek said.

"What are the odds that Rollo is selling us out as we speak?" Hound asked.

"Given our luck lately, I'd say pretty good."

"So what do we do?" Ellie asked.

"If these tunnels are intact, I can navigate us through them," Ben said.

"Then what?"

"That's a good question. I'm going to see if I can find Kayla with my magic. I think I'm starting to get the hang of this avatar spell. If I'm right, I should be able to find her just by thinking about her."

"Be careful," Homer said.

"Always," Ben said, sitting up to begin his meditation, reinforcing his circle before he began. His avatar sprang to life in his mind's eye with a single thought … and a moment after that, he was the avatar. He scanned the room. Homer was staring straight at him, but everyone else was oblivious.

Ben wanted to find Kayla, but when the thought occurred to him, his mind immediately leapt to Penelope. The world passed by in a blur and Ben found himself in a room, alone with Penelope. She was leaning over a large silver bowl full of water. As Ben floated closer, he saw a scene in the water. It took a moment before he realized that he was watching himself meditate.

Penelope was scrying on him.

"You just stay put," she muttered, waving a hand over the water.

The scene changed and she was looking at Kayla, sitting at a table, eating a meal. A man sat opposite her, watching her eat. He looked human, but he wasn't. She ate like she was hungry. He waited patiently.

"Hold on, baby girl," Penelope said. "I'm coming."

Ben looked through the water, saw the room where Kayla was and willed himself there—the world rushed by again, and he was standing in the room behind the man who wasn't human.

"I appreciate the meal, Grandfather," Kayla said. "But I can't tell you what I don't know. After I was snatched, I don't know where Ben went."

"You knew his plans, his objectives, his motives, yes?"

"No, not really," she said, with an off-handed shrug. "He always played things pretty close."

"Indeed," the man said, suddenly looking up with a brief hint of confusion before standing and facing Ben. "Quite impressive, yet ignorant, young Wizard," he said.

"Who are you talking to?" Kayla asked, looking around the room.

"Your friend is here, in spirit, as it were."

"Ben? Get out! He's dangerous."

"Too late for that," the Adara Patriarch said, smiling. "I was hoping you'd come around, but Kayla has persuaded me that you won't, so I'm afraid you'll have to go. The egg will be so much easier to locate without you protecting it."

Ben hesitated, a sense of confusion, and maybe even a bit of foolish curiosity, holding him in place for just a moment too long.

The Patriarch stepped toward him, transforming into a mule as he did, breathing fire at him.

Ben felt a warm sensation in his belly, followed by a sudden, terrible feeling of wild alarm, then a popping sound. The mule smiled as Ben floated past him and through the wall. He had no control, no volition, he was an observer in a powerless form, floating through buildings and people, drifting aimlessly through the astral landscape. The real world all around him was becoming less and less real with each passing moment.

He tried to guide his movement but nothing worked. He just kept falling sideways through buildings, houses, and people. A sense of fear began to grow in his belly. A certain, horrific finality began to seep into his awareness.

He was dead.

He bumbled through a building and floated up into the sky, tumbling slowly, his vision moving as he moved, causing the whole world to spin slowly around him. He saw the ground, then the horizon, then the sky—space, the void … the direction he was going. Fear gripped him, rising quickly into panic. He thought of Ellie.

Then Homer was there, silvery and translucent, his mouth gently but firmly clamped onto Ben's hand. Homer held on, but Ben could feel that he was slipping. He had no strength, no volition, no control over his body.

Quite suddenly, Homer transformed into a person that looked very much like an androgynous version of Ben. He was ghostlike, yet all but exuded a great sense of realness. He took Ben by the wrist, and the world flashed by. Then Ben was back in his body, jerking awake with a gasp.

"Oh, God, we thought you were dead," Ellie said, throwing her arms around him. "You stopped breathing. Your heart stopped." She looked him in the eye through building tears. "You died."

"Sort of," he said, holding her. "I'll be all right."

"I told you to be careful," Homer said.

"Who the hell are you?" Ben asked, virtually shouting in his mind.

"You'd be dead if I hadn't brought you back."

"Thank you … now who the hell are you?"

"I'm Homer."

Ben let go of Ellie and sat back, trying to process his near-death experience and to understand this new piece of the puzzle that was his dog.

"You should rest," Ellie said, guiding him to lie down.

Homer licked him on the cheek. "She's right, you look tired."

"One of these days, you're going to answer my questions," Ben said.

"I know," Homer said, getting comfortable, but offering nothing else.

"Wait," Ben said, sighing wearily as he levered himself back up. "Penelope knows where we are, and I know where Kayla is. Also, the Adara Patriarch is alive and well and he thinks he just killed me."

"Well shit, is that all?" Hound said, checking the door.

"The Patriarch … he's alive?" Derek said.

"Yeah, and he's a mule. Kayla's with him."

"Lies within lies," Derek said. "It's always the same with this family."

"We should probably be on our way," Hound said.

Ben nodded, accessing his augment and plotting a course through the tunnel system. "Looks like we can surface pretty close to another subway station."

"More tunnels?" Homer said.

"Afraid so," Ben said, deploying a hundred splinters as lanterns and proceeding into the darkness.

Rollo was right—the place was like a maze. Without his map, Ben would have become hopelessly lost in a matter of minutes. The only upside to the place was that it was empty and quiet. Half an hour later, they came to a ladder that led to a manhole above. Hound went first, leveraging the heavy steel plate out of the way and emerging into a street, several people looking at him suspiciously.

"We're clear," he said.

Ben came through next, carrying Homer to the surface in a blanket sling.

"I'm really getting tired of that," Homer said. "I am glad to see the sun again, though."

Ben scanned the people watching them emerge. "Let's go," he said, heading toward the nearby subway station. It was only a few blocks away. He was relieved to notice that the people on the streets took little interest in them, most walking with their heads down.

Like the other stations, this staircase had been covered over by steel plates. They reached it without drawing the attention of the Dragon Guard, a fact that Ben considered to be a minor miracle—one which ran out the moment he deployed his shield to cut through the steel plates.

One couple saw his tech, pointed and quickly turned to hurry around the corner.

"Won't be long now," Hound said, scanning the street for threats.

The plate took a minute or two to cut through, falling in half down the stairs with a clatter when it finally gave way. They descended quickly, knowing full well that they would probably be pursued.

Ben was again surprised to find that they didn't have enemy on their heels, but he kept a drone overhead watching behind them just to be safe.

They walked for several hours before coming to a station with an intact staircase to the surface. Ben crept up the stairs and found that this set had been covered over with steel plates and bricked up on the one open end as well. He backed away, returning to the tunnel and continuing into the dark.

They stopped to eat after another hour, taking care to keep the light low. The air was still and dank, occasional drips falling into still waters echoing down the tube.

"You think they're on to us?" Hound asked.

"Honestly, I'm surprised they haven't found us yet," Derek said.

"So, what's the plan?" Ellie asked.

Ben leaned forward and cleared away the space in front of him, drawing a rough sketch of town in the dirt, marking their current location and the building where Kayla was being held.

"We're here, she's there."

"Of course she is," Derek said, moving to orient himself better. "Yeah, we're screwed. That's cartage headquarters."

"Looked like she was on one of the higher floors, too," Ben said.

"Naturally."

"This tunnel runs right by that building," Ben said, making a line in the dirt.

"Cartage has probably cut tunnels from their headquarters into this system," Derek said.

"That would be convenient," Ellie said.

"Maybe," Derek said. "The access points are liable to be well secured and probably guarded."

"No more so than the front door," Ben said.

"Fair enough. I guess going in this way will draw less attention."

"How's security?" Hound asked.

"Pretty tight at the doors," Derek said, "but once we're inside the building, it's mostly an office. They keep a unit of guards on standby, but they're not very well armed."

"Sounds like getting in won't be a problem," Hound said. "Getting out…"

"Yeah," Derek said. "Especially if the Dragon Guard are alerted."

"Let's try to avoid that," Ben said.

Hound chuckled. "No sense becoming an optimist at his point," he said.

"Speaking of which," Ellie said. "Are we going to talk about what happened?"

"Not much to say," Ben shrugged. "The truth is, I don't really know what happened." He looked over at Homer.

"You died," she said. "Your heart stopped and you fell over."

"Maybe she's right," Hound said. "I don't pretend to understand magic, but whatever happened almost ended badly. Until you get a better handle on the why of it, maybe you should be more careful with your spells."

Ben nodded, his grandfather's admonitions about the dangers of magic springing to mind. With those thoughts came a pang of fresh grief.

He nodded.

"You should listen to him," Homer said. "I told you leaving your body was dangerous."

"And I'm still trying to figure out how a dog knows anything about this, not to mention how you pulled me back."

Homer laid his chin on Ben's leg and looked up at him. "I love you," he said.

Ben sighed, scratching his dog's head.

"Yeah," Ben said, nodding to Hound. "You might be right. I thought I had something with that spell, but I clearly don't understand magic well enough to even know what happened."

He got to his feet.

"We still have a ways to go, so we probably ought to get to it."

His mind went to work overanalyzing everything he'd learned. As was often the case, the enigma surrounding his dog remained the most perplexing question on his mind. He quickly dispensed with Penelope's spying—aside from the questions surrounding her magical scrying ability, it was only natural for her to be gathering information about him, especially in light of Kayla's situation.

They continued through the dark, moving more carefully when they approached boarding stations, but finding the tunnels mostly empty, save for the rats. After traveling for the better part of the day, they reached a barricade across the tunnel.

"Must be the quadrant line," Derek said.

The barricade was just that, large cement blocks designed to fit together into interlocking patterns filling the entire tunnel from wall to wall and floor to ceiling.

It looked nearly impassable.

Ben examined the barricade and nearby walls in close detail. After ten minutes, he went to the tunnel wall right where the barricade joined it.

"Cover your ears," he said.

He assembled all four hundred splinters into a large dart and directed it at the wall, accelerating it past the sound barrier in a matter of a few meters, hitting the wall with an even louder crack. The dart penetrated the wall, causing fissures in the concrete to radiate away from the point of impact. Sand began to pour out of the newly formed cracks.

Ben disassembled his splinters and called them back to his boots and belt.

Hound motioned for him to step back, wedged his axe handle into the crack in the wall and levered a section two feet wide, breaking it loose with a heave and leaping back to avoid getting hit by it as it fell. More dirt and sand poured out.

"My turn," Ben said, deploying a small shield and spinning it into a blade. He used the whirling blue disc to cut away the dirt, causing it to pile up in front of the rapidly growing hole in the wall, then turned the shield sideways and dragged it across the pile of dirt, spreading it out into the hallway before cutting away more earth. In less than an hour, they'd dug a narrow, but passable, tunnel around the barricade and into the northwest quadrant.

"Remember, cartage likes tunnels," Derek said.

Ben kept his light low, providing just enough illumination to avoid stumbling.

They walked in the dark for hours, moving slowly under the dim light, stopping frequently to listen for danger. The eerie quiet filled Ben with tension. He tried to turn his mind to any of his many other concerns, but the still, quiet darkness kept drawing him back to the present and the feeling of dread in the pit of his stomach.

"I hear something," Homer said, "very far away."

Ben stopped in his tracks, extinguishing the light.

"Something ahead," he whispered, switching his drone to thermals and zooming in until he saw the source of the noise. Nearly two kilometers ahead, there was an intersection with another tunnel, and it looked like a small army was traveling east. Men in formation marched by, rank after rank, interspersed with wagons in small trains of three or four.

Ben watched, expecting the procession to end at any moment, but it continued for several minutes.

"What's happening?" Hound whispered.

"An army's moving east," Ben said, still mesmerized.

A break in the ranks gave Ben a glimpse of an older woman who appeared to be in command. He reached out with his senses, feeling for magic. It was there, ever so faintly in the distance. Ben checked his circle and watched.

The last unit of soldiers passed. The Matriarch watched it go, accompanied by Lulu and Juju, as well as two men who stood like military officers, but wore no uniform or insignia. Ben realized that none of the other soldiers had any identifying marks or rank or badges or any of the things one might expect to see in the ranks of an army.

He briefly considered sending a dart, but thought better it. Several men led a half dozen horses into view; they all mounted up and rode off after the army.

Ben waited, watching the intersection. After a few moments, four men hung lanterns and took up guard posts at the four corners of the intersection.

"The army is on its way east," Ben whispered, "but they left some guards at the intersection."

"That's a long way to walk in the dark," Hound said.

"I have an idea about that," Ben said. "But right now, I want to know about that army."

"They're probably moving personnel and valuables out of reach of the Dragon Guard clampdown," Derek said.

"I wonder where they're going," Ellie said.

Ben accessed the map of the subway system and found that it crossed over a deeper NACC tunnel that ran north and south. It was close to an intersection with two other tunnels, one running east, the other headed southwest. He switched data feeds and examined the NACC tunnel system, nodding to himself in the dark, seeing that the eastbound road ran straight to Cheyenne, with no other major branches or intersections.

"Wyoming," Ben said, "with most of their muscle."

"So how are we going to do this?" Hound asked.

"Delicately," Derek said. "The less killing we do, the better our chances of forging an alliance with one or more factions within the family."

"So far the only Adara who ever told the truth was Kayla," Hound said. "Not sure alliances with these people is a good idea."

"No, but they're Kayla's family, so we'll tread lightly," Ben said. "Here's the plan."

Chapter 21

They had walked for hours, trudging through the pitch black. Ben had deployed his drone an inch in front of the bridge of his nose, closed his eyes and relied solely on the thermal feed to see, while his friends lined up, hand on shoulder, behind him in a single file. It was slow going, but they got close without notice. Ben stopped and knelt down. Everyone else followed his lead, watching the lantern lights in the distance.

Ben reached out, searching for magic ... nothing. He deployed a dart followed by a drone. The lantern light was dim. He was just over a hundred feet from the nearest guard. He sent his weapons, taking careful aim, four targets, one after the other, smashing each lantern in turn, plunging the world into absolute darkness.

He raced forward alone, Homer his only companion in this battle, his drone his source of vision. He approached the guards, each of them trying to figure out what was happening, flailing about or shouting for one of their companions to light a lantern.

Ben circled, moving in a crouch, quietly maneuvering to get behind his first target, then striking him hard in the back of the head with the butt of his sword, knocking him to the ground with a thud.

"What was that?" another guard said.

Ben moved toward him, angling to get behind him, sheathing his sword as he approached.

"Draw his attention," he said to Homer.

His dog circled in front of the man and growled, deep and guttural.

The man froze. "What was that?" he whispered.

Ben slipped an arm around his neck and took him in a sleeper hold, dragging him backward to the ground, setting his hold and applying pressure. The man struggled for a moment, his cries for help muted as he succumbed to unconsciousness. Ben extracted himself and began to hunt the next man. In the dark, they were helpless to defend against him.

Once all four were unconscious, he brought his light up enough to let his friends know that it was safe to approach. They found the small room that served as the guard shack and dragged the four men inside before binding and gagging them.

Ben checked his map. "This tunnel gets pretty close to Adara headquarters," he said.

"The access passage will be guarded or locked ... or both," Derek said.

Ben looked as far as his drone could see and found only straight passage and darkness. They set out again, much the same as before, hand to shoulder, following Ben. He kept two drones up, one right in front of his eyes, the other overhead, and zoomed in as far as possible down the tunnel. After an hour of walking, a light came into view, still very far away.

The approach was painstaking, but they arrived a dozen feet from the door, a dim lamp hanging on a hook beside it. They could hear the muffled voices of at least three men talking about drinking and how they planned to do more drinking later.

Ben sent a drone and a dart into the room, targeting the lantern. All three men stood up in surprise as the room went dark. Ben targeted the door and accelerated the dart to top speed, allowing it to shatter into individual splinters on impact, blasting the lock apart.

He smashed the lantern outside the door as he moved in, using darkness to his advantage, hitting the first man in the side of the head with a closed fist, stepping into the second man and shoving his face into the wall, rendering both men unconscious in seconds. The third man lashed out, Ben dodged and slipped in behind him, putting him out with a sleeper hold, then raised his lanterns.

"You're getting pretty good at that," Hound said.

"I never knew what a powerful advantage seeing in the dark could be," Ben said.

"I'll bet," Hound said.

Ben went to the door on the far wall of the guard room and sent a drone underneath it, scanning first with visual and then with thermals.

"One lantern, no guards," he said. "There's a staircase a hundred feet away."

He led the way, relying on the lantern to illuminate their path. The staircase ended in a landing with a switchback staircase. Ben sensed for magic. Finding none, he sent a drone up the staircase, six flights, ending on a landing with a locked, heavy steel door.

He left the drone in place and raised even more light.

"How many?" Hound asked.

Ben shrugged, shaking his head before heading up the flight of stairs. They stopped one staircase away from the top, resting for a moment. He looked for a way under the door, but the frame was made with exacting tolerances, scarcely a millimeter of distance between door and frame. Worse, there were no keyholes or handholds, just a clean painted sheet of heavy steel surrounded by stone.

"I can get through, but it'll be noisy," Ben said.

"If we want in…" Hound said.

"Yeah. You guys might want to stand back."

He deployed two shields, one to protect himself and the other to cut, beginning an inch above the steel door frame, slicing into the stone, creating a shower of sparks, but making steady progress, cutting a deep line across the entire width of the door in the space of two minutes. In another five minutes the door came loose, wobbling back and forth ever so slightly. Ben gave the door a little shove. When it wobbled back toward him, Ben grabbed it by the top and pulled it free, Hound taking hold as it fell so they could lay it down quietly. Ben breathed a sigh of relief when he saw another staircase and an empty passage.

"You know getting out this way will be difficult," Hound said.

"I know," Ben said. "Probably more like impossible."

"You got a plan?"

"Not yet," Ben said, with a shrug. "But I do have schematics for the building. I think I know where we'll come in."

He sent a drone up to the top of the stairs, finding another door, this one far less secure.

"That's a start," Hound said.

They climbed doggedly and quietly, stopping frequently to prevent their breathing from making too much noise. Ben sent his drone under the door at the top and found an empty room with a door on the far wall. He was able to break the lock easily with a dart. The far door was locked with a mechanism attached to the wall beside it. Ben pulled the lever and the door swung open, revealing an old furnace in a disused-looking basement. The only part of the scene that didn't fit were the hundreds of footprints leading through the dust and the secret door. The door closed seamlessly after they had passed into the room, becoming nearly undetectable—just another section of wall.

"I have our location on the map," Ben said. "There's a service elevator not too far from here."

"Wait a minute," Hound said. "You want to climb an elevator shaft? That's a long way up in the dark on a ladder that may or may not support us."

"I agree," Homer said.

"We need a way in, and the quieter the better," Ben said.

"There's got to be a staircase somewhere."

"Several, but they're more likely to be in use."

"Tell you what, I'll look at this elevator shaft," Hound said. "We can decide from there."

"Fair enough," Ben said, setting out quietly, leading with a drone out front, but still within his circle. The level was empty, but it had been recently used as an assembly point for a large number of people. They reached the elevator in short order ... or where the elevator should have been.

Ben stopped, switching to thermals with his drone and found a space behind the wall. After that, he found the way in fairly quickly ... another secret door.

Rather than an empty shaft, it actually had an elevator cart with a high railing and a set of crank wheels to power the ascent. Ben looked up into the darkness and saw that at a certain level, it stopped next to another elevator that continued up from there.

"I don't like this," Hound and Homer said at the same time.

"It's empty all the way up," Ben said. "This is our best chance to get to the upper levels undetected."

"I know, I just don't like it," Hound said, stepping into the cart and examining it dubiously.

They started to work the two wheels, rope moving around a set of gears pulling them crank by crank. Halfway up, they passed the counter car going down.

At the top of the ride was a platform with a single door … another secret door when viewed from the other side.

Ben looked up. The next elevator would take them to the top of the shaft. He went to the door and found a peephole. The room beyond looked like an office, and a nice one at that. A large desk sat near the door with a set of furniture wrapped around a fireplace along one wall and another entire wall made of glass, affording a spectacular view of the city. Ben stepped back and pulled the lever. Silently, the door swung open. He waited, listening as he sent a drone to the door on the other side of the office, moving underneath it and scanning the hallway—empty.

He motioned to his friends for silence, leaving the drone in place as he went into the room and straight to the desk.

He stopped a step away and frowned. The surface was completely clean save for a shallow wooden box in one corner and a pen and inkwell in the other. He reached out and felt nothing … maybe more than nothing … the absence of magic, a void space above.

His drone feed brought his attention back to the moment—people were coming.

"And this office?" a man's voice said.

"For visiting dignitaries, sir," a woman's voice answered. "It's yours if you'd like it."

Ben hurried back through the secret door with his drone and returned the lever to its original position. A whirring preceded the door's closing by a moment and then it slid shut and locked. Ben took up a position at the peephole.

A Dragon Guard dominus entered, followed by a nervous-looking woman with a clipboard and pen.

"Quite … palatial," he said, almost visibly sneering as he took in the room, walking casually to the windows and taking a moment to admire the view while the woman waited.

"Who was the last individual to use this office?" he asked, without looking away from the window.

"Um…"

He turned, smiling like a predator.

She went a bit white, then with a start seemed to remember that she was holding a clipboard. She referred to it and swallowed hard. "The Matriarch," she said.

"I see. And who was the person to use this office prior to that occasion?" She swallowed again. "The Matriarch."

He held his hand out and snapped his fingers, motioning for her to bring him the clipboard. She reluctantly obeyed. He took it with an insincere smile and perused it carefully, nodding to himself.

He handed it back to her, fixing her eyes with his. "Where did she go?"

"Who?" the woman managed, stammering a little.

He smiled again, facing her more squarely.

She stood before him trembling.

He lunged, taking her by the throat and walking her back across the room until she stopped against the wall. She shrieked the moment he grabbed her, then froze and went quiet. He stood very close to her, his cheek against hers, his mouth right next to her ear.

"Where did the Matriarch go?" he said, loudly, stepping back and releasing her as soon as he'd asked the question.

She flinched, looking at the floor. "I don't know," she said, timid as a mouse. "I heard rumors of a place to the west."

"Well, a whole cardinal direction," he said. "I guess that narrows it down somewhat. What else?!"

She flinched from his sudden shout. "I don't know … they took everything, everything important anyway."

"I see," he said, turning back to the window, losing interest in her.

She remained frozen in place, looking down at the floor and trembling.

"Go fetch my soldiers in the lobby," he said, smiling at her again. "You belong to me now. Do not disappoint."

Ben didn't think it was possible for her to become more pale, but he was wrong. She nodded tightly and left quickly.

He backed away, motioning for everyone to return to the elevator. They cranked slowly and quietly, lifting the elevator with the assistance of the weight of the counter car and an elaborate system of pulleys and gears. When they reached a platform halfway up, they slowed, coming to a stop and listening. There was another secret door with a peephole.

Ben motioned for everyone to stay put and eased up to the door, peering through the peephole. The room could have been a costume room for a traveling circus with a decidedly dark bent. It was full of black hooded robes, ceremonial knives, and restraints, among other, less savory, things.

Ben opened the door, waiting in the shadows and listening. He heard muffled chanting.

"Wait here," he whispered. "If it's her, we'll make a plan."

He slipped into the room, leaving the door ajar with Hound and Ellie watching the room through the crack. Ben moved quietly, slowly, scanning carefully, feeling magic flare toward an exit that looked like it went through a series of curtains. He glanced at the ordinary door on the other wall and felt nothing.

He headed into the curtains, slowing even more, constricting his circle even more. The chanting became louder and more guttural. Three voices repeated the same word over and over. Ben deployed a drone when he reached the last few layers of curtain, keeping it low and close as he moved it along the floor.

Three people, two women and a man, stood in a triangle around a magic circle carved in the floor and soaked in blood, some of it old and dried. They were all mesmerized by the spectacle taking place inside the circle.

A lump of black stone, almost like basalt, rough and unformed, rested atop an altar. A spiral of white smoke rose from the stone and formed into a porcelain head and face, slowly rotating, its perfect white skin marred by a dozen or so bugs that had partially crawled out of its perfectly black eye sockets and perched around the rims of its eyes.

It stopped rotating when it was looking straight at Ben. He froze.

"Hello, Benjamin," the demon said, its mouth not moving. "Come out where we can see you."

Ben called to Homer as he stepped into the room, expanding his protective circle to the edge of the circle carved into the floor. One of the three acolytes worshipping the demon fell within Ben's circle. A dart began to form.

"Hold!" the demon said. "I can make you powerful—more powerful than you could possibly imagine. Just give me the egg. I can feel its magic."

Homer came up alongside him. Hound was close behind.

"No," Ben said, his eyes darting from one threat to the next.

The demon's porcelain mask cracked in half and insects began flying out of the darkness behind it … black, dangerous-looking bugs with stingers—hundreds of them, all swarming in a cyclone within the confines of the circle. The bugs gradually assembled into the form of a man's face, larger than the porcelain face and vibrating with power and anger.

The acolytes broke and ran all at once. A moment later, the Warlock stepped out of the wall. Ben's mind seemed to freeze in confusion.

"Hello, Benjamin," the Warlock said with a cool smile. "It's so nice to see you again. You always bring me the best gifts."

He turned to the demon, smiling with genuinely sinister glee as he raised his dragon-claw staff toward it.

"You … you're not supposed to be here," the demon cried, breaking apart and transforming into a mass of flying insects, then re-forming a moment later, as if against its will.

"This can't be!" the demon shouted, fury and fear in its inhuman, buzzing wail.

The Warlock produced a bottle with his other hand, popping the cork off onto the floor and uttering a string of words that Ben didn't understand.

"You can't do this," the demon said. "I won't allow it!"

The demon's substance began to drain into the bottle, and the swarm of insects began to diminish.

"You know what happens when you fully manifest in material form," the Warlock said. "You know what you risk."

"Please! What do you want? I'll serve you for a thousand years. I'll keep you young. You can live like a king."

"I already am a king," the Warlock said, still holding the demon in place with his staff while drawing off its life force, such as it was, into the bottle.

"Please stop…"

The insects vanished and the white smoke began flowing off the hunk of black stone. It grew, flowing thick and quickly, a wail accompanying it throughout as the stone vanished into the smoke and the smoke flowed into the bottle. After what seemed like several minutes, the cork leapt off the ground and flew to the bottle, sealing it tight in an instant.

Ben wanted to act, to attack, but he stood rapt, held in thrall by the spectacle.

The Warlock put the bottle in his pocket and smiled at Ben with a courteous nod. "Beware your brother," he said. "He's close."

He stepped back through the wall, vanishing as quickly as he'd arrived.

"What the hell just happened?" Hound said. "I wanted to shoot him, but I couldn't."

"I don't know for sure," Ben said. "But I think the Warlock just captured that demon."

"I'm trying to figure out a way that that could be good," Hound said.

"I wouldn't spend too much time on it," Ellie said.

Ben took a quick breath and centered himself, setting aside the sensation of insanity at the edge of his mind and deliberately turning his attention to the task at hand.

"We have to move," he said, hurrying back to the elevator, pausing only long enough to close the secret door behind them before ascending again.

The next platform was the final stop. They reached it fairly quickly, noting that there were two doors, both secret and operated from the elevator side, as well as an open passage that looked like it ran parallel to a corridor.

Ben calmed his mind and reached out with his senses. After a moment, he found a barrier to magic … a circle, close, well-established and powerful … the null magic space that he'd been feeling. He focused on it, beginning to feel the details, the size and outline of it.

Nearly the whole floor, save a few spaces and passages on the periphery were protected, nearly invisible to his senses.

Ben felt a little thrill of fear at his enemy. The Adara Patriarch was within the circle and would become aware of Ben the moment he passed the threshold. He wondered if he would even have a chance to negotiate.

He withdrew his circle to a few feet and went to the door on the left, looking through the peephole into a large room, the one where his avatar had seen Kayla, and sure enough, she was there, locked in a well-appointed cage, bars and all. She looked comfortable and well fed, but irritable. Ben was relieved to see that she hadn't been harmed.

He went to the door on the right and looked through the peephole, seeing the Patriarch sitting at a desk, reviewing a sheaf of papers. A man with no uniform, but armed and capable-looking, stood before him. Neither of them seemed to be in a hurry.

The Patriarch looked up from the papers and leaned back in his chair. "Report."

"Our primary target is in town, though his current location is unknown. All vital assets are safely away. We believe the girl's mother may be in play as well."

"Really?" the Patriarch said, smiling with an approving nod. "Continue."

"The Dragon Guard are in the building, but so far, none have asked about the upper levels. It's strange."

"Indeed," the Patriarch said with a knowing smile. "Make preparations to leave tonight at full dark."

"Understood," the man said, leaving the room through the door on the far wall.

It was only because of his nod to someone off to the side that Ben even noticed the other man in the room.

"Your best bet is to wait," the voice off to the side said.

It was so familiar.

The Patriarch smiled with forced courtesy.

"Perhaps, but preparations need to be made."

"You're right," the man said, standing up and coming into view. "But I know my brother. He'll come for Kayla."

Frank … Hoondragon, black armor and all. Ben idly wondered where he'd gotten such well-fitting plate armor.

Voices from below drifted up the elevator shaft. The pulley started to turn. Hound looked over at the wheel moving, shaking his head in near disappointment as he pulled out his axe and closed with the mechanism. Ben stayed his hand, looking down into the basket.

It was Penelope and Rollo, with a dozen Dragon Guard in the elevator below them.

Ben waited for her to arrive, motioning for quiet as she came into view. She mastered her surprise quickly and stifled a protest when she saw the look in his eyes.

"We have soldiers behind us," she whispered.

"We didn't until you showed up," Hound said.

"Later," Ben said. "Rufus, get ready to hit them hard as soon as we enter the room."

"Got it," Hound said, going to the door leading to the room with the Patriarch and Frank.

Ben and Ellie went to the other door, Ben taking hold of the lever and looking over to Hound. They pulled as one, the secret doors swinging open silently.

Hound opened fire, blast after blast of buckshot spraying Frank and the Patriarch in rapid succession. Frank cried out in pain and surprise, covering his face with an arm, his black armor taking the rest of the pellets. He fell forward with a grunt, hitting the ground hard, moaning as he clutched at his side where he'd taken the most direct blast, curling into a ball with his back to Hound.

The Patriarch transformed into his true form in a blink, his batlike wings encapsulating him and forming a shield that seemed all but impervious to Bertha's bite. Hound stopped firing, taking a moment to reload a sabot round in the chamber and more buckshot behind it.

Ben and Ellie raced into the room where Kayla was imprisoned, sprinting to the cage door, Ben slashing at the lock with the Dragon's Fang, cleaving it easily. Kayla stood in surprise, then smiled as she raced to Ben, hugging him quickly and giving Ellie's hand a squeeze before heading for the exit. Ben pulled the door closed as Hound fired again. Frank cried out. The Patriarch cursed.

"That was a sabot round … hurts, don't it?" Hound shouted, adjusting the rounds in his weapon again.

"Kayla?" Penelope said, hugging her daughter fiercely the moment she saw her.

"Mom? What are you doing here?"

"I came to get you."

"With Ben?"

"No," Ben said, fixing Kayla's mother with a glare.

"Sorry about that," Penelope said. "We'll talk later. Right now, we have to go."

"Right," Ben said, looking past Hound into the room. Frank was still curled in a ball, lying on his side with his back facing Hound. The Patriarch was cocooned within his wings.

"We need to go up those stairs," Penelope said, pointing to the staircase on the far side of the room, past Frank and the Patriarch.

"Whatever we're going to do, it won't involve the elevators," Derek said, a knife in one hand and part of the elevator in the other.

Ben turned and watched the gears begin to unwind very quickly as the apparatus became unstable and flew apart, a cart full of Dragon Guard plunging to their doom.

"Right," Ben said, rushing into the room. He reached Frank quickly, lunging at him with his sword. Frank rolled aside, causing Ben's blow to glance off his armor, as he whipped his sword at Ben's legs. Ben jumped, avoiding the blow but putting himself in position for Frank to kick his feet out from under him.

Ben fell flat on his face as Frank scrambled to his feet.

Hound shot Frank in the side, the sabot round hitting his armor hard, crumpling him into a ball and blasting him into the wall, right next to the door. He hit hard and collapsed.

The Patriarch whipped his wings out, spinning quickly and causing everyone to duck before he crashed through the door into the room where Kayla had been held, turning toward the secret door and the elevator behind them.

Ben regained his footing and let the Patriarch go, turning toward the end of the room—the staircase, the door, and Frank, who was just coming to his feet, Hoondragon in hand.

The door next to Frank opened and a Dragon Guard came through, his rifle coming up as he saw Ben. A dart shot forward, taking the man in a blink, then going powerless just as quickly, the Patriarch's magic still potent enough to disable advanced tech.

Frank looked past Ben and his eyes went wide. He rolled through the door, shoving a Dragon Guard out of the way. Rufus fired a sabot round, tearing through the Dragon Guard's armor, slamming him against the wall outside the door. The soldier slumped to the floor, blood dribbling from his mouth and flowing freely out of the hole in his chest.

Ben moved quickly, closing with the next man to enter the room, stabbing him through the heart as he stepped into view, then kicking him loose through the door, slamming it shut, and throwing the bolt into place.

THE DRAGON'S FANG   181

"This won't hold for long," he said, motioning to the stairs.

Everyone raced for the staircase leading to the next level up, filing past Ben. Orange heat washed over the door, its bright glow shining above and beneath the door as the hall outside ignited. Ben followed Ellie up the stairs, hoping that the fire would at least slow the enemy ... and that there was some way off the building other than the quick way down.

He reached the next level and stopped in stunned amazement, standing mouth agape, with all of his friends. The top floor of the building was entirely without a roof. All four walls stood high and intact, but the ceiling was open to the sky. Moored in the middle of the room was an airship—an oblong balloon, faintly radiating the same null magic that Ben had come to see and feel as a circle cloaking magic.

He wondered if others could feel that as well.

"You want us to get into that?" Hound said.

"At the moment, it's this or death," Penelope said, gently guiding a reluctant Kayla onto the airship.

Ben threw up his hands, looking over his shoulder, listening to the door below burning through. "Shit, why not?" he said.

"Because we won't be on the ground," Homer said, following Ben with his head hung low.

"I really don't like this," Hound said, boarding and taking a quick look around.

"This is how they got me into town," Kayla said. "So at least I know it works."

Ben closed the gate and looked at Kayla's mother. "Do you know how to fly this thing?"

Penelope shrugged. "We're about to find out," she said, going to the controls. After a moment's examination, she nodded to herself before turning to Rollo. "Release the lines, just like I told you."

He pulled all four lines loose, one by one, the airship lurching gently higher as the last tether came free. They floated straight up, clearing the walls and emerging into the cool night air and a kind of silent darkness that felt all-encompassing.

A set of propellers on the back end of the ship began to turn, moving them slowly forward as they ascended.

"You guys came for me," Kayla said. "All of you."

"Of course we did," Ben said. "We got you into this."

"Yeah, that's sweet," Penelope said. "Can we talk about what happens next?"

"Mom," Kayla said, facing her mother. "Don't make this complicated."

"I want you out of this ... as far away from all of this as I can manage to get you."

"Not going to happen," Kayla said.

"This is bigger than you!" Penelope said.

"I know that! Do you?"

Ben walked to the railing and looked over. The basket was shaped like a boat, easily large enough for ten people, twelve if you didn't mind cramped sleeping arrangements. On the back end was a cabin, on the front was a raised platform with a cargo hatch beside the staircase. One hatch led to the hold.

The city looked small and peaceful below. It was so quiet, and so tiny. From so high above, Ben could almost imagine that the suffering below wasn't real. But a shriek rose up, ever so softly, and he knew in his gut that he'd just heard the last sound some poor soul would ever make.

Another sound drew his attention, much closer. He turned as the door to the cabin opened and the Patriarch stepped out onto the deck, his hands held up in peace, his form human. As he crossed the threshold, Ben felt his magical presence very strongly.

Hound stumbled to his feet, his eyes a bit wild as he raised Bertha.

"Hold," Ben said, deploying two darts and extending his circle to encompass the entire passenger space.

A strange look came over the mule's face. He composed himself quickly. "I offer truce and alliance," he said.

"What the hell is it with you people?" Ben said. "You always want to make nice after you screw us over. You tried to kill me!"

"No," the Patriarch said, "I did kill you. And yet, here you stand. Not only that, but you raided my compound and rescued Kayla. An impressive demonstration of loyalty, determination, and capability. I've clearly underestimated you."

"Great … I still don't trust you."

"Nor should you," he said. "But that doesn't mean we can't work toward similar goals. I've been planning a coup against the wyrm for some time now. When I succeeded in becoming a mule without his assistance, I knew it was only a matter of time before he discovered my secret, so I faked my death.

"In truth, the family has been far easier to manage from the shadows than it ever was in view of the dragon and the priesthood. At any rate, you've forced me to move more quickly than I would have liked. Perhaps it's for the best. Now that we have the same objectives, we might as well coordinate our efforts."

"Sounds good," Ben said. "Why don't you tell me your plan?"

The Patriarch smiled thinly. "I have assets in place," he said. "Enough to inflict significant damage on the priesthood, though not enough to destroy them."

"Tell you what, you get your people ready and I'll tell you when to strike," Ben said.

"It would help to know more about your intentions," the Patriarch said.

"I'll bet it would. Trouble is, I don't trust you, so there's no way in hell I'm telling you my plan."

"Ah … so you do have one, then?"

"This guy's trouble, Ben," Hound said, Bertha wavering only slightly.

"Indeed," the Patriarch said. "Consider the advantages of having House Adara behind you in this effort. I think you'll find that the advantages far outweigh the risks."

He looked out over the railing, nodding. "I think we're far enough from the priests in town that I won't be detected," he said, going to the railing.

"Grandfather," Penelope said.

He turned, smiling more genuinely than before.

"Who can I trust in the family?" she asked.

"Only those that you already trust, I'm afraid," he said, his smile broadening. "I was always proud of you, Penelope. You have a wonderfully devious mind. Your best route into the Mountaintop will be through Cheyenne. I'll see to it that all of the family's resources are made discretely available to you. Needless to say, don't tell anyone what you're really doing."

"I never do," she said. "Thank you, Grandfather."

"Don't thank me, child," he said, his smile vanishing, "I'm taking you to war."

With that, he vaulted over the edge of the railing and vanished.

Rufus choked back vomit, racing to find a bucket.

Chapter 22

"What the hell do you mean?!" Frank said.

"They aren't in the building," the Dragon Guard dominus said.

"You told me the building was secure."

"It was."

"Then how did they get out?"

"I don't know," the dominus said.

"Listen to me carefully, Dominus Killgrave," Frank said, stepping into the man. "Find them! Nobody leaves the building until you find them."

"Understood," Killgrave said, seemingly unfazed by Frank's behavior.

Frank shook his head, looking back up at the sky. "And figure out why there isn't a roof."

"Yes, Lord Hoondragon," Killgrave said.

Frank shook his head, snorting to himself and wandering off to find the stairs.

He'd had them. They were right here. And they got away … again.

It was Hound's fault.

Frank fumed about it as he descended to the ground floor, one staircase after the next. He grimaced and complained out loud to himself about his sore legs, but he always came back to Hound.

Rufus was supposed to be Frank's friend. He should have been on Frank's side.

Instead Rufus had shot him.

His new armor had saved him, but a few of the rounds that Hound had used had really hurt.

Rufus was one more thing that Ben had taken.

Frank thought he heard the scream of a wildcat. He stopped at the next landing, welcoming the excuse to rest while he listened.

After a moment, he continued to descend, reaching the ground floor upset about Hound's betrayal all over again.

This time he saw it, just a blur out of the corner of his eye, through a window, a cougar leapt up onto a roof across the street. He stood very still, breathing deeply, his eyes lost in thought. A quick nod and he was on the move again, heading out of the building and across the street.

He picked out the alley next to the building where the cat had gone and walked briskly to it, motioning for the soldiers on the street to hold position. Deeper shadow fell across his vision as he entered the narrow passage. He slowed, letting his eyes adapt to the darkness before proceeding.

He moved cautiously and quietly, searching the night for any sign of the Warlock, step by step, taking his time to listen and scan the darkness.

"Hello, Franklin," the Warlock said, sitting on a crate only a few feet away.

Frank leapt back so quickly, he nearly fell over. He scrambled to reach for his sword, but then changed his mind in midfall, flailing about to keep his footing. He managed after a moment of uncertainty to avoid falling and regain some measure of composure.

He faced the Warlock, one hand on his sword.

"That was … undignified," the Warlock said.

"What the hell are you doing here?"

"Looking for you."

Frank frowned, then looked back and forth down the alley. "Why?"

"I need your help."

"Doing what?" Frank asked, after a moment's hesitation.

"Defeating the dragon."

Frank looked at him intently, shaking his head. "I just don't know if you can win."

"That's fair," the Warlock said. "But consider the alternative—you go before the dragon empty-handed. After all, your brother has bested you every time you've faced off against him. Your chances to acquire the egg are dwindling by the moment."

"That's not true," Frank said. "My soldiers have them trapped in that building as we speak. It's just a matter of time…" His voice trailed off when the Warlock began shaking his head.

"Your brother got what he came for and then flew away," the Warlock said, smiling slightly while he watched Frank intently. "Quite extraordinary, although I don't believe it was a plan on his part at all. Rather it was a case of blind luck—perhaps even more interesting."

Frank started to tense, a slight quiver rippled through his voice. "What the hell do you mean, he flew away?"

"Oh, it's quite an ingenious contraption, really," the Warlock said. "I first saw it when the Adara Matriarch abducted the girl Ben was traveling with. Seems to generate buoyancy with heated air, though I detected a trace of magic when I got close to it."

Frank took a deep breath and let it out.

"Where is my brother?"

"Flying east," the Warlock said, with a helpless shrug. "They took off half an hour ago from the top of that building your men are searching."

Frank swallowed hard, shaking his head as he turned around and walked away.

"Shit!" he screamed, leaning over, hands on his knees, shouting at the ground.

A few moments later, two men came trotting up to the end of the alley. Frank waved them away, returning to the Warlock.

"What do you want? And what can you do for me?"

"I can free you from the wyrm."

"How?"

The Warlock pointed at the sword on his waist.

"What do you mean?" Frank asked, a bit defensively.

"I can draw the demon from the blade," the Warlock said. "It's only through the demon's influence that you are compelled to return to the dragon."

"But the sword would lose its power," Frank said.

"Yes…"

"No! I won't let you," Frank said, stepping back and shaking his head.

"Fair enough," the Warlock said. "It's your choice, and the offer stands."

"Is that all you've got?" Frank asked.

"Upon reflection, I'm certain you'll come to see that I'm offering you everything," the Warlock said. "With the dragon, you will never be more than a useful pet—always reminded of your inferiority. If I prevail, you will be a valued ally—respected and honored.

"And consider again the consequences of going before your master without his prize. Even if you do succeed, I hear that the wyrm is very particular about who he allows to wield that weapon you're carrying. Perhaps it would be helpful to consider our arrangement as a contingency plan."

"I want more," Frank said.

"Did you have something specific in mind?"

"Rufus Hound," Frank said. "He betrayed me. I want him dead."

"He's the large one helping your brother," the Warlock said, looking to Frank for a nod of confirmation. "I'm sure that can be arranged."

"What do you want me to do?" Frank asked.

"First, I need your assistance in casting a spell…"

"So you were saying, Mother?" Kayla said, breaking the stunned silence after the Patriarch had disembarked, midflight.

Penelope looked at her sadly, then went to her daughter and took her into her arms without a word.

Ben motioned with his head for Ellie to follow him to the cabin where the Patriarch had been hiding. It was a simple room with a built-in cot, a bolted-down desk and a lantern hanging from a hook on the wall. One wall was painted with a map of the central and western portion of North America and there were a number of locations marked, one of which was the building in Salt Lake where they'd found the balloon.

"You think we can land at all of these spots?" Ellie asked.

"Probably, I just wonder how many are manned by hostiles."

"There is that. At least we got out of town."

"Yeah, but I didn't get the chance to contact Kaid."

"All things considered, take the win," she said, reaching for his hand and smiling at him. "Getting Kayla out in one piece is impressive, forging an alliance with the people you rescued her from is amazing."

"If they'll come through when we need them," Ben said. "I'm not going to count on it, but I might try to use it to my advantage."

"What did you have in mind," she asked, lowering her voice to a whisper.

"I'm not sure yet, but I'm working on it," he said, leading her out of the cabin by the hand.

Penelope and Kayla were sitting together on a bench near the bow railing. Everyone else was sitting on the deck, save for Derek who was at the ship's controls.

Ben walked up beside him. "Any idea what you're doing?" he asked with a sidelong grin.

"Nope," Derek said, "but I kind of like it. It's peaceful up here. Penelope told me to hold this wheel steady and don't move any levers. I can manage that."

"There's a map of landing spots in the cabin."

"Oh good, we should probably pick one. We don't want to be up in the sky during the day."

"Right, let me talk with Penelope," Ben said, heading for the bow. He sat down next to Kayla and her mother with a respectful nod to each.

Penelope huffed.

"Kayla…" she started, trailing off, shaking her head. After she mastered herself, she fixed Ben with a glare.

"So now that we're at war, what's our plan, Mr. Wizard?"

"First we rescue Imogen's baby."

"See, Kayla said that, too. But I had a hard time believing her, because that's not a strategy. So what I'm hearing is that you've dragged my whole family into a war to rescue a baby that may or may not still be alive."

"That's the first part," Ben said. "After that, we'll regroup and plan our attack."

"Who's we?"

"I have allies. Some are quite powerful."

"Then where are they?"

"Attending to other tasks."

She started to protest but he cut her off with a raised hand.

"I get it, you're not happy. You don't want your daughter involved with this. I understand all of that. I don't want to be involved with any of this either, but I am, and so are you, and so is she. For a minute there, it even looked like your long-lost, risen-from-the-grave Patriarch was on board, too. So, what's it going to be?"

She took a breath, and then deflated, nodding with resignation.

"I guess there are worse reasons to poke a dragon than saving the life of a child," she said, her eyes going distant for a moment. "You think the baby is inside the Mountaintop?"

"I'd bet he's inside the palace, or some other well-protected facility."

"All right, I have some contacts in the city," Penelope said. "For now we need a place to set down for the day."

"There's a map in the cabin," Ben said, pointing.

"I'm on a special mission for our master," Frank said, holding up a small purse of coins. The two Dragon Guard looked at the money, and then at each other, nodding a moment later. They took the coin and vanished, leaving the entrance unguarded.

Frank eyed the staircase winding around and around overhead. He sighed.

The Warlock came up behind him, smiling before turning his attention to the Dragon Guard carrying a large metal collar. He pointed to the stairs and the man began to climb, the second of the two possessed men following behind them dutifully. The Warlock didn't wait for Frank. He followed a few moments later, hurrying to catch up, muttering about the burning in his legs with each step. He reached the roof in pain, his legs on fire to the point of cramping.

The Warlock stood at the edge looking out over the city. His arms were spread wide and he was breathing deeply.

"Invigorating," he said, when Frank approached.

"Like hell," Frank muttered. "What are we doing up here?"

"Casting a spell," the Warlock said, fishing a small flask out of his robes and handing it to Frank.

"What am I supposed to do with this?" he asked, taking the ornate bottle and examining it.

"I want you to pour the contents into the cistern," the Warlock said, pointing at the oversized water tank on top of the building.

"Why?"

"To poison the soldiers who drink the water," the Warlock said.

"Why?"

"I need their souls to cast my spell."

Frank frowned, blinking several times before responding. "That's pretty dark, even for you."

The Warlock studied Frank for several moments, appraising him carefully … visually examining him. "Perhaps I've misjudged you," he said. "I thought you were willing to do what it takes to get what you want. Was I wrong?"

"No, I just don't understand why you need me to do this. You're here, why can't you do it?"

"I want to see if you can be trusted," the Warlock said.

Frank fell silent.

The Warlock waited.

Frank nodded after a moment, took the bottle and went to the cistern, climbing the ladder and emptying the contents into the water.

"Excellent," the Warlock said, holding up a cloth bag as Frank descended the ladder. "Put the bottle in here."

Frank obeyed. "Now what?"

"Now you wait," the Warlock said, "while I make preparations."

Frank sat down with his back to the low wall that formed the perimeter of the rooftop. The Warlock went to work, first creating a circle and then sitting in the middle of it, chanting quietly for several hours.

Frank woke with a start. The sky was just beginning to show the color of the coming dawn. The Warlock stood over Frank, looking down at him.

"It's nearly time," he said.

"All right, what do you want me to do?"

"Nothing, but we will need to be ready to move as soon as the spell is completed."

Frank nodded, getting to his feet and stretching his legs.

The Warlock returned to his circle. There was now a makeshift altar in the middle of it with the large collar resting atop it. He placed a small, ornate bottle in the middle of the collar and began to chant softly in an alien tongue.

A wisp of white smoke began to form around the bottle, swirling slowly as it rose and formed a disembodied head with blackness behind its eyes.

"I have a bargain for you," the Warlock said.

"Release me!"

"No."

"I demand…"

The Warlock uttered a single word and the voice of the demon transformed into a wail of agony. The Warlock waited until it died down.

"I have a bargain for you."

"No … you must free me now!" the demon said, its voice sounding like the buzzing of angry bees.

The Warlock repeated the single word and the demon began to wail again. Again, the Warlock waited.

"I have a bargain for you."

"I will kill your entire line…"

The Warlock spoke the word again, inflicting torment on the demon.

"I have a bargain for you. Accept my proposal or I will seal this bottle that is your prison in stone and drop it into the ocean."

"No," the demon wailed.

"You will be a prisoner for millennia. Or … you could be free in ninety-nine short years. Your choice."

"Free me now!"

The Warlock shook his head.

"I guess it's the bottom of the ocean."

He started to turn away.

"No, please…"

"I have a bargain for you."

There was silence for a moment, a slight buzzing sound permeating the morning air.

"What do you offer?"

"One hundred souls in exchange for ninety-nine years bound up in this collar."

The buzzing grew, sounding more and more agitated by the second, but then it subsided.

"Agreed."

"Excellent," the Warlock said, turning to Frank and pointing at one of his Dragon Guard servants. "Kill him."

Frank frowned questioningly, snorting softly and shaking his head when the Warlock answered his unspoken query with an inscrutable grin. He drew

Hoondragon and drove it through the man's chest with a single thrust. The man grunted, slumping to his knees and falling onto his side.

The Warlock began his spell. Frank could feel the air grow colder as wispy streamers of shadow and light flowed from the dying man to the bottle. The sound of buzzing grew.

The city was coming to life, the soldiers barracked in the building below waking and making preparations for the day.

"More," the buzzing voice of the demon demanded.

"Submit and serve!" the Warlock said, beginning another spell in a completely different language, this one fluid and lilting, which sounded entirely incongruous coming from the Warlock.

The cork popped off the bottle and a streamer of white smoke flowed out, swirling around until it came into contact with the collar, where it was absorbed. When the smoke was completely gone, the Warlock switched languages again, uttering a single word loudly.

Silence fell, eerie and disturbing at a visceral level, as if death was in the air. Streamers of light and shadow began to flow up from the building, swirling around the collar until they were absorbed, one by one at first, but then all in a rush. The buzzing rose to a crescendo as the last soul was consumed and then silence fell again.

The Warlock placed the tip of his dragon-claw staff onto the collar and spoke a number of words under his breath. Frank felt a pulse of energy like a shockwave wash past him and then the Warlock stepped back.

"Flawless," he said to himself before turning to the one remaining Dragon Guard and pointing at the collar. "Carry that."

The man dutifully picked up the large, newly enchanted collar and looked to the Warlock for further instruction.

"Time to go," he said, collecting the bottle, replacing the cork, and heading for the door.

"So what now?" Frank asked.

"Now we go to the Mountaintop," the Warlock said.

"Then what?"

"Then we will begin to destroy the dragon's most trusted servants."

"How are we going to do that?" Frank asked.

"That will depend entirely on the weaknesses and vulnerabilities of the target in question."

"All right, so who's first?"

"Why, Noisome Ick, of course," the Warlock said.

Chapter 23

"It looks clear," Ben said.

"Are you sure?" Penelope asked.

"Yes, set her down."

She hesitated for a moment before she began working the controls of the airship, causing it to descend toward a clearing in the forest. It was one of the spots marked on the map, and perhaps not so coincidentally, it was just about a night's flight from Salt Lake.

Ben scanned the horizon, first with his eyes and then with his drone. It was clear, but that did little to alleviate the tension he felt. While an alliance with Adara would be highly beneficial if they would actually honor it, he wasn't convinced that they would. Worse, they had some knowledge of his location and his intentions. If the Patriarch was going to betray them it would probably be sooner rather than later.

The airship passed below the tops of the trees and his feeling of exposure diminished somewhat, but not entirely. While the airship was a quick and even comfortable way to travel, it also left them exposed.

When they were a few feet above the ground, Hound and Rollo slid down a set of ropes and tied the ship to a number of stakes they pounded into the ground. Once it was secure, Penelope deflated the balloon enough to ensure the ship wouldn't break free and float away.

"NACC technology detected," the augment said.

A series of data streams began flowing through Ben's mind. The third and final orbital weapon was online and passing overhead. The command codes and orbital schedule downloaded into his augment's memory as well as a message from Kaid.

"Hey, Kid, third weapon's up and ready. I see you already used one. Hopefully that solved our problem, but if not, I'll be coming to you in about a week. Stay alive until then, all right? Kaid out."

Ben smiled to himself.

"Penny for your thoughts," Ellie said.

"Kaid should be here in a week, and the third weapon is up and ready."

"That'll help," she said.

He nodded. "I'd still like to get a message to him."

"Maybe we should wait until he gets here before we make our move."

Ben shook his head. "There's too much in play right now. We need to keep going, especially if we're going to coordinate with Adara."

Kayla came up beside them at the railing.

"So how does this work?" she asked. "After they snatched me, I spent the whole time in the air trying to figure out how I was flying."

"That's a good question," Ben said, motioning to the balloon overhead. "It looks like they incorporated a circle into the balloon to shield it from detection, and I can feel some magic coming from below, so there's a good bet this thing is powered by some kind of artifact."

"Let's go take a look," Kayla said, heading for the hatch, peering down into the darkness after lifting it open.

Ben deployed a hundred splinters as lanterns, sending them into the hold ahead of him.

It wasn't a large space. Most of it was taken up by the mechanical apparatus that seemed to power the ship. On one wall was a small portal with an insulated handle and latch. Ben motioned for Ellie and Kayla to stand clear before he opened it.

Roaring heat poured out, filling the room with hot air. Ben looked inside, the heat nearly singeing his eyebrows, before he slammed the hatch shut again.

"What was that?" Kayla asked, lowering her hands slowly as the heat subsided.

"Looked like a knuckle joint," Ellie said.

"It was certainly a dragon bone," Ben said. "I think it was enchanted to produce heat, and a lot of it."

"A magic fuel source powering a tech machine," Ellie said. "Interesting."

They headed back up to the top deck. Penelope was waiting for them, hands on her hips.

"Tell me about your tech," she said, pointing to Ben's lanterns. "Where did you get it and what can it do?"

Ben looked at her for a moment, weighing his options, looking to Kayla for her input.

She shrugged. "You might as well tell her. She's probably going to see you use it anyway."

"I suppose that's fair," Ben said, motioning to a bench before beginning his story. He told her about Alturas and the base beneath it, about Kaid and the weapons he was deploying, and about his splinters and augment. She listened carefully, asking a few questions here and there, but mostly just absorbing everything Ben said. After he finished, she sat quietly for several moments before nodding to herself.

"I guess that explains how you're still alive," she said. "Also, it helps me understand why my headstrong daughter decided to tag along with you on your fool's errand."

Ellie chuckled to herself. "I have a feeling that you and my father are going to get along pretty well," she said.

"How's that?" Penelope asked.

"He thinks this is a mistake, too."

"Smart man. You should listen to him."

"I do ... when it suits me," Ellie said.

"Yeah, that seems to be going around," Penelope said, looking over at Kayla.

"We should probably get some rest," Ben said.

He slept poorly, and not just because it was daytime. He was getting close to his objective, and all of the risk associated with it. His mind couldn't seem to let it go, so he sat up and pulled on his boots.

"Can't sleep either?" Ellie said, sitting up beside him.

He shook his head. "I think I'm going to stretch my legs."

"Want some company?"

"Sure," Ben said, coming to his feet and offering her a hand.

They climbed down a rope ladder and set off for the edge of the clearing, walking slowly, holding hands.

"What did the Patriarch mean when he said that he'd killed you?" she asked, once they were a good distance from the ship.

Ben was silent for a moment while he decided how much to tell her.

"When I was out of my body, I found Kayla. Somehow, the Patriarch could see me. He attacked and … it was like I was suddenly disconnected, drifting helplessly, and then I was back. I'm not entirely sure how."

She stopped, turning to face him.

"Your heart stopped," she said, swallowing hard, her eyes suddenly glassy. "I've never been so frightened in my whole life."

He pulled her into his arms and held her.

"You can't do that again," she said into his chest.

"What?"

"Leave your body. It's too dangerous, and you don't understand what you're doing well enough to know how to protect yourself."

"I can't argue with that," he said. "I'll be careful, but it might be necessary."

"I don't like it."

"Me neither," he said. "I spent so much time figuring out how to cast that spell, and it turns out that I did it wrong. Unfortunately, it's one of the few things that I can do with magic. If it'll give us an advantage, I have to be willing to use it."

She frowned, nodding reluctantly. "But only as a last resort," she said.

"Deal," he said, motioning with his head for them to continue their walk.

"It's so peaceful here," she said. "I can almost forget how much trouble we're in."

"Almost," he said absentmindedly.

"What is it?"

"I wonder if the Sage could help me with my avatar spell."

"Maybe, but he's not here."

"No, but I could go to him with the spell. He can see my avatar. Maybe I could talk to him through my spell."

"I don't like it," she said.

A glint caught his eye. He walked over and picked up a gold coin, shaking his head.

"I can do this," he said, holding up the coin. "And I can feel your mind when we fight, but that's about it. I need more. I'm worried that the tech isn't going to get the job done. You saw how hard we hit him."

"Yeah, and we'll hit him harder the next time."

"And what if that doesn't work? What if tech just isn't enough to kill a magical being?"

She raised her hands, shaking her head. "Then we're screwed."

"Unless I can figure out how to use magic against him."

"You're making assumptions," she said. "You made the wyrm bleed. If he can bleed, then he can die."

"I don't doubt that, but the first hit only stunned him, and he disappeared a few minutes later. I don't know if that leaves us enough time to call down the next weapon. If I could use magic better, maybe I could interfere with his spell ... prevent him from vanishing before we can deliver the kill shot."

"If the Sage knew how to do that, he would have told you."

"Maybe I just didn't ask the right questions."

She pursed her lips and shook her head before looking up to check the position of the sun. "Well, if you're going to do it, you'd better do it now."

They went back to the airship and Ben began to prepare a magic circle.

Penelope watched for several moments before she sighed deeply. "What are you doing now?"

"Casting a spell," Ben said, without looking up.

"Care to be a bit more specific?"

"Not really," Ben said, finishing his work and inspecting the circle before closing his eyes and imbuing the magical diagram with the intention to protect him.

"I can't help you if I don't know what you're doing."

He sat down in the middle of his circle.

"Just going to visit a friend," he said, closing his eyes.

She huffed but didn't respond.

Ben descended into the calm places within his mind, quieting the mental chatter and reaching out for the egg.

"Are you sure this is a good idea?" Homer asked, interrupting his focus.

"I need more information," he said. "If you won't answer my questions, then I need to find someone who will."

"Just stay away from the dragon and his minions," Homer said. "I was almost too late last time."

"Are you ever going to explain that to me?"

Ben waited, his eyes still closed.

"Be careful," Homer said.

Ben started the process again, this time succeeding in projecting his avatar and transferring his consciousness into the mental construct.

Homer looked over at him and whined softly.

Ben flew straight into the air, surveying his surroundings for a moment, checking for danger before he thought of the Sage. His surroundings shifted and he found himself inside a bunker. The Sage was busy chiseling a circle into the stone floor. The wagon containing the jawbone artifact was parked nearby.

"Can you see me?"

The Sage looked up with a start, frowning for a moment before a look of alarm came over his face.

"Benjamin? Is that you?"

"Yeah, I was trying to create an avatar but somehow the only way I can make it work is to leave my body and become my avatar."

The Sage shook his head in dismay. "What you're doing is incredibly dangerous. The wyrm, or his priests, for that matter, can sever your connection to your body … instant death."

"What did I do wrong? This wasn't what I was trying to accomplish."

"You didn't fully form the identity of your avatar in your mind," the Sage said. "You have to imagine your avatar, personality and all, so vividly that it becomes real to you. It has to take on a life of its own within your imagination before you can transfer it into the light body that you've created for it."

"I was able to create this form relatively easily. Probably because my tech helped me see it in my mind's eye."

"Like I said, the light body is only part of the spell. Instead of creating a separate identity for your avatar, you've projected your astral body into it."

"So how do I fix it?"

The Sage shook his head, shrugging helplessly.

"I suspect that you'll have to deconstruct this form entirely and start from scratch. Since you've already projected into this light body, it will be nearly impossible for you to ever see this form as anything less than an extension of yourself."

"Well, shit," Ben said. "I was hoping for better news."

"I'm sorry I can't offer you more," the Sage said. "For what it's worth, we've secured this facility and are beginning to build the basis of a wizard's guild." He motioned to the large room.

"Where are we?"

"Under Mt. Rainer. Turns out, the NACC had a pretty good-sized facility here. Most of it's caved in, but there's still more than enough space for us to turn it into a base of operations."

"How's everyone else?"

"Well enough," the Sage said. "Dom's wife wasn't happy that Ellie didn't come home, but that was to be expected. We've had a few bounty-hunter types looking around for us, but none of them have survived finding us."

"It's good to know that you're safe."

"Ben!" Imogen said, coming into the room. "Is that you?"

He turned to see his aunt coming toward him.

"You can see me?"

"Faintly, but yes," she said. "The Sage has been teaching me how to feel magic. It's really subtle, but the more I work with it, the more sensitive I become. Any word about Robert?"

"No," Ben said, wincing inwardly. "We're on our way to Denver, and I think we've secured an alliance with House Adara. I'm hoping to be inside the city within a week or so."

"Hurry, Ben," she said, her voice catching. "I'm trying not to think about it, but…"

"I know," he said. "I'll bring him back to you."

She nodded. "Be careful."

"Wait," the Sage said. "Dom will want to know how Ellie is."

"She's good," Ben said, transitioning back to his body with a thought.

He opened his eyes.

Ellie was staring at him. "Are you back?"

"Yep, and apparently, I really screwed up this spell."

"You mean the one you just used to talk to a guy who's halfway across the continent?"

"That's the one. Pretty much any of the dragon's magical minions can kill me if I project anywhere near them."

"Well, it might not be the answer you wanted, but it's important information."

"I guess I can't argue with that," he said, coming to his feet and stretching. "I think I'm going to try to get some sleep."

"You mean like the rest of us are doing?" Hound mumbled from under the coat over his head.

Ben lay down, drifting off quickly. He woke as the ship launched into the sky, blinking the sleep from his eyes and getting up to look over the railing as the ship rose above the treetops and the dusky orange horizon came into view.

Penelope was at the controls. Most everyone else was asleep, save Derek, who was eagerly awaiting his turn at the helm once the ship reached altitude and the course was set. Ben lay back down, welcoming Ellie into his arms as she nuzzled closer.

He woke well before dawn, feeling better rested than he had in weeks.

"If the map on the wall is right, there's a farmhouse with an oversized barn near Cheyenne," Penelope said. "That's where we're headed."

"Sounds like there might be people living there. Any chance they'll be friendly?"

"Hard to tell," Penelope said. "Could go either way."

Ben nodded, his eyes going distant with thought.

"Look, I know we got off on the wrong foot," she said. "If we're going to work together, we're going to have to learn how to trust each other."

"Trust is earned by faithful action. Show me that I can trust you and I will."

She chuckled softly, somewhat bitterly, nodding to herself. "In hindsight, I probably should have made different decisions. But at the time, I didn't have all the information. Truthfully, I still think it would be better to turn around and fly as far away from this mess as possible."

"I understand exactly how you feel," Ben said. "I don't want to do any of this, but it has to be done. If we don't do it, who will?"

"Who cares?" she said. "The world is broken … it's always been broken. Even before the dragons came, we had war and suffering. You can't change that. Look out for your own and let the rest of world fend for itself."

"She has a point," Homer said.

Ben looked over at his dog.

"You sound like Dom," he said to Penelope. "At this point, I doubt there's anywhere I could go that the wyrm wouldn't find me."

"You're probably right," she said. "I just wish you hadn't dragged my daughter into the same predicament."

"He didn't drag me anywhere," Kayla said, untangling herself from her bedroll and joining them at the railing. "You know full well why I'm here."

Penelope nodded sadly, falling silent.

"We should be getting close," Derek said.

Ben deployed a drone a short distance away.

"I think I see the farmhouse," he said, switching to thermal imaging and zooming in. "Looks like just two people living there … and they have quite a few horses."

Penelope reclaimed the helm and began their descent, slowly bringing the airship down into one of the pastures near the barn while Ben guided her in. Once the ship was close to the ground, Hound and Rollo were the first to disembark, both of them going to work tethering the craft while Penelope slightly deflated the balloon to reduce the buoyancy.

Light grew in the bedroom of the house and shortly thereafter a man emerged, holding a lantern. He waved.

"Hello!" he called out.

Ben scanned him and saw that he was unarmed.

Penelope stepped forward as he approached. "My name is…"

"Stop," he said. "I don't need to know and I don't want to know. I got word you might be coming, with some pretty pointed instructions. I'll need two of you to give me a hand moving the ship into the big barn. The rest of you will find saddles in the small barn over there. Horses are in the paddock out back."

"Thank you," Ben said.

"Young man, your presence here is a threat to me and my wife, so I want to get this contraption out of sight and I want you and your friends to be on your way at the first hint of light. We clear?"

"Fair enough," Ben said, heading toward the horses without giving the man a second look.

By the time the stars began to fade, they were leading their horses away from the farmhouse along a very dark road with only a single lantern to illuminate their path. Ben was tempted to deploy some splinters to provide more light, but he didn't want to risk detection. He knew the chances of being discovered by the enemy were slim, but his anxiety seemed to be growing the closer he got to the dragon.

When the light of dawn overcame the shadow, they mounted up and rode for Cheyenne. Penelope led them around town, taking the better part of the day to approach from the east. Ben was frustrated with the delay, but he held his tongue.

They reached the outskirts of town and stopped at a roadhouse to feed and water their horses.

"You sure about this?" he asked Penelope, hesitating before they got close enough to be seen.

"This place is a smugglers' den," she said. "Nobody here is going to ask any questions because they don't want to draw attention to themselves."

"I don't like it," Ellie said.

"How about I go in and have a look around," Hound said.

"And a drink?" Ben asked with a knowing smile.

"How else am I supposed to blend in?"

"All right," Ben said. "Go take a look while we find the stable manager and see to our horses."

"You're wise beyond your years," Hound said, gently spurring his horse into a trot.

The rest of them went around back to the paddock and stable. A young man came out to greet them.

"Welcome, welcome, will you be staying the night?"

"No," Penelope said, smiling at the young man warmly and convincingly. "We just need to feed our horses and maybe have a bite ourselves."

"Very good," the young man said. "You can turn your horses out into the paddock. The price is a drake each."

She produced a small purse and counted out the coins, dropping them into the man's hand with another smile.

"They have a side of beef roasting inside," he said. "Another drake each will get you all you can eat."

"Sounds good," she said, leading her horse to the gate while the rest of them followed.

Hound returned before they were finished removing their saddles.

"Might want to rethink that," he said, handing Ben a sheet of paper.

It was a sketch of his face with a reward of ten thousand gold.

"Shit," he said, handing the sheet to Ellie.

"So much for a hot meal," she said.

"Yeah, I think it might be best to push on," Hound said.

"Agreed," Ben said.

The stablehand returned as they prepared to depart.

"Is something wrong?" he asked.

"Not at all," Penelope said, drawing him aside, away from Ben. "We just decided that we could make it into town before dark."

He looked up at the sky.

"I doubt it," he said. "The light is fading fast."

"Be that as it may, we need to be going."

"Suit yourself, but there are no refunds," he said.

"I understand," she said, smiling again.

He started to turn away, but stopped when he saw Ben.

"Your friend looks familiar," he said, frowning for a moment before his eyes went a bit wide. "Never mind ... I must be mistaken ... please excuse me."

He turned and stopped in his tracks, Hound standing in his path.

The stablehand looked around a bit wildly. "Please don't hurt me," he said.

"Well now," Penelope said, coming up beside him, "that will depend entirely on what you do next."

"If I yell, everyone inside will come running," he said. "There's a pair of men in there who were asking about your friend."

"That would be a mistake," Ben said, coming up on the other side of the man. "If you call out, we're going to have to kill everyone here, including you."

Hound pulled his coat aside and revealed Bertha, smiling humorlessly at the terrified young man.

"I don't want to do that," Ben said, holding up a gold coin. "So here's my offer. I give you this coin and you keep your mouth shut."

"The poster says you're worth ten thousand gold," he said.

"Well, well," Hound said, "look who just grew a pair."

Ben reached down and took the man's hand and pressed the coin into his palm, closing his fingers around it, but not letting go.

"The wyrm will never pay," Ben said. "I just did. Take the money and keep your mouth shut or I will kill you, right here, right now."

The young man blinked, nodding tightly.

"Don't even think about double-crossing me. I can see the wheels spinning in your mind. Here's the thing, you're just a guy doing a job, and I respect that. I don't want to hurt you, but the moment you become a threat to me and mine is the moment your life will end."

He looked down at the coin, then around at Ben and his friends, finally nodding.

"Also," Penelope said, "if you report us later, some pretty unfriendly people will want to know why you didn't speak up sooner. Think of this as the easiest job you've ever had. You just earned a small fortune to do exactly nothing."

He cocked his head to the side and shrugged. "All right, I won't say anything."

"Ever?" Ben asked.

He shook his head.

"Good, now put that coin in your pocket and go on about your business like any other day."

A few minutes later they were riding away, moving through the rapidly falling light toward town. As the day vanished, they dismounted and Penelope led them off the road to a small clearing that used to be someone's backyard. Now it was part of a young forest trying to reclaim what was once a neighborhood.

"Wait here," she said.

"What do you mean?" Ben asked.

"I'm going into town to smooth the way."

"Why don't we all go?"

"Because I don't have all of the necessary arrangements in place yet," she said.

"I'm going with you" Ben said.

"No, you're not," Penelope said. "Do you think that roadhouse is the only place with your face tacked to the wall? You stay here. I'll be back in a few hours."

Ben started to protest, but Kayla stopped him.

"Ben, this is what she does. Let her do it."

"All right," he said, looking at Penelope, "but I want you to take Derek with you."

"If you say so."

She and Derek disappeared into the night, leaving the rest of them to wait in the dark. Ben tried to sleep but couldn't, so he turned to meditation to calm his nerves, focusing on his coin, more because it was familiar than because he needed the money.

Penelope and Derek returned at midnight, slipping into camp almost silently. Ben might not have noticed if Homer hadn't warned him.

"Time to go," Penelope said. "Everything is in place. Follow my lead, stay quiet and don't make any light."

She led them along a trail that had once been paved, a long time ago. As they approached a train yard, bustling with activity even at this late hour, she stopped in the shadow and gestured for everyone to wait.

A few minutes later, a Dragon Guard patrol passed by, none the wiser. Once they vanished, she led Ben and his companions through the yard, past a number of clearly disinterested workers, and into an enormous warehouse that was missing both end walls where the tracks entered and exited. A nervous-looking man was waiting for them between two rows of rail cars.

"Hurry up," he whispered harshly. "We don't have much time before the night shift comes on. Leave your horses."

They gathered their things and followed the man to a train car. He retrieved a ladder from beside a nearby job shack and propped it up against the car, motioning impatiently for them to climb.

Ben carried Homer up and found that the car was filled with coal, save a section at one end that had been dug away to reveal a hatch into a lower compartment beneath the cargo. Boards were in place and braced with more lumber to keep the coal from covering the hatch.

"Inside," Penelope said.

"I don't like the way this place smells," Homer said.

"Me neither," Ben said, climbing down into the cramped space and reaching up to lift his dog down beside him. The entire lower half of the car was a secret compartment. There were a few small barrels of water and a box of food as well as some blankets and a small lamp.

"How does this work?" Ben asked Penelope after everyone was inside.

She closed the hatch without answering. A moment later the sound of coal pouring in over the exit filled the compartment and then everything went quiet.

"We're in for the duration," she said. "This car is due to depart for the Mountaintop at dawn. It'll take about a day to get there."

"How do we get out?" Ellie asked.

"One of my operatives in town will come for us."

"It's a bit cramped, but it beats the hell out of flying," Hound said, claiming a spot on the floor and settling in for the night.

Chapter 24

The night shift came on and started assembling a train, car by car, often moving several to get at one, then moving them again. Not only was it disturbingly noisy, they also found their car being moved frequently.

Ben tried to sleep, then he tried to meditate. Finally, he settled on worrying about all of the things that might go wrong.

"Stop it," Homer said. "Don't lend your emotion to visions of defeat."

"What do you mean by that?"

Homer didn't respond.

Ben changed his focus and accessed his maps of Denver, reviewing the layout of the town and considering his options. Ultimately, he decided that his course would probably be dictated by events out of his control, and he would deal with them one at a time.

He woke with a start when the train started moving. This time it began very slowly and built speed. Ben wondered about the steam engine pulling them—he'd never seen such a machine, but then he'd never seen a hot-air balloon before either.

The day passed slowly, the tedium and discomfort wearing on everyone. The rhythmic noise of the tracks passing beneath them drowned out their voices and made conversation impossible. The periodic screeching of the brakes as the engineer negotiated the winding mountain rails ensured that sleep was interrupted, if it could be had in the first place. That well-rested feeling that Ben had enjoyed just a day earlier vanished like a puff of coal dust in the wind.

The train slowed, then slowed again, finally coming to a stop. Workers were busy all around them. Ben felt his anxiety rise. He was in the Mountaintop. All things considered, it was a genuinely stupid place to be.

The car moved, back and forth, then one car came unhitched, the muffled curses of the crew just feet away as they struggled to work the mechanism. It seemed to go on for hours, being jostled about, pulled back and forth. When they weren't being moved, other cars were in motion, creating a constant background of thud and clank.

The commotion died down gradually, finally fading away. Ben wasn't sure what was worse, the noise and proximity of the workers or the dread of waiting in silence.

Tap, tap, tap…

Ben's heart caught in his throat. He held his breath.

Penelope tapped twice.

Tap.

Silence.

Then digging. Scraping and shoveling.

Then light.

"Hello," a young man said, sticking his head into the compartment. "We should hurry."

Ben frowned, realization coming to him in a rush.

"Juju?"

"Someday you're going to have to tell me how you do that," Juju said. "Right now, we have to go."

Ben shared a look with Ellie before heading for the hatch, lifting Homer out before he climbed up and offered her a hand.

The yard was deserted. The coal at one end of the car had been dug away and held at bay with boards as before. Once they were out, Juju closed the hatch and removed the boards, shoveling the coal back into place.

"What happens next?" Ben asked.

Juju pointed to a wagon. "I'll need one of the big ones to give me a hand," he said, gesturing vaguely toward Hound and Rollo.

Rollo followed Juju's instructions, lifting the boards lying in the wagon bed and using them to create a large box of sufficient size for them to crawl inside and lie down.

"In you go," Juju said, once the top board was in place and the supports were set, a row lengthwise on each side of the bed and one down the middle.

Ben climbed in first, followed reluctantly by Homer. Once everyone was inside, Juju nailed the end board in place about a foot shy of the tailgate. The wagon moved slowly, stopping for a moment while coal was poured in over the entire box, duplicating the trick with the rail car.

Then they were off. The ride was bumpy and uncomfortable, but they moved through the early morning traffic without a problem—a cart transporting coal, entirely expected.

The noise of town faded, gradually being replaced by countless birds chirping and an occasional crow cawing. Then there was only the sound of the wagon on the road. They stopped, started again, stopped and started again, then stopped. A large door closed. The tailgate dropped open and coal poured away from the end of the box. Then the end was pried off and they clambered out, breathing deeply and getting a lungful of coal dust.

Ben coughed, his spit was black.

Juju motioned for them to follow him upstairs. The second floor was sparsely furnished, but relatively spacious. The curtains were drawn, but Ben could see trees through the cracks.

"This is a carriage house on the empty side of a large estate," Juju said. "This man I've taken is a willing participant who is being well paid for his assistance. The Patriarch wanted me to tell you that."

"How close is town?" Ben asked.

"We're on the outskirts," Juju said. "I have a map on the table."

Ben checked their position, recording the map into his augment and running a comparison with his pre-dragon maps, updating them as needed.

"What are your orders?" he asked Juju.

"To bring you here safely and quietly, to provide you with this location to use as an operations base, and to facilitate whatever other assistance you require to destroy the wyrm."

"Excellent," Ben said. "I'll need to begin with reconnaissance."

"My sister can assist with that," Juju said.

"I'm sure she can, but I'm going to need to take a look for myself."

"As you wish," Juju said. "Weapons are prohibited in town—a policy that is strictly enforced."

"That complicates things," Ben said.

"We could go at night," Hound said. "You can see pretty well in the dark."

"Stalker-enforced curfew, full dark 'til dawn," Juju said.

"So, broad daylight it is," Ben said.

"I might have another option," Penelope said. "But I need to know your target … specifically." Her eyes flicked to Juju, almost imperceptibly.

It suddenly occurred to Ben that he and the Patriarch, and hence Juju, had different immediate objectives. He needed time to think.

"Do you know where the dragon is right now?" Ben asked.

"Last report had him deep under Cheyenne Mountain in an old NACC base," Juju said.

"What do you think it would take to draw him out?" Ben asked, musingly, as he leaned over the map.

"You, out in the open … a bunch of dead priests might do it. Hard to say at this point."

"Let's do both," Ben said, without looking up. His finger landed on a spot in the wilderness some distance from the city. "We need to draw the dragon to this location."

Juju frowned, hesitating for a moment, before speaking. "Unlikely."

"We kill a bunch of his people and then run there," Ben said. "He follows. Once he's out in the open, I can hit him."

"Perhaps, but it's risky."

"Life is risk," Ben said.

"And you won't entertain the idea of a strike on the Mountaintop?" Juju asked. "That would certainly get his attention."

Ben froze, a deep frown on his brow. He shook his head slowly. "I'm not going to kill all of those innocent people. We have to lure him away from the population."

"As you wish."

"Tell me how to act and blend in," Ben said.

Juju took a moment to think about it and then began describing the customs and laws they would need to comply with. Half an hour later, Ben felt like he had some idea of just how oppressed these people really were. And they thought of themselves as the powerful. In truth, they were just upper-class slaves—well-treated pets that the wyrm occasionally snacked on.

The place was a den of informants, spies, and hidden agendas—a dozen different families and organizations vying for power and advantage with the priesthood and the Dragon Guard at the top.

"I have papers," Juju said, going to the desk and retrieving a stack of bound leather wallets. He tossed them on the table. "Find one for a man."

Ben selected one, reading all of the information on the document and shaking his head in dismay. "These are pretty specific."

"The Guard doesn't mess with people very much unless someone rats you out. Regardless, it's always better to have papers," Juju said. "But keep looking, there should be one or two that you could pass for."

It took four sets of papers before Ben found one that sounded most like him. His profession was listed as a tracker.

"Give me a minute to prepare the wagon," Juju said, heading for the stairs.

As soon as Juju was out of sight, Ben whispered to Penelope, "I need a way into the palace, quietly. See if you can make that happen while we're out."

She thought about it for a moment before nodding.

"I know a guy," she said. "I can also give you a look inside, but only once."

"Magic?"

She nodded again.

"You coming?" Juju yelled from downstairs.

"Find a way in, we'll look later."

"Don't get caught," Ellie said, laying her hand on his arm.

"I'll do my best."

Ben kept his head down and his eyes up while Juju drove the wagon into town. He'd insisted on using the cover of the man he was occupying. Ben went along. He didn't really want to rely on Juju but he also didn't want to arouse suspicion.

He'd given Ellie his sword. It made him feel like something was missing, and not just in a physical sense—he could feel the difference in the magical field that he was immersed in … it was more alive, less aggressive.

He wondered how much the magic influenced his decisions or colored his thoughts. No wonder his grandfather had been so wary of magic.

Juju drove the cart easily, like a man on the way to pick up a load of supplies who wasn't in a hurry to get there. Ben felt his patience wearing thin, but he remained silent and watched, frequently reinforcing his circle.

Juju nudged him when the palace came into view.

The wall was twenty feet high, surrounding a complex of dozens of buildings and many acres of grounds. A road encircled the entire expansive estate. Ben could feel magic radiating faintly from the walls, but he couldn't determine the enchantment's purpose.

He watched, recording every perception into his augment for more detailed analysis. Juju drove like it was any other day. Nobody bothered them. A few Dragon Guard posted at busy intersections directed them through traffic along with everyone else, but mostly nobody gave them a second look.

Ben started to think about the last few days and how much ground he'd covered. While the journey had been uncomfortable, the smugglers' route had gotten him farther, faster, than the direct route ever had.

He paid more attention when they passed the section of wall that formed one side of the building that housed the nursery, almost certainly where they were keeping Robert. Ben made sure to get a good look at the buildings nearby as well.

"There!" Frank whispered harshly. "There he is. I knew he'd show up here."

"Indeed," the Warlock said, "your incessant complaining for the past three hours notwithstanding."

"If you'd given me my rifle back, I could shoot him right now."

"Doubtful," the Warlock said, peering down at Ben. "Besides, you abandoned your rifle, and our alliance, in the middle of a battle, thus forfeiting any claim. I recovered the weapon and it now resides in a safe place."

"Sometimes I wonder why I'm working with you."

"I seem to recall that it had something to do with your survival," the Warlock said.

"There he goes!"

"Your suspicion has been confirmed," the Warlock said. "He will move on the child. All that remains is to set the trap."

"Yeah, about that," Frank said. "You said you'd tell me about the trap we've been working on for Ick."

"Very well, the players are already in motion. The mould you planted in the basement of the chapel was the very same mould that I used to forge the dragon collar. I've arranged to have it discovered and reported to the Dragon Guard. That will precipitate an investigation. A member of the chapel staff will provide incriminating testimony that will lead to a search of the priest's quarters, which will in turn produce the bottle of poison used to kill the soldiers in Salt Lake.

"The priest of this chapel is a staunch ally and known confidant of Noisome Ick. What the dragon will see in one look is that this man isn't capable of casting the spell in question, that in fact, only a small number of priests in his service are capable of such a magical feat, and Ick is the only one allied with this particular priest. Faced with such tangible and irrefutable proof of betrayal, coupled with a clear effort to conceal the collar's creation, I expect that the wyrm will eat his faithful servant.

"Do my machinations meet your approval?"

Frank forced a quiet laugh, shaking his head. "That's quite a plan. Why couldn't you tell me that before?"

"Because before, you could still screw it up."

Frank glared at him.

The Warlock smiled back. "Learn the lesson," he said. "Information is power. Don't give it away easily."

Frank huffed, looking back to the road below. Ben was gone.

"For example, you now have proof of your brother's presence and intent. What will you do with this valuable information?"

"I should have followed him."

"No."

"What do you mean, no?"

"Not should have ... will. What will you do?"

Frank went silent, staring off at the nursery.

"Well?"

"I don't know. All I can do is wait for him to come back."

"Surely, you can do more than nothing. There must be some action you could take that would move your agenda forward."

"He's gone. What do you want me to do?" Frank said.

"I want you to think. I want you to make a plan. I want you to be cunning and devious and dangerous. I want you to be worthy of my association."

"You know, you tell me you want to be allies, but then you talk to me like I'm lesser than you. I don't see you doing anything."

"No, you don't, and neither does your brother. As we speak, my cat is tracking him back to his friends while my shadow is scouting the nursery. The child is there, and the place is well guarded."

"You could have told me," Frank said, somewhat sullenly.

"Would it have made a difference?"

Frank didn't answer.

"We're being followed," Ben said.

Juju looked behind them, then all around. "I don't see anyone."

"No, you wouldn't," Ben said. "Take a ride through town."

"Are you sure that's wise? You are a very wanted man."

"True, but if we head straight back, we'll give away our location."

"To whom?" Juju asked. "I don't see anyone."

"It's not a person, it's a cat," Ben said. "It's stalking us, but it won't be able to follow us if we go through the more populated parts of town."

"How do you know any of this?"

"The same way I know you're Juju and not some wagon driver."

Juju seemed to consider it for a moment, then turned away from the direct route to the safe house.

Ben kept his head down and his mind alert, feeling for any source of magic. He felt a strong presence, approaching fast. He turned his attention to his circle, holding his breath as a mule flew past, soaring several hundred feet overhead.

When he reached out again, the stalker was lost—too far away to feel.

"I think we're clear," he muttered without looking up.

Juju adjusted course, following behind another wagon loaded with casks. They meandered through town, Ben occasionally feeling the presence of an artifact, most of which seemed to be owned by either priests or very well-dressed people usually accompanied by a number of armed men.

He kept his senses alert until they pulled into the carriage house and closed the door. Hound and Ellie were waiting when they rolled in.

"Get what you need?" Hound asked.

"I'm not sure," Ben said, motioning for them to follow him upstairs.

"The place is more imposing than I had expected," he said, studying Juju's map. "We could attack and probably kill a few priests, but we would be exposed and I think Juju's right about drawing the wyrm out like that."

Juju nodded respectfully to Ben.

"I think we need to wait for Kaid. He'll bring weapons that will give us a whole new range of options."

"And who is this Kaid?" Juju asked.

"He's the guy that gave me these," Ben said, deploying a hundred splinters and forming them into a dart.

"I wondered about that," Juju said. "Very well. When is this man Kaid due to arrive?"

"Within the week," Ben said, hoping to hear from him much sooner than that.

"And in the meantime?" Juju asked.

"We gather more information. Maybe we can figure out where the priests sleep—or better yet, where do they congregate to worship?"

"There's a large temple within the palace grounds. The priesthood assemble there every morning at dawn."

"Sounds like a target," Hound said.

"Agreed," Ben said. "Now we wait."

"I hate that part," Hound said, wandering away from the map table.

"In that case, I need to tend to a delivery for the estate," Juju said. "Appearances and all."

Ben watched out the window as Juju drove the empty wagon away, waiting until he was out of sight before turning to Penelope.

She smiled, holding up a tiny opaque vial. "I need a large dish or a puddle."

"How about a horse trough?" Ellie asked.

Penelope considered it for a moment and shrugged. "That should work."

Everyone followed her downstairs, gathering around the trough, watching as she removed the stopper and held the vial upside down over the water. Moments passed before a drop began to form on the lip. She shook the vial and the drop splashed into the water. She quickly replaced the stopper and put the vial away.

The surface of the water became silvery, almost reflective.

Penelope whispered a word as she slowly dipped her finger into the water. After a moment, they could see an image of the stables and themselves on the surface of the water. Then the scene shifted rapidly, moving thousands of feet into the sky, turning and surveying the city, picking out the palace and moving there in a blink.

"There," Ben said, pointing to the building in question.

The view fixed and stopped for a moment. The building was two stories and perfectly square—just over a hundred feet on a side. The back was part of the palace wall, and the main entrance was on the opposite wall. There was a forty-foot courtyard in the middle of the building, with a balcony walkway all the way around the second level. The side entrance shared a dead-end alley with the building right next door.

The view shifted. Ben watched, recording every moment for detailed analysis. Penelope was thorough and methodical in her search. She started on the top floor, moving from room to room. One side was servants quarters. The other side was the nursery.

Ben felt his breath catch when his nephew came into view, napping in his crib, the only child in the entire building. But not the only person. Ben counted a dozed Dragon Guard, five servants, three nurses, and one more nurse that was actually a mule. By the time Penelope's magic had run its course, Ben had a clear picture of the entire building, including guard locations.

"That was a neat trick," Hound said. "Where do you come by something like that?"

"It was payment for services rendered," Penelope said. "I'm afraid I can't say more than that."

Hound smiled, chuckling.

"Any luck getting us into the palace?" Ben asked.

"I can get three of us in," Penelope said. "I don't have a way out though."

"We'll figure that out later," Ben said. "Tell me about getting in."

"I know a guy who's a bread-delivery man. Every morning, he loads up freshly baked bread and he delivers it to most of the buildings in the palace compound, including the nursery. He can fit three people under his load without drawing attention.

"He'll make his delivery to the nursery, then turn around and deliver to the library next door. Since it's so early, there's nobody there to receive the delivery so he has a key to a storeroom. You will wait there for half an hour after he leaves.

"He wants five gold."

Ben dug his coin pouch out and poured out four coins. He'd spent a lot bribing and buying transportation, often spending freely. Now, he was short—and there was only one coin left, his lucky coin. He pulled it out of his pocket, rubbing the face of it with his thumb, a pang of loss and grief in his belly as he carefully laid it on the table with the others.

Penelope gathered them up.

"We'll need to get there before dark and stay the night in the driver's carriage house. Also, we need to know who's going in."

"We are," Hound and Ellie said in unison.

"What do you want the rest of us to do?" Kayla asked.

"Stay here and make sure Juju doesn't cause any problems," Ben said.

"Hold on," Penelope said. "I should be going with you. The man is my contact, and I have a lot of experience at this kind of thing."

"No," Ben said. "I can almost guarantee there's going to be some fighting. Take us to your man and then come back here."

"You still haven't mentioned how you plan to get out."

"She has a point," Hound said.

"Off the roof," Ben said. "We tie off and slide down into the street right at dawn, just as everything gets busy."

"That exit plan could use some work," Hound said.

"At the moment it's our best option," Ben said. "The baby's on the second floor, so we're halfway there. Take the two guards on the roof and we're outside the walls."

"Not saying it can't work, just looks a bit thin," Hound said.

"I know," Ben said. "I'm hoping Kaid will show up soon."

"Now *that*, is an exit plan."

"Either way, we need to make our move," Ben said. "The longer we stay here, the more chance we have of being discovered."

"I guess I can't argue with that," Hound said. "When do we leave?"

"The best option would be to have Juju drive us there," Penelope said.

"He might want an explanation," Ben said. "One that I'm not prepared to give him."

"We'll tell him we have a plan to assassinate Ick," Penelope said with a shrug, "but we have to go tonight. It's plausible enough that he'll go along for as long as he needs to."

Chapter 25

Ben sat with his knees to his chest, focusing on his circle. Homer was pressed up next to him, much to the consternation of the bread man. White cotton bags full of warm bread were piled on top of them.

The wagon stopped at the gate, the back door opened. Muffled voices exchanged pleasantries, the door closed and they started moving again.

"Data burst received … decompressing…" the augment said.

"Hey Kid, looks like you're walking right into the belly of the beast," Kaid's voice said in Ben's mind. "I'm overhead and I'm ready to assist as needed. Maintain radio silence until you really need me. The moment you broadcast, that place will spin up like a pissed-off hornet's nest. And remember, if you need a ride, I'm going to need you to keep the magic off me. I sure hope you know what you're doing, Kid. Kaid out."

"Back to plan A," Ben said. "Kaid's overhead."

"Nice," Hound said, his voice muffled through the bread.

Ben counted the stops, the door opening for each, a bag of bread or two taken by the driver. The sense of tension grew as they neared their target. Ben replayed the layout of the building in his mind, noting where each guard had been, planning his course to the room where Robert was being kept.

The wagon stopped. The door opened. The bread man put a finger to his lips as he gathered bags of bread, then closed the door. Ben listened intently to the conversation with the guard. Courteous and professional on both sides. The wagon jostled as the driver jumped back onto the seat, then it turned around, coming up to the library service entrance.

The door opened.

"Wait for a moment," the bread man said. "I'll open the door first."

Ben moved toward the back of the wagon, reaching out with his feelings, and finding magic from two sources, both familiar.

A mule in the nursery—entirely expected.

Hoondragon in the library.

Ben chided himself for not predicting that Frank would lay in wait for him here.

"Trap," Ben said. "Frank's here."

They piled out quickly, Ben scanning in all directions for a threat while reaching out with his feelings for magic. Hoondragon felt like it was higher. Ben looked up as Frank stepped into view from the roof of the library, flanked by six Dragon Guard, all with rifles at the ready.

"I've been waiting for you, Ben," Frank said through his helmet's face shield. "You've lost. I can burn you with a word. Surrender and I'm sure my master will make it quick."

"Your only master is your own ego," Ben said. "The dragon is going to see that in about five seconds. Your only chance out of this is to lay that sword down and walk away."

"No!" Frank shouted. "Why does everyone want me to give up my sword?" he asked the man beside him. "Anyway, surrender or die. At this point, I don't really care."

The bolt on the service door of the nursery slammed open, followed by the door.

A guard stepped out. "What's going on out here?" he demanded.

"Go!" Ben shouted, sending all of his splinters overhead and forming them into a shield as he turned and raced for the door.

Ellie reached the startled guard first … he was halfway through drawing his sword when she stabbed him in the throat, a quick jab withdrawn the moment it hit. She crashed into his breastplate with her shoulder, knocking him backward. He stumbled and fell on his butt, his hands going to his throat in a futile attempt to prevent his lifeblood from draining away.

Ben reached the door two steps behind Hound. Fire and heat washed down behind him, engulfing the entire alley in orange, splashing over the surface of the shield as Ben dove through the door. He deconstructed his shield and re-called his splinters as he came to his feet and surveyed the room.

Aside from the door they'd entered through, there were three doors leading out of the room, two on the far wall and one on the wall to his right. Ben already knew his route. He passed Ellie as she was lowering a guard to the ground, the tip of her blade guiding his dying body to the floor from underneath his chin.

Ben kicked the door, stepping into the courtyard and scanning the scene. It was exactly as expected. He was on one end of a walk that ran the length of the wall and ended in a staircase leading to the second floor. An identical path ran along the wall to the right, ending in the other staircase to the second-floor balcony. A pair of Dragon Guard were posted on each staircase, one at the top and one at the bottom.

Ben picked the two guards that were most immediately in his way and sent two darts to kill them. Both men fell a moment later, then those two hundred splinters went dead. He raced forward, closing the distance to the stairs. He noted that Bertha fired. Data in the background.

He was close now. He'd been working and fighting and bleeding for this for so long, it almost didn't seem real. He hit the stairs. Ellie was right behind him. He could feel her mind seamlessly meshed with his. Bertha fired again. A man yelped. Someone was ringing a bell.

His plan was coming apart, but he couldn't give up now, he was so close. He reached the top of the stairs, the feeling of magic very close now. His two hundred disabled splinters came back to life, re-forming into two darts. Bright orange flared behind him as he reached for the door latch.

"You son of a bitch," Hound shouted from the bottom of the stairs, firing two rounds in rapid succession. A man on the roof grunted, then fell into the courtyard with a thud followed by a groan.

Ben opened the door.

"Hello, Benjamin," the Warlock said, cradling baby Robert in one arm and holding his staff in the other, black magic actively swirling around the claw.

For a moment Ben was stunned, simply unable to reconcile what he was seeing with what he expected to see, but then he regained control.

A dart leapt at the Warlock, coming apart harmlessly as it passed the threshold of the magic circle burned into the floor around him.

Ben stepped forward.

The Warlock raised his staff. "Think carefully. Do you really want to engage me while I hold this child?"

Ben stopped, the point of the Dragon's Fang never wavering.

"You know what I want," the Warlock said. "I trust that you still have the summoning stone that I gave you."

He smiled with a sense of deep satisfaction, turned and stepped through a portal that Ben hadn't even noticed because it was sideways to him. He rushed forward just in time to see the Warlock wave as the doorway quickly shrank and then vanished.

"Shit!" Ben shouted.

"There's more coming," Ellie said.

Ben raced back to the top of the stairs. The one remaining guard on the roof was still ringing the alarm bell. Hound had killed the rest—four corpses scattered across the courtyard.

He opened a broadcast channel.

"Emergency evac. Under attack. Come in hot and fast."

Simultaneously, Frank rushed into the courtyard from the side entrance, followed by six Dragon Guard. A mule burst from a door halfway down the second-story walkway … it turned on Ben and pulled back to hurl a javelin.

Ben thrust two hundred splinters forward, forming a shield just as the mule threw the weapon at him. It hit with such force that it broke the shield and hit Ben right in the chest. He flew back, landing hard, a sharp, dangerous pain where his ballistic shirt had stopped the javelin from penetrating, and a dull ache where he'd landed on his butt.

The mule drew back and threw again. Ben re-formed his shield and angled it at forty-five degrees to the direction of impact, causing the javelin to be deflected and embed itself into the wall.

Ben shoved his pain aside and staggered to his feet as a grenade exploded. He glanced over and saw the remains of most of Frank's Dragon Guard sprayed around the yard. Frank was down and there was still smoke rising from the spot where Hound's grenade had hit.

Ben surged forward, closing with the mule. Another javelin hit his shield and violently deflected into the wall beside him. His circle crossed the mule. Ben sent two darts—one targeting each arm. Two loud cracks added to the tumult of the battle as Ben's darts accelerated past the sound barrier and hit the inside of the mule's elbows, one a fraction of a second after the first.

Each dart exploded into its constituent splinters on impact, violently tearing the mule's arms off at the elbows. It shrieked, pain and shock transforming into rage and fury in an instant. It pulled back to breathe fire. Ben didn't hesitate, racing toward the monster, positioning his shield to defend as needed—and it was. A gout of flame shot toward him, hitting his shield and running its course in a second or so, but delivering enough heat that his splinters were flashing warnings in his mind's eye.

He transformed the shield into a swarm of splinters and sprayed them into the mule's face, blinding and disorienting it as he covered the last few steps, the Fang back and ready, coiled for the strike.

It was flawless. His blade pierced through the mule's heart and two inches out its back.

"Look out!" Ellie shouted from behind Ben.

He looked over just in time to see a Dragon Guard aiming straight at him. The weapon fired. Orange death rushed toward him. Ben rolled toward the wall, pulling the dying mule, still impaled on his blade, in front of him. He yanked his blade free and dove to the side, trying to miss Homer as he skittered to safety as well. The fire hit the mule across the back, its one wing providing the moment of cover that Ben needed to get clear. That section of the balcony went up with a whoosh.

Hound was at the base of the stairs. Frank was on his feet and moving toward him. Ellie was facing off against half a dozen Dragon Guard that had gone up the far staircase and were approaching along the second-floor balcony. Six men were also coming for Ben.

"I want them alive!" Frank shouted, forestalling the man aiming his rifle at Ellie.

Ben moved to the corner of the building, the path he'd come from cut off by fire, the path before him occupied by enemies. The first two men to cross into Ben's circle died a moment later, his darts whirling in the air like angry bees.

Ellie waited for the first soldier, danced past his blade and stabbed him in the face. He fell back. A moment later, she was in a pitched battle against two men fighting side by side.

Ben sent a single dart weaving its way through the grey matter of the four men still advancing on him. Once they were dead or dying, he sent his dart across the courtyard, quickly but methodically killing the five men attacking Ellie.

As he maneuvered his dart from one target to the next, felling them with headshots, one by one, the sound of Bertha firing rapidly nagged at his attention. He killed the last man and looked down to see his brother standing in front of Hound, the bloody tip of Hoondragon protruding from Rufus's back. He stood, back arched in pain, Bertha on the ground beside him, blood dribbling from his chin, eyes wide.

Everything seemed to slow down. More Dragon Guard were coming, a dozen more arriving in that moment, but none of that mattered. Ben watched in stunned, surreal helplessness as Frank yanked the blade free.

The big man-at-arms slumped to his knees, both hands holding in his guts. Frank looked up at Ben, his armored mask inscrutable, but his intent clear. He raised his blade and brought it down, cleanly taking Rufus Hound's head.

For what seemed like a long time, Ben stood there staring at the headless corpse of the man who had stood by him from the beginning, all out of loyalty to

his grandfather, a loyalty that Ben didn't even understand, and there he lay …
dead.

"This is on you, Ben," Frank shouted, pointing the dripping blade of his
black sword at him.

"Do something or you're going to die," Homer said.

Ben snapped out of his daze as four more men reached the top of the
stairs, all four turning toward him. Four more were advancing on Ellie, backing
her up toward the staircase. She turned and ran, reaching the stairs as Frank neared
the top.

Ben sent two darts, both targeting the back of his brother's sword hand,
both hitting, the second succeeding at knocking the sword from his grip. Ellie
seized the moment, stabbing high, forcing him to raise his shield as she took hold
of the railing with her free hand and kicked him in the chest. He toppled over
backward and slid down the stairs, landing on top of Hound's corpse.

"Look out!" Ben shouted.

Ellie turned just in time for a Dragon Guard to hit her in the side of the
head with a closed fist. She fell like a bag of beans, going still, her mind going
quiet.

Frank regained his feet. "You've lost!" he shouted. "Just give up,
already."

A mule landed in the middle of the courtyard as another dozen Dragon
Guard flowed in.

"Burn him!" the mule commanded.

Dragon-fire rifles came up.

Ben deployed his remaining two hundred splinters as a shield on the
courtyard side and raced for the stairs leading to the roof. Flames hit his shield,
splashing in front and behind him. He leapt over a puddle of fire between him and
the staircase, glancing up and seeing Homer already at the top.

He kept his shield on the outside of the railing, defending against another
wave of flames. Once he was on the roof, he deconstructed the shield and re-called
the splinters, glancing to see them flow up over the edge just in time to see the
mule launch, rising twenty feet above the roof as its malevolent cat eyes locked
onto Ben.

Telemetry data began to flow into his mind, describing the descent and
landing place of the skiff. He took note as he re-formed his splinters into a shield
at the edge of his twenty-foot circle and used it to deflect the mule aside and
behind him as the monster tipped forward into an attack dive. It snarled, tumbling
awkwardly and crashing to the ground, then coming back to its feet with alarming
speed.

The Dragon Guard ringing the bell noticed Ben and reached for his rifle.
Ben splintered the shield and sent a dart at the soldier, even as he tried
unsuccessfully to re-call the splinters that he'd used to attack Frank's hand.

Fire washed across his path. Ben skidded to a stop, glancing back at the
mule, now ten feet off the ground and gaining altitude, then glancing at the fire. A
whoosh of heat and air flared the fire, but then extinguished it. The skiff landed

not twenty feet in front of Ben, coming down hard enough to crack the stones of the roof. The back door dropped open.

The mule roared. Ben could feel the tech-dampening magic pulsating from the creature as he focused his power on the skiff.

"I'm helpless in here," Kaid said, a hint of panic in his voice.

Ben raced onboard, two steps behind Homer. He felt stabbing, almost debilitating guilt and cowardice as he projected his shield and communicated to Kaid to launch.

As the skiff was lifting off, a mule futilely breathed fire onto its shields. Then a roar broke the predawn chaos. As the back door closed, Ben caught a glimpse of the wyrm.

The dragon was coming.

Ben felt a wave of magical power hit him like a shockwave, nearly collapsing his circle. He redoubled his focus, clearing his mind and bringing his entire concentration to seeing the circle around the ship, protecting, concealing, and defending them from any and all magical threats.

Another wave of magic hit them, this one harder and longer. Ben held for several seconds, but then the sheer force of the magic shattered his concentration. His circle failed.

The skiff began to descend.

"I'm losing power!"

Ben reestablished his shield, knowing that the dragon was just going to overpower him again. The thought came and he implemented it in a microsecond, taking control of the skiff's laser and directing it at the dragon at full power.

The wyrm roared, but the force of his mental attack against Ben's circle lessened. The skiff shot straight into the air. The dragon launched a moment later, gaining altitude on them rapidly. Ben refocused the aim of the laser and started tracking him with it. At first, the dragon flinched, rolling aside, then he began casting a spell, black smoke forming a dense cloud all around him.

Now Ben was tracking a cloud, and it was gaining on them.

"How high can this thing go?" he asked.

"Suborbital," Kaid said.

"Good, get there faster."

"We're already at max acceleration."

The door separating the personnel cabin from the cargo cabin opened. Ben took a seat next to Kaid at the helm, scanning the instruments, his eyes landing on a rearview camera.

The black cloud was gaining on them.

"Can we go faster if we're not going up?"

"Yep," Kaid said, working the controls.

A whirring from somewhere behind him tugged at Ben's attention, but his eyes were fixed to the screen showing the approaching black cloud of death.

They started forward.

Ben could feel the magic pressing against his defenses.

"Can you shoot him with something else … anything else?"

He focused on his circle.

"Hang on," Kaid said.

Ben could see the operation unfold in the data readouts in his mind's eye, not that he was paying attention.

A missile detached, falling toward the dragon and the cloud of unnatural black smoke enshrouding him. The laser flashed a moment later, detonating the rather large ex-plus charge right in the dragon's path. The explosion caught him full in the face, blasting away the cloud of black surrounding him and blasting the dragon away from them. He fell tumbling for several seconds before he regained control.

The explosion hit the skiff, causing it to lurch forward. Ben's augment indicated that the shield was holding. He kept focusing on his circle, withstanding another two assaults from the dragon as they gained altitude.

Then they were in low orbit. Gravity all but vanished. Kaid rolled the ship so they could see the world.

Ben looked up and lost all sense of himself—instead he became the experience, stepped so fully into the moment that he forgot he was a person, let alone one with a name. In that moment, the vast, incomprehensible scope of reality challenged his sanity. The beauty of the world hanging like a blue jewel in the black brought a lump to his throat and a moment later he was weeping uncontrollably.

"Whoa ... Kid?" Kaid said, uneasiness in his voice. "You all right?"

Ben wept, surrendering to the sadness, the loss, the grief, and the soul-crushing terror of even thinking about Ellie in the hands of his enemy. The rational part of his mind told him that this was foreseen. He'd been expecting it to happen.

Yet, now that it had, he wasn't sure he had the strength to even stand up, let alone go fight a dragon.

Hound's death was still beyond Ben's ability to comprehend. He could see the horrific beheading of his friend—in fact, he couldn't stop seeing it, and even still, he didn't fully believe it. He couldn't.

Kaid took a slow deep breath and let it out. "I can see that you've been through a lot..." he started, clearly uncertain.

Ben wiped the tears from his face, very deliberately pushing his grief aside while making himself a promise to give it the attention it deserved at a later date.

"Release data," he commanded his augment, streaming all of his records, files, and experiences over the past several weeks to Kaid. He waited a moment for the transfer to complete.

"The short version is, we hit the dragon with an orbital weapon at Battle Mountain and made him bleed, but he was able to use his magic to get away. We came here to rescue Imogen's baby, but the Warlock got there first and took him. Frank killed Rufus and took Ellie. I walked us right into a disaster."

Kaid was quiet for a moment.

"What's our next move?" he asked, gently.

"We pick up our people and get the hell out of here," Ben said, sending the coordinates of the carriage house with his augment.

"Looks like the dragon is still circling. We'll wait a while, maybe 'til dark. Go lie down in the doc … it'll check you out and give you a booster shot."

Ben didn't ask. He was too tired and defeated to care. All he wanted was oblivion. He pushed a button on the wall and a panel slid up, then a shelf slid out, complete with a rather firm pillow. He lay down. The shelf withdrew into the wall and the panel slid closed. Readouts began to flow across his mind's eye. He deactivated them and tried to meditate. Sometime later, he woke when the doc opened up and the shelf extended into the cabin.

"How're you feeling?" Kaid asked.

"Better but still not very good."

"I reviewed your adventures—the highlights at least. You've been busy. I especially liked the part where the dragon flies through the air and bounces. I had to watch that a few times."

Ben's expression remained sullen.

"Losing people under your command is never easy," Kaid said. "But it is part of war, and that's what this is."

Ben nodded, less convincingly than he would have liked.

"It'll be dark soon," Kaid said. "I'll need your head in the game if we're going to go back down there."

Ben nodded, more firmly this time as he took his seat beside Kaid.

"Is Kayla down there?" Kaid asked.

"Should be," Ben said.

"Good, I can send her a message, tell her to be ready. I don't want to be on the ground any longer than necessary."

Ben concentrated on his circle, willing it to protect against magical detection and against tech-dampening spells. They came down gently, compared to the last landing Kaid had made, setting the craft just outside the door to the carriage-house stables.

Kayla, Derek, Penelope, Rollo, and Juju were standing in the dark looking at the skiff as the back door flopped open. Ben didn't get up, instead maintaining his concentration.

"Hey folks," Kaid said. "Good to see you again, Kayla, Derek. Time is short, so if you're coming with us, then come on."

Kayla didn't hesitate.

Her mother caught her by the hand. "Are you sure about this?"

"Absolutely," Kayla said. "Mother, this is Colonel Kaid. Colonel, this is my mother, Penelope Adara."

"Pleased to meet you, ma'am," he said with a respectful nod. "Now, I don't mean to be pushy, but we're exposed and vulnerable, so I'd like to be on our way."

She nodded once and followed Kayla and Derek into the skiff with Rollo close behind.

Juju didn't move.

"Ben says to tell your Patriarch to attack when the ground shakes," Kaid said, returning to the pilot's seat as the door closed.

They lifted off a few moments later, gaining altitude quickly. Ben felt magic in the distance, but nothing directed at them. His anxiety faded a few minutes later when they were at suborbital altitude and cruising toward Mt. Rainier.

Chapter 26

"Ah, there you are," he said, smiling down at her.

Ellie blinked the double vision from her eyes, trying to see the man kneeling over her. Her sight came into focus as the pain in her cheek registered. She groaned, gently probing the side of her face.

All of it came rushing back to her. She looked around frantically, searching for Ben.

He was gone.

Her heart sank as she took in the dozen or so Dragon Guard surrounding her.

"My name is Noisome Ick," said the greying, slightly built man kneeling over her. "I'm told that your name is Ellie."

She sat up, scanning for a weapon.

He stood, smiling at her. "You have been disarmed. Not that a weapon would do you any good at the moment."

The air stirred. She looked up and saw the dragon land on the roof of the nursery, his catlike eyes peering down at her. She locked eyes with the beast and her breath caught in her throat. Despite her desire to show no fear, she couldn't help the trembling that overcame her in the face of such a terrifying creature. The intelligence in his eyes was only overshadowed by the malice she saw there.

Ick looked up at the wyrm, nodding solemnly.

"As you wish, Master," he said, seeming to respond to some unspoken command.

The dragon launched into the sky.

"Hey, what about me?" Frank said, as the dragon disappeared, the sound of his wings beating the air fading into the distance.

Ick turned slowly, eyeing Frank curiously. "You have failed, Sword Bearer."

Frank seemed on the verge of saying something intemperate, but caught himself.

"It's not my fault," he said. "How was I supposed to know that my brother has a spaceship?"

Ick smiled thinly, regarding him without answering for several moments before he turned back to Ellie and smiled more warmly.

"Can you walk?" he asked.

She frowned, levering herself to her feet, still a bit shaken but able enough. She nodded, scanning her surroundings again, looking for any hope of escape and finding none.

"Excellent," Ick said. "Please, come with me."

"Wait," Frank said. "What about me?"

Ick turned back to him as if he'd forgotten about him entirely.

"You will come as well," he said, not bothering to wait for Frank's response before turning back to Ellie.

She was staring at Hound's severed head, his dead eyes staring back at her. She swallowed her pain, closing her eyes and looking away.

"Where's Ben?" she asked.

"I was hoping you could tell me," Ick said. "My master would very much like to meet him. I must say, he has proven to be quite resourceful … and far bolder than expected. Alas, that he would expend such effort and resources to rescue an infant child only serves to highlight his naiveté."

"I think you mean his humanity," Ellie said.

"No … I mean to say that he is a foolish child playing at a game that he simply cannot win. Please, come."

Several Dragon Guard stepped closer to punctuate the polite command. She followed reluctantly.

"Where are you taking me?"

"To the palace," Ick said. "My master will determine your worth to him and dispose of you as he sees fit."

She stopped in her tracks.

A Dragon Guard shoved her forward.

Ick raised a hand to his men, forestalling any further contact.

"You can walk with me and we can have a civilized conversation, or my men can carry you. Either way, you will face the judgment of your god."

She burst out laughing, albeit bitterly and somewhat forced. "God? Your master isn't a god, maybe a demon, but certainly not divine."

Ick smiled, laughing softly. "Godliness is a function of power," he said. "My master will live for a thousand years and he wields a power beyond human comprehension. You will stand helplessly before him as he decides your fate. Divinity doesn't enter into the equation."

He gestured for her to continue.

She glanced at the men surrounding her and started walking again.

"Excellent," Ick said. "Now, tell me about your beloved."

"No."

"Once again, I have many ways of compelling your obedience," Ick said. "Though I would much prefer a simple conversation."

She walked in silence.

"How does he prevent detection of the egg?" he asked.

She didn't answer.

"I can sense the artifact that you have incorporated into your sword," he said. "I suspect that you can feel its power as well. Yet the egg, a far more potent item, is beyond my senses, even when Benjamin carried it right into my master's palace.

"Then there's the question of the technology that he's brought to the fight. Such sophisticated devices should be easy for my master to defeat, yet they remain functional in his presence."

"Maybe your master isn't as powerful as you think," she said.

"Oh, child, I fear that you will find out just how powerful my master really is."

She stopped again. This time the soldiers surrounding her stopped as well.

"Why would you sell out humanity?" she said. "Why would you side with a monster like the dragon, do his bidding, kill for him?"

"Power," Ick said with a shrug and an almost confused look. He gestured for her to continue walking, only continuing when she complied.

"I was the Chief Healthcare Officer for the NACC," he said. "It seems like a lifetime ago … in many ways I suppose it was. I had some measure of power, but not enough to do all that I wished to do. The bureaucracy was stifling. Even in such a lofty executive position, I had many others to answer to, far too many. It was almost impossible to accomplish anything. Quite frustrating, I must tell you.

"Then, one day, a man came to see me about the dragons. At first I didn't believe him, but he offered proof. Once I understood what was coming, I resolved to serve a new master, one with the power to make things happen without endless meetings or consensus. Those early days were quite exciting, the possibility of discovery always lurking at the edge of my mind. Ultimately, my master and his kind were victorious, and I was rewarded for my loyalty."

"You killed the whole world," she said. "How can you even live with yourself?"

He shrugged offhandedly. "The world was broken. It was teetering on the edge of war and financial ruin. There were simply too many people to be effectively ruled. Something had to be done to establish order—in many ways, the dragons are our salvation."

"Salvation? Are you kidding? How can mass murder be salvation?"

He nodded thoughtfully.

"Many died, yes. But their sacrifice was necessary to usher in a new era. Humanity will go forward into the future, serving a god that is worthy of their worship. Unlike all of the false gods of the past, the imaginary beings conjured from the minds of men to compel servitude, our new god is real, flesh and blood, power and magic, all embodied in a being who is actually capable of working wonders in the world."

"What you call wonders, I call atrocity," she said.

"Isn't ultimate peace worth a bit of blood?"

"A bit? Peace?" she said. "What the hell are you even talking about?"

"Imagine a world without war, without scarcity, without strife. Imagine a world where everyone knows their place and purpose. It's a beautiful future that we are working to build."

"Maybe it looks pretty good for someone who lives in a palace," she said, gesturing to the looming structure before them. "But it sucks for everyone else."

"Admittedly, we're still in a transition period, in large measure because of people like you and your friends. Once the world is pacified and comes to accept the new order, there will be peace and prosperity like humanity has never known before."

"Fat lot of good that does the nine billion people you killed."

"The cost of progress," he said.

She opened her mouth, then shut it again, shaking her head as Ick led her through the palace gates. Several attendants were waiting.

Ick stopped and faced her.

"You will go with these people. They will prepare you for your audience. If you cooperate and obey, you will be treated with dignity and courtesy. If you resist, you will be met with force."

He reached out to touch the lurid bruise on her cheek. She flinched before he made contact.

"You are quite beautiful. It would be a shame to see you suffer any further injury."

He turned to Frank. "You will also prepare for your audience, Sword Bearer."

"My name is Hoondragon."

Ick smiled thinly. "That remains to be seen."

"For what it's worth, he's an asshole and a liar," Ellie said. "I wouldn't believe a word he says."

"You bitch," Frank said, taking a step toward her. Several Dragon Guard intervened quickly, stopping him in his tracks. "What the hell are you trying to do?"

She leaned forward, looking him in the eye, past the soldiers between them.

"I'm trying to get you killed, you piece of shit," she said very deliberately.

Frank stared at her with fury dancing in his eyes.

Ick chuckled, his smile almost sincere. "I genuinely hope my master spares you, Ellie," he said, turning away and walking off briskly, leaving her and Frank surrounded by soldiers and functionaries.

Two young women bowed to Ellie.

"Please come with us, My Lady," one said. "We will see to your bath and gown."

She started to protest, but the fear in the young woman's eyes stopped her. She nodded instead, following behind them. Four soldiers escorted the women as they made their way through the palace to a large, lavishly appointed suite.

"Please undress," one of her attendants said.

"I'll draw you a bath," said the other.

Ellie took a deep breath and let it out slowly while she looked in the mirror. Her clothes had disappeared while she bathed. Now she wore a simple white linen dress with nothing underneath save a pair of slippers. Her attendants had spent an hour grooming her, brushing her hair, cleaning the road grime from under her fingernails, and finishing with a yellow ribbon woven into her hair.

She had tried to engage the young women, to draw them into conversation and gain some information about her circumstances, but they were resolute in their unwillingness to discuss anything except her preparations.

For a moment she almost smiled at the reflection in the mirror—she looked like a princess. A knock on the door brought her back to her terrifying reality.

"Ah, you look quite lovely," Ick said, smiling warmly. "My master will be pleased. It's time."

She started trembling, took a deep breath, raised her chin and set out with purpose.

Ick silently led her through the palace until they arrived at a huge set of double doors, a passage clearly designed with the dragon in mind. Two Dragon Guard, wearing much more ornate armor than most, opened the door, revealing a cavernous room.

Ellie shivered for a moment until the sound of footsteps drew her attention and Frank came around the corner. He was dressed in a black linen robe and was carrying his sword in its scabbard. Two Dragon Guard trailed behind him.

He stopped in his tracks when he saw Ellie.

"What's she doing here?"

"Same as you," Ick said, gesturing for them both to enter the room.

When she saw the hesitation in Frank's eyes, Ellie set out into the enormous chamber with feigned confidence, scanning the room as she walked.

The doors closed behind her, dimming the already poor lighting even further.

"That will do," Ick said, after she'd crossed nearly half the room.

She stopped and turned around. "Now what?"

"Patience," Ick said, gesturing for Frank to stand a good twenty feet away from Ellie and taking his place between them.

She felt his arrival before she saw him … magic pulsing in her with each heartbeat.

The air stirred at the far end of the room, something moving in the shadows—then faintly glowing eyes peering out of the darkness.

She forced herself to breathe, glancing over at Frank and taking some comfort in the paleness of his complexion.

The dragon advanced quickly, bounding toward them with a grace and quickness that seemed unreasonable for his size, stopping a dozen feet away, his barbed tail flicking around behind him like that of an angry cat.

He stared intently at her, and she stared back, willing herself to hold her ground, to show no fear. His head extended toward her, his giant snout approaching slowly. She stopped breathing and started trembling, but didn't flinch or step back.

He nudged her, knocking her onto the ground like a plaything before withdrawing and turning his attention to Frank, who fell to his knees the moment the wyrm's eyes fixed on him.

"I swear to serve you, Master," he said, a tremor rippling through his voice.

"Stand up," Ick said.

Frank looked up at the dragon, then back down, his trembling becoming more pronounced.

Ick chuckled mockingly. "Is that fear I smell?" he said.

Frank didn't move.

"Rise and face your master, or die on your knees," Ick said.

Frank seemed unsure, coming to his feet hesitantly, still not looking the dragon in the eye.

"Good," Ick said. "Report."

Frank looked around quickly, panic in his eyes.

Ick reached out toward Frank, his hand clenching into a fist quickly. Frank stepped forward as if in the grip of some invisible power and began to speak. He told of his efforts to capture the egg, his attempts to kill Ben, and his collusion with the Warlock.

Ellie smiled at the look of terror on his face as he detailed how he and the Warlock had conspired to frame Noisome Ick for the creation of the collar. After several minutes of listening to his forced confession, Ick released the magical grip he had over him and Frank fell to his knees, weeping and groveling.

"I didn't mean it," he said. "It wasn't my fault. The Warlock made me do it. Please don't kill me…" His voice trailed off into uncontrollable sobbing.

Ick snorted derisively, turning to Ellie. "How would you deal with such failure and treachery?"

"Give me my sword and I'll show you."

Ick smiled, nodding approvingly. "I suspect that you would," he said, turning back to the dragon, as if hearing some unspoken command, then nodding as he turned back to her.

"You've heard the old saying that what you don't know can't hurt you. Few clichés are more wrong. In this case what your beloved doesn't know is going to kill him … and you will be the instrument of his doom, my dear. Your bond to him, that magical connection you share, the one that makes you such a formidable team in a fight—that will be his undoing. You see, you and he are soul-mated, forever linked."

Ellie looked around a bit frantically, her eyes landing on Frank's sword.

"Yes, now you are coming to see your ultimate defeat," Ick said. "That magical link you share can be used against you. My master will summon a prince of hell, a demon of power and darkness like nothing this world has known for many millennia. His servant will crawl inside you, taking your mind and your will … and your soul."

Ellie lunged for the sword, trying vainly to avoid Ick, but the high priest was faster, transforming in a blink into his true form, seven feet tall, batlike wings, and talons for fingernails. He snatched her up by the throat, lifting her a foot off the ground and stopping her in her tracks, holding her helplessly for a moment before tossing her to the floor and reverting to his human form again.

"Once my master's servant has claimed your soul, the demon will travel along the link to your beloved, burning the soul out of his body as well, claiming him as a puppet. In the end, your Benjamin will kill everyone you love and then hand-deliver the egg to my master."

She shook her head, wiping a tear from her face before regaining her feet.

"You'll fail," she said. "Ben will come for me, and when he does you and your master will die."

She wished her voice sounded more confident.

The wyrm started laughing, a most unsettling sound.

"It's unfortunate that it's come to this," Ick said. "I find that I've grown fond of your bluster and your façade of courage, even though I can smell the fear on you."

"I'm pretty sure that smell is coming from him," she said, motioning toward Frank and reclaiming her composure.

Ick started laughing.

"I think you might be right," he said, shaking his head sadly at Frank. "Stand and be judged, Sword Bearer."

Frank stayed on his knees, shaking his head tightly, clenching his eyes shut.

The dragon's head shot forward, stopping just a few feet from Frank with a roar so loud and terrifying that Frank toppled over backward, a stain spreading across the front of his robe as he scrambled backward, clambered to his feet and ran for the door.

Ick watched calmly, a sparkle of genuine mirth in his eyes as he shared a glance with Ellie. She watched Frank run away, propelled by terror and panic.

The dragon sprang over their heads, lithe and nimble, pouncing on Frank like a cat on a mouse, snatching him up in a single bite and swallowing him whole.

In one moment, Franklin Boyce was no more.

Ellie forced herself to start laughing, tipping her head back and pouring all of her fear and uncertainty into her mirth until it became real. Tears streamed down her face as she laughed.

The wyrm turned, moving toward her with more speed than she would have liked, but she held her ground. His snout got closer to her, and still she laughed. When he came within striking distance, she lunged, hitting him on the end of the snout with her bare fist, and cursing at the pain of landing the blow. The dragon flinched back, his head coiling like a snake as if readying to strike.

"Go on, kill me!" she shouted.

The dragon's head darted forward, but instead of snapping her up, he roared, the sound and force of it enough to cause her to stagger backward, covering her ears against the onslaught of noise.

Abruptly, the sound stopped, the dragon launched into the air, gliding into the darkness filling the far end of the room. And then he was gone.

Noisome Ick casually picked up Hoondragon by the scabbard and turned to face Ellie.

"Please, come, we'll be making a small trip," he said. "The ritual my master will be performing requires special preparation and a sizable quantity of treasure."

Ellie froze, a hint of a smile ghosting across her face, a faint glimmer of hope igniting within.

"Let me guess, the wyrm's treasure hoard is inside a cinder cone."

Noisome Ick frowned.

"How could you know that?"
She didn't answer.

Chapter 27

Benjamin didn't talk during the trip, instead he sat quietly in the copilot's seat and focused on his circle. It wasn't really necessary, the circle was all but automatic at this point, but it gave him something to think about other than what he was going to say to Dom and Imogen.

The journey took mere hours. Under any other circumstances, he would have welcomed such speed, but today he wanted to go anywhere but to his destination.

Information streamed through his mind as Kaid brought the skiff down out of the sky and maneuvered it to an open area a hundred feet from the Rainier bunker entrance. The ship gently touched the ground, its landing studs settling into the soil. Kaid powered down and opened the back door, the ramp lowering slowly, admitting the cool early-morning air.

Ben didn't move.

"Are you all right?" Homer asked.

"No."

Homer put his chin on Ben's leg and looked up at him with his big brown eyes. "You'll get her back," he said.

"Maybe ... or maybe I'll get her killed and deliver the egg to the dragon."

"You can't think like that," Homer said.

"Even if it's true?"

"Benjamin, you chose this course," Homer said. "Now that you've suffered the reality of war, the loss of it, the pain of it, you feel like you can't go on ... but you can because you must."

Ben put his hand on Homer's head and swallowed the lump rising in his throat.

He heard people outside, footsteps. Then Imogen was there at the back of the skiff, both hands over her belly.

"Did you find him? Is my son alive?" she asked through tears streaming down her face.

Ben couldn't answer, the words simply wouldn't come. All he could do was face her helplessly.

"Is he dead?" she asked, a look of unfathomable horror in her eyes.

Ben shook his head, tears beginning to roll down his face as well. He tried to speak again but the pain in his chest was too much to overcome.

Imogen sobbed, nearly falling save for John who was there to catch and support her.

Ben sat back down.

Kaid looked at him with hard but sympathetic eyes. "I know how bad this sucks, Kid. I've lost people. Right now, you feel broken. But that'll pass because it has to. You'll get up and go inside and tell your friends and family what happened, then you'll tell them what you're going to do about it. All the while, you'll feel like you're dying inside, but you'll do it anyway, because you have to."

He shook his head. "I'm not sure I can do this anymore."

"I am," Kaid said, offering his hand.

Ben looked at it for a moment as if he wasn't sure what to do with it.

"So the wyrm has my daughter, then," Dom said, standing just outside the door, his eyes fixed on Ben.

All he could do was nod helplessly.

Dom closed his eyes, clenching his jaw tightly, before walking away.

"Come on, Kid. We have work to do." Kaid reached down and gently, but firmly, lifted Ben to his feet.

"I'm sorry, Ben," Kayla said. "But Kaid's right. We're not done yet. I miss Rufus too, and when this is all over, I'm going to curl up in a ball and cry for a week. Right now, we need to plan our next move. We have a dragon to kill and we need you if we're going to have any hope of success."

"Success…" he said, as if the word was unknown to him.

"Come on," Kaid said, putting an arm around his shoulders and guiding him out of the skiff and toward the bunker entrance.

Ben walked numbly, every step feeling like it brought him one step closer to his doom. In the back of his mind he wondered at the absurdity of it—he could rush into battle, risk life and limb with little more than an elevated heart rate, but the idea of recounting the events that led up to Hound's demise and Ellie's capture seemed like death itself.

Zack was coming out of the bunker entrance just as they reached it. The moment he saw Ben, he gave him a big hug. "I'm so glad to see you," he said. "I've been really worried."

Ben nodded dumbly, struggling to hold back his tears. Zack winced at the pain in Ben's eyes.

"Come on, I'll show you the way," he said, leading them into the mountain.

The bunker entrance was dark, a light in the distance the only illumination until Kaid put a dozen splinter lanterns overhead. The route they took through the bunker was a blur. Ben put one foot in front of the other until he was standing in a room filled with people, all of them looking at him.

He scanned the room, his eyes falling on Imogen first. She looked broken, emotionally spent. His sense of numbness and detachment intensified. The look of anger and fear on Dom's face was next, an indictment of Ben's choices. He'd made the man a promise—a promise that he hadn't kept. He could rationalize it by telling himself that Ellie had made the choice, but if he was being honest with himself, he had wanted, maybe even needed her to be with him. Her strength and determination had centered him, but more than that, her love had always given him something worth fighting for.

Then his eyes landed on Gwen and he almost broke. She fixed him with a look of such uncompromising ferocity that he wasn't even sure he could stand in her presence, let alone report his failure.

"Snap out of it," Homer said. "You got through your grandfather's death, you can get through this. Besides, Ellie isn't dead, and you know where the dragon is going to take her, so do what she told you to do and use it to your advantage."

Ben looked down at his dog, sitting beside him, looking up with his big brown eyes. He took a breath, nodded to himself and then scanned the crowd again. There were many faces that he didn't know, people who had joined his cause, people that were depending on him, looking to him for leadership and maybe even salvation. In his mind, he detached from the bottomless pit of despair and loss that threatened to swallow him whole and stepped forward.

"My name is Benjamin Boyce…"

He proceeded to recount his journey, beginning with the orbital strike at Battle Mountain and ending where he stood. He spoke without emotion, neither embellishing his successes, nor glossing over his failures. The room was silent, every person present hanging on his every word. When he finished, the silence felt like a death sentence … and then Imogen sobbed and ran for the door.

All of the emotion that Ben had been holding back came rushing forth. Before his composure broke, he left the way he'd come and wandered outside the bunker until he found a small knoll with a view of the rising sun. There were just enough clouds to light the sky with orange and red as the world came back to life.

Homer lay down next to him without a word.

Ben let go and wept.

He sat there for a long time, letting his seemingly endless pain and fear flow out of him until he was spent. Once his emotions had run their course, his mind cleared and his sense of purpose returned.

"You've got incoming, Kid," Kaid's voice said in his head.

Ben looked around and saw Gwen coming his way. A little thrill of fear returned. Of all the people, she was the last one he wanted to face.

She came up and sat down next to him but didn't say anything for what seemed like a long time.

"A sunrise like this is almost enough to make you forget what's happening … almost," she said.

Ben nodded.

"I'm sorry about your friend."

Her words were gentle, almost soothing. A fact that did nothing to assuage his guilt or alleviate his anxiety.

"Thank you," he said. "Rufus was a good man."

They fell silent again for several more moments.

"Do you love my daughter?"

Ben blinked a few times, then turned toward her.

"Yes, more than I ever thought possible."

"Good, Ellie deserves someone who loves her fiercely. Now, I want you to listen to me."

Ben nodded, that feeling of anxiety returning in a rush.

"I want you to reach down and grab a hold of your balls and squeeze real hard—remind yourself that you're supposed to be a man. And then I want you to go get my daughter!"

Ben nodded, looking down at the grass. His indecision and emotional paralysis seemed to lift and he felt a sense of calm purpose settle over him. Ideas and plans began to form and flow through his mind.

"I'll be in shortly," he said. "I just need a few minutes to collect my thoughts."

"Fair enough," Gwen said. "But don't take too long. Everyone in there is afraid. They all seem to have a different plan and they all think their plan is the only way forward, but none of them is the Wizard."

And that was the crux of it.

He knew what he had to do, and he also knew that precious few of his friends and allies were going to understand or accept his decision, yet it had to be done.

After Gwen had vanished into the bunker, Ben found the glass bead that the Warlock had given him and placed it on a rock.

"Are you sure about this?" Homer asked.

"Yeah, I think I am. We need a win … I need a win."

He crushed the bead with the butt of his knife, and noted the hint of magic that emanated from it. Moments passed. He began to doubt … and then the Warlock appeared before him, a translucent projection smiling at him knowingly.

"Are you ready to make a deal?"

"I am," Ben said, coming to his feet. "The child, alive and well and unharmed for the egg."

"Excellent, Benjamin. I knew that you would make the right decision," the shimmering projection said, as it faded out of sight. A minute later a window in the fabric of space opened up not ten feet in front of Ben.

"Interesting," the Warlock said. "You're not anywhere near where I thought you would be."

"Show me the child."

"Very well, right to the business at hand." He motioned to someone and a man clearly possessed by the Warlock's magic stepped into view holding little Robert.

"And now the egg," the Warlock said.

Ben lifted the shoulder strap over his head and removed the dragon's egg. He looked at it for a moment, reevaluating his decision and coming to the same conclusion that had led him to this moment. He stepped forward, coming to within a few feet of the portal, taking care to maintain his circle close enough that it wouldn't disrupt the Warlock's magic.

The possessed man stepped through and held out the baby. Ben took the child and handed over the egg.

The Warlock smiled widely when the egg was placed in his hands.

"Well done, Benjamin. You've just ensured the dragon's defeat and saved your blood in the process. You have the makings of a great leader. I hope that one day we will become allies, perhaps even friends."

Ben snorted derisively. "Well, you know what they say, hope on one hand…"

He turned and walked away, cradling Robert in his arms.

He could feel the magic of the egg vanish as the portal closed behind him, leaving only the sharp and pointy feel of the Fang's magic. He smiled down at the child and the baby smiled back. Certainty of purpose flowed back into him with each step.

He could hear the argument and bickering taking place in the main hall of the bunker even before he reached the threshold. He was ten steps into the room before the argument turned to murmuring and then to silence as he crossed the distance to Imogen.

She stood, hope and fear in her glassy eyes when she saw him approaching. Her hand went to her mouth as tears began streaming down her face.

Without a word, Ben gently handed the baby to her. She sobbed as she held her child to her breast, then she held him out to look at him and started laughing through her tears.

"You brought him back to me, just like you promised," she said, putting her free arm around Ben and pulling him into an embrace. "Thank you, Ben, with all my heart, thank you!"

He held her for several moments until the Sage broke the silence.

"How is this possible?" he asked, the expression on his face revealing that he knew exactly how.

Ben disentangled himself from Imogen and faced the roomful of people.

"I gave the egg to the Warlock in exchange for Imogen's baby."

The Sage looked at him in utter dismay.

"How could you? You had no right! That egg was our only hope…"

"Stop talking," Ben said, holding up one hand. "That egg isn't our salvation, it's our doom. Before the sun sets, I'm going to pick a fight with the dragon and I don't want that egg anywhere near me when I do."

"You could have left it here!" the Sage said.

"With you, you mean," Ben said. "No, I gave it to the one person in this entire world who has any chance of keeping it from the dragon … and I got something priceless in return."

"All the world for a single child," the Sage said.

"Oh, shut up," Dom said, forestalling any further protest. "It looks to me like he made a pretty good bargain." He looked over to Imogen, lost in her baby's eyes.

"I agree," Gwen said, stepping up next to Dom. "So what's our plan, Benjamin?"

He took a deep breath, surveying the expectant and fearful faces, all looking to him for leadership.

"Colonel Kaid, what weapons have you brought?"

"I thought you'd never ask. The skiff has a laser and a rack of nine ex-plus missiles. I brought you a set of Mark-Three Close-Battle Armor and I've got a locker full of plasma rifles and a box of ex-plus charges. On top of that, there's me and those two pounders up in orbit."

Ben was accessing the specifications for the battle armor before Kaid had finished speaking. As the capabilities flowed through his mind, a plan began to take shape. The armor was a fully contained, airtight suit equipped with a vacuum generator and a gravity drive. It was armed with a flamer on the left wrist, a twenty-millimeter shotgun on the right wrist, and a bank of individually targeting, antipersonnel missiles across the back of the shoulders. The armor plating could shine so brightly that no human eye could look at it without suffering damage. It could project a six-foot-diameter force shield similar to his splinter shield, only much more robust. And finally, it was equipped with a force sword—six feet of energy blade projected around a scaffolding of specialized splinters that could be deployed on command.

All in all, it was an impressive piece of tech.

"I think we can work with that," Ben said. "Is there any way that you can generate an electrical charge? A big one?"

Kaid frowned, nodding after a moment's thought. "Several different ways," he said. "What did you have in mind?"

"I'm pretty sure that the dragon is vulnerable to electricity," Ben said. "I just need a way to deliver it."

"Wouldn't that be a bitch?" Kaid said. "We tried everything we had, but I don't think we ever tried that. I can rig a cluster of splinters to produce a pretty good jolt, but you'll have to get close."

Ben drew the Fang and laid it on the table.

"I want to turn this into a spear and wire electricity into it," he said. "Also, is there any way to modify those missiles to deliver a shock?"

"I think I can manage that, but the tech won't work anywhere near the wyrm."

"Actually, I think I have a solution for that," Ben said. "I want to grind a piece of dragon bone into powder and add it to some paint. Then I want to paint magic circles onto the missiles and the skiff and have everybody here who can feel magic join together to consecrate those circles."

"You think that'll work?" Kaid asked.

"I think it might," the Sage said. "The wyrm can break the protection of most any circle if he's close enough, but it might buy enough time for the weapon to hit."

"I'm game," Kaid said. "But it'll take all day to modify all the missiles."

"Just do two," Ben said. "We'll set them to fire as a salvo, one arc missile followed by three ex-plus. If the electricity works, he won't be able to stop the ex-plus from detonating."

"I like the way you think, Kid," Kaid said. "Kayla, how do you feel about flying the skiff?"

She blinked. "I don't know how."

"Oh, you don't have to know how to fly, it does all that. You just have to tell it what to do, and those eye drops I gave you make you the perfect person for the job since you're the only one besides me and Ben who can actually interface with the computer."

"In that case, I'm in," Kayla said.

"Now hold on," Penelope said, pushing her way through the crowd. "I'm going to need a lot more information before I let my daughter pilot a spaceship."

Kayla chuckled. "Come on, Mom, we have work to do. I'll explain while we make some paint."

Kaid looked at Ben. "We'll need to install an upgrade to your augment so you can interface with the armor."

"I need to sit for a minute first," Ben said. "I want to see if I can find exactly where they're taking Ellie."

"Fair enough," Kaid said, "I'll be out at the skiff. Join me when you're ready."

Ben nodded, scanning the room for a quiet corner. He sat down and looked around. Several people were watching him, but none approached, so he closed his eyes and cleared his mind.

"If I get separated from my body again, can you bring me back?" he asked Homer.

When Homer didn't answer, Ben opened his eyes. His dog was lying next to him, looking up at him with an expression of worry that Ben had never seen before.

"What's wrong?"

Homer whined softly.

"I need to find Ellie, and there's only one way I know how to do that."

"I know, but what you're doing is incredibly dangerous," Homer said. "If you get too close to the dragon, he will see you and he will kill you."

"Last time I got separated, you brought me back."

Homer hesitated before answering.

"Yes, but Homer nearly died."

Ben felt a thrill of fear race up his spine. Maybe more than any other thing, the idea of losing his dog terrified him.

"What do you mean? You are Homer."

"Yes and no. If you get separated, I can bring you back, but I'm not sure that Homer will survive."

"I don't understand."

"No, but I think maybe it's time that you do. I am not your dog, I am your guardian angel," Homer said.

Ben sat very still, the implications of the statement leaving him stunned

"When you were very young, your grandfather sought out a prophet and bargained with him to look into your future. What he saw frightened your grandfather so badly that he enlisted the aid of his own sacred guardian angel to summon me.

"Normally, we tend to stay in the realm of spirit and only intervene in the most extraordinary of circumstances. Often, a person will live their whole lives without ever becoming aware of us. But in rare cases, such as yours, the danger to our charge represents a much larger danger to the world and to humanity.

"Since we are beings of light, we live in a vastly higher vibratory state, which means that it takes a great deal of energy for us to manifest effects in this much denser three-dimensional time-space environment that you think of as reality. For me to live here with you, I needed a flesh-and-blood host.

"Homer graciously allowed me to share his life, to live within him so that I could be here with you and watch over you throughout the course of your life. But Homer is a dog, and he has already lived far longer than his normal lifespan.

My presence is the only thing preserving his life. When you were separated from your body and I came to save you, I had to leave this vessel. Homer nearly died as a result."

Ben sat, slack-jawed. So much fell into place. So many questions that he had pondered during the course of his life were answered. But there was still one more.

"Why didn't you tell me any of this before?"

"To protect you," Homer said. "If you had known my true purpose and origin, you would have undoubtedly felt emboldened and immortal—an unfortunate delusion of youth would have become a greater source of danger because of my presence. To serve my purpose, you had to remain ignorant."

Ben thought it over, remaining silent, his eyes staring off into space for several minutes. It all made sense, in the sort of way that he would have never believed before his world had been upended.

"Why tell me now?"

Homer whined again softly. "You are quickly approaching the turning point," he said. "You will either succeed against the wyrm or you will fail. Either way, my purpose here will have come to an end."

Ben felt like someone had plunged a dagger into his heart. Homer was his best friend and his most trusted companion.

"What are you saying?"

"You know what I'm saying, Benjamin."

"No…" he whispered, trying unsuccessfully to swallow the lump in his throat. For the second time in one day, he felt like his entire world was crumbling around him.

"I don't want you to go," he whispered, barely able to form the words.

"I know, but you have to understand, Homer is suffering. He's already outlived his normal lifespan by many years and he longs to return home. My presence and his love for you are the only things that sustain him."

"Oh, God," Ben said, tears flowing freely as he put his face in his hands and sobbed.

Homer put his chin on Ben's knee. "I will always be with you, even when you can't see me or talk to me, but Homer's time here will soon be at an end."

Ben felt a pain like nothing he had ever known, like a part of him was dying.

"Are you okay?" Zack asked.

Ben looked up at his friend and shook his head.

"Come on, let me take you to a room so you can be alone for a while," Zack said. "People are watching, and they kind of need you to be strong right now."

All of the practical concerns in the world seemed small and pointless until he saw Gwen watching him and remembered just how much was resting on his shoulders.

He sniffed back his tears and nodded, following Zack into a hall lined with closed doors. Zack fished a key out of his pocket and opened the door to a medium-sized room, sparsely furnished but comfortable enough.

"This is our room," he said. "Olivia won't mind if you use it for a while."

Ben blinked, the realization coming over him all at once.

"You and Olivia are together?"

Zack smiled like the sunshine, nodding proudly. "I don't quite understand it myself, but I've never been happier."

In that moment, all of Ben's despair and fear and uncertainty was washed away by the simple joy he saw in Zack's smile. His friend was in love ... and no tyranny, no evil, no supernatural enemy could diminish that most powerful magic of all.

"I'm happy for you, Zack. You deserve this."

"I don't know about that, but I'm sure going to hang on with both hands."

Ben smiled, taking Zack into his arms and hugging him tightly. "Thank you," he whispered.

"For what?" Zack said, stepping back with a questioning frown.

"For reminding me what I'm fighting for," Ben said. "I'll be out shortly."

Zack nodded, closing the door and leaving Ben to his work.

He sat down on the bed and closed his eyes.

"I love you, Homer," he said. "If I get separated and you die saving me, know that you are the best thing that ever happened to me."

Homer jumped up onto the bed and curled up next to him.

"I love you, too."

Ben took a deep breath, and with a force of will, set his emotions aside and focused on his breathing, quieting his mind and forming the image of his avatar, both with his imagination and with his augment. It took a while, but eventually his awareness transferred to the being of light that he had created with his imagination.

He thought of Ellie, but imagined seeing her from a distance. In a blink, he was thousands of feet up in the sky, looking down at a road leading away from the Mountaintop. Three wagons accompanied by a hundred Dragon Guard moved down the road at a steady pace.

Ben followed the road, looking for the cinder cone he expected to find, and he wasn't disappointed. The open top of the hollowed-out volcanic vent stood out against the brown and green of the surrounding terrain. The dragon perched on the lip of the opening was the giveaway.

When the wyrm looked up at Ben, he willed himself back to his body, opening his eyes and looking over at Homer.

"I'm still here."

He stroked his dog's fur, struggling to set aside his feelings so that he could do what needed to be done.

Before he stood, he accessed his augment and searched his maps of the area around Denver to find the cinder cone, marking its exact location and sending the coordinates to Kaid with a thought.

"Hey, there you are," Zack said, as Ben entered the main room. "Liv had an idea. We want to know what you think."

"All right," Ben said.

Zack held up a piece of plywood that had been cut into a circle about five feet wide with the center hollowed out. A foot-wide section of board formed a ring that had been carefully painted with paint mixed with ground-up dragon bone. Ben could feel the faint presence of magic emanating from it.

"Maybe this can protect Colonel Kaid from the dragon's magic," Zack said.

Ben smiled, nodding approval. "Let's find the Sage and see if it works."

"He's out at the skiff, painting magic circles on the nose cones of the missiles."

"Perfect, come on," Ben said, motioning for Zack to follow.

"Ah, there you are, Kid," Kaid said, when Ben stepped into the back of the skiff. "Got your mind right?"

"For now," Ben said, glancing down at Homer, right by his side as always.

"Good enough. You ready to try on your new armor?"

"Yeah, but first Zack has something for you."

Kaid frowned dubiously.

"Can you use your splinters to hold this up around you?" Zack asked.

Kaid shrugged, detaching several hundred splinters to lower the circle over his head.

Ben laid his hand on the circle and consecrated it.

The Sage came into view at the door to the skiff.

"Huh, quite ingenious," he said. "We've tested my ability to deactivate the missiles painted with circles and your plan seems to work. I'm assuming that this circle is designed to provide the same protection for Colonel Kaid."

"That's our hope," Ben said.

"Very well," the Sage said, focusing and muttering a number of words under his breath. "Give it a try."

Kaid floated a foot off the ground, smiling broadly. "Nice," he said.

"Indeed," the Sage said. "I believe we're about finished with the painting, though it might be wise to reinforce the consecrations."

Ben looked at the circle surrounding Kaid and smiled.

"Hey, Zack, can you cut a piece of board a foot on each side and draw a circle on it with that paint?"

"Sure, what are you thinking?"

"I want to attach three or four ex-plus charges to it and put it into a satchel."

"I like it," Kaid said. "While he does that, let's get you up to speed on your armor. Also looks like you're down a few splinters."

Ben felt the handoff in his mind as Kaid transferred two hundred splinters to him.

Chapter 28

"We're approaching the drop point," Kayla said from the pilot's seat.

After Kaid had installed the new software into his augment, Ben could operate the powered armor as easily as he could use his own hands ... it was almost like an extension of his body.

He had briefed Kayla, Derek, and Kaid on his plan, then took a few minutes to say his goodbyes to everyone else. Many offered to come with them, some were even angry that he wouldn't let them, but all offered their heartfelt wishes for his success.

He played out the events of the past months in his mind. Everything he had done, all that he had lost, had brought him to this moment. He had expected to be afraid, terrified even, but he wasn't. Instead, he felt unusually calm, a quiet certainty settling over him as he reviewed his plan in his own mind.

"Are you sure about this, Kid?" Kaid asked.

"Yeah, I'm sure. Ellie is down there. And so is the wyrm."

"All right, then," Kaid said. "Give me ten minutes to get spun up and then do your thing."

"Thank you," Ben said, picking up his helmet. "We would've never had a chance against the dragon without you."

"Right back at you, Kid."

Ben looked down at Homer, curled up in a corner looking back at him. He swallowed the pain that threatened to shatter his resolve.

"I love you," he whispered, turning away and seating his helmet into place.

He and Kaid stepped through the bulkhead door and it closed behind them.

"Pressure check," Kayla's voice said in his head.

Ben consulted the readouts in his mind's eye ... all green.

"Check," he said, looking over at Kaid.

They nodded to one another as the air in the rear compartment began to be pumped out. Moments later, the door dropped open, revealing a stormy, late afternoon sky.

Ben checked the Dragon's Fang, now an eight-foot spear thanks to the steel rod affixed to the butt of the sword, complete with a vacuum generator and a number of fully charged capacitors capable of delivering a deadly jolt of electricity.

"All good?" Kaid asked.

"All good," Ben said.

"See you on the flip side, Kid," Colonel Kaid said, launching into the open sky, his magic circle held in place with an intricate web of splinters and force fields.

Ben waited, counting the seconds, monitoring Kaid's progress as he took his position high over the cinder cone and began to deploy his splinters as an impressive array of weapons.

He checked his equipment one last time. His armor and all of its built-in weapons were showing green, his satchel charge was over his shoulder, and the Dragon's Fang was in hand. Four hundred splinters were affixed to his gauntlets. He reinforced his circle and shifted the armor's color to dark grey.

"Kaid just flashed the signal," Kayla said.

"Thank you," Ben said, stepping to the edge of the ramp and looking down at the world so far below. He picked out the opening of the cinder cone and stepped off into the sky. The sensation of falling was at once exhilarating and terrifying. His most basic and animal nature screamed in the back of his mind, while his augment calmly displayed his rapidly changing altitude.

His focus narrowed and his mind cleared. The past and future vanished in the face of the eternal now. He smiled as the feeling of aliveness permeated every fiber of his being.

The world raced up at him. He adjusted his descent with slight movements of his arms and legs, his eyes never wavering from his target.

He felt the magic below him before he saw any hint of the enemy inside the darkness he was aiming for. Then it pulsed, dark and potent, but not directed at him. The dragon was doing something else, something dangerous.

His augment offered a warning that he would soon begin deceleration. He noted it in the back of his mind while his concentration remained focused on the yawning blackness rushing up at him like the abyss.

He checked his circle and his armor's systems one last time before the gravity drive began slowing his descent, the initial deceleration bleeding off speed so rapidly that he nearly lost consciousness, as expected and even planned for. With his speed in check, he passed through the opening in the cinder cone and activated his armor's brilliant illumination, flooding the entire cavernous chamber in stark white light.

The scene was as he expected, nearly exactly as he had foreseen with the aid of the Oculus, but not quite. The dragon was there, crouching on one side of an enormous magical circle. Within the circle was a pile of gold and gems that would have embarrassed even the greediest of men. Opposite the dragon was an uneven mound of dirt and rocks with a wood post embedded in the center.

Ellie wore nothing but a white dress, her hands tied to the post behind her back. She averted her eyes from his light, closing them tightly, but he could feel her mind touch his as the battle was joined, filling him with hope and purpose.

Off to the side, Noisome Ick stood in his true form, watching the spectacle from a distance.

Shadow was swirling within the circle as some dark and evil force began to take shape. Ben could feel the threat it represented through his connection with Ellie. She feared it more than she feared the dragon.

All of this registered in a fraction of a second. Ben adjusted course, aiming for the wyrm, the Dragon's Fang pointed at the beast's neck, the blade crackling with blue-white arcing electricity.

The dragon roared, his head snapping up toward the light even as he clenched his eyes shut to shield against the brilliance of Ben's armor. A gout of fire erupted from the dragon's maw, but his aim was off. Ben deployed his shield at an angle to protect against the edge of the flame, skirting the dragon's attack and picking his target, the base of his enemy's neck.

The wyrm flinched at the last moment. The Fang struck him in the shoulder, sinking to the hilt through nearly impenetrable scales, driving deep into his flesh, electricity crackling and dancing over the dragon's entire body as it made its way to the earth.

Ben felt the magic permeating the entire chamber diminish to nearly nothing save the now familiar feeling of the Fang's presence. The wyrm thrashed, a spasm overtaking him. Ben was thrown clear, jerking the Fang free but not before tearing into the dragon's flesh and widening the wound.

Ben tumbled through the air, propelled by the inhuman strength of the wyrm, slamming into the wall and falling to the ground. In spite of the armor's protection, it felt like the impact had bruised every inch of his body. Warnings flashed yellow in his mind's eye. He ignored them, rising into the air with a thought.

Another warning flashed. He reacted without thought, rolling in the air to bring his shield between him and the incoming grenade.

Noisome Ick had Bertha.

The grenade hit the shield, a loud crack echoing within the chamber, but the impact was absorbed and deflected. Ben turned just in time to see the dragon leaping toward him like a cat. The creature's magic was still diminished, but his ferocity and raw strength were very much intact.

Ben evaded, shooting straight up, but not quickly enough. The dragon swatted him, hitting his leg and sending him flipping through the air. While he struggled to right himself, he reached out for the grenades still housed in Bertha's magazine, activating the charges with an override command. The explosion was deafening, even through his armor. He felt the shock of pain through his connection with Ellie as the sound hit her.

The dragon roared again, trying to breathe fire at him, but failing for a lack of control over his magic. Electricity was the key. He sent the data stream to Kald and the skiff in case he failed and they were left to continue the fight without him.

He regained control, turning hard in midair and accelerating toward the dragon, meeting him in flight, his spear striking again, but again, the wyrm was able to avoid a fatal blow and instead only suffered a deep wound along the side of his body, the electricity pulsing into him. His body tensed, his wings failing to provide lift. Ben let go of the Fang, leaving it embedded in the wyrm's side, current flowing into the beast, leaving him stunned and helpless as he crashed to the ground.

In the midst of the melee, Ben saw the remains of Noisome Ick, broken and bleeding on the ground, the grenades in Bertha's chamber having done their work.

He turned his attention to Ellie, extinguishing his light, and deploying two hundred splinters as a blade ahead of him. His tech severed her bindings a moment before he reached her. She was disoriented from the light and noise, but she responded to his arrival by throwing her arms around him and hanging on for dear life. He carefully wrapped one arm around her, tight enough to hold her to his chest, but not so tight that he might hurt her.

With his free hand, he pulled the satchel charge loose, dropping it into the circle with the swirling darkness, and flew for the Dragon's Fang, still protruding from the side of the crackling and twitching wyrm. Ben snatched the blade free and launched into the sky, his shield deployed beneath him as he fled the battlefield.

"Minimum safe distance achieved," the augment flashed in his mind.

"Detonate," he commanded with a thought.

A flash of light from below was followed by a crack that seemed to shake the world, four pounds of ex-plus filling the cinder cone with fire and force.

Ben looked down.

The wyrm shot out of the cold volcano like a bullet from a gun, tumbling up toward him with alarming speed, an outcome that Ben hadn't considered. All too soon, the wyrm regained control, scanned the sky and found him.

"Engage," Ben said, broadcasting the command to Kaid and the skiff.

The wyrm gained on him with impossible speed, breathing fire, a great and ferociously hot gout of flame rising up to meet the shield that was trailing just beneath them. He would have survived without it, but Ellie would surely have burned to death in his arms.

A beam of light shot out of the sky, hitting the dragon and drawing his attention toward Kaid. A moment later a shot from a plasma cannon tore past them, narrowly missing the dragon. The second shot hit, sending the wyrm tumbling once again.

Ben checked the position of the rapidly descending skiff, adjusting his trajectory to meet it at an altitude that wouldn't kill Ellie from the cold or lack of air. He looked back down in time to see the dragon regain control and begin to ascend toward them.

A pulse of magic washed over him, nearly collapsing his circle. He turned his focus to maintaining his protections. Another stream of plasma nearly scored a direct hit, but the wyrm spiraled at the last moment, narrowly avoiding the attack.

Ben's augment began tracking the salvo of missiles the skiff had launched, four missiles, one after the other targeting the dragon. Ben launched a swarm of micro-missiles, knowing that the wyrm would easily defeat them, but also knowing that they would provide a vitally important distraction.

The dozen tiny weapons, each a kill shot against a human being, flew unerringly toward the wyrm, but all twelve lost propulsion as they got close.

Then the arc missile hit, releasing a jolt of electricity powerful enough to deep-fry an elephant. The wyrm lost muscle control, and then began to lose altitude. The next three missiles hit, one by one, each exploding with shattering force, each blasting the wyrm farther and farther away, each doing damage, though not nearly as much as Ben would have liked, but enough to give him time to reach the skiff.

He landed in the rear compartment and gently set Ellie down, then turned and launched into the sky.

"Bring her in and run like hell," he said, his augment relaying the command to Kayla and Derek.

Without looking, he knew that the back door closed rapidly and the compartment pressurized as the skiff began to gain altitude and distance. An enormous weight lifted and his mind cleared.

Ellie was safe.

Now for the wyrm.

A sentiment that the dragon seemed to share. He was coming again, battered and bleeding, but still fierce and powerful.

Ben felt the magic before he saw the darkness concentrating around the wyrm. It pulsed, a wave of power like nothing that he had ever felt before. He braced for it, focusing on his circle, willing its protection to hold. In the first moment, he thought that it would, but then it began to falter. He brought his full concentration to bear, but his circle broke, his tech failing a moment later, his suit losing power and locking up, his gravity drive shutting down.

And then he was falling.

This time the sensation was all the more real, the fear and rising panic nearly overwhelming his common sense. He tried to reactivate his circle, but the wyrm had him in his spell, a dark cloud of magic surrounding him. He was powerless, and all too soon, he would be dead.

As he fell, tumbling helplessly, the world and the sky alternating in his field of vision with dizzying speed, he saw that the dragon had turned his attention to Kaid. Bolts of plasma shot past, each lighting up the world, but the dragon avoided them far too easily, spinning and spiraling with more speed and grace than seemed possible. Each second brought the wyrm closer to the Colonel.

Ben struggled to focus past his fear, willing his circle back into place, but the darkness was preventing him, a magic beyond his understanding.

He fell helplessly, each flash of the world larger and closer than the last, each flash of the sky showing the dragon closing on Kaid as the Metal Man fired his lasers and his plasma at the wyrm with little effect.

"I guess I'm coming home with you, Homer," Ben thought.

And then Homer was there with him, a disembodied spirit, only slightly visible, but present nevertheless. Ben felt an infusion of magical power flood into him, and the darkness surrounding him evaporated.

He thrust all of that power into his circle, bringing the protective barrier back into place and then reactivating his armor. As it came back online and he regained control, now just a few hundred feet from the ground, he turned toward the dragon and accelerated back into the fight.

He watched the wyrm dodge a plasma round as he closed on Kaid.

"Call the orbital strike when the wyrm hits the ground," Kaid said in Ben's mind.

The twin rings of spun-up plasma above and to each side of Kaid lost cohesion, spraying blue hot death in every direction. Kaid's oversized laser cannon lost power, then disintegrated into a shower of deactivated splinters.

Ben watched helplessly as Kaid formed a sword with his splinters and moved to engage the wyrm in close combat, his circle holding as he closed. He slipped past the dragon's fire, rolling to the right as he slashed with his sword, cleanly severing the dragon's wing in half a moment before the wyrm snapped at him, catching him in midair with his powerful jaws.

All of the hope and certainty that Ben had felt just moments before vanished in a blink, replaced with the horror of watching his friend falling to the earth, clutched in the dragon's mouth.

Then the second missile salvo hit, the arc missile sending a surge of electricity into the wounded dragon's body, followed by three explosions, each striking true. The dragon was falling freely, seemingly unconscious, yet he still held Kaid's body in his mouth.

"Kaid?"

Nothing.

Ben tried to access Kaid's armor, but there was no signal, no power … only silence.

The dragon stirred. He struggled to regain control, one wing out and slowing his descent into a spiral.

Ben was gaining, but not quickly enough. He watched as Kaid came apart in the dragon's mouth, his head and shoulders falling away in one direction and his legs falling the other. Fear, horror, and sadness flooded into his belly yet again as he watched one more friend die. With an act of will, he transformed all of that emotion into cold rage and determination.

He calculated the wyrm's trajectory, gauging where the beast would hit the ground and then activating the orbital weapon, calling it down on top of his enemy, then changed course, moving to gain safe distance from the coming storm, signaling the skiff to get clear as well. The dragon hit, bouncing, tumbling through trees and finally coming to a rest.

"Sixty seconds."

Ben continued to gain altitude as the red streak flashed past him. It hit with such thunderous power that Ben was once again shocked by the magnitude of what he had unleashed onto the world—a force so great and terrible that it could erase a city in a blink. Too much power for anyone to possess.

The flash was blinding, to eyes and sensors alike. The sound and shockwave hit him like a wall. His armor protected him, but only just. For the second time, he felt like his entire body was bruised by the impact. A mushroom cloud began to rise into the sky. Ben searched for the dragon, reaching out with his mind and his tech.

A sinking feeling overcame him when he saw the wyrm falling through the sky, flipping end over end away from the point of impact, his one good wing completely burned away, his body trailing smoke, but still, unbelievably, intact.

Ben began to move, calculating where his enemy would land, beginning to wonder if the dragon could be killed. The beast hit over a mile away from the edge of the pillar of smoke rising from the impact site, his body tumbling across a patch of earth that had once been farmland, before coming to a rest.

Ben closed, watching for any hint of life.

The dragon twitched, flopping over, wounded, perhaps even fatally. But that wasn't enough. Ben needed to be sure that he was dead.

As he watched, closing with all possible speed, a window in the fabric of space opened up and the Warlock strolled through. Ben watched with incredulity and fury as his other enemy flopped a collar around the dragon's neck while two men secured ropes to his body.

Ben watched helplessly, his tech providing him with a close-up view as the Warlock motioned and the ropes went taut and dragged the wounded and collared dragon through the magical portal.

Light flashed from the skiff, its laser targeting the Warlock, but his magic easily dispersed the attack. He looked up at Ben with a broad smile, waved and then stepped through the portal as well, the magical rip in space-time vanishing a moment later.

"What the hell?" Kayla's voice said in his mind.

Ben wanted to rage at the world. All they had done, all they had lost, their enemy on the brink of defeat … and now this.

"Pick me up," he said, adjusting course to rendezvous with the skiff. "Set course for these coordinates and burn with all possible speed as soon as I'm onboard."

"Copy," Kayla said.

Ben landed in the back compartment, commanding the door to close as he stepped inside.

"Pressurizing," Kayla said.

"No, leave it like it is," Ben said. "I need to be able to launch quickly."

He was lying and he knew it, but he needed some pretense to avoid going into the forward compartment because he knew what he would find and he didn't have the strength to face it, not until he was done.

"Ellie? Is she all right?"

"Derek put her in the doc. She'll be fine."

"Good, let me know when we get close," he said.

"You sure…"

"Please, Kayla … just get us there as fast as you can."

Ben turned his mind inward, focusing on his coin, the most familiar image he could conjure, the most comforting … the one place that he could put his mind without it wandering into darkness.

Time passed quickly, almost as quickly as he would have liked.

"Approaching coordinates," Kayla said.

Ben brought his mind back to the moment, accessing the trajectory data of the final orbital weapon and finding exactly what he was afraid that he would find—it wouldn't come into firing position for another couple of hours.

He accessed the skiff's sensors and focused in on the spot where he knew the Warlock would be. The place where he had come into the world, his grandfather's hiding place for the egg.

Things had come full circle.

"Be ready with the last missile," he said.

"What are you going to do?" Kayla asked.

"Bluff," Ben said, opening the back door with a thought and stepping out into the sky.

The Warlock had built a log wall around the spot where he had originally arrived. His portal was open again and a number of people, all white as albinos, were beginning to stream through, his clan from his world, where magic was understood and practiced. He had the egg and a collared dragon, and he had his staff.

Ben descended, reinforcing his circle as he closed, igniting his brilliance as he got within a few hundred feet, landing with a thud while everyone shielded their eyes. He reduced the light his armor was producing to just enough to make the Warlock's people shield their eyes. He peered through the portal into their world, the sky was dark and filled with ash and soot, the sun a red blotch in the sky, setting through an open stone window in the Warlock's keep.

Ben retracted his face shield, glancing at the still-smoking dragon, lying helplessly beside the Warlock.

"Hello, Benjamin," the Warlock said. "Have you come to offer me your fealty?"

"No, I've come to tell you that you've lost."

"Is that so?" the Warlock said. "I have the egg, the dragon in a collar, and my clan is arriving to conquer your world as we speak. How have I lost?"

Ben sent the launch signal and pointed to the sky.

The Warlock frowned, hesitating for a moment before looking up.

"You saw what I did to the dragon," Ben said. "I'm about to do the same thing right here, right where you and your people are standing."

A spasm of rage contorted the Warlock's face, but he mastered it quickly.

"You really should reconsider, Benjamin. We could be great allies. In spite of your continued insolence, I have much respect for you. Call off your weapon and I will give you anything you want."

Ben thought of Homer, dismissing the idea in an instant.

"I couldn't call it off if I wanted to. In about ninety seconds, this patch of dirt is going to be nothing but a fiery hole in the ground. And to be honest, I hope you're still standing here when that happens."

A flicker of doubt danced in the Warlock's eyes. "Then why come down here and warn me? Why not just do your worst?"

"Two reasons," Ben said. "First, your people didn't do anything to me or mine. They don't deserve to die for your sins."

The Warlock snorted, shaking his head. "You are far more compassionate than a true leader should be, Benjamin. And your second reason?"

"I wanted to look you in the eye and tell you that I beat you. You've been ahead of me at every move, but it's always the last move that counts most."

Realization spread across the Warlock's face and then he smiled, genuine mirth and perhaps even joy overtaking the tightness that had marked his expression since Ben pointed out the weapon falling toward them.

"Well played. I've enjoyed our game," he said, turning to his people and barking a series of commands in a very different language. "I look forward to seeing you again, Benjamin. And in truth, this adventure has been a triumph that my people will tell stories about for centuries. I will bring them a breeding pair of dragons and this device you call a rifle—both treasures of incalculable value."

The Warlock's people began to drag the wyrm through the magical portal, obeying their leader's commands without question or hesitation, all of them filing back into their world.

"If you ever come back here again, I will kill you," Ben said.

"I wouldn't have it any other way," the Warlock said, stepping through the rip in the fabric of reality and waving with a smile as the portal closed. And just like that, his enemies were gone.

Ben launched into the sky and let the missile blast a hole in the ground where the Warlock's circle had been. He landed in a clearing not too far away and sat down on a log, taking off his helmet and gauntlets.

He was trembling when the skiff landed. The door fell open like a sentence and then Ellie emerged carrying Homer, tears streaming down her cheeks.

Ben put his face in his hands and wept.

Epilogue

"We are gathered here today to join these two couples in marriage," the Sage said.

Ben stood with Ellie, Zack with Olivia. Both of the women looked far too beautiful for either of them, but Ben didn't mention that. In the months that had followed Homer's death, Ben had grieved. He had wept until he had no tears left, for his grandfather, for Rufus, for Kaid, and for Kat, but most of all, for Homer. There was still an emptiness within him, a place that he doubted even Ellie's boundless love could fill, but he had come to terms with it.

Homer had been an uncommon blessing, a gift that Ben had taken for granted far too often. It took a while to get past the crushing sadness, but once he did, he came to remember Homer with a profound sense of joy and privilege.

Now, on this day, he was simply grateful—for his friends who remained, for the ones who had fallen, and for the love of his life who was standing next to him, radiant and glowing with joy.

The ceremony was simple—two souls joined with a pledge of love and loyalty. In truth, Ben knew that it was all a formality. He had given himself over to Ellie the moment they had joined minds during a sword fight that seemed to have taken place a lifetime ago. None of that diminished the happiness of the moment.

There was still a war to fight. They were still important leaders in the struggle against the remnants of the dragon's dying empire—but without the wyrm, it was only a matter of time before humanity fully reclaimed the world from the mules that remained.

After the words had been spoken and the food had been eaten, the party gathered around the fire and the stories began to flow as easily as the drink. Ben listened to the embellished tales, enjoying his friends' enjoyment. And then came his turn—it was time to tell his story. He nodded to himself, taking Ellie's hand as the silence fell over the crowd, all eyes on him, all ears awaiting his version of humanity's salvation.

"I want to tell you the story of how my dog Homer saved the world…"

The End

Made in the USA
Las Vegas, NV
22 January 2023